# ALL THAT GLITTERS ISN'T GOLD IN CRIPPLE CREEK . . .

### GREED
*has already led to the murder of one man
and the tragic deaths of six others.*

Phillip LaFarge. The owner of the Rattlesnake mine is the one responsible for the cave-in that kills six workers. A cold-hearted, selfish man, he knowingly endangers the lives of men in an effort to save money...

### A DECEITFUL COVER-UP
*costs one man his job and reputation.*

Casey Daniels. A man of morals, his concern for human lives gets him fired when he refuses to sign off on plans for a mine that he knows are unsafe. When the cave-in has people blaming LaFarge, he frames Casey...

### A KILLER EPIDEMIC
*has been rapidly claiming the lives
of the children in town.*

Maureen Kramer. Left a widow by the accident at the Rattlesnake, she is heartbroken when—still mourning the loss of her husband—her only child falls ill with the killer disease...

DI026134

This work is a creation of Siegel & Siegel Ltd.

CRIPPLE CREEK

A Berkley Book / published by arrangement with
Siegel & Siegel Ltd.

PRINTING HISTORY
Berkley edition / June 1997

The Putnam Berkley World Wide Web site address is
http://www.berkley.com

ISBN: 0-425-15850-0

BERKLEY®
Berkley Books are published by The Berkley Publishing Group,
200 Madison Avenue, New York, New York 10016.
BERKLEY and the "B" design
are trademarks belonging to Berkley Publishing Corporation.

10 9 8 7 6 5 4 3 2 1

# CRIPPLE CREEK

## DOUGLAS HIRT

BERKLEY BOOKS, NEW YORK

*For Ed, Gayle, and Ashley*

# ONE

"YO, MACK! HOLD UP A MINUTE," CASEY DANIELS CALLED from the ticket window of the Colorado Midland Railroad depot. Wedging his leather portfolio under his left arm and grabbing up suitcases in both hands, Casey hurried down the steps of the baggage platform of the Florissant Station and started across the tracks.

The sudden shrill of the locomotive's steam whistle caught Casey off guard and he scrambled off the right-of-way as a spurt of steam ruffled his trouser legs and the hissing, black engine's four big drivers began their slow, first revolution. Macklin Deats had been climbing onto the seat of his freight wagon when Casey's shout had stopped him. He stepped back off the iron rung, grinning as Casey was unceremoniously shooed off the tracks by the train's whistle. Casey hurried down Station Street, hoofing it to the end of town and the tall frame building there with the long sign across the door: DEATS SHIPPING COMPANY.

The building shone in the lowering sunlight, wearing a new coat of white paint, Casey noted as he skipped out of the way of a buckboard drawn by two tired horses. To his right the window shades of the Hundley Stage Line building were drawn down and the door closed—just as the Colorado Midland ticketing agent had informed him they would be only a few minutes earlier. The big Concord stagecoaches were not there, and neither were the half dozen freight wagons usually loading up with supplies bound for the mines in the District.

He made his way down the narrow street, the weight of the bag in his left hand dragging him down a bit and giving him the appearance of a sailor romping along the sloping deck of a plunging schooner. As Casey neared Deats's warehouse he caught a glimpse of a bright yellow freight wagon hidden in the shadows of its wide double doors.

"You're in an almighty hurry, Casey," Deats said when Casey drew up. "What's got you going?"

Casey set one of his suitcases upon the road, puffing like the locomotive that had just passed him by. "I missed the stage, Mack." He shook his head in mild amazement. "You'd think Hundley would arrange his schedules to coincide with the comings and goings of the train."

The freight man shrugged his beefy shoulders, spat a stream of tobacco juice onto the ground, and laughed. Though not a tall man, Macklin Deats was built every inch as stout as a woolly bison. It came with the work. Daniels, at five feet eleven inches, stood over Deats by a good four inches, but Macklin Deats easily possessed twice his strength.

Deats said, "The stage pulled out of here almost an hour ago, and the way I hear it, John Hundley figures Haggerman can damn well run his trains to match *his* schedule. Neither will to give an inch. Hundley must have more business than he needs."

"Maybe, but Haggerman is rich. He can afford to be stubborn. One of these days Haggerman is going to put John *out* of business."

Deats grunted and frowned. "Him and me both."

Casey glanced over at the sound of the suddenly sober words. There was a brewing storm cloud of concern in Deats's eyes. "You seem to be doing all right for yourself, Mack. This building has never looked better."

"Oh, I'm making money hand over fist—now. What with all that booming prosperity going on over in the District, I'm riding high. Bought me a new wagon and six more mules. But it ain't gonna last, Casey. Nooo-siree. If I was a smart man, I'd hustle my butt up there and stake me out a claim or two— like Matt Sterrett done, and Lankford, and Castello, and a dozen more men from parts hereabout. Haggerman is bound to push that railroad of his into the District sooner or later, if for no other reason than to haul his own gold out. And when he does, there goes my business, and Hundley's, and every other freight hauler's around as well."

Casey said, "The District is only starting to prove out, and it might prove a bust after all this excitement dies down."

Deats gave a short laugh. "Not likely, Casey. A man in your line of business ought to know that. This boom is here to stay."

Casey grinned and adjusted his narrow-brim hat. "I got to admit it's looking pretty good. You were just about to leave. I take it you're heading up to the District?"

Deats inclined his head at the gleaming steam engine lashed down tight onto the freight wagon. "That just came in on the noon train. Bound for another one of them sawmills popping up like spring flowers. Next year you won't find nary a tree left in whole District." He whipped his hat off his head and sleeved the sweat from his brow. "Go ahead and throw your things aboard, Casey, if'n you want to ride along. But I gotta warn you, I'm gonna be late getting into the District tonight. You might just want to curl up on some of them sugar sacks in back of Frank Castello's store and wait for the morning stage."

Casey tossed a suitcase behind the seat and hefted the second one in back with it. "Nope, I'll ride along with you." He climbed up onto the wooden seat. "I'm kind of anxious to get back. Before I left, I drew up shoring plans for a drift off of

LaFarge's third tunnel. The timbers should be in place by now, and I'll want to inspect them before LaFarge puts men into that tunnel.''

Deats climbed up onto the seat next to him and grabbed a handful of reins. ''Seems like lately I've been hauling more folks up to the District than old Hundley. I ought to go into the people-freighting business.'' He grinned, winked, then turned the team of fourteen gray mules away from the tall building and cracked a bull whacker's whip over their ears. ''Come on, Sal, move your butt. Maggie, step along with her.'' The mules strained at their harnesses and the heavy wagon moved away from the warehouse.

They turned south onto a rutted road, and once they were under way, Deats offered Casey a bite off his twist. Casey declined, fishing a pipe and pouch of tobacco from inside his jacket instead. When he got it burning he settled back for the long ride ahead.

They passed a carriage parked alongside the road, and a little distance away two men and two women were poking around in the dirt with sticks, collecting petrified wood, Casey figured. The place was loaded with the stuff. He'd even collected a few samples himself when, as a ten-year-old boy, he had come up here with his father in the summer of '74.

It was eighteen years ago that Wood and Ben Requa had first poked around the District for gold. It hardly seemed that long ago now, yet so much had changed in the intervening years. Colorado Springs had grown up into a real city. The Arapaho were no longer bothering the ranchers. His father had sold their ranch to J. F. Seldomridge and now sheep grazed where their cattle had once cropped the high-plains grass.

*They call that progress,* he mused.

Casey grinned to himself. Well, *some* folks called it progress. He wasn't so sure, but the money from the sale of their land had helped put him through school. There was some progress in that. And his father and mother now operated a feed store in Canon City. The work was easier, and the income steady.

Casey had attended the State School of Mines and after graduating with his degree in mining engineering had gone to work for the United States Geological Survey, acquiring the experience that he'd need later to work in private industry. The "Survey" was a little like graduate school for most young hopefuls with the ink barely dry on their ME degrees. Two years of that was enough for Casey. Pete McGuire had snagged him out of the government job and hired him on to work his played-out mine near Leadville, Colorado. That job lasted all of three months before Pete's operations went bankrupt, and Casey moved on.

He spent two years building railroads in Central City and Black Hawk, and another year and a half engineering a dam and pipeline to bring water to a struggling mining camp west of Breckenridge. But these had all been Johnny-come-lately jobs. Casey had missed the real *booms*—missed them by as much as two dozen years in some places.

Frustrated by that, he considered relocating to someplace far away, and perhaps exotic; the Witwatersrand in South Africa intrigued him. That was the move he'd been pondering when the telegram from Phillip LaFarge arrived offering him a job at his Rattlesnake mine in the fledgling Cripple Creek Mining District. Cripple Creek just might prove to be his last shot at a real mining camp, and since he was out of work anyway, he'd jumped at the chance.

It was a man named Sam Stepton, he learned later, who had recommended Casey for the job. Stepton was a self-taught engineer whom Casey had worked with some years back near Leadville.

LaFarge's offer had come just four months ago, and in that short time Casey had seen enough of the District to be convinced that Cripple Creek was shaping up into a real boomtown. And he was in the middle of it, getting in at the beginning.

"So, Casey, what have you been up to?" Deats asked, glancing at the suitcases behind the seat. "Traveling?"

The question pulled Casey from his reverie. Deats went on, "With all that digging folks are doing around Battle Mountain, I'd have figured LaFarge would keep you too busy for you to go off traveling."

Casey noted the thinly veiled disapproval in Mack's voice. It was common knowledge that most folks frowned upon the way Phillip LaFarge ran his business. But Casey tried to stick strictly to his own job and not get involved in the rumor-spreading. He said, "I had to go up to Golden, to use their laboratory."

Deats lifted an eyebrow. "Laboratory?"

"I've been running tests on some samples of sylvanite I discovered in the new tunnel Mr. LaFarge is digging. I've found minable quantities of calaverite, which you know is a gold-tellurium, often associated with chalcedony, fluorite, and certain sulfides. I wasn't certain of its concentrations, and thought it might profit Mr. LaFarge to know just how much calaverite we might be talking about."

Deats gave him a vaguely blank look.

"It won't be long before we have the proper instruments to analyze samples for most of their ore contents, but right now, the resources available in the District are somewhat limited. Of course, there is always the simple, tried-and-true method of—"

Deats threw up his hand and said, "I can tell you're about to get off on one of your technical explanations, Casey, and whenever you do that I start to get this sudden urge to be alone with my mules. My mules I understand."

Casey grinned. "Sorry. Let's just say that I've been away on business."

"That's all you needed to say in the first place." He cracked his whip over Sal's left ear.

The mules pulled the wagon up the wide valley, towards Cripple Creek. The sun lowered over Casey's right shoulder. Long shadows stretched across the road and gathered beneath pine trees that grew in wide swaths, running in and out of the bowls and valleys of grass where cattle grazed.

Darkness moved down the mountain, swallowing rocks and trees. A cold, thin crescent hooked its way up over the peaks, dragging with it a million stars, like frosting upon a chocolate cake. Casey buttoned up his wool jacket against the night chill, and as the wagon rumbled along he recalled the first time he'd come this way with his father, and that wonderful summer and fall of 1874 as they, along with a hundred other men, dug that first tunnel in Arequa Gulch. He smiled to himself recalling Ben Requa's consternation when he discovered that someone had put an "A" in front of the gulch that had supposedly been named in his honor.

They had not found any gold that summer eighteen years ago. Thinking back on it, Casey was certain their tunnel— they had named it the Lone Tree Prospect Tunnel—had been off the mark by only a few feet. What if their aim had been a mite better? He tried to imagine what the District would look like today if gold *had* been discovered there nearly two decades earlier.

Well, it hadn't been a complete waste of a summer. It had, after all, ignited the spark within a ten-year-old boy that had flamed into a career, a career that in its own roundabout way had brought him back to the place where his life had taken that turn.

Casey lingered among the pleasant memories until his eyelids grew heavy; then, nodding, he dozed on the wagon's rocking seat.

Gray against the star-filled sky, the brisk night wind snapped the great expanse of canvas sheets like a bull whacker's whip. The Whosoever Will church, by far the largest tent building in the infant town of Hayden Placer, stood on a platform five feet off the ground. Its foundation was a hundred pilings driven into the rocky earth, looking for all the world like a wharf with the tide run out. Two separate flights of steps brought Sunday worshipers to the platform in front of the wooden front door. At the rear of the tent the ground rose until the back door-flap opened out onto nearly level ground— as level as any piece of ground in Hayden Placer, or Fremont for that matter.

Scattered nearby were other tent buildings—some with sides of rough-hewed logs, others with no sides at all. One or two of them showed the pale yellow glow of a coal oil lamp flickering behind their sheets, but most were dark this time of night. Not far away rose the imposing frame bulk of the Hotel Clarendon. Its upper windows were mostly dark, but the street-level windows and doors spilled light out into the night and reflected dimly off the Whosoever Will's gray sheets.

Beneath the tent, in the gloomy underworld, Elvin Tate hunkered beside one of those hundred pilings. Two feet overhead, the rough-hewed board floor of the church brushed his hat. At his feet was the rubble from the newly dug holes that held the pillars. Elvin shivered in the chill night wind threading between the pillars. He pulled his thin jacket closed at the throat with his right hand as he stared out at the only slightly brighter landscape tilting away from the church.

Elvin cussed softly beneath his breath. His legs were beginning to cramp. He shifted his weight. He could feel the thick envelope tucked inside his jacket. A wave of regret, mixed with apprehension, swept over him.

*How had he ever allowed himself to be talked into this?*

He'd asked himself that question half a hundred times over these last few days, and the answer had always been the same.

*Money.*

That ancient temptress who had led humans down the path he was now traveling for more centuries than man could reckon. Money, and maybe a chance at the good life it could buy.

Just the same, there was a bitter taste in Elvin's mouth, and a knot in his stomach that made him wish he had never gotten involved . . .

*How had he ever allowed himself—*, he'd begun for the

half-a-hundred-plus time when a sound snapped his head around. His view shot past the pilings to the road beyond the tent church. They were coming. His heart pounded his chest. He tried to swallow and discovered a lump caught in his throat. Beyond the forest of pilings two men were striding up the street—not much more than silhouettes moving among the shadows. Elvin could not make out their faces. He saw only that one was short and bulky and the second man was somewhat taller. They came directly to the tent and stopped at the foot of the stairs.

"Where is he?" one of the men said quietly, his boot scuffing the stair tread as if he was scraping something off its sole.

The other man didn't reply at first, then in a guarded voice called, "Elvin. You here, Elvin?"

Beneath the tent, Elvin Tate steeled himself, put on a brave face, and said, "I'm here. Who are you?"

The men bent and two faces peered at him under the platform. Elvin unfolded himself from his place at the piling and, crouching low, stepped out into the open. He didn't recognize these men, but that meant nothing. He had never spoken to anyone in person, except once to that pretty lady who had first contacted him. Later she had passed messages to him as they'd strolled past one another along Myers Avenue, but they'd never spoken to each other.

"Who are you?" he asked again, trying not to show his nervousness.

"Never mind that," the shorter man said. "You got it?"

Elvin's cheek had begun to quiver. He hoped that they didn't notice in the dim light. "Yeah, I got it."

"Lemme see."

Elvin reached towards his jacket, which had fallen open. Then he stopped, his eyes narrowing suspiciously. "You have the money?"

The taller man gave a quick laugh, took a bulky envelope from his pocket, and slapped it into Elvin's left hand. "It's all there. See, we trust you."

"Sure we do," the short man added. "Now it's your turn to trust us."

Elvin squeezed the fat envelope in his fist and managed to smile. Some of his fears melted away. "OK. I got it." He passed his own envelope across to the short man. It was not nearly as thick, but infinitely more valuable than the two thousand dollars he had received for it.

The man checked its contents. Satisfied, he glanced at his partner. "It's here."

"Everything?"

"Looks like it, but only LaFarge will know for sure."

Elvin said, "Now that you got what you want, I'm gonna leave."

The short fellow shifted his view, and in the dim light Elvin saw that his nose was crooked, as if it had once been broken. "Sure, go on . . . Only, don't you want to count it first?"

Elvin had been so nervous, he'd completely forgotten to check the contents of the fat envelope. Now he broke the seal and, fumbling, extracted a sheath of hundred-dollar banknotes. He quickly counted them.

"It seems to be all here," Elvin said, looking up. The shorter man was grinning oddly; his friend had moved around, putting himself at Elvin's rear. All at once he knew what they had in mind. Elvin wheeled about, tried to dodge past the taller man.

The man shifted too, and as he moved his hand slipped into his pocket. There was a click and a sliver of steel flipped out, glinting in the pale light coming from up the street.

Elvin sidestepped and leaped backwards as the stiletto lunged forward. It caught his coat sleeve. Behind him powerful hands grabbed his arms. Elvin banged his head back, connecting with solid bone. The short man cried out and Elvin dodged the lunging blade.

The stiletto came in again. Elvin threw up his hands to guard his face. The sharp blade sliced into the envelope and across the palm of Elvin's hand; a flurry of hundred-dollar banknotes fluttered in the air. For a brief instant Elvin Tate was stunned by the loss, and by the sudden gush of warmth flowing down his wrist, but in the next instant he was leaping backwards, with that long knife making slashing passes inches from his belly.

Then Elvin's back slammed up against the pilings of the Whosoever Will. The knife wavered before his face like a cobra about to strike. Elvin sank to his knees. His eyes gaped and filled, his pleading came out in an unintelligible blathering, and his bowels let loose.

Then the cobra struck.

Barney Mays yanked the blade free and wiped the blood on Elvin's jacket. "Now what, Olly?" he said, folding the stiletto and tucking it away in his pocket.

Olly retrieved his hat, which had been knocked off, and rubbed the bump rising on his forehead. He studied the dark buildings nearby, where a few lights showed. Satisfied that no one had seen their deed, he said, "First let's gather up this money before it's blown clear across the mountainside."

The two men scrambled after the tumbling bills, recovering most of it and letting the wind carry off the rest; it couldn't be helped. Olly shoved the wad into his pocket and inclined his head at the body lying by the Whosoever Will. "Take him away from here."

"Where?"

"Hell, I don't care where. Dump him somewhere where he won't be found. There are five hundred holes dug into this District. One of 'em should be deep enough to bury him in."

The taller man frowned and said, "While I'm finding a hole, what are you gonna do with that pocketful of money?"

"It will be here when you get back, you suspicious son of a bitch."

A slow grin spread to the shadows of Barney's face. "It better be," he said, and whether conscious or not, his hand patted the pocket where the stiletto lay. He hefted Elvin to his shoulder and staggered under the weight into the night.

Olly took one last look around before leaving. He was certain no one had witnessed the murder—well, almost certain.

A half dozen paces down the road a woman stepped from an alleyway between a small log cabin and a tent.

"How long have *you* been there?" he asked.

Lisa Kellerman had the kind of looks a man likes. Olly eyed her pinched waist, the upward swell of her bosoms filling the bodice of the canary yellow dress, her long, slender neck, and the nearly perfect face that appeared as if it had been carefully released from a block of white alabaster by the hands of a sculptor. Lisa not only had good looks, but she was always eager to please a paying customer, and for some reason that Oliver Sawyer had yet to discover, she'd taken an interest in him that seemed to go beyond mere business as usual.

They had enjoyed each other's company for about three months now, almost from the very day he had watched Lisa step off the Florissant Stage at the Continental Hotel. Lisa had wasted no time setting up shop on Myers Avenue, and Olly had been one of her first customers. Since then they had been together almost every night. Olly knew Lisa better than any other man in the District, and he knew that her aspirations went far beyond the one-room crib she currently occupied.

"Long enough," she said.

Olly grunted and continued on his way. She fell in step at his side. "Now what?"

"You're starting to sound like Barney."

"I like Barney. Where did you send him?"

"To dump the body—and you'd like anyone so long as they wear pants, Lisa."

"I like you, Olly," Lisa cooed.

He laughed. "A whole lot more than last night I'll bet, now that I got two thousand dollars in my pocket."

"We can go somewhere and talk about that, Olly."

"Talk?" He stopped and raised a skeptical eyebrow.

She folded her arms around his neck, peered into his dark eyes. "Or whatever . . ."

"I like 'whatever' better."

"You hurt your head." She touched the bump gently, kissed it. "Come to my cabin and I'll make it all better for you, Olly dear."

"I ain't got a lot of time."

"We don't need a whole lot of time, Olly." She took his hand and led him off the road . . .

# TWO

MACKLIN DEATS PULLED HIS TEAM TO A STOP ON A LEVEL stretch of road and nudged Casey in the ribs. "A fine traveling companion you turned out to be. You've been snoring away ever since we crossed Four Mile Creek."

Casey came groggily awake, stretched his legs in the cramped foot well, and shifted upon the hard seat. "Sorry, Mack," he said, yawning. "I've been traveling since yesterday morning. Where are we?"

Deats hooked a thumb at the dark cone of a hill rising to the right. "Mount Pisgah is just over thataway."

"Oh!" Casey came full awake now. Fremont and Hayden Placer lay just over the next hill. He straightened his jacket, shivering in the cool mountain wind blowing steadily, and glanced at the pine-covered hillsides, slowly recognizing the place now. "Why are you stopped?"

"Need to let the mules blow a mite. It's been a long pull to here, and I don't want them stumbling on the other side, on their way down." Deats reached under the seat and came up with a brown paper bag. "Hungry? Got some corn dodgers here. Some fried chicken too."

Casey hadn't thought of it until just then, but with the mention of food he realized he was hungry; actually, "famished" might better describe the emptiness in his belly, he decided. He'd eaten a turkey sandwich on the train from Denver that morning, and that was all. How long ago had that been? He turned the enameled dial of his watch towards the night sky. It was nearly eleven-thirty now. That would make it over twelve hours. He crunched down a hard dodger and followed it with a long pull at Deats's canteen. The food only made him more hungry.

"You ready?" Deats said a few minutes later, watching Casey lick the last of the fried chicken from his fingers.

"I'm ready to get into town and buy me a real dinner."

Deats laughed and cracked his whip. "Git up, Sal. Move your tail, girl." The animals started ahead. "The only place I know of where you can get a decent meal this late is the Continental or the Clarendon."

"I'll toss a dollar."

"Humph. I take my meals more seriously than to leave them to the toss of a coin. I'd take the Clarendon. They got a chef down from Denver City to do their cookin'."

"All that means is that they charge forty-five cents for a decent meal instead of thirty."

Deats laughed again. "A skeptic, I see. How 'bout we both stop at the Clarendon and I'll make a believer out of you."

The freight wagon topped the ridge, and as it started down the other side the valley opened up below, forming a bowl rimmed with high ridges. From this vantage point, Casey was struck by the bright glare along the length of Bennett Avenue from the newly installed electric arc lights. Beyond that lone, bright slash, Casey could just make out the rudimentary scratching of a town below—the more or less straight furrows destined to be streets, the scattering of lights and buildings tossed together, more a matter of expediency than deliberate design. That it was actually two towns growing up side by side, each vying for dominance, was impossible to detect from up on the ridge—or from down in the middle of Bennett Avenue, for that matter.

Fremont, the first town site platted in November of '91 by the Denver real estate investors Horace Bennett and Julius Myers, occupied the Broken Box Ranch property. Three months later Hayden Placer was officially platted: 140-acre placer claim, ostensibly staked out by Ed De LaVergne, Harry Seldomridge, Fred Frisbee, Frank Howbert, J. C. Plumb, Judge Sam Kinsley, and H. C. McCreery for the purpose of finding gold. These seven Colorado Springs businessmen and politicians *were* looking for gold, all right—the sort of gold that came from selling ground, not from digging holes in it. If their method of acquiring the land wasn't exactly legal . . . well, setting up bogus placer claims was a common enough method in the booming mining camps across the West to get your hands on a lot of land quickly.

Casey was amazed by the changes that less than a year of prospecting had wrought. The once prettily wooded hillsides were now scarred with ragged swaths where the lumberman's axe had felled fodder for the hungry sawmills springing up throughout the District. Even in the dark, with a feeble moon overhead to light the land, the pockmarks of the gold disease were evident everywhere. Daily, new cabins were sprouting where pine trees had once gripped the rocky soil with their tenuous roots. Hastily erected tent buildings were giving way to the more permanent-looking frame or log structures. Casey wondered if these shacks—if the towns themselves—were going to be just as tenuous.

Boomtowns were like that: exploding in a whirlwind, chewing up the land like some monster gopher gone mad, and then just blowing away. Casey had a momentary pang of regret, remembering this place as it had been eighteen years earlier when he and his father and a hundred other men had tested the valley for gold and had found it wanting. The pang passed. There was work to be done here. Money to be made by the wheelbarrowful—no, by the boxcarful. And he was going to be part of it!

Macklin Deats snapped his whip and sang out his curses to the mules as they came onto the muddy, rutted track named West Carr Avenue. The freight wagon rumbled past dark buildings and flapping sheets of canvas, through the town of Fremont. West Carr became East Carr, and that was the only indication they had that they had passed through Fremont and were now in Hayden Placer. Deats turned onto Main Street and then onto Pikes Peak, hauling back on the reins and bringing the eights to a stop in front of the Hotel Clarendon, where he set the brake.

In spite of the late hour, light, music, and the sounds of people spilled out of the hotel. Casey and Macklin climbed down to the street—a sidewalk was in the plans—and went inside to become part of it.

The Hotel Clarendon, perched on the corner of Pikes Peak Avenue and Bison Street, had opened on the 20th of April. It was the biggest building in the District, and so new that the smell of fresh pine boards still permeated the hotel, in spite of the barrels of paint required to cover the walls. Fine, imported carpets covered its wooden floors and paintings graced its walls. The Hayden Placer group had built the Hotel Clarendon with one goal in mind: to surpass the luxurious Continental Hotel that Joe Wolfe had opened that January. To that end they had brought in sixteen thousand dollars' worth of furniture to make it the classiest guest house and meeting place in the whole District. It boasted a billiard room, a bar, the finest dining room in all of Cripple Creek, and an elegant ladies' parlor with a glistening black grand piano. It also offered 125 sleeping apartments, hot and cold running water, and electricity! The District's coal-fired generator had been put into operation one week before the Clarendon opened its doors.

The Hayden Placer group had roundly upscaled Joe Wolfe's place, but the final indignation to Joe Wolfe's hotel was when several of the regular stage lines had adopted the Clarendon as their terminus.

Phillip LaFarge looked across the long dining room, with its two dozen tables spaced neatly about, being waited on by a frenzied, inexperienced hotel staff. Out the window to his left, the glow of oil lamps through canvas roofs of nearby restaurants gave the appearance of luminescent globules of swamp gas scattered across the black mountain landscape.

He reached inside his jacket for a cigar, discovered the pocket empty, and frowned, recalling that he had smoked the last one at his office near the hoist shack of the Rattlesnake mine. He sipped his coffee, eyeing the door and the steady stream of men and women flowing through it.

"Would you want somethin' more to eat, Mr. LaFarge?"

He shot a quick glance at the waiter who had materialized at his elbow. "I'll have some more coffee, and bring me a cigar while you're at it."

The door opened again and Bob Womack and the sheriff, Peter Eales, stepped in from the night. Bob was a tall, stoop-shouldered man, and although always amiable, he seemed in particularly good spirits this evening. He and Pete aimed for the bar, with four or five men in fresh clothes tagging along. LaFarge didn't know them. New arrivals on the afternoon stage, most likely; men from Colorado Springs who had a warm home, fat wife, and thriving business to go home to once their grubstake ran out. Obviously they had sought out Womack. Everyone who came to the District first scouted out Bob Womack. He was, after all, a celebrity, the man who had discovered gold here, and Bob was never one to turn down a chance to take men on a tour of the District and to tell his story—especially if someone was oiling his tongue with whiskey.

LaFarge wondered how the former cowboy ever found time to work his own claim. The Womack Placer reportedly contained a fair amount of gold ore, but gregarious Bob Womack seemed more interested in being the District's chief unofficial greeter and tour guide than in working his claims.

LaFarge's cigar and coffee came. He glanced at his watch, then at the door again. His rough nails rapped the table impatiently. More men joined Womack and Eales at the bar.

Sitting alone at a table across the room, the somber Winfield Scott Stratton moodily contemplated a half-full glass of whiskey. LaFarge was mildly surprised to find him here. Stratton was a loner, preferring to remain in his cabin on his claim on Battle Mountain. His claim, the Independence—named because Stratton had staked it out on the Fourth of July—was not far from LaFarge's Rattlesnake.

He did not know Stratton well. The slightly built man with the big white mustache kept pretty much to himself. He did know that Stratton had been searching for his pot of gold for more than twenty years, digging holes in Colorado from Ouray, in the San Juan Mountains, to Leadville. Stratton's Independence had showed some yellow—enough for the man to have invested all his money in equipment and a small crew—but so far its production was not encouraging and LaFarge figured that like most men who came to the District, Stratton had just about had his fill of digging holes in this rocky ground and was probably right now deciding if he should pack up and return to Colorado Springs. Stratton was a carpenter by trade, and the income from that line of work was at least steady.

"I'm late."

LaFarge took his eyes off Stratton, fixing them upon the man standing before him. "You're an hour late, Mr. Sawyer," he said sharply. "What took you so long?" LaFarge did not offer the man a chair, but Oliver Sawyer pulled one back anyway.

He was a short man in a light gray wool jacket over a brown broadcloth vest. He wore a dusty bowler hat, and the wire spectacles perched upon the bridge of his nose made his eyes huge and round. He did not have the look of a miner, and to the casual observer he might have been mistaken for an attorney, or perhaps one of the many speculators in mining stocks arriving daily. But Oliver Sawyer was neither of these, and a more studious observer might have wondered about the bulk of his shoulders, the big, callused knuckles, the crooked nose that had obviously been broken more than once, and the slight bulge in his coat beneath his left arm.

"I had business of my own to see to."

LaFarge sniffed the air. "You've been drinking."

Sawyer laughed briefly. "That was part of it."

LaFarge's frown deepened. "Are you drunk?"

"No, and it wouldn't make no difference if I was."

"What did you do to your head?"

"Walked into a tree."

LaFarge gave a short laugh. "Like hell you did, Olly. Where is Barney?"

Sawyer shrugged his bulky shoulders. "He was busy last time I saw him. I ain't his keeper."

LaFarge pulled deeply at his cigar and held the smoke a moment. Oliver Sawyer had never been what a man might call "cooperative" even in the best of situations, and LaFarge could see that this evening he was particularly combative. He blew an impatient cloud into the already smoky room. "Well, did you get it?"

Sawyer tossed the envelope onto the table.

LaFarge grabbed it up and greedily stripped the papers from it. He studied them, turning them to the chandeliers overhead. They were exactly what he had hoped for. He methodically returned them to the envelope, and then to his pocket.

"Did you have any trouble?"

Olly waved down a passing waiter and ordered a whiskey. "No trouble. Mr. Tate was most accommodating."

"He took the money?"

"Sure he took it. He had no complaints."

"Then what?" LaFarge was irritated that he had to pull this

information from Sawyer. The man was most infuriating at times—but most useful as well.

"He took it and left. What else is there to tell?" Sawyer looked down at his callused knuckles and began to massage them with his left hand.

LaFarge studied him a moment, drawing thoughtfully at the cigar. "That was it?"

"What else did you expect him to do? Weren't that the agreement?"

LaFarge peered at the curl of smoke coming from the cigar between his fingers. "Yes, that was the agreement. He didn't happen to say where he was going, did he?"

Olly grinned and looked up from his rough hands. "Naw, he didn't say a word. Just left real quick. I don't figure we'll be seeing any more of Mr. Elvin Tate around these parts. Now, about my pay?"

For a long time Sam Stepton just stood there, not moving, wondering what he ought do about it. In the end, Sam decided to do nothing—except to forget it. He stepped away from the privy and retraced his steps to the darkened tent where his wife, Sharon, slept.

As Sam slipped into bed, Sharon stirred, mumbled something in her sleep, then drifted again into light, even breathing beside him. But Sam could not sleep. A vision of what he had just seen flashed through his brain like a vivid nightmare.

"What's the matter?" Sharon asked groggily after his tossing had awakened her.

"Hm? Oh, er . . . I can't sleep." Sam dared not tell her. She'd insist that he tell Sheriff Eales. But how could he? He'd heard Sawyer mention LaFarge's name. He'd seen the two men together so many times that it did not surprise him. Just the same, squealing on one's boss was a sure way to find oneself out of a job, and at his age, pounding the streets for work was the last thing he needed.

Sharon went back to sleep, but Sam lay there awake, staring

at the ceiling. A half hour later, he crawled out of bed and
stood at the door, gazing up at the dark ridge beyond town.
In the distance came the sound of a piano playing and the
buzz of voices. It was useless to try to sleep now, and dressing
quietly, he went out into the night.

Sam Stepton entered the Hotel Clarendon and stared a moment at the table across the floor. Somehow he wasn't surprised to see LaFarge and Olly Sawyer talking there; it only
confirmed what he already suspected. He paused but an instant, hardly long enough for anyone to notice, then hurried
across the room and mingled with the men standing at the bar.

Casey Daniels ordered a plate of liver, fried onions, and a mug
of beer. Macklin Deats grunted disapprovingly and when the
waiter slanted an eye his way, proceeded to arrange for the
delivery of a thick steak, mashed potatoes with rich dark
gravy, and a side of beans smothered in green chili. His drink
of preference was whiskey—a double straight up.

Casey figured it was Deats's way of showing his disfavor
with his choice.

"No wonder you're skinny as a rail, Daniels," Deats huffed
when the waiter left. "Here I'm going out of my way to in-
troduce you to real uptown victuals and what do you go and
order? Liver and beer!"

Casey grinned. "Your sacrificial act has not gone unnoticed
or unappreciated, Mack, but midnight is not the time for me
to be packing away the volume of food you are obviously
better suited to carry."

Deats huffed amiably and patted his belly with affection.
"Leastwise a stout wind ain't gonna blow me over, Daniels."

"No," Casey admitted. "But then I don't need the use of
a skip hoist to help me out of bed in the morning either."

Deats stifled a chuckle.

The beer and whiskey arrived and the two men washed
down the dust of the trip. Over the rim of his mug Casey spied
the face of a man he recognized. Peter Kramer strode across

the room, grinning, and stuck out a big, rough hand. He had the firm grip of a man who worked hard for every dollar he earned. "Where the hell have you been the last week, Casey?" he said.

"I've been out of town doing some work for Mr. LaFarge." Casey pushed back a chair with his foot. "Sit down and tell me what's new."

"Oh, nothing much. Same job, different day. I'm down another dozen feet on my claim, but working for Mr. LaFarge cuts into the time I can put in."

Kramer was a big man with the equally big arms that came with swinging a drill hammer all day. His young face was usually smiling, and his sandy hair seemed forever in a state of confusion beneath the dusty celluloid bill cap.

"Well, at least you have money coming in while you develop your own claim. You have a good location, Peter: it won't be long. Did LaFarge get the new shoring built?" The project had been on Casey's mind since he'd left the gold camp over a week ago and put it in Sam Stepton's hands to oversee. It had been a particularly tricky design, because of a density difference between two layers of rock where the volcanic intrusion, that had given birth to the gold in the Cripple Creek Mining District, had flowed between an unusually soft sedimentary rock. Casey had considered different shoring techniques, finally discarding all the textbook designs and drawing a clean-paper design of his own.

"They finished with it this morning," Kramer said.

"I'll inspect it tomorrow morning, then."

Kramer laughed. "LaFarge already put men into that shaft today, Casey. I figure if he thinks it's OK, then it must be so. Besides, Casey, you designed it and as far as I'm concerned, you're the best mining engineer in all of Cripple Creek."

Casey frowned. "I appreciate your vote of confidence, Peter, but I had wanted to inspect it before he put any men down there. He'll need me to sign off on the plans if he wants the union's blessings."

Peter Kramer laughed. "What union? A bunch of unorganized miners milling around like lost sheep. A tiger made of straw. There's no bite in 'em."

"You a member?"

"Naw. I got better things to do with my time." Peter's eyes brightened suddenly. "I finished it, Casey."

"Finished what?" Casey had to do some fancy mental footwork to catch up with Peter's sudden shift.

"That little house I've been building all spring. I sent Maureen a letter three days ago telling her it's finally finished. I told her to sell everything and come on out, now that we have a place to live. I sure miss her, and Margaret." Peter's face was glowing, and it had nothing to do with the stark, bright glare of the electric light fixtures suspended from the ceiling. "Why, the way Fremont and Hayden Placer are growing, in no time at all there will be schools and churches, and all kinds of nice stores for a lady to shop in. Every day men are sending for their women to come to town. You see as many women as men stepping off the stagecoaches. It's the women who will turn this rough mining camp into a place fit to raise children."

"How old is Maggie?"

Peter gave him a crooked grin and said, "Call her Maggie to her face and she'll give you the evil eye for sure. Her name is *Margaret*! *Margaret* will be eight come August. I can't wait for you to meet her, Casey. She's got her mother's eyes, blue as cornflowers. Have I ever showed you her picture?"

"Oh, I think you might have, Peter. Maybe once or twice."

Peter grinned. "A man can never be too proud of his family, I reckon." Then he spied a friend across the room. "Someone I got to see, Casey," he said, standing. "I'll talk to you later." Peter Kramer wove through the tables, pulled back a chair at one of them and sat down.

"OK, so what's the matter now?" Deats said, studying him. "You look like someone stepped all over your favorite hat."

Casey frowned, then said, "Nothing's the matter except . . ."

"Except . . . ?"

"I had told Mr. LaFarge I wanted to inspect that shoring before he put men down into the tunnel."

"Oh, is that all. Well, if it makes you feel any better, I understand that Mr. LaFarge does pretty much what Mr. LaFarge *wants* to do. He ain't well thought of among most businessmen. I won't haul freight for him, and frankly, I'm surprised a man like you—a man with integrity—would work for him."

Casey winced. Working for LaFarge had not been easy at times. He had had to look the other way more than once when it came to some of Phillip LaFarge's business practices, but so far none of LaFarge's double-dealings had touched upon his job as a junior mining engineer beneath old Sam Stepton.

Deats said, "You know how he got his hands on the Rattlesnake in the first place, don't you?"

"I've heard rumors, but that's all. I've learned to believe only half of what I hear, and that with a skeptical ear."

"Yeah, I know. You didn't believe me when I told you this Hotel Clarendon served the best food around."

Casey grinned and speared the last of the liver with his fork. "I'm still not convinced of that, Mack."

Deats made a face. "Well, how much can any man do to make *liver* not taste and feel like old shoe leather? Anyway, the Rattlesnake was one of Matt Sterrett's original claims. He'd staked it out and put his name to it like he should of, but he never got around to registering it. He laid claim to another piece of ground at about the same time and filed a lode claim on it; Pride of the Rockies, he named that one. This happened early in '91, before Count Pourtales came to spy out the District and then turn the camp on its head. You know about that, don't you?"

"Of course I do," Casey said, although he really knew little about those first hectic months after Bob Womack had discovered gold at the head of Poverty Gulch. He did know, however, that Bob's reputation for cheap whiskey and ladies of dubious reputation, and the Mount Pisgah hoax of a few years earlier, had dampened anyone's enthusiasm to take his story seriously, even though Bob had the assayed ore to prove his claim. That chunk of gold-bearing rock spent months gathering dust in the window of the J. F. Seldomridge and Sons grain store on South Tejon Street until Ed De LaVergne spied it and recognized it for what it was. Ed asked some questions, made some quiet plans, and then with his partner, Fred Frisbee, took a quick trip up to the Broken Box Ranch on Cripple Creek to check it out.

Mack rolled his burly shoulders and pressed his forearms to the table as he leaned closer. "After the Count went and bought Steve Blair's Buena Vista claim, suddenly anyone with any cash at all to invest was a-pourin' it into Cripple Crick. Matt Sterrett sold his Rattlesnake claim to a speculator from Florence by the name of Sandie Cantwell. Well, on his way back home, Cantwell met up with LaFarge on the Santa Fe Stage at Ben Requa's store in Fountain. No one knows what happened, but before the stage reached Pueblo, one of the passengers by the name of Mueller was dead from a knife in the belly and the sheriff was hauling Cantwell off to jail.

"They had stopped at Midway Station, and it happened while the folks were off stretching their legs. Someone said Cantwell had done the deed. There were no real witnesses, none that had actually seen Cantwell murder the poor fellow. But everyone aboard said that Cantwell and Mueller had come to words and nearly to blows. Well, Cantwell was the only logical suspect, and I believe he would have paid for the deed at the end of a rope if Mr. LaFarge hadn't showed up at the jail a day or two later with the alibi Cantwell needed. LaFarge said that Cantwell had been with him the whole time, never left his sight. He had another man there with him to back up the story, too."

Casey said, "It seems odd that they didn't speak up right away."

Mack gave a short laugh. "You ain't the only one who

thinks that. But Mueller had no kin nobody could find and the matter went away. The funny thing is, when a crew arrived to start working the Rattlesnake claim, it was Mr. Phillip LaFarge who was the major stockholder, not Sandie Cantwell. And another thing. The fellow who first pointed a finger at Cantwell—he's a gent named Barney Mays, and it wasn't long before Mays showed up here, in the District, along with the other passenger that supported LaFarge and gave an alibi to Cantwell. A man named—''

Mack's words stopped and his mouth dropped as his view shot past Casey's left shoulder. Casey turned. A man was rising from a chair across the room—short, burly, wearing a gray suit and a dark bowler hat and, as he turned a bit of lamplight glinted off the spectacles perched upon his lumpy nose. It was only after the man walked away that Casey saw that the second fellow at the table was his boss, Phillip LaFarge. Casey looked back at Mack.

Mack cranked his mouth shut and a small, satisfied smile moved across his lips as the man in the gray suit walked out the front door. ''The man's name is Oliver Sawyer, and that was him who just left.''

''It is still only rumors and hearsay, Mack.'' Casey glanced back over his shoulder in time to see LaFarge stand and make his way across the room and out the door as well.

''Maybe, but there comes a time when a man needs to look closely at them rumors—especially when the facts all add up. What time you got, Casey?'' Mack asked all at once, changing the subject.

Casey took out his watch and said, ''A little after one o'clock.''

Mack finished off his whiskey, pushed his plate back, and scrubbed his mouth with the linen napkin. ''I suppose I ought to move my wagon and catch some sleep. I'll need to unload that steam engine early and get back to Florissant before noon. If I dally too long up here, old Hundley will have corralled all the business from the Midland's morning train. Got to make hay while the sun shines, you know.''

"Good night, Mack. And thanks for the ride into town.''

"Night, Casey.''

Macklin Deats left and Casey strolled to the bar and shouldered up beside Sam Stepton. Sam didn't notice him at first. His eyes were turned towards the now empty table where Phillip LaFarge and Oliver Sawyer had sat only a few minutes before.

"You're up late, Sam,'' Casey said.

Sam Stepton looked over with a start. After a moment he relaxed and fixed a tight grin to his face. Casey didn't know how old Stepton was, only that he'd been working the mining camps long before Casey was born, and that he had two grown boys who owned a farm of some kind in California. Sam was hatless tonight and his white hair was wild and tangled, as if he'd not brushed it in a while. His face was nut brown and creased, with a black smudge on his right cheek that Casey knew had come from an explosion some years back in the silver mines around Aspen.

Sam gave a short laugh. "I couldn't sleep tonight, Casey, so rather than to toss and turn and keep Sharon awake, I got dressed and came here instead.''

Casey thought he detected a note of concern in Sam's voice, but perhaps not. Sam was a man who wasn't happy if he didn't have something to worry about. Mostly Sam Stepton worried about his work, even when work was through for the day and he was supposed to be relaxing.

"When did you get back?'' he asked.

"I just rode in with Macklin Deats about an hour ago. In fact, those are my bags over by the door. I haven't been back to my cabin.''

"That's a long hike this time of night,'' he said dourly.

"I could have caught a ride with Mr. LaFarge a few minutes ago, if I had thought of it.''

Sam seemed to go cold for a moment. "Well, if you don't

find a ride tonight you can come up with me in the morning.''

''Thanks. I heard you got the new shoring in place, Sam. How did it go?''

Stepton looked away from him. ''Oh, it went all right, Casey.'' His voice was oddly distant, matching his gaze.

Casey waited, but Sam remained staring into the distance. ''Did you have any trouble with the extra overhead stringer?''

''I said it went all right,'' Sam said impatiently. He pushed away from the bar. ''I better get back. Been out long enough.''

Casey watched Sam leave, wondering what he had said to rile him. He shrugged it off, blaming it on the lateness of the hour. Sam was probably tired, as he was, and indeed, it was time he found his way home as well. He had the new shoring to inspect in the morning, and he wanted to get it finished before LaFarge sent the first shift down.

Casey left his beer on the bar and gathered up his grips. Outside, he flagged down a dilapidated phaeton heading towards Battle Mountain and hitched a ride to his cabin.

# THREE

MAUREEN KRAMER HUDDLED UNDER THE BLACK UMBRELLA as she hurried down the rain-slick sidewalk through a shadowy canyon of brick and concrete. A brilliant white flash arced across the stormy sky, momentarily blinding her. Almost at once a drumroll of thunder rumbled like a freight train about to run her over. Maureen's vision came back. Ahead, beyond the opaque curtain of driven rain, the feeble splotches of light from the widely spaced street lamps wavered before her.

Maureen clutched her shawl tighter while her other hand gripped the umbrella, which fought her like a wild animal in the icy wind off the lake. It was a wind that cut to the bone. Cold . . . wet . . . with none of the feel of summer.

She hated Michigan.

She hated the wet, cold winters.

She hated the frigid winds off Lake Huron, Lake Saint Clair, and Lake Erie.

She hated the dirty city, with its depressing, perpetual clouds of smoke from factories that never closed, and the soot and fumes of the thousand chimneys.

But there was another reason Maureen Kramer hated Detroit, and as she hurried through the driving rain and crashing sky towards the dark six-story brick apartment house at the end of the street, the dread swelled within her.

Maureen shoved through the heavy green door and pushed it closed against the wind. She stopped just inside, shivering and shaking her umbrella. To the right was the staircase that wound round and round. Her sister's apartment was up on the sixth floor. To Maureen's left was a desk and a threadbare chair resting on a bare pine floor.

The sleepy clerk had glanced up from his paper as the icy wind whistled through, flickering the feeble flame of a gaslight. He didn't offer a cheery hello—he didn't offer any hello at all. He merely stared at her in his peculiar way that made Maureen's skin crawl whenever she returned home to her sister's apartment. She knew her red hair was rather startling, but Swink's thoughts were obvious, and they had nothing to do with the color of her hair, the shape of her comely face, or the fair complexion with which she had been cursed. He might have been intrigued by her heavy Irish accent, but she didn't really believe that either.

She shook most of the rain out of the umbrella, then collapsed it. "Good evening, Mr. Swink," she said out of common courtesy, and because whenever she spoke directly to him, Gorham Swink took those probing eyes off her and returned them to the wrinkled newspaper that was always spread open upon the desk. Swink was a tall beanpole of a man who shaved whenever the spirit moved him—and the spirit never moved him two days in a row. In the summer he wore a dirty undershirt regardless of the weather, and in the winter he never appeared without the raveling dark blue sweater which made Maureen think that at one time he might have been a sailor. Like she, Gorham Swink lived with a sister; a flaccid, obese woman who never bathed and rarely left her apartment.

Why there should be a desk in an apartment house had at first confused her, but then Bridie had told her that some of the rooms were let by the week to workers at the nearby Hoffman's Steel Works. And there were the boatmen, too, who needed a room for a few days until their ship steamed out or until they could find a new berth.

"Evenin', Mrs. Kramer," Swink said, returning his eyes to the newspaper as she had hoped he would.

Maureen glanced up the long winding flights of steps. They reminded her of a coiled serpent, and up there, at its head, were the fangs. Her heart thumped her ribs. It wasn't as if it was her fault, she told herself angrily, starting up the stairs at an even pace, in no hurry. There was only one person up there that she cared to see, and if it hadn't been for Margaret she'd have left a long time ago. She should have gone with Peter when he took off for the gold camp, in spite of his warnings. She'd have gladly faced the hardships of the new Cripple Creek Mining District rather than remain here with her sister and her rum-loving husband.

Maureen reached the top floor, steeled herself against what might greet her beyond the door, took the knob in hand, and went inside. The little apartment was depressing—just like Detroit itself. Its single window looked out onto the next building, so close beside them that only at high noon did anything resembling daylight manage to filter down. And they were on the top floor! Maureen imagined that the window on the ground floor, where Swink and his grotesquely fat sister lived, had never known the feel of full light upon its wavy, sandcast glass panes. To the left was Bridie and Ralph's bedroom, and across the eight-foot-long living room was the kitchen. The gaslights in the apartment needed cleaning; their smoke only added to the stink of the city.

There was a single oak table standing on a fading carpet. Against one wall was a couch where Maureen slept, and beside it a pile of blankets bunched up and shoved into a corner where Margaret slept. At the moment, though, Margaret was sitting upon a straight-back oak chair, looking at a picture book in the naked flickering flame emanating from a black iron pipe in the center of a chipped plaster sconce molded to look like a seashell.

"Mommy!" Margaret said, hopping off the chair and throwing her small arms around her mother's waist.

Maureen dropped to one knee and gave the girl a giant hug. If it weren't for Margaret, life here would be unbearable. "How is Mommy's little lady?" she asked. Through the kitchen doorway, Maureen could see the shadow of Bridie moving around. The odor of cooking food filled the little place like an oppressive wet blanket. There was no cigar smoke, so apparently Ralph had not yet come home from Hoffman's.

Margaret had inherited Maureen's beautiful red hair and bright blue eyes, but unfortunately she had gotten her father's nose, a bit overlarge. Maureen felt certain the little girl would grow into it. She had Peter's chin though, which more than made up for the slight imperfection. But she had plainly inherited Maureen's strong jaw, and her even stronger will. It was only after Margaret had been born that Maureen had begun to appreciate the trials and tribulations she must have put her own mother through. Raising a headstrong child was no easy task, and doing it without a husband around to help made it doubly hard. *It was a test from God, to be sure*!

"I'm all right, Mommy," Margaret said.

Maureen held her at arm's length and studied the little face. "Your words say one thing, darlin', but the tone in your voice says somethin' else. Now out with it."

Margaret shrugged her shoulders beneath the gray sack dress. "It's just that I get tired staying indoors all day long—"

Suddenly the window flared and the building rumbled and shook from the thunder. Maureen and Margaret leaped, and when the explosion had passed they looked at each other and laughed. Maureen said, "With weather like that, inside is the safest place to be."

"I know, but even when it isn't raining, Aunt Bridie makes me stay inside."

"I know, darlin'. We are living in a rough part of the city. Bridie only does what she thinks is best."

Margaret pouted and said softly, "She's just mean. She doesn't like me."

"Now, that's not true," Maureen said. "Bridie has never had children and she doesn't quite know how they are, that's all."

"You're a-drippin' on my floor, Mau."

Maureen looked up. Bridie was in the kitchen doorway, her arms folded and holding a long wooden spoon in her right fist. Bridie O'Connor had Maureen's face and hair, but she was heavier by twenty pounds, and five years older as well, and at thirty the strain of life had begun to settle deeply in her face; a face perpetually sculpted into a frown. Maureen knew that part of Bridie's unhappiness lay in a barren womb. Bridie had long ago given up any hope of having children. But the other side of her unhappiness had mostly to do with the man she had vowed to share her life and bed with.

Still, at least she had a place of her own, as she continually reminded Maureen, with a husband who brought home his pay once a week—all except that portion which found its way into the till of McNulty's Saloon.

Maureen stood and looked at the small pool of muddy water under her feet. "I'm sorry, Bridie. I'll wipe it up."

"You best be believin' you will, deary."

Maureen pulled her shawl from her shoulders and carried the umbrella past Bridie, who moved aside to let her into the kitchen. She put the umbrella on a hook on the back door where it could drip, then came back with a rag and cleaned every trace of water from the stained pine-board floor. When Maureen finished, Bridie put herself in the kitchen doorway, blocking her sister's way, and held out a hand.

Maureen knew precisely what she wanted. She reined in her sudden anger and then, fixing an innocent smile upon her lips, placed the wet rag in Bridie's hand.

Bridie threw the rag across the room. "You won't be thinkin' it so funny when I toss you and your kid out into the street, deary Mau."

Maureen bit her tongue. She wheeled and found her hand-bag in the shawl's folds, then fished out two coins and pressed them into Bridie's hand.

Bridie made an attempt at a smile, and failed. "It's only fair, Mau," she said, trying to sound reasonable. "When you get paid, we get paid. You can't expect me and Ralph to feed and house you and your kid and not get paid for it."

"Peter sends you money once a month," Maureen shot back. Her temper was on the verge of exploding, and she struggled to keep it caged, for once let out it could be a fear-some beast.

Bridie dropped the coins into the pocket of her dress. "I told you when you married that man, Mau, that he was goin' to bring you nothin' but grief. He's a lazy fool, like a boy who never grew up, who runs off to strike it rich in Colorado, or wherever else the cry of gold is to be heard. As much as I regret saying so, Mau, you are better off here with me and Ralph. At least you're with family. You make a little money at that penny store, and that's more than most women can say for themselves."

Margaret was watching them with big eyes and a peculiar tightness around her mouth that had only first made itself known upon her young face after they had moved in with Bridie and Ralph. As the weeks and months stretched out, Maureen had watched her daughter pull deeper within herself. In the beginning, Margaret would cry herself to sleep at night, wrapped in the safety of Maureen's arms, but after a while the tears stopped. Now there was only that taut stare as she with-drew somewhere deep inside herself—somewhere she could deal with the pain and stress on her own terms. Somewhere that even Maureen was being excluded from.

Maureen did not want Margaret to see another fight. She submerged her pride, turned her back to Bridie, and lifted Mar-garet into her arms.

"Now, darlin', tell Mommy what you did today." Maureen wondered if Margaret could sense her stress and despair, and prayed she hadn't. They sat on the sagging couch, where Margaret showed her a picture of a cat on a picket fence that she had drawn. Maureen pretended to look at the picture while watching Bridie out of the corner of her eye until her sister disappeared back inside the kitchen.

Ralph O'Connor came in then, pushing the door shut behind him. He stood a moment on slightly spread legs, as if trying to keep the rest of his body from swaying. His face was flush, and his nose glowed slightly. Ralph had gained a lot of weight in the last couple of years. His once tight belly now overflowed his pants and strained his suspenders. He never bothered anymore buttoning the shabby black vest that he wore every day—it would have been fruitless to try. As he stood there, Maureen thought that he looked shorter than he had that happy day in June fourteen years earlier when he and Bridie had exchanged vows at St. Mary's Church back home in County Cork.

Ralph held a battered lunch pail in one hand and two or three envelopes in the other. He blinked as if the feeble light stung his eyes, then gave Maureen a crooked grin. "Helluva rain, ain't it, Mau?"

"Yes it is," Maureen said flatly. How could Bridie talk about Peter as she did when her own husband came home every night nearly falling-down drunk!

"Ralph!" Bridie screeched from the kitchen. Her glowering face loomed in the doorway. "You've been drinkin' again!"

"Aw, Bridie, it weren't but just a wee nip at McNulty's."

"McNulty's! I swear, Ralph, if it weren't for your 'wee nips' Liam McNulty would be out of business for sure. It's you and fools like you what are payin' for that grand apartment of his and all them fancy clothes his wife wears!"

"Aw, be charitable, darlin'. Don't be startin' in on me again. I just stepped through the door."

" 'Stepped'? Hah! More like you stumbled through, and barely able to keep from tippin' over."

" 'Tis not like that at all, Bridie.'' Ralph walked unsteadily across the room and reached for her.

"You stay away from me, you drunken fool.''

"What? Not even a little kiss? Ain't you glad to see me home?''

She moved out from his groping arm. "I warned you, Ralph O'Connor. You keep your hands off me or I'll—''

"Or you'll what?''

Bridie scowled and left the room, then came back with a broom.

Maureen moved to the edge of the couch and wrapped her arms around Margaret. This scene was taking an all-too-familiar course—one Maureen had had the misfortune to witness more than two dozen times in the year and a half that she and Margaret had lived with her sister and brother-in-law.

"Now, what is it you're intendin' to do with that floor sweeper, darlin'?'' Ralph's voice took on a menacing tone.

Bridie cocked the broom over her shoulder like a bat. "If I'm lucky I'll knock some sense into that thick skull of yours, Mr. O'Connor.''

Ralph threw back his head and laughed.

Bridie swung.

Ralph ducked. He was remarkably agile considering his inebriated condition. He stepped inside Bridie's arms and his fist came up. Maureen clutched Margaret to her breast as the smack resounded in the small room. Bridie staggered back against the doorjamb, then immediately rammed the broom handle into Ralph's stomach. He grunted, buckling, then grabbed it, and the two of them played a tug-of-war game with the broom. Ralph won, and Bridie stumbled across the room into the wall.

Maureen clutched Margaret tighter, trying to stay out of their way.

"You're a big, brave man hittin' a woman!'' Bridie screeched, snatching up a boot that had been sitting next to their bedroom door. Ralph ducked too late, and the boot glanced off his forehead, opening a gash. It sailed on into the kitchen, where something crashed to the floor.

"Woman, you try my patience!" Ralph dove across the room, wrestling Bridie to the floor. They tumbled across the tattered carpet, cussing and swinging and leaving a trail of blood and spit. Bridie's fingernails slashed Ralph's face while his big fists bruised her cheeks and bloodied her nose and mouth.

Maureen felt Margaret whimpering against her. She backed into a corner, as far from the flailing arms and legs as she could get in the tiny room.

Finally Ralph stood, shaking, sleeving blood from his cheek. He glared down at Bridie, who scooted up against the wall, holding her bloodied face in both hands, her tears leaving streaks in the smears upon her face. His angry eyes shifted, riveted a moment upon Maureen; then, turning heavily, he left the apartment, slamming the door shut.

Maureen went to Bridie, but her sister pushed her away, crawled into the bedroom, and closed the door.

The apartment was in shambles. Margaret was shaking in the corner, where she half buried herself in the blankets and pillow.

"Mommy?"

Maureen turned away from the mess. Margaret was big-eyed and as white as face powder.

"It's all right now, darlin' " Maureen said.

"Aunt Bridie was bleeding real bad."

"It looks worse than it really is, I think."

"Will she be all right?"

"Of course she will. You'd think Aunt Bridie would learn by now not to badger Ralph when he's been drinkin'." Maureen tried to encourage her daughter with a smile. "Now look at this mess they left us with. Think you can help me clean it up?" When Ralph left as he just had, he hardly ever returned home until the next day. And Bridie would probably remain in her room for the night.

Maureen would bring her a basin of warm water and a towel—but that would be later. At the moment, she knew her sister would refuse any aid. Bridie was stubborn, and she had a temper as well—both traits that she and Maureen shared.

Maureen set about putting the kitchen in order. The crash she had heard had been a beef stew, and it was now spread across the floor. Maureen shut off the gas burner and began to clean the mess.

From the other room, Margaret suddenly cried, "Mommy!"

Maureen dropped the mop and rushed back into the living room. Margaret was holding one of the envelopes Ralph had brought home.

"What's wrong, darlin'?" But she could see the child was excited, not frightened.

Margaret shoved an envelope into her hand. "It's a letter from Daddy!"

*Dear Maureen,*

*You can hardly believe how hectic life is becoming here in the camp. People coming and going in such frenzy all the time. Every day more new faces stepping off the stagecoaches from Florence, Florissant, and Colorado Springs. Whenever I stop to watch all these people I think of that time we went to Mr. Barnham's Greatest Show on the Earth, and Margaret got lost. Remember when we found her by the elephants? She had no idea she'd become separated from us, all she cared about was whether or not I could buy her an elephant, and could we keep it in the lot behind the apartment. That day was all so confusing—and so is this place, Maureen. But there is such excitement and expectation in the air that one hardly notices.*

*What's coming of all this bustle is a fine town—well, two towns, but I can explain that to you later. There are new stores going up on Bennett and Myers and Carr Avenues every day. Go off for a week and a half and*

*you'd come back not recognizing the place! The towns
are putting up polls to carry electricity right into the
stores. It is already on Bennett Avenue where electric
carbon arc streetlights make the street nearly as bright
at midnight as it is during the day. Soon it will be into
peoples houses as well. We even have a Telephone
Exchange! It's enough to make your head whirl, Maureen! There are churches going up too. You'd love St.
Peter's Catholic Church. And with the churches, there
are schools opening up, and talk of a water works now
being planned. By the end of the year we should have
drinking water out of a pipe! Doesn't that sound grand?*

*I have more news too. I've found promising color on
my claim. It ain't much yet, but I've talked to a good
friend, Casey Daniels, who is a mining engineer at the
Rattlesnake. He says that what I have found is a gold-
bearing float just like Bob Womack found before he
struck his lode at Poverty Gulch! It is a great encour-
agement, and keeps me working the claim after I'm done
working for Mr. LaFarge.*

*But now for the best news of all. I have just finished
building us a house, Maureen, and I want you and Margaret to come out as soon as you can! It ain't much as
far as houses go, but it's what most folks in Cripple build.
It has a solid wood floor, and a wooden front with a door
and a window too! The sides and top are all canvas for
the time being, but I'll be replacing them as I can afford
it. It's up in Hayden Placer, but folks generally just call
it Cripple Creek after the District. It's a nice place, Maureen, not like Fremont. It don't allow gambling or dance
halls, none of them frail sisters homes neither. All them
things that Fremont is encouraging.*

*I can't wait to see both of you. You have no idea how
much I miss you. Hope all has gone well living with your
sister. I know it ain't been easy. But now you can come
out to Colorado, and a house of your own. Please come*

*soon. Wire me as to your arrival so as I can meet you at
the stage when it comes in. I love you.*

*Yours faithfully,*
*Peter*

Maureen read the letter aloud. Margaret clapped her hands
with glee and the fight of a few minutes before was instantly
forgotten. "When can we go, Mommy? Can we leave today?
Please?"

"No, darlin', we have to make preparations." Maureen tried
to sound in perfect control, but inside she was bubbling over
like Margaret. She was finally going to be able to leave Detroit
and join Peter. Colorado, she had read, was a beautiful place
of wide tawny grasslands and blue towering mountains, where
fragrant pine trees and emerald glens were everywhere for the
eye to see. Peter had written often in his letters, of the pleasant
summer in the mountains, when the ground warmed and pine
needles smelled sweeter than perfume. He'd written just as
often about the fierce winter as well, but right now, Maureen
didn't care.

"What preparations?"

"Well, we have to pack all our clothes. Then there is that
little bit o' furniture in storage; I'll be wantin' to ship it out.
I'll have to give Mr. Johnson notice that I'll be quittin' his
penny story . . . and there's the post office too. I'll need to tell
them so they will know where to forward any mail."

"How long will all that take?" Margaret sounded daunted
by the long list of things to do.

Maureen squeezed her daughter's arms. "It won't take that
long, although it might seem like it. No more than a week or
two, I should think—enough time to give Mr. Johnson proper
notice, you understand."

"I'm going to write Daddy a letter right now and tell him
we are going to be there in two weeks!"

"You do that, darlin'. And when you're done I'll add my
note to it. Meanwhile, I'll get busy cleanin' up this mess."

• • •

The head-frame to the Rattlesnake mine stood against the night sky like the skeleton of some grotesque beast. Phillip LaFarge pulled his carriage around back of the hoist shack, unhitched the horse from its traces, put it in a corral down at the edge of the claim, away from the works. He took the path up to the dark mine office, which also doubled as his sleeping quarters.

The works were abandoned this late at night. It rankled him that the mine was not yet producing enough gold for him to keep it operating around the clock. The board of directors were on his back, pushing him to show more than the mountain was willing to give. It rankled too that the next claim over, James McKinnie and Frank Peck's Black Diamond mine, had already turned into a paying property. LaFarge liked to think himself a success already, but the truth of the matter was, he was barely making payroll.

As he strode up the steep trail to the office, LaFarge renewed his determination to have the biggest mine in the District, and at any cost. Instinctively his hand went to the pocket containing the thick envelope Sawyer had delivered to him, and a thin slash of a smile chiseled itself in the sharp features of his face.

He unlocked the door to the mine office and put a match to the lantern on the corner of his desk. The flame pushed the shadows back into the corners of the room. He pushed aside the clutter and removed the papers from the envelope, spreading them flat. Among the half dozen sheets there was a three-page engineering report of a mineral survey of the Black Diamond mine, apparently copied from the original in Elvin Tate's own hand. LaFarge read it carefully, comparing it with the reports his own consulting engineers, Sam Stepton and Casey Daniels, had prepared on the minerals of the area.

Next was a page titled: *Cross-section through Black Diamond vein system.* It had been copied from a much larger drawing, but Tate had been careful to include all the tunnels and drifts, and a legend; gold-bearing veins in red pencil, the basalt dikes in black, and the phonolite dikes in brown. On one side was a scale of the levels. The mine was down to 150 feet already.

He retrieved a plat of Battle Mountain from his files and oriented it to the cross-section of the Black Diamond claim. It was a standard lode claim: 1,500 feet long and 300 feet wide, running northeasterly up the side of Battle Mountain. At its northernmost corner the Rattlesnake claim touched it, running generally northwesterly. LaFarge studied the drawing and compared it with a similar diagram of his own mine. A frown worked its way slowly onto his face. It was just as he feared: The vein he was working was the *same* vein McKinnie and Peck's crew were working; they were just coming at it from different ends. But the distressing thing was that if the engineering reports were accurate, the vein apexed on the Black Diamond claim! That meant that according to the bothersome Apex Law, the vein belonged to Peck and McKinnie!

LaFarge took a cigar from the humidor on his desk and bit down on it, thinking. His most expedient course would be to work the vein until its ownership was found out, but then he'd have to abandon the work, and there would be months of litigation. There was only one sure way to protect the vein, and that was to acquire his rival's mine.

He studied the plat again. The claim on the far side of the Black Diamond was owned by Jimmie Doyle, James Burns, and John Harnan. They were no threat. The "Three Jims," as they were affectionately referred to around the District—even though one of them was named John—had filed on the tiny tenth of an acre, and had built a shack on it. But as far as LaFarge—or anyone else, for that matter—knew, those three just squatted on that postage-stamp-sized claim. No one ever saw them doing much work.

To the south, Sam Strong's Strong Mine might pose a threat. Sam was pulling lots of gold out of the ground, but according to the cross-section in front of him, LaFarge's vein ran away from Strong's claim.

The only other threat to LaFarge's hoped-for empire was that recluse carpenter from Colorado Springs, Winfield Scott Stratton. Stratton's Independence mine barely made enough to cover expenses. He had only a small crew working the mine, and it seemed to LaFarge that unless Stratton made a big strike soon, the slightly built, white-haired man was destined to return broke to his carpenter shop in the Springs.

LaFarge leaned back in his chair and blew a cloud of cigar smoke at the ceiling. There had to be a way; there always was a way for a man daring enough to seize the opportunity. He poured himself a whiskey and rolled the glass in his palms as he considered various possibilities, but nothing satisfactory came to mind. He put the problem temporarily aside, finished his drink, locked the valuable papers Elvin Tate had stolen for him in the company safe, and went to bed.

# FOUR

A HUNDRED FEET BENEATH THE GROUND, THE QUIET DARK-
ness plays games with a man's senses. He feels disconnected,
as if treading a world beyond his own. Perhaps this is what
Venus was like, Casey mused, moving alone through the darkness, with only the beam of his safety lamp connecting him
to the real world. And if it should go out? Casey grinned to
himself. That would be unlikely, but if it should, he could
always find his way to the skip—the metal box in which the
ore was hauled up—by feel if he had to. As of yet, the tunnels
being driven through the District were not all that extensive—
not like those of Leadville or Aspen, where men had burrowed
into the ground for decades.

Casey stepped carefully over snaking rubber hoses and the
iron rails of the ore carts. The rolled-up engineering drawings
were tucked under his left arm, his right hand swinging the
beam of his lantern from the floor a few feet ahead of him, to
the walls pressing nearby, and finally to the ceiling shoring
three feet overhead. He was working his way through the long
passageway of the Treasure Trove Tunnel, nearing the La-
Farge Drift Number Three, which was cut to explore a smaller
vein that LaFarge had dubbed the Princess' Necklace. It was

there that they'd encountered the disconformity which had forced Casey to design an elaborate shoring to support the soft ceiling.

The beam of the lantern picked out the new cut thirty feet ahead. Behind him a soft tapping against basalt walls made him stop and listen. Casey wasn't a suspicious man, but no miner—no matter how pragmatic he claimed to be—could ever completely ignore those deep, distant sounds that sometimes come out of solid rock. Miners called them Tommy-knockers, little mischievous omens of impending disaster. Casey didn't know precisely what caused the eerie sounds, but he suspected it had something to do with shifting pressure within the rock around him. Blasting a tunnel through ancient stone tended to cause the rock to adjust to the new stresses.

Just the same, Casey swung the beam of the lamp back along the dark corridor that he had just come from. As he suspected, there was nothing back there.

He started forward again, swinging the beam up a winze, or passageway, that connected this level to the one above which LaFarge had abandoned when the vein ran out. Silent blackness swallowed the beam of his light; a slight breeze spilled down, stirring the heavy air here below.

Casey turned into the new drift and stopped again, listening. From nearby came the slow, steady sound of dripping water, echoing in some small pool. It won't be too long, he thought, before LaFarge was going to have to install pumps. He started into the new works, his light glancing off the new shoring.

What Casey saw made his jaw go suddenly rigid. Quickly the beam leaped from the ceiling braces, to the timbers against the walls, and then back again. For an instant Casey wondered if he hadn't stepped into the wrong tunnel, but he knew he had not. Now he steadied the beam on the timbers overhead. It was all standard square set shoring! Casey pushed deeper, stumbling over the hoses of the new pneumatic drills snaking along the floor. Overhead, the crumbly rock ceiling remained unsupported. He had carefully designed a system of timbers that would have held that rotten granite in place, but what LaFarge had built instead was the open box-work typical of normal shoring—fast, easy to put up, and cheap.

Casey's anger rose as he gripped the rolled engineering drawings in his fist, crushing them. At the end of the drift where the timbers stopped, his light glanced off the pile of rock the miners had blasted the night before, waiting for the morning crew to shovel out. LaFarge, in his hurry to gouge out the gold-bearing rock, had completely ignored his plans!

Suddenly Casey understood why Sam Stepton had been so evasive the night before. Casey wheeled and scrambled back along the tunnel, heedless of the dangers of the dark, his view riveted upon the single spot of bobbing light illuminating the uneven floor ahead. He rang for the hoist operator on the surface and stepped inside. The skip started upward, clattering like a bucketful of stones. Overhead, a rectangle of light grew steadily larger.

It cleared the shaft and came to an abrupt stop. Casey bounded out. Two dozen men were there in the shack, waiting for the skip to take them down into the mine. Peter Kramer was one of them, talking with three or four other men, a battered lunch bucket in hand. Peter grinned at him as he passed and said, "Boy, is LaFarge mad that you're holding up the works!"

Casey only vaguely heard Peter's warning as he strode out the shack with long, angry strides and headed directly for the mine office. He pushed through the door without knocking and slammed the roll of drawings down upon LaFarge's desk.

"You changed them!" he exploded, pushing his fists onto LaFarge's desk and leaning forward. "You changed my designs for the Princess' Necklace drift. Why?"

LaFarge had been studying an engineering drawing when Casey burst in. Sam Stepton was there as well. LaFarge straightened up and leaned back in his chair, putting extra distance between himself and Casey. He bit down on the cigar between his teeth and his dark eyebrows came together.

"Whatever are you talking about, Mr. Daniels?"

"You know damn well what I'm talking about. My engineered trusses were not built. Instead you had standard box set shoring built. I want to know why!" Casey's view shifted momentarily towards Sam Stepton, and the older man looked away from him.

LaFarge's sharply chiseled features remained unmoving, as if cut into stone instead of flesh. Only his dark eyes moved, then his lips, as he took another long, easy pull at the cigar.

"All right," he said finally. "I had Sam change them."

"Sam?" Casey glanced at the old mining engineer who had been responsible for bringing him to the Cripple Creek Mining District in the first place. Stepton still refused to look him in the eye. "Why?"

"I'm not in the habit of explaining my decisions to my employees, Mr. Daniels."

Casey's anger roared back. "Perhaps not, but you will damn well explain this one to me."

LaFarge considered a moment. "All right. I'll tell you why. What you designed for that drift was too complicated. It would have taken twice as long to build, at twice the expense. I'm running a business here, Mr. Daniels, and the whole point is to make a profit. I won't if I sink thousands of dollars into some elaborate timbering when simple methods will work just fine."

"Simple methods!" Casey could hardly believe what he was hearing. "I've written a complete report on what we encountered down there—"

"Yes, yes, I know," LaFarge said impatiently. "Soft tuff and crumbly breccia—I read your report. But I don't see where it is any different from what has been found in a dozen different mines in the District, Mr. Daniels. Sam reevaluated the structure and says the simple timbering will work."

"Sam? But Sam isn't a geologist. He hasn't been schooled

in engineering . . ." Almost at once, Casey regretted the words. It was true—Sam had none of the book knowledge that he had; had never attended any school to study the subject. But he had worked in mines all his life. Sam possessed untold knowledge of mining—the little things mining schools never get around to teaching. He'd learned them through experience, just as man had for thousands of years.

LaFarge said angrily, "Sam has forgotten more than you know, Mr. Daniels. He's been working mines since before you were born, and I'll trust his judgment. I don't care how many degrees you hold from fancy schools."

Casey glanced at the old man again, but Stepton still refused to look him in the eye. "What you say is true, Mr. LaFarge: Sam's one of the best. But in this case I feel he is wrong— and you as well. What Sam has built down there is not safe. I can't see risking men's lives over a few thousand dollars' worth of lumber and labor. I won't sign off on it."

LaFarge allowed an easy grin to move across his sharp face. "Sam here will sign off on them, won't you, Sam?"

Throughout the encounter Stepton had refused to join in. Now he said quietly, "Yeah, I'll sign 'em, Mr. LaFarge."

LaFarge's victory was complete. The grin broadened and he took another long pull off the cigar, blowing smoke defiantly at the ceiling. "You see, Mr. Daniels, I don't need your signature."

Casey stiffened, drawing himself up to his full height. "It appears that you don't," he answered tightly. "And it appears that you don't need my services as an engineer, either. I won't work for a man who puts profit above concerns for the men who work for him. I quit."

LaFarge shrugged his shoulders. "Very well." He stood, crossed the room to the safe, and drew Casey's pay from a big black cash box that he kept there. "This will cover what the Rattlesnake owes you to date, I should think," he said, pushing thirty dollars in gold across the desk at him.

Casey put the coins in his pocket. He gave Sam one last

look, but still the old man's eyes remained averted, staring down at the floor of the office. Casey turned back to the door and slammed it shut behind him.

Phillip LaFarge casually removed the crumpled drawings that Casey had left on his desk and set them aside. "You will see to these later, Sam, won't you?"

"Yes sir, Mr. LaFarge." Stepton was sick inside. It wasn't as if he had wanted to overrule Casey's findings. LaFarge had said flatly that the project was too expensive and that he wanted it reworked. Casey was a bright young engineer, and Sam genuinely liked him.

Sam was a sixty-year-old mining engineer with no degree in today's world. He would find himself pitching hay down at the livery stable, or sweeping floors if LaFarge fired him. Hardly a noble ending for a life of hard work. Sure, he and Sharon had had a good life, but that had meant spending almost every dollar he'd ever made. They had a little money put away, but not enough for him to be able to afford to lose this job. What could he have done but exactly as LaFarge had told him to do?

"Good. Now, back to business at hand, Sam. I want a crew to start working the Princess vein day and night. I'll have Mr. Madigan pull men off the first level and put them down there as well. We will work them around the clock."

Sam was confused by LaFarge's sudden change in plans. Only two days before LaFarge had wanted extra men on the first level, to scrape out the last of a fading vein there. Now all of a sudden he was putting every man down on the lowest level.

Sam noticed the line of the vein that LaFarge had apparently added to the geologists' drawings. "Where did you get this new information from, Mr. LaFarge? What makes you think that vein is gonna run off in that direction?"

"Call it a hunch, Sam," LaFarge said cryptically. "Now that Mr. Daniels is no longer with us, it will be up to you to keep up with the assay reports. See that you keep me appraised of our progress."

"Of course, I will. Is there anything else you wanted to see me about?"

LaFarge rolled up the sheets of drawings and returned them to the safe, closing the heavy door after them, but not scrambling the combination. "No, that's all for now."

"I'll get to work then." He started for the door.

"Oh, Sam—"

Stepton stopped and turned back.

LaFarge's smile spread like oil across water. "Don't say anything about what I've just shown you, will you, Sam?"

He wouldn't have, of course, but LaFarge's question struck him as odd. Did LaFarge not trust him? Why would he question him now?

"No, 'course I won't tell nobody, Mr. LaFarge."

"Good. And the disagreement between Mr. Daniels, hm?"

"That ain't none of my business either—or anyone else's."

"Good. You're a reliable man, Sam. I'll put something extra in your pay envelope Friday."

"Why, thank you, Mr. LaFarge."

LaFarge grinned. "You take care of this mine's business, and this mine will take care of you." LaFarge opened the door for him.

Sam stood outside looking across the torn-up mountainside. To his left was the growing pile of mine tailings and the hoist shack beneath a timber head-frame that stood black and stark against the brilliant blue Colorado sky. With an uneasiness weighting down his spirits he started across the rocky ground towards it.

Casey Daniels walked down the long slope of Battle Mountain to his little cabin near Wilson Creek, above the fledgling community of Lawrence. Lawrence wasn't much of a town yet, merely a few scattered cabins below the creek, but there was an extraction mill there where they were experimenting with the chlorination refining process, a slaughterhouse, a few commercial buildings, and the beginnings of a brickyard. Not far away was the cabin of Jimmie Doyle and James Burns. Casey knew them to be a friendly pair, along with their partner, John Harnan. They had a small claim not far from LaFarge's Rattlesnake but, despite having erected a little shanty on the plot, the Three Jims seemed to do very little digging on the claim.

Casey hitched his horse to a heavily sprung mountain wagon and by the time he had driven into Cripple Creek, his anger had subsided some and he began making plans for finding another job. There were plenty of mines in the district, and he figured it shouldn't be too hard to find another one to work at. Bob Womack was sitting out in front of the Clarendon when Casey pulled up.

"Mornin', Casey. Step on down from that rig of yours and pull around a chair," Womack said.

Casey tied his horse to the hitching rail and stepped up to the boardwalk that skirted the front of the hotel. It was one of the few buildings in town—in either town—that had such a convenience.

"My, I jest can't get over how tall you'd grow'd, Casey. I can't get it out of my head that you were jest a fresh-faced kid the first time your pa and me and old Ben Requa come up here to dig that hole. You remember it?"

"Sure I do, Bob." Casey could have almost guaranteed that the first words out of Bob Womack's mouth would have referred back to that expedition in the summer of '74. Actually, Bob had only worked the diggings a few days before wandering back down the mountain to Sunview, his father's ranch. But Casey and his father had stayed the whole summer and fall, until the company of prospectors broke up. "Why aren't you working your claim, Bob?"

Bob was a tall willow-switch of a man with stooped shoulders and a great mustache. Casey figured him to be in his late forties or early fifties by now. These days Bob always wore dusty green corduroy overalls and an equally dusty bowler hat, but Casey remembered him differently. When Casey first met him in the early seventies, Bob had been a dashing young man beneath a wide sombrero, wearing chaps, high-heeled boots, and one of Colonel Colt's six-shooters on his hip. Bob could ride like the wind and drink whiskey all night. Casey hardly ever saw Bob on back of a horse these days, but the man sure could drink. He didn't wear the six-shooter anymore either. Sheriff Pete Eales had made it clear that he would confiscate any guns worn into town and sell them for money for the school fund.

Bob said easily, "Oh, I'm just waiting for the stage from Hayden Divide to come on down that hill, Casey."

"Expecting someone?"

Bob grinned crookedly, and Casey suspected that perhaps he had started his drinking early today. "Naw, nobody in particular," he said. "Jest curious to know who it will bring today."

"How is work going on your claim?"

"Oh, I'm making progress at it, Casey. Figure to git to work on it hard next week."

For Bob Womack, there was always a "next week."

Two men strolled past and slapped Bob on the shoulders and congratulated him on discovering Cripple's gold. Bob's eyes beamed. He stood and slapped them back. They all laughed and exchanged pleasantries, and everyone was happy. Although Bob would never admit it, Casey figured that having discovered gold was reward enough for him.

"I'm going inside for a beer, Bob. Care to join me?"

"That's right friendly of you to offer, Casey," he said, holding the door for him. "Ain't it kinda early for you?"

"Not after the morning I've just had, Bob."

They went through the lobby, past the express and stage line offices, and into the dining room, cutting across to the bar just beyond another door. Casey ordered two beers.

"You ain't saying much, Casey, but I can sure see you're worried about something."

Casey considered how much he should tell him. No matter how much he disagreed with it, LaFarge's business was none of Bob's, or the town's. "I just had it out with Mr. LaFarge."

Bob Womack gave a short laugh. "I've been wondering how long it was gonna be before you and that man locked horns. I hear he ain't an easy man to work for. What was it about?"

"It doesn't much matter. What does matter is that I quit the Rattlesnake, and now I'm out of work."

"Hm. No wonder the long face. But don't fret too much over it, Casey. A man like you won't have trouble finding another job. Not in this District."

Finding another job didn't concern Casey as much as the slipshod manner in which LaFarge was running the mine. He was putting good men down that hole in unsafe conditions. But as long as a man with Sam Stepton's experience and reputation was there to back LaFarge up, there wasn't much he could do about it—except try to put it out of mind. Perhaps he was being overly cautious? But how could you be too cautious when dealing with men's lives?

"I'm not too worried about it."

"If you need me to put in a good word for you, I will, Casey."

Casey grinned. "Thanks."

"In-in fact," Bob went on, his tongue loosening some, and loosing with it the slight stutter that came on whenever he got excited . . . or drunk, "I know that Sam Strong is pulling pay dirt out of his mine faster than he knows what to do with it. He's paid off all his loans, I'm told, and he's even eyeing a hunk of real estate down in Texas somewhere. You should go talk to the man. His Strong Mine ain't but a few hundred yards from LaFarge's Rattlesnake, so's you'd still be close to your cabin."

Casey sipped his beer, thinking it over. The Rattlesnake was LaFarge's concern, not his. After all, he couldn't go around policing everyone's claim, he told himself. Casey was suddenly feeling better about the situation. "I'll do that, Bob. I'll go talk to Sam this afternoon." He finished the beer and dried his mustache with his sleeve. "Well, I got some business to see to."

"Th-thanks for the beer, Casey."

On his way out he spied Joe Wolfe coming down the stairs from the floor above. Wolfe could be instantly picked out in a crowd by the wide, flat-brimmed black hat that he preferred to the more modern bowler. His suits were always black, and generally a stunning purple vest resided beneath them. Joe smiled so easily and freely that it made folks wonder what joke he'd just heard—or was replaying inside his head. Joe was a small man, possessed of boundless nervous energy. Casey couldn't recall ever seeing the man frown, even when he was losing at the faro tables. Joe's black eyes always sparkled when they looked at you, as if you were the most important person in the world just then. You couldn't help but like the man, even though it was generally known about town that Joe Wolfe was a promoter of the first order, and that it was best to keep a tight fist on your money clip when he was around.

Casey took his hand. Joe's grip was strong in spite of his small size. "Morning, Joe."

"Casey, you're looking damn good. My God, if I had your height, I'd be murder with the ladies. I haven't seen you around lately. Been busy?"

"I've been out of town. Got back in last night."

Joe laughed, and his heavy gold watch chain bounced merrily upon that purple brocade vest. "Bet you hardly recognized the place when you got back."

"Who can keep up with it? In the last four months Bennett Avenue has exploded from a few scattered buildings to a solid strip of storefronts. Myers Avenue, too, and they are working mightily on turning Carr Avenue into one solid track of lumber as well."

Joe's smile was infectious. "Damn, is it the most amazing thing I ever did see?"

Casey said, "What are you doing here at the Clarendon, Joe? Checking out your competition?"

"Competition? Hell, Casey, this hotel ain't competition— at least not anymore. I just became manager!"

"What have you done with the Continental?"

Joe chuckled. "They built this place thinking they were going to put one over on old Joe Wolfe," he said, obviously satisfied with himself. "Well, I got to hand it to them, they sure did move uptown, and I saw right off that my Continental was going to play second fiddle to it. Now, I don't play second to no man, Casey. You know that, so I up and leased the Continental and came here to manage the Clarendon." Joe winked and leaned closer, lowering his voice. "Actually, Casey . . . and keep this under your hat, but I wanted to get a real close peek at this place and see how they done things. I intend to build another hotel what will make the Clarendon stand up and look twice. And I'm going to build her down in Fremont, where there aren't any silly rules about saloons and parlor houses like they have up here at Hayden. It will be the damn finest hotel in the whole District, Casey, and it will be called the J. H. Wolfe! Yes sir, the finest tables, the best whiskey, and the prettiest and friendliest girls around, you wait and see. I've already bought that lot on the corner of Bennett and Second."

"Big plans, Joe."

He winked again. "My plans are only just beginning, Casey. Well, I got to get about business. Talk to you later." Joe gave him a wave over his shoulder as he headed for the hotel office.

Casey walked down into Fremont. Overhead was a maze of wires; telegraph and those that carried the electricity from the new steam generator. In the distance a steam whistle from one of the mines drifted down from Bull Hill into the valley. On the corner of Bennett Avenue and Third Street a transfer wagon was selling drinking water at five cents a bucket or fifty cents a barrel. Plans were in the works to pipe water from Beaver Creek into the town, but with two separate municipalities involved, it was going to take until the winter, or possibly the following year, before the lines were finally run.

At every corner down the length of Bennett Avenue was a new streetlight, and midway between the blocks, an electric arc bulb hung from a wire suspended across the street. For all its primitive buildings and rough appearance, Hayden Placer, which everyone just called Cripple Creek, and Fremont were really very modern communities. Western Union's telegraph lines had connected the towns with the outside world that March, and shortly thereafter telephones had arrived, though in limited number. There was still no central exchange, but Casey was certain that once the exchange was built every business in town would have one, and he had no doubt that if the boom lasted long enough, there might even be a few homes with them as well. The wealthy mine owners would certainly insist on having one of the newfangled gadgets on their parlor walls.

On the south side of the street the repair work on seven buildings that had been destroyed in an April fire was nearly complete. That fire had occurred the week Casey arrived in town. The buildings involved had been flimsy board, canvas, and log affairs. What replaced them were sound buildings featuring mill-sawed clapboard, large windows, and carved millwork decorations. Between Bennett and Carr an opera house was taking shape, crowding out one of the few vacant lots that remained. Casey stopped to watch carpenters clambering about the framework of what would soon be the Cripple Creek Stock Board and Mining Exchange.

Yes, Cripple was booming, and Casey felt good just being a part of it all. Sure, he was out a job, but another was certain to come along soon. This morning, which had started out so gloomy, had suddenly brightened. Nothing really bad could happen when so much building and commerce was going on all around him.

Well, at least that was what he believed as he stepped into the A. A. Ireland Real Estate Building, where the Bank of Cripple Creek was located.

# FIVE

LISA KELLERMAN SLIPPED FROM UNDER HIS HEAVY ARMS AND climbed out of the bed. Oliver Sawyer lay among the crumpled sheets, his breathing irregular, marked occasionally by a sudden gasp and then some small settling-out snores.

She looked down at herself in the light that filtered through the curtained window. Sawyer's sweat of the night before, and then of earlier that morning, had dried upon her skin and a few dark hairs from his chest still clung to her breasts and belly. She brushed at them halfheartedly and frowned. She had needed a bath days ago. She would have to see to it sometime today.

Lisa slipped into a sheer, peach chiffon robe, tied it loosely about her waist, and opened the curtain. Morning light streamed through the single window, falling upon the rough wooden floor and glinting off the brass bed frame. It brightened every corner of the one-room crib, but even so, it was a dreary shack. In one corner was a battered dressing table, in another hung her six dresses, each one as pretty as the next.

*Men took no heed in properly undressing a woman.*

She glanced at the yellow dress upon the floor. Sawyer was no different from the rest in that respect. Lisa drew in a breath, let it out as a soft sigh, and picked the dress out of the rumpled pile of clothes hastily discarded the night before when Oliver Sawyer had come back from his meeting with Phillip LaFarge. She shook out the wrinkles as best she could and examined it for fresh signs of wear, then carefully hung it among the others. They all needed mending, they all needed washing—and that took money.

Lisa hated being broke all the time. She stood at the window and peered up Myers Avenue at the fancy new parlor houses being built there. "Someday," she whispered. She sat at her dressing table, studied herself in the cracked mirror, parted her red hair, and frowned at the dark roots beginning to grow out.

"Someday soon," she said, tugging a brush through the matted hair.

Behind her, Sawyer stirred and gasped for air, then settled down again in his restless sleep. Lisa was always amazed, and somewhat amused, by men. Each and every one of them was alike. They'd go after it like it was to be their last chance in this life, and finally they'd explode in a moment of ecstasy . . . and always too soon! Then a few minutes of heavy breathing followed by some tepid groping, and they'd be asleep.

She watched Sawyer turn upon the sheet, his naked body marked and scarred by who knows what.

"Someday soon," she promised herself again, lighting a cigarette and pouring whiskey into a glass.

"What time is it?" Sawyer mumbled.

"Late." Lisa plucked the cigarette from between her lips and with the same hand took a long sip of whiskey.

Sawyer rolled over, looked at himself naked in the morning light, and pulled a corner of the sheet over himself.

Lisa laughed. "Now's a fine time to think about that. Where was your modesty last night when you were bouncing and turning all over me? Now roll out of that bed and get dressed. I've got things I got to do today."

Sawyer stood and stretched. Lisa was amused. In his suit

and hat he was kind of cute, she thought . . . in a pugnacious sort of way. But now, stark naked to the world, Oliver Sawyer was a short, pale, lumpish creature whose muscle had begun to sag and settle about his waist.

He slipped on his shorts, drove his legs into his trousers, then looked over his shoulder at her. "What are you giggling about?"

She took another drink. "Nothing. Now hurry it up."

Sawyer dressed, put his glasses on, and looked at himself in the cracked mirror as he folded an arm through his suspenders.

"They say clothes make the man," Lisa said softly, but loud enough for him to hear.

He shot her a narrow glance. "Taking care of a woman like you is what makes a man, Miss Kellerman, and there ain't no one in this here District that can do it better than me, and you know that."

Lisa laughed, put her arms around his neck, and kissed him hard on the lips. "You're the best, sweat pea. That's why I keep letting you back in my bed." She turned away and threw the rest of the whiskey down her throat. His hands moved to her hips and up her waist, and briefly cupped her full breasts beneath the chiffon gown. She sidled out of his grasp.

"No, no more. Not now. I told you, I got things to do."

He grinned. "All right—for now. But I'll be back." He dug the wad of bills he'd taken from Elvin Tate the night before and peeled a five-dollar note off, dropping it upon the dressing table.

Lisa grabbed his hand before he was able to return the money to his pocket. "You know, Olly love, I could be so much more a woman to you if you wanted me to."

"You'd like some of this, wouldn't you?"

"Did I hear you say last night that there was two thousand dollars there?"

He laughed. "You're a greedy bitch."

"I'm not greedy, sweet pea. I'm ambitious." She placed his hand gently between her breasts.

He glanced around the shack and grinned. "Yeah, I see your ambition all over the place, darling. A real Taj Mahal you got here."

Sawyer turned to leave, but her fingernails dug into his wrist. He looked down at them, then up at her wide brown eyes. "I thought you said you had things to do."

"I do," she said, suddenly serious, releasing his hand. "Sit down." Lisa poured another whiskey for herself and one for Sawyer. "I got a business proposition for you, Olly."

He tasted the drink and made a face. "A mite early for this sort of thing. What sort of business proposition?"

Lisa leaned against the edge of her dressing table and propped a foot up on the seat of the chair, allowing the robe to fall open slightly. "I don't intend to stay a two-bit sporting lady all my life. In fact, I don't intend to stay in this line of business at all—at least not on this end of it anyway."

"Yeah, I know, darling. You got your big plans."

She lit another cigarette and flipped the match into a porcelain honeypot sticking out from under the bed and badly in need of emptying. The smoke burned her throat as she drew it deeply into her lungs and let it out in an impatient blow. It,s like the whiskey, helped soothe her nerves.

"Yeah, I got plans, but I don't have the money."

Behind the thick lenses of his eyeglasses, Oliver Sawyer's eyes widened impossibly large. "OK, now I get your drift. You think this two thousand dollars is going to let you buy your way to respectability? Well, forget it, darling, I ain't paying two thousand dollars for a screw no matter how good you are."

Lisa's laugh was short and scornful. "Oh, come on, Olly. You have more imagination than that."

He bolted out of his chair and slapped the whiskey glass out of her hand, sending it crashing against the wall. "Don't you never use that tone with me, darling. Your face is far too pretty. I'd hate to have to do something about that."

"Sit back down, Oliver!" Her voice wavered, but she was determined not to let Sawyer intimidate her.

He hesitated, then returned to the chair.

"That's better. I'm not asking you to give me the money, Oliver. But I am going to invite you to invest it. Of course, I can always find someone else if you don't want to."

"Invest? What is it you have in mind?"

"Someplace where I can set up business."

"What do you call *this*?" His hand swept past the shabby dressing table and the splintering walls where building paper kept the wind from blowing through the cracks.

She laughed again, the bitterness showing. "This? This one-room crib? I'm sorry, Olly, I guess I figured you all wrong. It might be better if I did start looking for another partner."

"Wait a minute . . . wait a minute." Sawyer pursed his lips, thought it over, and nodded his head. "Suppose you tell me exactly what it is you have in mind."

"A parlor house, Olly. The finest parlor house in the District!" In spite of her need to remain completely professional, Lisa could hardly contain her enthusiasm for the idea.

Sawyer leaned forward. "You're serious, ain't you?"

"Hell yes, I'm serious! I've already talked with Melvin Sowle, the agent representing the Myers and Bennett real estate office, about buying a lot on Myers Avenue. There ain't but a couple left and I have to move quickly if I'm going to get one of them. Commercial lots are already fetching nearly a thousand dollars apiece, and I have my eye on one near Fourth Street. But"—Lisa paused to choose her next words carefully—"but I *persuaded* him to sell it to me for five hundred dollars. He said he would, if I could come up with the money in three days." Her long lashes fluttered innocently. "In fact, Mr. Sowle is part of that business I have to tend to today." Then she laughed. "Who knows, after this afternoon I might even get him to lower his price to four hundred. But

I got to move fast, and I ain't got five hundred dollars—not all of it, at least.''

Sawyer stood, paced a step or two, then turned and said, ''I don't know, darling. You're talking a lot of money. Buying the land is only the beginning.''

''I know that, but with a paid-up lot I won't have any trouble finding investors.''

''Hm. What's in it for me?''

''You'd be a partner. You'd be entitled to a share of *everything*.'' She made it clear that she would be included in that.

''I don't know. This money ain't all mine, you know. It's half Barney's.''

''All I need is five hundred bucks, for cryin' out loud! You got at least that much.''

He slipped the holster and revolver over his shoulder and adjusted it under his armpit, then covered it with his jacket, and finally settled the dusty derby upon his head. ''I don't know, darling. I'm gonna have to think on it a while.''

''Dammit, Olly! I told you I don't have any time. I got to come up with the money by the day after tomorrow or Sowle will sell the lot to someone else. Dammit, Olly, are you so blind that you can't see a great deal when it hits you between the eyes? Hell, I reckon those eye spectacles don't do nothing for you after all—except make you look like a damn bug-eyed fish!''

Sawyer took two quick steps. There was a sharp crack and Lisa landed against the wall before catching herself. Blood stained her hand when she took it from her face.

''I warned you about that mouth of yours, darling,'' Sawyer growled. ''You take care what you say from now on. I ain't gonna warn you again.'' Sawyer yanked open the door and strode angrily away.

Lisa watched from the open door as he disappeared up Fourth Street, then slowly closed the door and sat in front of the cracked mirror, looking at herself. She held a rag to her bleeding lip. "Oh, Olly," she said, and buried her face in her arms.

Casey Daniels paused on the single, wide step outside the bank to watch the heavy traffic on Bennett Avenue rolling by. He didn't remember there having been so many people in town when he'd left less than a week and a half ago.

Up the hill to his left, where Bennett Avenue swept around and merged with Carr Avenue, came the high-pitched squeal of brakes. In the next moment one of Hundley's big Concord stagecoaches came rocking into view, throwing up a rooster plume of dust in its wake as the sixes came galloping past Pisgah Cemetery. The coach charged down the long hill from Pisgah, brake shoes squealing, racing towards the edge of town carrying a full load. The passengers stuffed inside seemed to overflow it through the windows—the overflow having scrambled up onto the top of the coach, where at least five men clung desperately to the iron luggage rack.

The coach hit the town limits in a flurry of chicken feathers as the frightened birds scrambled madly to clear a path for it. A high-kicking mule bounded off the road one step ahead of Hundley's horses, and as the mighty coach careened onto Myers Avenue, it picked up three dogs at its wheels, racing along, nipping at their spokes.

Casey lost sight of the coach once it turned onto Myers, but he could hear the pounding hooves a block away, and then the sudden squalling of its brake shoes as the driver brought the heavy coach to a stop. A moment later a cloud of dust rose over the top of the Continental Hotel and drifted out over town.

As usual, a goodly number of folks up on Bennett Avenue succumbed to the force of gravity and began flowing downhill towards Myers, to stretch their necks at the new arrivals. Watching one of Hundley's big Concords come charging into town was great sport for the idle. Casey caught a glimpse of Bob Womack long-legging it down from the Hotel Clarendon.

Poor Bob. He loved to watch the stagecoaches arrive, and with the increasing number of stages coming into town daily, Bob was having a devil of a time deciding at which hotel to station himself to be able to greet the newcomers. Casey laughed to himself. No wonder he had no time to work his claim.

Casey went next door to the Central Meat Market, and bought half a pound of beef for his dinner. Tucking the brown paper bundle under his arm, he crossed Bennett to catch a view of the coach down on Myers before heading back to his rig up at the Clarendon. He hadn't gone but one block when a man in a great, blind hurry rounded the corner and crashed into him. He staggered from the unexpected blow and the beef plopped heavily to the dusty street.

"Why don't you watch where you're goin'!" the fellow snarled, adjusting the spectacles that had been knocked awry upon the bridge of his nose.

Casey was struck by the immense black eyes magnified behind them. This was the same man that Macklin Deats had pointed out to him the night before. Mack had said his name was Oliver Sawyer, and now, after a good night's sleep and without the intervening haze of cigar smoke, Casey knew that he'd seen this man, Sawyer, occasionally around the Rattlesnake mine and in LaFarge's office more than once.

He was a short man with strong shoulders, a short neck, and a belligerent scowl that told Casey he would like nothing better than to crush someone's nose to pulp—anyone's nose at the moment.

Other than the affair at the mine that morning which had left him presently unemployed—a minor downturn to a man with Casey's drive—the day was shaping up nicely, and he could see no good reason to ruin that now.

"Sorry," Casey said, and bent to rescue his beef from the dirty street.

But Sawyer wouldn't let it go at that. "Look at me, mister!"

Casey had a sinking feeling, and suddenly he knew that he wasn't going to so easily avoid this fellow. He let the package remain and turned slowly to face the man. "What is it you want?"

Sawyer came forward a step. Casey caught a glimpse of his fists bunching at his sides, and he caught the whiff of whiskey upon his breath when he spoke.

"I said look at me," Sawyer demanded again.

"What exactly am I supposed to be seeing?"

"You think I look like a damned bug-eyed fish too?"

Those big, dark eyes behind the thick spectacles were indeed startling, and perhaps, Casey had to admit, one might describe them as "bug-eyed." But to say so now would not be prudent.

"Well, now I wouldn't exactly say that—"

"What exactly would you say?" Sawyer moved in closer, pure hatred smothering in his pug face.

"I'd say that someone has got you all riled up, and now you're looking for someone else to take it out on." A small crowd of men gathered around them, but Casey dared not take his eyes off Sawyer.

"I'm not looking anymore, mister," Sawyer said through clenched teeth, and suddenly his left fist shot out.

Casey was waiting for it, and easily sidestepped the jab. He was limber, and his long legs gave him an advantage over Sawyer.

Sawyer's second punch went wide as well, which only stirred up the fires within him. He hunched into a fighting stance, and his next blow shot out like a cannon ball, clipping Casey along the side of his head.

Casey darted to his left, light-footed and quick, and drove a fist through Sawyer's defenses, smacking the man in his chin. The spectacles popped up against his forehead, then slid back onto the bridge of his nose. Casey followed with a cut to Sawyer's gut but found only close knitted elbows guarding that part of his body. Then Sawyer plowed in and Casey fended off the volley as best he could while backpedaling into the street. He took a jab to the ribs, and another to the chin that momentarily stunned him, but he kept weaving and dancing, just out of reach of Sawyer's fists. Sawyer was powerful, but he lacked endurance, and slowly Casey's fists began to find openings in his defenses. Casey hadn't fought much since going off to school, but growing up on a ranch on the eastern plains of Colorado at a time when the Arapaho still raided and plundered taught a boy to be quick with his fists as well as his mind. His father had drummed it into his head that when push comes to shove, you don't stop until your opponent is down and unable to do you damage. He drove Sawyer to the ground, and as the man's defenses crumbled Casey finished him off with an uppercut that sent the fragile spectacles sailing and Sawyer reeling headlong onto the street.

Casey straightened up, drawing in a breath that seared his lungs. He had a bloodied lip, but that was the only damage he could find as the spectators drew in for a closer look. One of the men slapped him on the shoulder. Casey looked to see who it was. Macklin Deats was standing there grinning.

"Best damned fight I've seen in all of a week, Casey."

Casey grinned, shook the sting from his fist, and worked his fingers, grimacing. "It wasn't half bad, was it, Mack? Could have turned out a lot worse." Casey glanced at Sawyer, who turned groggily in the street and began to feel around him searchingly.

"What started it all?"

"I don't know, Mack." Casey patted his lip with his shirtsleeve and frowned at the bloodied stain that it left. All at once a dozen men were asking questions. Casey dunked his head in the watering trough and shook the water from his hair. Someone found Sawyer's spectacles for him.

Sawyer put them on, hooking them over his ears.

Breathing still brought fire to Casey's lungs. Mack snatched his hat from the ground and handed it back to him.

Then someone cried out a warning. Casey swung about in time to see Sawyer drawing a revolver from under his coat.

His huge eyes blinked behind the lenses as he brought the weapon up and steadied it.

A boot kicked out and the revolver flew from his hands. Sawyer came about then froze where he was sitting, staring up at Sheriff Pete Eales's six-shooter, steadied in both hands not twelve inches from the crown of Sawyer's head.

"Keep your hands right where I can see them, mister," Eales said. Eales was tight as a fiddle string, and Casey held his breath as the two men regarded each other. Sawyer's thinking seemed to clear in a mighty hurry, as any rational man's would looking up the barrel of a .45 Colt revolver.

Sawyer spread his palms skyward to show Pete that they were empty. "Hey, I didn't mean nothing, Sheriff. I guess I lost my temper."

"I'd say you did." Eales backed up a step, his revolver remaining on Sawyer. He glanced at Casey. "Who started this here ruckus?"

Casey was not a man who passed blame to another, especially when there was always the outside chance that the fight could have been avoided if he had done something differently—in this case, chose his reply more carefully. "No one started it. That fellow had a bad start on the day and I must have said the wrong thing."

A weathered-looking miner with gray chin whiskers and a crooked back called out, "I seen it, and it was that there fellow on the ground what threw the first punch."

"Is that right, mister?"

Sawyer stood and brushed the dust from his black jacket. "I don't remember."

Eales frowned. "Well, maybe a few days in the county jail might sharpen your memory, mister."

"All right. Yeah, I started it. I just had a fight with my woman, OK?"

A low chuckle worked its way through the men standing there. Even Eales smiled. "Well, I know how that might set a man on the wrong track," he said, retrieving Sawyer's revolver from the ground and looking it over. "What's your name?"

"Oliver Sawyer," he mumbled.

"Well, Mr. Sawyer, civilized men learn to control their passions—even where womenfolk are concerned."

"It won't happen again, Sheriff."

Eales tucked the revolver under his belt. "Let's hope not. I'll not take you in at this time, but I will be keeping my eye on you. Get in trouble again, Mr. Sawyer, and you will find yourself cooling your heels in my jail." Eales turned to the crowd. "All right, everyone, break it up now. You're blocking traffic."

There were a dozen freight wagons, phaetons, buckboards, and horses and mules bunched up and waiting to pass. Macklin Deats's freighter was one of them, loaded with crushed ore to be taken back to Florissant for the trip down to the mill at Colorado City. As the men cleared off the street, drivers whistled and cracked their whips and got moving again. Eales started away as well.

"Hey, what about my revolver?" Sawyer said.

"We got ordinances about carrying a weapon in town. Most men know that, and them that don't lose their iron." Eales pulled the revolver from his belt. "This is a pretty nice Smith & Wesson break-top. It'll fetch maybe five, six dollars for the school fund. Consider it a donation towards the education of our kids, Mr. Sawyer." He grinned. "Have a nice day."

Sawyer's scorching glare burned into the back of Pete Eales's vest, then turned upon Casey. He held it there a moment before wheeling around and bounding angrily down the street, back towards Myers Avenue.

"If I was you, Casey, I'd keep my eye on that one. It's plain to see he has no regards for you." Macklin Deats climbed back aboard his freighter. "It don't take no Injun scout to see that that man has a mean streak clean to the bone and wide as a Denver City street." He took up the reins and toed off the brake. "See you around, Casey." With a whistle and a crack and a cuss at "old Sal," Macklin's wagon rumbled slowly away.

Casey found his half-pound of beef smashed into a bloody mess in the street. He left it there for the dogs that came trotting up from the stagecoach they had just chased into town. They eyed the treat hungrily. "You fellows have at it," Casey said, and as if they understood, the dogs pounced upon the meat.

Casey brushed the dust from his clothes, frowned at the long rip in the back of his shirt and the bloody stain on its sleeve. On his way back to his wagon bought a copy of the *Cripple Creek Crusher* from a boy hawking newspapers on the corner of Carr and Fifth. He had developed an ache in his left shoulder and a purple bruise on his cheek by the time he arrived back at his cabin. At three o'clock he walked up Battle Mountain to Sam Strong's mine.

Sam, a hard-drinking, hard-fighting former lumber hauler from the Springs, had considerable respect for a man who could hold his own in a fistfight, and since he had no particular love for Phillip LaFarge, or any of his friends, it was no wonder Casey made a favorable impression, and by four o'clock he had hired on at the Strong Mine as a consulting engineer.

All and all, Casey decided when the six o'clock shift whistle sounded beneath a spurt of white steam that shot into the blue sky, it had not been a bad day. He made his way home, thinking of the thick slab of beef that had gone to fattening the local canine population. In sharp contrast to the disastrous morning, the afternoon had gone splendidly, and he couldn't allow even the loss of his dinner to spoil the mood.

He strolled the few dozen feet from his cabin down to Wilson Creek and lifted an old birdcage, weighted down with a boulder, from the water. Inside was his cache of Coors bottled beer, nicely chilled by the mountain stream. He popped the wire stopper and took a long pull as he climbed the hill back to his cabin. Inside, he chewed on a heel of hard bread and unfolded the newspaper he'd bought earlier.

The headline pitched his high spirits headlong into sudden concern.

DIPHTHERIA OUTBREAK IN CAMP; TWO CHILDREN DEAD

The article told of two boys who had died, and about a playmate of theirs down with a fever. Casey remembered other horrible outbreaks in other camps. Dr. Whiting, according to the newspaper story, advised fumigating all tents and cabins and avoiding contact with other people—he issued an especially stern warning on child-to-child contact—at least until he could determine the extent to which the disease had already spread.

All of a sudden, the day was proving out to be something less than splendid.

# SIX

ELEVEN DAYS AFTER MAUREEN KRAMER RECEIVED THE LET-
ter from Peter telling her the time had come to join him at the
Cripple Creek Mining District, she had terminated her job with
Mr. Johnson at his penny store, retrieved her few precious
belongings from the warehouse compartment where Peter had
put them in storage over a year before, and had them sent
ahead to Hayden Placer. She visited friends whom she would
most likely never see again, then packed a few worn carpet-
bags and an ancient steamer trunk with clothes. Hidden among
the clothes, and carefully protected, were the china dishes with
fine gold rims that had been a wedding present from her par-
ents, sent all the way from Ireland; and among the few pos-
sessions she truly cherished.

Peter sent money for the train tickets and when the day
came, Margaret awoke before sunrise and lay upon the floor,
fidgeting in her sheets.

Their train was not to leave until eleven-fifteen that morning, and the station was an easy ten-minute walk from the
apartment building.

When Bridie came sleepily out of her room, Margaret was
up in a flash, and the two busily prepared breakfast. Maureen

listened to their talk. Bridie's surly mood had mellowed gradually since Peter's letter had arrived, although her older sister made it plain she thought little of Maureen's husband.

"A man what would run off to the gold diggin's and leave his wife and child for another to care for is a sorry excuse for a husband and father."

Maureen bided her time, counting the days, and held her tongue. Ralph still came home drunk three nights out of six, but there had been no more bruises and spilt blood over it. Bridie, too, was biding her time.

Although Maureen never spoke of it, she knew that buried deep inside Ralph was a restless, pacing animal that wanted to burst free. He had once admitted as much while under the influence of a pint and a half of beer. He had told her that he secretly envied Peter's resolve and determination, but knew his own shrew of a wife would never permit him such a grand adventure.

An uneasy truce had made the household less of a battlefield, although the tension had risen to intolerable levels and Maureen knew that her leaving was the best thing that could have happened to the four of them. How Bridie and Ralph resolved their problems was their concern, not hers.

Maureen had her own problems to resolve . . .

Through the kitchen doorway she watched Margaret, still in the long nightgown that brushed the tops of her bare toes as she stood there trying to help.

Yes, leaving was the best thing that had happened to them, and she vowed that no matter what the future held, she would never again put Margaret—or anyone else—through that kind of hell.

Ralph emerged from the bedroom a half hour later looking as if he hadn't slept well. He mumbled a hello as he filled a cup with coffee and slouched against the kitchen door frame drinking it down. Bridie put out a plate of eggs, bacon, and fried potatoes. Ralph ate them with little appreciation. He'd been drunk the night before, and still feeling the sting of that poison this morning.

Afterwards, he took his lunch bucket from the counter and hunkered down near Margaret and told her to take care of her mother, and have a grand adventure, and write him a letter about it and the gold camp when she had time to. He said his good-bye to Maureen next and wished her happiness.

He merely glanced at Bridie as he left for work.

They ate a hardy breakfast, cleaned up the dishes, and packed a lunch of sandwiches, pickles, and apples for the trip. The two sisters spoke little as they worked side by side in the kitchen. Margaret put on her brown traveling frock and studied herself in the mirror, adjusting the straw bonnet that Maureen had bought just for the occasion. At nine o'clock a man on a one-horse dray arrived for the steamer trunk and grips. They loaded the luggage and paid him seventy-five cents to haul them to the train depot and deposit them with the baggage clerk. At ten, Maureen said good-bye to Bridie at the apartment's battered green door. There were no emotional embraces, no tears of regret at the parting, merely a perfunctory farewell and a "Write us a letter when you get there." But Bridie's request lacked the fire that Maureen had seen in Ralph's eyes when he'd asked Margaret to do the same thing.

Maureen and Margaret each carried a single bag, Maureen toting the wicker basket with their lunch as well. When she looked back after a dozen steps, Bridie was gone and the green door was shut.

At the train depot, Maureen sent a wire to Hayden Placer, addressed to Peter Kramer, telling him of their expected arrival. Right on schedule, the train steamed away from the station, and Maureen felt the weight of the place melting away as the smoky skies of Detroit fell behind them and the lovely green forests of Michigan began to crowd the tracks. Farms and villages swept past, and the air was sweet, hot, and humid.

For a while mother and daughter kept their noses pressed

against the windowpanes of the coach car, but soon Margaret got weary of counting telegraph poles. They ate their lunch, chatting about the trip that lay before them: Cripple Creek, and Peter's claim, the Lucky Irish, and the Rocky Mountains far to the west. Margaret strained at the window to catch a glimpse of them, and Maureen laughed.

"We are not even yet to Chicago," Maureen said. "Be patient, my darlin'."

At Chicago they transferred to an Atchison, Topeka, and Santa Fe chair car and slept in the straight-back chairs. They ate breakfast at a Harvey House at one of the stops along the way on the great, sweeping plains of America's heartland. Margaret was all gaping mouth and wide eyes as a million square miles of grass raced past the window, with nothing more than the flickering of the telegraph poles and an occasional farmhouse to break the illusion of vastness.

Maureen sipped delicious coffee from the Harvey concessionaire who prowled the aisle, and allowed Margaret to buy an all-day sucker from the candy butcher. They ate lunch in a splendid dining car where prompt young ladies in crisp white aprons served them. All the attention made Maureen feel almost regal, and she had to laugh at herself when she remembered that the sixteen dollars in her handbag was all the money she had.

Once Maureen became comfortable with this small, confined world racing along two shiny rails, she permitted Margaret to wander farther afield and explore the coach cars along the length of the train. Margaret picked up some friends her own age and they tried the door handles of all the lavatories, which were usually locked. They drank gallons of water from the ice water fountains, and a nice black man at the shoeshine stand gave them each a shiny penny when they stopped to talk to him.

The two-day trip was a first-class adventure all in itself, and Maureen half regretted that Ralph had missed out on it. But she knew that Bridie would never permit him any more than he already had. Maureen had begun to develop a great sense of peace about joining Peter in the Cripple Creek gold fields, helped along by the fact that she had not seen that pinched, worried look flash across Margaret's face even once since they'd left! For the first time in months, Margaret was happy . . . and so was she.

At the terminal in Pueblo, Colorado, early the next morning, Maureen and Margaret switched trains again for their trip north to Colorado Springs. The air was clean and dry, and it seemed to suck the moisture from Maureen's skin. She had never experienced such complete lack of humidity back east and she had not been prepared for it. Later, as the train steamed north, she decided the dryness was not at all unpleasant. The temperature had climbed as a naked sun burned through a perfectly clear sky, and although she was hot, there was very little perspiration to contend with. Back east she would have been drenched by this time, but here in Colorado, her forehead was merely damp as the moisture evaporated almost immediately.

The Santa Fe terminal in Colorado Springs was a big, dark brick building. Their luggage was loaded onto a cart and the porter wheeled it out front, then waved over a black hack drawn by two chestnut horses. The driver jumped down, inquired as to their destination, helped the porter manhandle the trunk onto the floor of the hack, between the two seats, and in no time they were rattling along the streets of Colorado Springs. They left the city limits behind and almost at once were in Colorado City. Fifteen minutes later their luggage was being transferred to a cart, then another baggage car.

Inside of an hour the big, black 2-8-0 engine of the Colorado Midland Railroad chuffed and spun its drivers and crawled away from the terminal. Looking back, Maureen watched the big stone roundhouse, with its six massive engines, disappear around a bend. It seemed an awfully busy place, she thought.

A shabbily dressed man came down the aisle and sat on the

bench across from them. He grinned and doffed his hat, setting it on the seat beside him. His hair was nearly snow white, but the man was obviously not much older than forty. "Good afternoon, ladies," he said.

"Good afternoon, sir," Maureen answered.

"My name is James Burns."

"Pleased to meet you, Mr. Burns. This is my daughter, Margaret, and my name is Maureen Kramer."

"Hello, Maggie."

She looked from the window and said firmly, "My name is Margaret, sir."

"Oh, well pardon me, Miss Margaret."

Margaret said, "All right," and resumed her study of the passing landscape while Maureen held back a small smile.

James Burns grinned and said to Maureen, "Kramer? Now what is a woman with such a lovely Irish accent doing with such a Teutonic name as that?"

"It is my husband's name. And I might ask, what is a man with as proper an Irish name as Burns doing speaking like a Yankee?"

He laughed. "I have to admit my sin. I was born here in the States, ma'am. Portland, Maine, to be exact."

Almost at once the hills rose about them as they entered Ute Pass, and the engine slowed and struggled up the steep grade, snaking along the mountainside.

"We will be making some pretty steep grades, ma'am. It's three percent between Divide and Florissant."

Three percent didn't sound like very much to her, but what did she know about railroads anyway? "Is that a lot, Mr. Burns?"

"When she's hauling really heavy loads they sometimes have to hitch up a second engine. And on her way down Ute Pass they have a man stationed in a shack whose only job is to switch runaway trains onto a siding track."

"That sounds quite dangerous. You speak as if you've ridden this train often, Mr. Burns."

"That I have, Mrs. Kramer. I have a little claim up in the District, but my home is in the Springs."

Maureen's interest was suddenly piqued. "You are a miner then?"

Burns nodded his head. "I scratch at the ground, all right— me and my partners, that is."

"Have you made a strike yet?"

For an instant Burns's face lit up, then the fire faded from his eyes and he shook his head. A heavy frown dragged down the corners of his white mustache. "No, no, it's sad to say. We have a little piece of ground all sandwiched in by big claims. It's barely big enough for the three of us to turn around on without bumping into each other. We're down about forty feet but other than traces of sylvanite, it is a bust."

"Then why do you keep working at it, Mr. Burns?" This was something she'd never understood about the men who went into the gold fields. She'd never understood Peter's tenacity, or the pull that gold had over him. Why, when they dig and sweat and turn up nothing but worthless rock, she'd always wondered, do men still keep at it until they've poured their last dollar into a worthless hole? She didn't know the reason—perhaps no one did—but she was certain that this Mr. James Burns was tainted with the same kind of insanity that had infected her husband and a million other men.

But although Mr. Burns was obviously a hopeless case— just like her Peter—he seemed a gentleman of the first order, and easy to talk to. "My daughter I and are goin' to the District as well, Mr. Burns."

"Are you now?" He smiled. "The District is a booming place. Women and children arriving every day." He slanted an eye at Margaret. "You'll have more playmates than you can count, young lady, and they are opening up a school this fall, I hear tell."

Margaret removed her face from the window only long enough to return the smile.

"My husband's name is Peter—Peter Kramer. Perhaps you know him, Mr. Burns?"

James Burns thought a moment, then said, "There are so many men in the District it is hard to know them all, but the name has a ring to it. Maybe if I saw him I'd know him."

"Perhaps you shall," Maureen said. "He works for one of the mines, but he has a claim of his own that he also works."

"Indeed, and who does he work for?"

"His name is Mr. LaFarge—"

"Oh, yes. The Rattlesnake. I know the mine well—it is only a few hundred yards from our claim."

Maureen detected disapproval in his voice, but she let it pass. "And what is the name of your claim, Mr. Burns?"

"It's the Portland, ma'am, named after my hometown. And now that I think about it, I do recall your husband. A tall man with yellow hair?"

"Yes, that is Peter."

"As far as I know, he's a fine man. A hard worker. A man has to be to work his own claim and another man's as well."

"He has built us a house in Hayden Placer."

"And I'm sure it is a fine house. Cripple Creek is where all the best citizens are living."

"Cripple Creek? Isn't Cripple Creek the name of the *District?* And why are all Peter's letters posted from the town of Fremont?" She frowned. "It is all very confusin'."

Burns laughed aloud. "Not near as confusing, I daresay, as it is going to be."

Now, that certainly was an odd thing to say, Maureen thought. And what was it she had said to amuse Burns so, anyway?

The engine slowed to a stop at the Florissant station, spilling its pressure through hissing cylinder cocks and engulfing the terminal platform in hot steam.

James Burns stood and leveed his hat back upon his white head. "It was a pleasure to meet you, and you too, Miss Margaret. Perhaps we will meet again."

"I will look forward to seeing you in Cripple Creek, sir. Good day to you, Mr. Burns."

Burns merged into the flow of disembarking passengers filling the aisle.

Maureen and Margaret gathered their bags and followed Burns into the crowd of men and women working their way to the door at the front of the car. On the platform, Maureen and Margaret moved out of the way of the crowd and looked around. The terminal was busier than any other she had seen the whole trip, and that included the bustling Chicago station as well. Below the depot were five or six freight wagons, each pulled by eight to fourteen horses, lined up to receive freight being off-loaded. Folks poured off the train and scattered out to different parts of the town. Florissant consisted of one wide main street and three smaller streets radiating north from the Midland right-of-way. There might have been three or four east-west connections, and that was all.

Maureen caught a glimpse of James Burns heading towards the edge of town in the company of quite a number of other men. Their destination, it was clear, was a building sporting a big sign saying:

JACK TURNER'S SALOON
The only legal whiskey in Florissant!

"Well, isn't that just like a man," Maureen said under her breath.

"Where do we go now, Mommy?"

She unfolded Peter's last letter, which had contained fifty dollars and instructions, and read the final paragraph. "It says here we're to book passage aboard a stagecoach at the Hundley Stage Line."

"Where is that?"

Maureen folded the letter back into its envelope and returned it to her handbag. She studied the little town, not immediately picking out the place she was looking for. "Well, this Florissant, Colorado, is not a very large place. We will find it with no trouble.'' She took Margaret by the hand and stepped down from the platform to the gravel right-of-way.

Castello Avenue appeared to be the main artery of business in Florissant, and she started her search there. They passed plenty of busy buildings along the way: Frank Castello's general mercantile store and post office, a barbershop, Stevens and Derby's meat market, and Wilson's billiard hall. She discovered a drugstore, and a boardinghouse run by W. L. Childs. Her searching took her past the Ore Grand Mining and Milling Company, and F. W. Bartlett's taxidermy shop. Heading back towards the railroad station, Maureen paused to marvel at the big freight wagons of the Deats Shipping Company, and she was about to step into the *Crystal Peak Beacon* newspaper office to ask directions when she spied Hundley's sign ahead.

''Ah, there we go, darlin','' Maureen said, tugging Margaret firmly along behind her. Already a long line of men stood outside Hundley's doors and three huge Concord stagecoaches with teams of six horses each waited out front. They were filling with passengers quickly.

Maureen got in at the end of the line, and those that came up behind seemed impatient that she was there at all. The men gave no regard to her, or to the ears of a little girl as their coarse language waxed colorfully.

''Just pay them no mind, darlin','' she told Margaret. ''Some men are no gentlemen at all.''

A young man in the dusty green corduroy overalls that marked him as a miner said, ''It's not a gentleman I'll wager you really want, now is it, sweetheart?''

''I beg your pardon, sir! I'll thank you to watch your tongue in the presence of my daughter!'' Maureen's eyes glistened like chunks of blue ice and she felt her cheeks reddening. It always happened when she got angry, and at such times she cursed herself for her fair skin.

He laughed and glanced at a friend. ''A fiery temper to match that red hair of hers. You reckon it's her real color? I know a sportin' lady or two down on Myers Avenue about that same hue.''

Maureen was embarrassed, especially in front of Margaret, who looked more confused than anything else. ''Why, I never—''

''Oh, I'm sure you must have a time or two, or you wouldn't have a kid, now would you?'' he quipped, pushing his chest out some as his friends laughed, encouraging him. ''I know of only one women who ever had a kid without doing it, and you don't look like no Jew—''

A hand clasped him by the shoulder and wheeled him about so quickly that he was still laughing when the fist flashed out. The sound of knuckles against chinbone was like a firecracker as the fellow staggered back and spun around, sprawling into the dusty street.

The line of men fanned out. Maureen recovered from the shock to see James Burns standing there. He shot her a glance and said, ''I'll see to his manners, Mrs. Kramer,'' and with that he raised the man off the street and swung another fist into his midsection. ''I'll not have you degrading a decent woman, nor will I stand by while you blaspheme the Blessed Virgin!'' He hauled back, but the man moved his face in time, twisting out of Burns's grasp.

''Kenny, Bob!'' the man called, staggering back. The two men who had been in line with him, momentarily stunned by the sudden arrival of Burns on the scene, came out of their stupor and moved in to encircle him now.

Burns turned in a slow circle, wheeling his fists like a prizefighter, trying to keep all three in view at once. Maureen was on her toes, rocking like a prizefighter as well, her fists bunched, her teeth clenched, as if it were she in the middle of it.

''Look out behind you, Mr. Burns!'' she shouted suddenly.

Burns ducked, twisted about, and connected with an upper cross. Quick as a cat, he sidestepped as a fist sailed by.

"I got me a quarter eagle what says Jimmie takes all three," a fellow standing nearby said to another.

Maureen glared at him. "Shame on you for bettin' money as though this was only for sport! Someone ought to go and help him!"

The fellow gave her a gap-toothed grin. "That's Jimmie Burns, ma'am. He don't need no help."

"But it's three against one!" she shot back. "And they are half his age!"

The fellow only chuckled. A sharp crack brought her head around to see the first man on the ground again, holding his jaw. Burns indeed did seem to be holding his own. He was still circling, trying to keep his opponents in sight. But he was starting to breathe hard and slowing down a bit. His hat lay crushed on the ground and his white hair gleamed in the sunlight.

One of the men snuck in a punch that set Burns back on his heels, and at that instant another came up behind him. Maureen shouted a warning a moment too late. They had his arms pinned as two of them moved in for the kill.

"Looks like I'm gonna lose my five dollars," the betting man said unhappily.

Maureen glared at him. "And it would serve you right!"

They laid into Burns with no mercy. Maureen could stand it no longer. Glancing about, she spied a man at the head of the line with his leg wrapped in plaster, leaning upon a crutch. She dashed to the front of the line and yanked the crutch away. "Sorry," she said, turning and diving into the fray. The crutch swung, slamming one of the men in the kidneys. He let out a cry and his knees buckled. Then Maureen cocked the crutch over her shoulder in the manner she had seen Bridie do a time or two with a broom handle when Ralph came in drunk.

"You little wench!" her victim growled. "I'll teach you to stick your nose into a man's fight."

"Begorra!" Maureen hissed back. "You try it, mister, and you'll find your noggin split open like a ripe pumpkin for your effort!'' The crutch circled ominously above her red hair, which had worked its way free of the pins and now fell in front of her eyes and mouth.

Burns arched back upon the fellow pinning his arms, and lifting both feet, he planted his heels square in the face of the single attacker facing him. Bone crunched and blood spurted. Burns's weight toppled the third fellow, breaking his grip as the both men fell to the ground.

Maureen's attacker suddenly dove under the spot where he had calculated the crutch would be. But Maureen had seen through his ploy and drove the tip of the wooden peg straight forward, catching him in the gut with all her weight behind it. If there had been a point on the end of the crutch instead of a flat, steel cap, she would have run him through instead of merely knocking him out cold.

Maureen wheeled about to aid Burns, but by this time he had the matter well in hand. He grabbed the man's shirt and sent this final attacker into oblivion with a short, powerful punch that laid him out flat and left the front of his shirt behind, still bunched up in Burns's fist.

Burns straightened up, flexing his fist. He grinned at her and said, ''You're a scrapping woman, Mrs. Kramer. I'm only glad we were fightin' on the same side.''

''Thank you for helping us, Mr. Burns. Ah, you are a-bleedin'. Does it hurt?''

He dabbed his forehead with a handkerchief, and winced. ''Only a little.''

''We should wash it out.''

''Don't have time if you are going to get a seat aboard one of Hundley's stagecoaches. They're filling up fast.'' Just then the clerk put out an ''All Full'' sign and closed the window.

''I'll find us another ride, Mrs. Kramer,'' Burns said, and taking up both Maureen's and Margaret's grips, he angled across the street and led them to the Deats Shipping Company.

Deats grinned at her and took her small hand into his big, rough paw, shaking it as he would have a man's. ''I saw it all through the window. It was a grand fight, and I'm somewhat of an expert on fights, you see, having stood in on my fair share of 'em over the years. You swing a mighty dangerous crutch, Mrs. Kramer.''

"Margaret and I seem to have missed the stage, Mr. Deats.''

"Well, I'm gonna be heading up to the District in 'bout half an hour. The three of you are welcome to ride along—that is, if two of you won't mind sitting atop four spools of hoist cable—and it won't cost you ten bucks a head like Hundley charges.''

"Ten dollars!'' Maureen had no idea the ride would have been so expensive. She closed her mouth, recovered from the shock, and said, "I don't even have that much money. I'd say that missin' Mr. Hundley's expensive stagecoach was a blessing in disguise, to be sure.''

"To be sure, Mrs. Kramer,'' Deats said.

# SEVEN

THE FREIGHT WAGON ROLLED DOWN THE LONG HILL PAST PIS-
gah Cemetery as the late afternoon shadows stretched far out
in front of the fourteen-mule team. The town below was a
mottled patchwork of grays and browns, with white splotches
of a tent here and there. The buildings seemed concentrated
along two streets. Burns had described the towns to Maureen
on the ride out and she suspected that those would be Bennett
and Myers Avenues, and although the lapboard shops and
banks and saloons stood shoulder to shoulder nearly the entire
length of the street, there was something temporary and
tossed-together in their appearance—almost as if no one truly
believed they would be needed five years from now. To the
north and east, about fifty tents clustered together and seemed
to make up an annex to the town.

"Fremont below," Macklin Deats said, stepping on the
brake to slow the heavy wagon on the long slope down into
town.

"Where is Hayden Placer . . . er, I mean, Cripple Creek, Mr.
Deats?" Maureen asked, her quick eyes darting up and down
the bowl below and the low ridge of hills that hemmed it in,
trying to take in everything at once. There appeared to

be something of a geometrical orderliness to the town, she decided, at least at its heart, but the buildings and tents on either side of it were scattered about in no apparent plan.

"You can't tell no difference between Cripple and Fremont, ma'am," Deats replied. "They both jest sort of blend together at the edges. But if you look out yonder to the east where the town climbs more steeply . . . that there is Cripple Creek, or Hayden Placer. Both names will let folks know where you're bound. That big building there, that's the Hotel Clarendon. It's in Hayden. It's got the best food in town, but it ain't the cheapest place. It's got a bar too, so's a man can get a drink if he wants to. They get away with that 'cause they don't call it a 'saloon.' "

Deats turned his team onto the lower of the two wide main streets and said, "This here is Myers Avenue. It's developing something of a seedy reputation, as it seems to attract more than its fair share of saloons and gamblin' houses—and there's the cribs up yonder too. There at the end is the Continental Hotel. That's where I'll put you and Mr. Burns off, because that's where the Florissant stage makes its stop. If you got people waiting for you, that should be where you'll find 'em."

"You have been most helpful, Mr. Deats. How can I ever repay you?"

"Shucks, ma'am. It's jest what folks in these parts call being neighborly." Deats hauled back on a fistful of reins and yelled, "Whooa there, Sal! Maggie, you mind your manners now!" The lug-sole boot on his left foot shoved the brake forward and the heavy wagon came to a stop.

The hotel was a narrow, two-story frame building. Its false front was of lapboard siding with four plain double-hung windows, and above its wide double doors was a glass transom. A simple sign between the two upstairs windows said:

THE CONTINENTAL

Macklin Deats set the brake and while he climbed down, Burns leaped over the side and lifted Margaret to the ground. Then he came around and helped Maureen.

"Let me help you into the hotel with that bag."

"Thank you, Mr. Burns, but you have already done a kingly job of helpin' Margaret and me. I don't want to be puttin' you out no more." Maureen was searching the faces of the men standing outside and those coming through the doors. A fellow called to Macklin Deats and the two shook hands like long-lost brothers. "I was hopin' my husband would be here," she said, disappointment showing in her voice. She looked hopefully at the busy street and storefronts.

James Burns glanced around. "I was expecting one of my partners to be here as well, Mrs. Kramer, but I suppose when I did not arrive on the stage—"

"Maureen!"

She looked over at the hotel. Peter jumped off the board-walk, grinning as he hurried around the team of horses. He swept her up in his strong arms and gave her a hug that took her breath away. Suddenly all her worries vanished and she was contented, albeit somewhat embarrassed by his open display of affection.

"Margaret!"

Maureen felt their daughter become part of the embrace. Then Peter put his wife at arm's length and looked at her.

"My darling, how I have missed you."

"It is good to be here," she managed to say through her joy.

"Did you have a good trip?"

"It went just fine, Peter."

"I heard about the ruckus in Florissant. My God, I wish I'd been there to see it."

"You heard?"

Peter laughed. "That is all they were talking about on the last three stages. When they said it was a pretty, redheaded

Irish lady that snatched Ben Whipple's crutch away and used it to batter a bully into the dust, I knew it had to be only one person—my wife.''

There was genuine pride in Peter's voice, and Maureen laughed in spite of herself. ''The man was about to hurt Mr. Burns, who had so graciously come to our aid. What else could I do?''

''I heard about that too.'' Peter took Burns's hand into his own and gave it a heartfelt shake. ''Thank you, sir. The folks off the stage said it was Jimmie Burns who stood in for Maureen's honor. Once we heard it was you, we figured you'd find a way to get Maureen and Margaret up here today. That's why Mr. Doyle waited around.''

Burns said, ''Jimmie's still here?''

''He's in the Continental. We were having a beer when someone said Mack Deats had just pulled up with a woman and child aboard.''

''Well, James, it's about time you got here,'' a young fellow said, standing in the doorway of the Continental Hotel.

''Jimmie,'' James Burns said. ''Good of you to wait around for me.''

Jimmie Doyle was about half Burns's age, with thick brown hair and a full mustache; a handsome fellow, Maureen thought as he stepped to the edge of the boardwalk and looked down at his partner. ''I heard you had yourself a rip-roarin' time in Florissant.''

''Ah, Jimmie, it was wonderful, and the whole time I was wishing you could have been there. You would have enjoyed yourself—and I could have used the help.''

''From what I hear, you had a fine helper in Mrs. Kramer.''

''She was brilliant, Jimmie. But I know how you love a good fight.'' Jimmie Doyle stepped down off the boardwalk, staggering a bit as he walked. ''The wagon is parked around the corner,'' he said with a crooked grin on his face. ''Come on along now and let's get going.''

James Burns tipped his hat to Maureen and said, ''I reckon

young Jimmie is in a hurry to get back to the diggings. I'll see you and your husband around town sometime, I'm sure. And Miss Margaret,'' he said, hunkering down and taking the girls hand in a businesslike manner, ''it was a pleasure having your company on the ride up.''

Margaret smiled at him. ''Can I come see your mine someday?'' she asked.

''Well, it ain't much of a mine, yet, but you're welcome anytime your pa wants to bring you up.'' He stood. ''Good day to you, Mrs. Kramer, Mr. Kramer.'' James Burns started up Myers Avenue, where Jimmie Doyle was waiting for him.

When he had gone, Maureen said, ''Mr. Burns is such a nice man.''

''I ain't never met the man before, but him and a Mr. Stratton and a few others are well spoken of in the District.'' Peter grabbed up their bags and said, ''Well, how would you two like to see your new home?''

''Is it far away?'' Margaret asked.

''No, sweetheart. It's just up the hill.''

''It's in Cripple Creek, also known as Hayden Placer. It's where all the finer folks live,'' Maureen said, proudly showing off some of her newly gained knowledge of the rough mining camp that was to be her home.

''I wouldn't have built a home for my family anywhere else,'' Peter said. ''Now, come along.''

On Bennett Avenue an open buckboard driven by a man in a black coat and an old fashioned stovepipe hat passed by. Peter stopped suddenly and stood there looking as the wagon pulled up in front of Lampman's Funeral Parlor. In back of the buckboard a man and woman clutched the sideboards stiffly. The man's face was drawn; hard as flint, and white as chalk. The woman was sobbing into a handkerchief wadded up in her fist. Between them was a body wrapped in a white sheet. Although no part of it could be seen, Maureen knew by the small size that it must be the body of a child.

She looked back at Peter and found him staring at Margaret.

"What is the matter, Peter?"

He shook his head, as if coming out of a trance. "Oh, it's nothing, Maureen," he said, staring across the street as the man lifted the body into his arms. The woman clung to him, seemingly unable to stand on her own, while the driver in the tall hat opened the door to the parlor.

Maureen looked back at her husband. His face held an odd expression, as though he was deeply worried about something.

"Do you know them, Peter?"

"Hm? Oh, no."

"Then what is the matter?"

He seemed suddenly impatient. "Nothing is the matter, Maureen. It is always sad to see someone so young as that die."

"I wonder what happened to him."

"I don't know," Peter said sharply—too sharply, she thought. "Come, let's go home." He hustled them away from there and up into Hayden Placer, to the little tent cabin he had built for them.

Peter remained in a somber mood that evening, unable to shake the fears that had settled upon him—and not just upon him, but upon the whole District since the first news of diphtheria had erupted into the community.

He glanced at his daughter.

Maureen and Margaret were delighted with the little two-room house he had built for them, and even the obviously disappointing aspect of a canvas roof over their heads instead of a solid tin one, like the house next door had, hadn't dampened their enthusiasm. Peter promised them a tin roof by winter, and that seemed to settle any of Maureen's concerns.

Even so, he could not shake the picture of that little body being carried into Lampman's Funeral Parlor. It was the children who were most susceptible. In the last week and a half, he had seen a dozen bodies arrive at Lampman's wrapped in a sheet, and the outbreak of diphtheria had showed no signs of running its course.

Maureen and Margaret had jumped right into cleaning the place, sweeping the rough floorboards and arranging the furniture, which had arrived only two days before. That evening, Maureen carefully unpacked her precious dishes and set them in a cupboard above the porcelain sink. Peter had bought the sink in Colorado Springs and fixed it up to drain into a dry well outside the house.

Peter watched Margaret going about the job of cleaning as if she knew precisely what was required of her, all the while Maureen keeping an eye on her progress, giving her hints on how to do this or that, and making comments like, "This house does not have round corners," when Margaret got a bit careless with her scrubbing or sweeping.

All in all, Peter was more contented now that they were all together than he had been in over a year . . . yet whenever he looked at Margaret, his heart would sink and he'd recall that little body in the back of Lampman's buckboard. Perhaps he should have written them and told them not to come once the epidemic became known? He had missed them mightily, but right now he wished they were somewhere away from this killer disease.

He would have to tell Maureen about it—but not tonight, not right now. She'd learn of it soon enough.

"What is troublin' you, darlin?" Maureen asked him later that evening, after they had eaten a fine dinner of Maureen's special beef stew. "You've been worryin' about somethin', I can tell."

"Nothing," he lied, glancing away. "It is only that I am tired tonight, that's all. I've been awake since five this morning, working first at Mr. LaFarge's Rattlesnake mine, and then at my . . . I mean our claim up on Bull Hill."

She studied him a moment. The newly sawed floorboards filled the little cabin with the almost overwhelming odor of fresh pine. "I would very much like to see *our* claim as soon as you have the time to take Margaret and me to it."

"And you will. Tomorrow when my shift is over at the Rattlesnake." A sudden excitement came into Peter's voice. "It's got real good possibilities, Maureen. My mining engineer friend, Casey Daniels, he looked the place over and thinks there might be a good lode vein running under it. And when I strike it rich, I will build you and Margaret a ten-room house in the best part of town, with three floors and hot and cold running water from pipes right inside. And a proper roof over your heads as well." He smiled a moment, then the smile faded. "Of course, until that time comes, I will have to keep working for Mr. LaFarge."

"You don't care much for the man, do you, Peter?"

"He drives his men hard, pays them poorly, puts only enough money into the mine shafts to make them workable, and is stingy as Scrooge with the candles and kerosene."

A concerned look crossed her face. "Is the mine safe?"

He grinned and tried to put her at ease. "It's as safe as any in the District. Left up to his own devices, I reckon LaFarge would run a tricky mine, but he's got a good engineer. Sam Stepton is an old hand at mining. He's been working them since he was a boy. And my friend that I've told you about, Casey Daniels, he designed the shoring in the new Princess drift where we are working now."

"You speak a lot of this man Casey Daniels. Who is he?"

"Like Mr. Stepton, he's a mining engineer, but unlike Sam, Casey went to the State School of Mines. He's got graduation papers and everything, and he knows his business. He's what I've heard some mine owners call the 'new breed of modern mining engineers.' He's about my age, maybe a year or two older. I think you'll like him once you meet him."

"He's good at what he does?"

"He's the best. I'd trust him with my life."

"It sounds as if you already have." She gave him a kiss upon his tangled sandy head, a discreet one, for Margaret was sitting upon a three-legged stool watching them. "If the man's as good as you claim he is, then I promise not to worry about

you when you go down that deep hole in the mornin'. If Mr.
LaFarge is the miser you claim, then it is good to know there
is a man like Mr. Daniels there to keep an eye on things.''

Peter gave her a faltering smile. He did not want to distress
her about Cripple's dark side just yet. So, he did not mention
the diphtheria that was snatching the lives of the children . . .
nor did he tell her that Casey Daniels had quit the Rattlesnake
mine more than a week earlier.

Maureen packed Peter's lunch bucket for him early the next
morning, and at six-thirty he kissed her good-bye at their cabin
door and jumped onto the back of a buckboard which had
slowed for him. In the box behind the driver half a dozen other
miners had crowded in, and were talking about the day to
come, or the day just past. They picked up three more miners
along the way before turning onto the freight road to Battle
Mountain, which lay two miles southeast of town.

''Your wife made it into camp, I see, Peter,'' one fellow
said.

''Yes, yesterday evening.'' He'd found a place in the corner, and sat with his knees drawn up and the lunch bucket
beneath them.

''Lots of women and children startin' to show up in the
District,'' another man added.

''The District is getting that permanent look,'' a third man
said, and made it sound as if permanence was a thing to be
avoided.

Peter looked around at the faces. ''Where is Kilmer?'' he
asked when he discovered that one of the regular riders of the
buckboard was missing.

For a moment the buzz of the two or three different con-
versations died down, then someone said, ''He ain't goin' to
work today, Pete. His boy come down with a fever and a red
throat last night. Doc Whiting was there this morning. I don't
know how Whiting ever finds the time to sleep these days.''

No one said anything for a while. Every miner in the District knew the symptoms of diphtheria by now. Peter instantly thought of Margaret, and his happy mood vanished like a morning vapor beneath a hot sun.

"It's a rough deal," Peter said soberly. "I hope his boy makes it."

The talk turned to a favorite topic, the upcoming election of the town mayor. George Carr, with the help of Bob Womack as his campaign manager, would be running against Dr. Whiting, and it was generally agreed that Carr would be the victor. As managers of the Broken Box Ranch, George and Emma Carr had, after all, housed and fed most of the early arrivals in the District at one time or another.

Work in the mine replaced the worry of the diphtheria epidemic that was ravaging the children of the District above their heads. There was a pile of rubble from the previous shift's blasting to clear out first thing. They worked at it in the feeble light of their candles and lanterns, shoveling the rubble into ore carts and then moving it to the skip to be lifted to the surface, where freight wagons would collect it and haul it down to Florissant.

At the noon call, the miners set aside their shovels and picks. Propping candles and lanterns on rock ledges, between the rails, and atop a pile of ties waiting to extend the rails deeper into the new hole, they settled down for half an hour's rest and lunch.

Peter showed them the meat pie that was carefully wrapped in a red checkered cotton napkin. It was still almost warm, having been baked just that morning. "Maureen and Margaret came in late yesterday, and look at this. Today I've a clean house and a lunch fit for a workingman!"

"And a lot cozier bed too, I'll wager," another man added.

Peter felt his cheeks redden, but he laughed with them too.

An older miner named Claude Parker lifted his candle and held it closer to Peter. "Taking on a bit of color, ain't you, lad?"

"It's only a reflection off of this here red napkin," Peter came back.

"Reflection my hind end," Claude said.

Someone said, "Hey, boys, quiet it down a bit. I hears something."

They cut their easy banter and listened. Far off, almost as if through solid rock, came the faint sounds of tapping, mixing eerily with the distant hollow echo of dripping water. A gust of wind from a nearby winze made the candle flames dance about on their wicks. They sat there straining to pick out the source of the faint sound. When no one could, a Cornish miner named Edwin Dabble said in a whisper, "It's the Tommy-knockers out for some mischief, mates."

There was not a sound among them, except for breathing and a soft scraping as they shifted on their rocky perches, adjusting the wicks of their safety lamps.

After a few more minutes the tapping stopped, and try as they might, the only sounds they could hear were the soft sighing of wind through the tunnel and the far-off clatter of a skip coming down the elevator shaft.

"I think they've gone off to play somewhere else, mates," Edwin said, still whispering.

"And good riddance to them," Peter added.

Someone gave a short laugh. "Annoying bastards, ain't they?"

Another man grunted. No one was in any mood for the friendly teasing of a few minutes earlier.

"Hell, I think I'll get back to work," someone said.

They all closed their lunch pails, corked their canteens, and gathered up their tools.

Peter shut and latched his pail as well. A pebble fell from the roof and clattered off its tin lid. A moment later a second pebble smacked him upon his dusty cap. He brushed at his hat, annoyed, and stood, but didn't give the incident another thought as he went back to work with the others.

That afternoon they exchanged their shovels and picks for

steel drill bits and nine-pound sledgehammers. By the end of the day they had bored seven drill holes in the rock face: three in a triangle at its center about two feet apart, an edger hole at each side, a reliever hole at the top, and the lifter hole at the bottom. They packed them with carefully calculated charges of dynamite and cut and timed their fuses to set off the center charges first, followed an instant later by the side and top charges, and then finally the lower lifter charge that, if everything went right, was supposed to toss the rubble out into the tunnel.

They all left the tunnel and rode the skip to the surface. The blaster stayed behind, and when the miners were safely away from the drift he put fire to the fuses.

"Fire in the hole!" he called out, scrambling back to the elevators and ringing for the hoist operator.

A couple of minutes later a low rumble shook the ground as the dynamite brought the face down precisely as figured and extended the Princess' Necklace drift another five feet.

His shift through, Peter normally would have headed straight for his own claim, the Lucky Irish, and worked it until nightfall, but this afternoon was different. His family was here now and he was anxious to get home to them.

In the ground far below their feet, a massive cloud of pulverized rock was slowly settling throughout the long, pitch-black tunnels. Only a few moments before it had rushed through them as if driven by a tornado, filling every crack and crevice, every drift and winze, with choking dust. Now, as it slowly coated everything in a fine gray powder, near the blast-face in the Princess' Necklace drift the ceiling began to tremble and pebbles rained down past the shoring overhead. The thick, wood braces strained, creaking and cracking like a rifle shot as the weight of more than one hundred feet of mountain began to shift slightly. The timbers bowed. It was not enough for any human eye to see, of course, but now suddenly the timbers were bearing a thousand times the weight they had borne only a few minutes before.

An hour later the raining pebbles had ceased. The air had cleared, and a grainy gray coating had settled upon every square inch of the tunnel. The creaking timbers were silent as well, and everything was back to normal . . .

# EIGHT

CASEY DANIELS HALTED HIS WAGON ON THE ROAD AS PETER Kramer strode down Battle Mountain from the Rattlesnake mine, his lunch pail swinging at his side.

"Yo! Peter!" Casey called out.

Peter looked around, spied him, and waved. "Casey!" He picked up his pace. "Maureen and Margaret came in yesterday."

"You've been wanting that for a long time now."

"It's good for us to be together again. I haven't seen you around lately. How is Mr. Strong treating you?"

"Sam Strong is a fair man. He lets me do my job and respects my decisions. I can't ask for much more than that."

"I understand he's a fair hand with the cards, too."

"He likes the wheel best, and wins pretty regular when he isn't drinking. You heading to your claim?"

"No, not tonight. Maureen and Margaret are here!"

"Hop aboard. I can only stand my cooking for so long, then I've got to do something about it."

Peter stepped up into the little wagon and Casey slid over. Just the same, with Peter's big arms and shoulders, the two of

them were squeezed shoulder to shoulder upon the narrow
seat.

"You ought to get married, Casey. That will take care of
the cooking problem."

"Isn't that sort of like curing a hangnail by cutting off the
finger?"

Peter laughed. "It's all in your point of view. Now me, I
like marriage. I like to know that when I walk through that
door this evening, Maureen will be waiting for me with a smile
on her pretty face, and a big hug. And that the house will be
sparkling clean and smelling of pine soap, and filled with the
wonderful odors of cooking pastries and meat."

"Hm. Well, I'm not saying that I wouldn't consider mat-
rimony—that is, if the right lady ever came along—but it isn't
a thing I'd go searching for, not like I would, say, a new
fishing pole, or a Greener bird gun."

"You just wait. Someday the right lady *will* come along
and you'll forget there ever was such a thing as fishing or
hunting."

Casey grinned. "That would have to be some kind of lady,
all right."

"Now, first thing we have to do is to find the meat market,
darlin'," Maureen had said earlier that afternoon as she tied
Margaret's sunbonnet in place with a big ribbon bow beneath
her chin. "We'll buy a fine roast, some potatoes, and perhaps
even canned beans, if they have any. Your father will be hungry when he gets home after a long day in the works."

"Then we can look for pretty cloth, Mommy?"

"Then we can look for material. Heaven knows, we both
can do with a new dress."

"And a candy store too?"

Maureen frowned. "Maybe. If we see one while explorin'
this new town. But mind you, darlin', no more than one
penny's worth." Maureen adjusted her own bonnet before
turning sideways to examine herself in a steel mirror on the

wall. Then she took up her handbag and she and Margaret went into town.

Cripple Creek was more of a residential community than a commercial one. Maureen had seen that immediately upon arriving. There was the big Hotel Clarendon at the corner of Bison and Pikes Peak, a tent church, a lumberyard and a brickyard doing a brisk business, the Elite Laundry, S. A. Peiffer's bottling works, two stables, half a hundred cabins in various states of completion, and that was about all. But below them only a few hundred feet was Fremont, a place churning and bubbling with business. The skeletons of tall buildings rose against the startling blue sky at half a dozen different locations, and horses, mules, and wagons filled the streets. People were everywhere. She took Margaret by the hand and they walked along near the edge of the rutted road.

In Fremont, boards had been hastily laid down right on top of the ground in front of most of the buildings; a sort of rolling boardwalk that Maureen found almost more effort to navigate than to walk along the slightly more even grade of the road. Crude telegraph polls lined both sides of the street every fifty feet or so; four lines from the electric utility company, seven wires of the telegraph company, and perhaps even telephone lines as well. Maureen had heard that telephones had already arrived in the District, although she hadn't yet seen one.

Margaret craned her head back to look up at the wires, and at the globes of the electric arc streetlights that hung from them at every intersection. Then she gawked at the storefront show windows. On the lookout for a candy store, no doubt, Maureen surmised.

Maureen paused in front of the De LaVergne Furniture Co. Beyond the narrow window was a beautiful walnut dressing table, and while Margaret fidgeted at her side, Maureen lingered, her eyes running an imaginary hand over the polished, curved front and testing each of the six drawers. Atop it was a tall mirror. Maureen peered at it and sighed wistfully, re-

calling the small, dull, steel mirror that Peter had nailed next
to the doorjamb. A woman and a little girl about Margaret's
age were making their way from the back of the building. The
woman stopped to speak to a man there, but the little girl
stepped out into the sunlight and blinked.

"Hello," Margaret said.

The girl looked over. "Hello, what's your name?"

"Margaret."

"Hi, Margaret. I'm Mabel Barbee. Where do you live?"

"In a cabin up there on Silver Street." Margaret pointed.

"We live in the tent camp on the west side. My father is a
prospector."

"My daddy has his own claim."

Maureen heard the boasting in her daughter's voice, but said
nothing. There was time enough later for a lecture on pride
going before a fall. Right now, she was pleased to see Margaret making a friend.

"Someday my father will be rich," Mabel said. "He
witches for gold."

"Witches for gold? You mean like looking for a water
well?"

"Yes, only he's looking for a gold mine instead."

Maureen said, "How long have you lived here, Mabel?"

"Oh, not long. We have only been here a week."

"We've only just arrived too," Maureen said.

"Have you got a horse?" Margaret asked.

"No. Have you?"

At that moment the girl's mother emerged from the store.
She was a pretty woman, with auburn hair and about Maureen's age, but when she saw the two girls together her face
went white. "Mabs," she said, "come away from that child
at once!" And with that, she pulled the little girl roughly away
from Margaret.

Maureen was startled, and the woman must have seen her
surprise, for her sudden harsh expression softened then and

she said, "I'm sorry. I did not mean to be rude."

"What has my daughter done?" Maureen asked, telling herself to keep her fiery Irish temper under control.

"It's not anything your daughter has done," the woman said. "It is only because of the epidemic, that's all."

"Epidemic?" Her anger died and instinctively she hugged Margaret to her side. "What epidemic?"

"You don't know?"

Maureen shook her head. "We only just arrived last evening."

"Diphtheria. It has broken out all over town. Many of the children have died these last two weeks."

For a moment Maureen could not speak. She shook her head as if dumb, then managed to say, "I had not heard."

"It is true. If you have just arrived, then you must keep your child from the other children."

"But how can you do that?"

The other woman shook her head sadly, and there was a helpless note in her voice. "Yes, I know. It's an impossible task, and even if you should be able to, the diphtheria is in the air." She paused, then said, "My name is Kitty Barbee."

"Maureen Kramer," she replied distractedly.

"I'll tell you the truth, Mrs. Kramer, I am so angry at my husband Jonce for allowing me to come here with Mabs that I've hardly said ten words to him."

"Why didn't Peter tell me——?" Maureen recalled the small body in the back of the undertaker's buckboard, and the way Peter had looked at Margaret. "He knew! He knew all along that there was diphtheria, and he did not tell me!"

"Isn't that just like a man," Kitty said.

Maureen's anger rolled back with a vengeance. "Well, *this* man is a-goin' to have the devil to pay when he comes home tonight." She instantly abandoned the idea of cooking Peter a fine meal and hauled Margaret home, ignoring her pleas to stay and look for a candy store. Once home, Maureen paced the floor of their little cabin, shaking with anger and rehearsing what she would tell Peter. Margaret moped at the windowsill, watching the pleasant afternoon sun sink farther to the west. Maureen knew that same helplessness that she had heard in Kitty Barbee's voice.

A little boy ventured out of the door of a tent cabin down the street but Maureen told Margaret she was forbidden to play with him—forbidden to play with any of the children in Cripple Creek.

"As soon as your father gets home, I'm goin' to have him take us away from this place."

Margaret's eyes filled. "You are being just like Aunt Bridie," she said. "Aunt Bridie never let me go out and play."

Maureen took her daughter into her arms. The last thing she wanted to be to Margaret was like her sister.

"I don't want to go away, Mommy. I have a new friend now."

The threat had been an empty one. She would not leave Cripple Creek. She had no place else to go, and nothing on God's green earth would ever drive her back to Detroit. She told Margaret so, and tried to explain about the diphtheria, and although the little girl claimed to understand, Maureen knew that she really had no comprehension of what danger there was in the disease.

"Are you real mad at Daddy?"

Maureen bit her tongue. Mad? She was infuriated! But it would do no good for Margaret to see that. "For sure, that man will have some answerin' to do for himself when he gets home, darlin'."

"Will you hit him with a broom?" the little girl asked cautiously.

"No, not with a broom, darlin'. I've something a mite more devastatin' than a broom."

Margaret looked worried. "What is it, Mommy?"

A small, satisfied grin moved briefly across Maureen's lips—the first since she'd heard about the dreadful epidemic—and she said, "My tongue, darlin'. And it's sharp and ready."

Casey Daniels pulled his wagon to a stop in front of Peter's cabin on Silver Street, one of two dozen tiny dwellings on these lots that had been some of the first to sell. Most of the cabins had canvas or sod roofs. A few had sturdy tin. Every home appeared, in one way or another, to be still under construction.

"Come on in and meet my wife," Peter said. "Maybe the smell of home cooking and the sight of a really pretty woman might change your mind about marriage. Who knows, you might even get invited to dinner."

Casey set the brake. "I wouldn't want to impose—after all, this is only her first full day here. But I will come in and meet this exceptional woman. After all that you've told me, I don't know why you bother looking for a gold mine. Sounds like you've already found one."

Peter laughed, opened the door to the cabin, and went inside.

"Begorra! Mr. Kramer," Maureen exploded in his face, "you have got some answerin' to do to me, and I better not hear no fancy tongue-waggin' either!"

Peter drew up in the doorway, caught off guard. Maureen came at him, her finger wagging viciously, her cheeks as crimson as the locks of hair pinned atop her head.

"W-What?" he tried to say.

"How could you bring your daughter and me to this place knowin' that it was infested with a deadly disease? If that ain't the works of a thoughtless man, I don't know what is. Saints, you are lower than a drunken fool in a ditch."

"But I—"

"And the worst of it is, you didn't even tell us! What were you a-figurin' we'd do, Mr. Kramer? Wait until Margaret came down with the fever and was burnin' up with it?"

"No, Maureen, I—"

She planted both her hands upon her hips and leaned into him. "My sister thinks you're a worthless dreamer, and now I have got to agree with her. You *must* have been dreamin'—

and your head full of cotton—not to tell us." She narrowed an eye at him. "Or was it whiskey that you were full of?"

"No, honest, Maureen. I've not had but a thimbleful now and again."

"Then my sister *is* right, and you have no idea how that hurts me." She advanced, backing Peter out the doorway and onto the walkway. "I'm so angry at you, Peter Kramer, that if you know what's good you, you will find someplace to be other than here—"

Maureen glanced up and saw Casey standing by his wagon, grinning. As soon as he realized he'd been discovered he hid the smile. She straightened up and quickly touched her hair in place, then nervously brushed at her dress. The crimson in her cheeks deepened.

Peter saw the chink in her attack and seized upon it. "Er, Maureen, this is my friend, Casey Daniels. You remember I told you about him? He . . . he gave me a ride home from the mine."

Discovering Casey standing there had clearly thrown her off her stride. "It is a pleasure to meet you," she said briefly, the lie as transparent as window glass. Maureen was obviously not pleased to meet anyone at this moment.

"Mrs. Kramer," Casey said, tipping his hat. "I . . . I think I have come at a bad time. If you'll excuse me, I will be going."

"No, no, stay," Peter said quickly. He would have implored the devil himself to stay if it meant keeping Maureen from his throat until he was able to explain himself.

"No, I'm sure I need to be on my way . . . somewhere." Casey climbed up on the seat of his wagon. "I'll see you sometime, Peter. Ma'am, it has been a genuine pleasure."

Casey turned his horse away quickly and started the wagon down the hill before Peter could see his huge grin.

Oliver Sawyer slouched in the chair at a back-corner table in Johnny Nolon's Saloon, staring at the long brown envelope that trembled in his fingers. He reached for the beer mug on the table. It was his fourth beer—or was it his fifth? He'd lost count. It must have been his fifth; no man could get drunk on only four beers! Of course, he'd had a dozen drinks since morning anyway, so what did a beer or two—of four or five—matter?

Sawyer's blurred vision shifted back to the envelope, and a bit of moisture gathered at the corner of his eye.

*I'm a damned sentimental fool. What's gotten into me, anyway?*

He tried to straighten up in the chair, but slipped back and laughed at himself. He managed to tuck the envelope back into the inside pocket of his jacket. The room made a couple of spins.

Grinning, Sawyer eyed the beer mug, extended a hand, and missed. He made a minor course correction and this time he was successful in wrapping his fingers around the handle. Once he was certain he had a good grasp upon it, he cautiously brought the mug to his lips, banged his teeth upon the rim, and didn't feel any pain. The idea that he might bash his teeth out and not even know it struck Sawyer as funny, and he giggled into his beer, bubbling around the edges of the mug and dribbling on his vest.

He drained the mug and slowly set it back, being careful not to miss the table. That would have been embarrassing.

Barney Mays came through the batwing doors and stood a moment with the bright light outside at his back. Glancing around the room, he spied Sawyer in the corner.

"Pull ups a chair, Barn," Sawyer said.

"I figured I'd find you here. They told me at the Ironclad Dance Hall that McMicken tossed you out because you were drunk. So, I figured that if McMicken kicked you out on your ears there was only one saloon keeper left in Fremont softhearted enough to let you stay, and that had to be Johnny Nolon."

Sawyer's battered face widened in a grin. He jabbed himself

in the cheek with the tip of his finger, then tried again and managed to push the spectacles up his crooked nose. "Johnny give me dis table alls to myself. Says I can stay here s'long as I don'ts makes no trouble."

Barney shifted uncomfortably in his new suit of clothes, ran a finger around the tight shirt collar. "Damned things ain't never gonna get broken in." He turned to the bar and flagged the bartender. "A couple more beers over here, and hurry it up." He looked back at Sawyer. "New clothes ain't worth shit until they get broken in proper, Olly. And then they ain't new."

"Get a li'l jingle in your pocket, Barney, and alls you can do is carp."

"At least I ain't drowning myself in every beer joint in town. What's gotten into you, anyway? This last week you haven't been sober for two hours. You wake up drunk, you go to bed drunk. This ain't like you, Olly."

Sawyer grabbed the table and heaved himself forward, resting his head upon his thick forearms.

"You ain't still stewing because that fellow kayoed you last week, are you?"

Sawyer's head snapped up. "No, I ain't! And he didn't kayo me, and don'ts yous forget dat. He gots in a lucky jab, dat's all. Anyways, I ain't done wids him yet. I gots his name, and his number is comin' up one of these days. Yous can count that on . . . er, count on that."

"Then what is it? This foul mood you've been in started right after that—" Barney stopped, then suddenly seemed to grasp the answer. "It's that woman, ain't it, Olly."

Sawyer's eyes were welling again.

*Dammit! It's the booze making me sentimental,* he told himself.

He managed to push himself straight and to remove his spectacles, then patted his eyes with the dirty sleeve of his jacket. "Damn light through them windows hurts my eyes."

"Sure it does, Olly."

He glanced up, not certain how Barney had meant that. "It's a fool that lets a woman get under his skin."

"You wouldn't be the first man it has happened to, Olly. And you ain't gonna be the last."

"She's nothing but a two-bit whore."

"Maybe, but I've seen the way she looks at you, Olly. She's in love with you. That's plain as daylight."

Sawyer frowned, then reached inside his jacket and took the envelope from his pocket.

"What's that?"

A tic in Sawyer's face momentarily drew a corner of his mouth into a grin. "That woman—she got dis crazy notion to start her own parlor house. She asked me for a loan to buys some land down on Myers." His lips sagged into a frown. "Then we had the fight and I ain't talk to her since." His thoughts drifted off into a whiskey-and-beer fog.

"So, what is that?"

Sawyer blinked and looked down at the envelope in his trembling fingers. He clasped his hand to stop the tremors. "I'm a fool, Barn. After me and Lisa had our fight, I started to drink. Kept it up for a day or two, den I went over to the real estate fellow and plopped my money down and he write me ups this deed for the land."

"You bought it for her?"

"Kinda crazy, ain't it."

"She don't know about it?"

Sawyer picked up his empty mug, then looked at the bar. "Where the hell is that beer you ordered, Barn?"

"It'll be here. When are you gonna tell her?"

His head lopped down between his arms again. "I don't know. I ain't talked to her since that day."

"Why not talk to her now?"

He looked up. "Think I ought to?"

"What's stopping you?"

"I don't know. Maybe I'm still sore—maybe she's still sore."

Barney gave a short laugh. "How long you gonna carry a grudge? Besides, you show up on her doorstep with that deed in hand and you are gonna have one grateful lady. Mark my words."

Sawyer's eyes widened a bit behind the thick lenses. "You thinks so?"

"Give it a try. What can you lose? Besides, Olly, that woman is really crazy for you."

The bartender started over with the beers, but Johnny Nolon intercepted him and brought the drinks to the table himself. Nolon was a short, soft-spoken man, always impeccably dressed. His saloon was famed for serving the best whiskey in town and having the most honest gaming tables.

He set a beer in front of Barney, then turned a concerned eye on Sawyer. "How are you feeling, Oliver?"

"I'm feelin' . . . no pain."

"I thought that might be the case. You want a place to sleep? I have a cot in the back room. I can get you something to eat."

Sawyer stood and grabbed the table to keep upright as the room did a spin or two. "Naw, Johnny. There is something I got to do now." Sawyer looked at the beer. "Hey, yous drink that, Johnny. Barney's payin'."

"Well, thank you, Oliver," Nolon said.

"Tink nothin' of it, Johnny."

"Be careful on the street, Oliver."

Sawyer wove a crooked trail to the door. Outside, he leaned against the door frame and squeezed his eyes. The sun stung like a handful of sand flung into his face, and it took a minute before he could see clear enough to cross Bennett Avenue. He wove his way through the traffic, ignoring the wagons that rumbled past and the cusses the angry drivers directed at him, bumped down Fourth Street, halting against a utility pole on Fourth and Myers to steady himself. Putting his eye on his destination across the way, he wallowed out onto Myers Avenue and down the center of it.

Sawyer dropped anchor at the front door of Lisa's crib. He steadied himself. He eyed the window, saw that the curtain was drawn, ignored that fact, and pounded his fist upon the door.

"I'm busy," Lisa's voice called beyond the door after a moment.

"It's me—Olly."

"Go away."

Sawyer glared at the door. "Who you got in there with you?"

"Ain't none of your business."

Sawyer squinted in the window but could see only darkness beyond the curtain. "Kick him outta that bed and opens this door for me, Lisa."

"I can't do that, Olly. He's already paid me."

"Oh, dammit, Lisa. Give him his money back. I gots something important I gots to tell you."

"I said go away, Olly. I ain't got nothing I want to say to you."

"Oh, yeah!" Sawyer backed up, lowered his bull shoulder, and drove forward. The door splintered before him and burst the lock from the jamb. Inside, he wheeled to a halt before crashing into Lisa's dressing table on the opposite wall. Lisa was in the bed, her arms folded angrily across her breasts. Besides her was a spindly gent, stark naked except for his socks.

Sawyer thought the fellow looked vaguely familiar, but he wasn't sure. And besides, it didn't matter.

"Is . . . is this you boyfriend?" he asked Lisa.

"No he ain't. And I'm going to call Sheriff Eales if he don't leave this very minute."

Sawyer picked the fellow's trousers off the floor and tossed them to him. "Here, get dressed, then *git*."

"Olly, you ain't got no right to do this," Lisa told him.

"You and me, sweetheart, we gots some talking to see to."

"Talking?" She lifted a skeptical eyebrow. "Business, or *pleasure*?"

"Maybe both." He glanced at the interrupted customer, who was hopping around one-legged as he tried to pull his trousers on.

"You're drunk, Olly. I don't like being around you when you get drunk," she said.

Sawyer looked back at the man and narrowed his eyes behind the spectacles. "Hurry it up, mister. You can put them boots and shirt on outside." He planted a foot on the man's rump and drove him headlong out the door, then turned back to Lisa.

She let her arms fall, revealing her breasts. Even in his drunken state he felt his body responding to her. "Dammit, Lisa, I've missed you."

"Yeah? Well, the way I remember it, it was kind of your choice." Her hand went to her face, where the faintly purple stain of a bruise remained.

He sat on the corner of the bed and started to speak, then was suddenly aware of the crowd gathering on the street outside her door. Lisa pulled the sheet up. He levered the door back in place, ramming the back of a chair under the knob to hold it there.

"Hey, sweetheart. I'm sorry about that. Looks like it was a real shiner."

"Cost me some business."

"Not too much, I hope."

She shrugged her bare shoulders. "So, what is it that was so important that you had to bust down my door and kick a paying customer out? He'll want his money back."

"So, give it to him."

"Just like that? Like I got bags of money tucked away under my bed," she came back angrily.

"Someday you will."

"Yeah, I know. But not with your help. And how much did you have to drink, anyway?"

"You still thinking of starting up your own place?"

"Oh, is that why you come here? To rub salt in old wounds? They say opportunity only knocks once. Well, it has knocked, Olly, and it has gone on to someone else's door. My land has a SOLD sign on it. It went up last week, and if you had really cared about me, or what I wanted to do, you would have seen that by this time. Or have you, and that's why you're here? You gonna tell little Lisa Kellerman how you told her so? How she's gonna stay a jerkwater two-dollar whore for the rest of her life—short as it might be? If so, you can leave right now. My life will be a lot easier without you in it, Olly."

He went to the window and pulled back the curtain. Most of the crowd outside had wandered away. Up Myers Avenue a block away was the only remaining lot. All the others had been built on. "You're right, sweetheart. There is a big SOLD sign right there in front."

She threw off the sheet and slipped into a wrinkled, fawn-colored chintz robe. Lighting a cigarette, she turned back to him. "I think you better go now, Olly."

The curtain fell lightly back in place.

"I come to discuss that business deal with you."

"Didn't you hear me, Olly? Or was I talking to these four lousy walls here? What's with you, Olly?"

"A partnership, sweetheart."

She sat on the wobbly chair by the dressing table and poured herself a drink. "What are you talking about?" came her unsteady voice. Then she tossed back a long drink.

"The same deal you offered me."

Lisa blew an exasperated cloud of smoke at the ceiling.

"You and me, sweetheart. We'll build us the finest parlor house and saloon in the District."

"You *have* had a lot to drink, Olly. What do you propose to build it with?"

"Close your eyes?"

"What?"

"Just do it. Dammit, if you question everything I says I'm gonna blow up."

She studied him a moment, then shut her eyes. "What are you doing?"

"You'll see. Okay, now open them."

The long paper dangled unfolded in front of her face.

"What is it, Olly?"

"The deed to that lot on Myers, sweetheart. *I* bought it. I bought it for you."

For the first time that he could remember, Lisa Kellerman could think of nothing to say. Her breath caught and she said, "Olly, *you* bought it?"

"I bought it."

Lisa reached for the paper. He snatched it back before she could grab a hold of it. "Conditions, sweetheart."

"What conditions?"

Sawyer was in control again, and he liked the feeling of that. "Condition number one. We are partners, equal. Fifty-fifty, right down the middle."

"Agreed."

"Condition number two. You don't work the line no more. You hire girls to do that. You and me, we have an exclusive. Understand?"

Lisa sat there stunned, then suddenly screamed, "Oh, Olly! I love you!" She threw her arms around his neck and dragged him into her bed as the deed fluttered to the floor.

# NINE

THE DIPHTHERIA SPREAD UNBRIDLED THROUGH THE TWO LIT-tle mining towns of Cripple Creek and Fremont, and the month of August saw a steady procession up the hill to the Pisgah Cemetery. Most of the caskets being delivered to Oscar Lampman's undertaking parlor were of a diminutive size. The epidemic brought the building of the log schoolhouse to a standstill. And even if it were to be completed and ready to open its doors by the beginning of the fall year, it was common knowledge that no parent would dare risk sending his or her child to it.

Cripple Creek/Fremont had become a prison for healthy children, who were forced to stay inside their houses, or in their yards, and were forbidden to play with any child who might be suspected of carrying the dreadful bacteria. And since *every* child was suspect, that summer of '92 seemed to drag on endlessly.

Maureen worked doubly hard at keeping her daughter healthy, scrubbing the house spotless, doing the laundry every day, and boiling the drinking water she bought from vendors on the corners at five cents a bucket. Although Doc Whiting had said the disease was not in the water, Maureen was convinced that it was, and she would press Peter on that matter to the point of distraction. She argued endlessly for a central water works that would bring clean water from the high mountains surrounding the District.

"I don't understand why they don't just build the damn water works," she exploded in frustration one morning while packing Peter's lunch bucket.

"It's not that easy, Maureen," he tried to explain. "We are dealing with two separate municipalities, each with their own interests—"

"And please tell me, Mr. Kramer, what could be of more 'interest' than the health of our children? There are at least fifty dead, and more sick!"

Peter shrugged his shoulders. "I can't explain it," he said. "I don't know that much about politics—" he began to say, but Maureen cut him off.

"I've had it up to here with the petty bickerin'. We have us two towns with two different administrations where all common sense says there ought to be only one. If you have no interest in politics, Peter, then maybe it is time *I* learned what is a-goin' on here."

Maureen immediately sat at their table and composed a letter to the editors of the *Cripple Creek Crusher, the Prospector,* and the *Daily Miner.*

Peter left for work as she completed her scathing note to the men of the two city councils about what she considered the complete nonsense of insisting on two municipalities operating in the space of a few hundred acres. She accused them of engaging in petty political infighting while necessary services—specifically, clean water—went by the wayside. When she had finished, she carefully folded the note and tucked it into her handbag.

If nothing else, she felt better after having written out her anger. After breakfast she put her hat on and checked herself in the pitiful mirror tacked to the wall. She thought of the lovely dressing table at De LaVergne's Furniture Co. Perhaps someday, she said to herself as she glanced up at the sagging canvas roof. Peter had promised her a new roof by winter, but so far the money had not been available for it, and she knew that money for a dressing table with a *real* mirror was going to be a long time coming.

"Margaret," she called as she gathered up her handbag and Margaret's hat. "Come in, darlin', we are goin' into town."

"Margaret?" She looked out the window at the little mound of dirt and gravel where Margaret had been playing only a few minutes before. It was now abandoned, except for the doll sitting on a chair made of scrap lumber that Peter had built for her.

Maureen stepped outside and called a third time. Then she spied Margaret up the street, playing with a little boy named David Shore. The Shore family, in Maureen's opinion, gave David far too many freedoms. They allowed him to roam the town in spite of the epidemic, and never seemed to care how late it was before the boy came in. Maureen never once had heard his mother, a thin Cornish woman named Delsey, call for him or summon him with a dinner bell like every other parent along Silver Street did with their children.

"Margaret!" she called sharply. This time the girl heard, and started home at once. As she got closer, Maureen could see the worried look upon Margaret's face.

"What were you doing talkin' to that little boy?" Maureen scolded.

"I'm sorry, Mommy."

"What on earth made you do that, Margaret? You know about all the children sick and dyin' of the epidemic!"

Margaret looked down at her dusty black shoes and frowned. "He said he caught a frog down at the creek. He had it in a lard tin at his house and said if I wanted to see it I had to come over."

"A frog? Mercy, child. In the house this very minute, young lady."

While Maureen heated water on the stove, she had Margaret

get undressed. She filled the sink, scrubbed Margaret's hands, arms, and face with green lye soap, and made her put on a clean dress. When she had finished, Maureen took Margaret by the shoulders and looked her sternly in the eyes. "I pray that no damage has been done, darlin'. Now listen to me. I don't ever want you wanderin' away from the house—at least not until this dreadful plague has passed us by. Do you understand?"

"I don't have anyone to play with, Mommy."

"My, you are headstrong, child. I don't know where you get it from. You can play with Mabs."

"But only when you call on her mother," Margaret came back with a pout.

"Maybe so, darlin', but this scourge isn't going to last forever. Doc Whiting says that once the weather cools down, the disease will have run its course. Until then, I do not want you playing with the other children—except Mabs, of course, for her mother feels the same way as I. Now, darlin', promise me you will obey me."

"I promise," the girl answered unhappily.

"Good. Now, put your hat on. We need to go into town and deliver a letter to the newspaper offices."

"Why did you write a letter to the newspapers?"

"In hopes the editors would publish it and maybe knock some sense into the bullheaded officials of Cripple Creek and Fremont."

Maureen and Margaret walked down into Fremont and stopped a while on Bennett Avenue to watch a crew of men working the road between Fourth and Fifth Streets.

"Well, it is about time they did something about that sloping avenue," she said to Margaret. "It's a danger to both man and beast. This Cripple Creek Minin' District is as mixed up and impatient as my uncle Paddy back in County Cork. He was in such a hurry to build himself a wagon shed that he never took the time to make the measurements fit the cart.

When he had finished, the door was so narrow he couldn't get his cart through it.''

''What did your uncle Paddy do, Mommy?''

''Why, the only sensible thing he could do, short of tearing out the shed. He cut two inches off each side of his cart and it just squeezed through. And that's just what the people of Cripple Creek have to do now.''

''Cut two inches off a cart?''

Maureen laughed. ''No, darlin'. They have to cut it off the *street*. You see, they were in such a hurry to put buildings up and to start makin' money, they never bothered to measure the street. Now to make everythin' fit, they must cut fifteen feet off one side of the street, and build a wall to hold up the other side . . . just like my impatient uncle Paddy. Come along, darlin'.''

Maureen and Margaret walked into the front door of the *Cripple Creek Crusher*. E. C. Gard, the editor, politely listened to Maureen's complaint, then took a minute to read the letter she had composed.

Gard cleared his throat when he had finished and said, ''If I were to print this as you have written it, you could draw some fire from the powers that be.''

''And fire they'd be deservin', Mr. Gard. This petty bickerin' is only hurtin' the women and children.''

''Hm. Well, I agree with you. But there are men who already know that. Consolidation is inevitable, it is only a matter of time.''

''But we don't have time.'' She pulled Margaret closer to her side. ''Pisgah graveyard is fillin' up with the bodies of children who have run out of time.''

''Well, Mrs. Kramer, I've spoken with Dr. Whiting. This epidemic has nothing to do with the water supply. It comes from contact. This town has grown so fast and people are so packed in right at the moment that there is no way to avoid an epidemic of this sort. We aren't the first town to be so stricken. Epidemics have become almost an expected pattern in mining camps throughout the West."

"Does that mean you won't print my letter, Mr. Gard?"

He thought a moment, then said, "I will print it so long as you allow me to edit some of the strong accusations."

"You won't be changin' the meanin' of none of it now, will you?"

"No, of course not. I'll only tone it down some so that certain men in power will read it with an open mind instead of becoming defensive."

"Very well then, you may edit it, Mr. Gard. And thank you very much."

She and Margaret visited the office of the *Prospector* next. A horrible racket was coming from the place as she stepped through the door. A man was stretched out on his back under the black press which clanged like a cracked bell under the repeated pounding of a hammer.

"I am lookin' for Mr. McCrea, please," she said.

The pounding continued, ringing in her ears.

Maureen raised her voice. "I am lookin' for Mr. McCrea, please."

The clanging stopped, and the man wiggled out from under the press, dropped the hammer, and stood, wiping his dirty hands upon his ink-splattered overalls. "What was that, ma'am?" he shouted.

"I am looking for Mr. McCrea," she repeated at a normal level.

"I'm McCrea," he said, still shouting.

Maureen handed him her letter. "I would like you to print this in your newspaper."

He looked it over, then laughed.

"I do not see anythin' funny in it, sir."

"Mrs. Kramer. You obviously have no grasp at all on politics—and that is what this is all about. Your letter displays passion, to be sure, but it lacks depth, and understanding. I suggest you stick with cooking and raising children, and leave the politics to men.'' He handed the letter back to her.

Maureen's cheeks flamed. "I'll have you know, Mr. McCrea, that because politics *is* left up to men we have this very problem today.''

"Indeed, Mrs. Kramer? Good day.'' He turned back to his work.

Shaking with anger, Maureen grabbed up Margaret's hand and stormed outside . . . and nearly ran down Casey Daniels.

"Oh!'' she said, startled.

Casey tipped his hat. "No harm done, Mrs. Kramer.'' He noted her ire and said, "Are you all right?''

Since that day Peter had first brought him over, nearly a month earlier, Casey had come by the house on three or four occasions. They'd had dinner once, and the other times he and Peter had spent the evening talking of mining, the merits of various gold ore refining methods, and what the future held for the District if Congress should move from the silver standard to the gold standard, as it was rumored might happen.

"I am not all right,'' she answered, her anger rushing back. "That Mr. McCrea refuses to print my letter to the leaders of our two squabblin' municipalities.'' She thrust it into Casey's hand.

As he read it, Maureen scowled at him. If he dared laugh he would certainly not be welcomed back in her house again, whether he was Peter's friend or not. But Casey didn't laugh, and nodded his head slowly as he finished it.

"I think you have a good point here.''

"You do?'' She wasn't prepared for that.

"I do. We are being governed by two mayors, two different sets of rules, and one police officer to enforce them. As your letter says, neither town wants to relinquish its power, yet to run a water line from Beaver Creek, they both have to sit down and begin agreeing on some things. It's high time they see the handwriting on the wall and consolidate.''

Maureen felt suddenly better. "I see you are a sensible man, Mr. Daniels.''

He laughed. "Well, some would argue with you on that point. Which way are you heading?"

"The *Daily Miner,* and if that editor laughs me out of his place I'll . . ." She stopped, not knowing how to continue without losing her dignity in front of this man.

"I'll go with you, if you like."

"Thank you, but I wouldn't want to be puttin' you out."

"Not at all. I'm heading that way myself."

"In that case, I accept."

Along the way, Maureen remarked on all the saloons and gambling houses going up. "You'd think drinkin' whiskey and gamblin' was all that was important to a man." Discretion prevented her from mentioning the opium dens and brothels.

"Most men work hard all day, and afterwards want to play just as hard. The family men go home, but when you have no home . . ." He left the thought unfinished.

"You are speakin' of yourself?" she asked.

He grinned. "Me? I never was much for gambling, Mrs. Kramer. Money is too hard to come by to throw it away at the wheels or tables. Most of these miners will never amount to anything, because they spend money as fast as they earn it. Of course, that will all end once they get married and have a wife to be accountable to for their wages. Then everything changes."

He sounded like a sensible man to Maureen, but she did not tell him that she thought so. She stopped in front of the skeleton of a two-story building. "Look there, Mr. Daniels. All that money going into a fancy saloon when what this town really needs is a school."

"They are building a school," he said.

"Aye. Have you seen it? A tiny log house, and the buildin' of it has stopped since the epidemic. Meanwhile look at what we have here." She pointed at a sign driven into the ground at the corner of the lot. "LISA AND OLLY'S SALOON. Such a grand building for sinnin' in."

•   •   •

Inside the half-finished building, Lisa Kellerman studied the roll of plans in her hands. She paced off the rooms where now only bare timbers stood, waiting for the laths and plaster to be applied. She knew exactly how much space would be enough, and she had made certain the architect had not allotted one square foot more than was necessary for a bed, a dressing table, and a wardrobe. After all, her girls weren't going to be giving dancing lessons up here. Enough floor space to get from the door to the bed was plenty . . . and by cutting down on that, she was able to squeeze an extra room into the floor plan.

From the loan the bank had given them to build the place, Lisa had taken out enough money to purchase a rack of new dresses, four pairs of shoes, and a half dozen hats. She had put some money down on a new single-seated phaeton too, although for the moment she had to rent a livery horse to pull it. But she had no doubts that within a year she would own her own animal as well.

She glanced around and found Olly by the corner, looking through the open studs at the street below. Lisa stepped carefully around a carpenter's toolbox, keeping the hem of her new green taffeta dress well out of reach of the teeth of a protruding saw, and stepped up beside him, wondering what had riveted his attention. She glanced at the two adults and the little girl on the street. The woman was quite attractive she thought as she noticed the glint of her red hair in the sun. Lisa wondered who she might be. "You know them, Olly?"

"Huh? Oh, no. Ain't never seem 'em before, sweetheart."

"Why were you staring at them?"

"I wasn't. Hey, you hungry?"

"There isn't anything else I can do now until the workmen get back from lunch, I suppose. Yeah, I'm hungry, Olly. You offering to buy, sweet pea?"

"Sure, sweetheart. Let's go."

They started down a ladder to the first floor, since the staircase was not quite finished, and as they did so, Lisa noticed Sawyer still watching the couple and the little girl. Her curiosity was piqued, and she decided to investigate the matter later. If nothing else, this tall, stunning woman with the red hair might make a perfect addition to the business she intended to build.

They broke from their work at the noon bell. Peter found a comfortable niche in the wall and spread the red checkered cloth across his knees. In the flickering light of eight candles and the soft glow of four lamps, he bit into the tasty meat pie and washed it down with a long drink of water from his canteen.

Sam Baroni let out a long belch that echoed down the Princess' Necklace tunnel and said, "What's got you down, Peter? You've been sporting a long face ever since you showed up for work this morning."

Edwin said, "I know the look, mates. Old Peter here is having woman trouble."

They laughed. Peter said, "It's not like you think."

"You don't know what I'm thinking, old boy."

"You're partly right."

"See, what did I tell ye?"

Peter glanced up at the shadow-contorted grins in the flickering candlelight and said, "Maureen has got it in her head that this epidemic is caused by bad water. She's been harping on it for weeks, and this morning she decided to do something about it."

Claude said, "That could be dangerous, Peter—letting a woman poke about in the business of men."

"I know. But you don't know Maureen. If I told her to keep out of it she'd scalp me like a wild Indian."

"Sounds like that woman needs to be put in her place."

Peter frowned. "You're free to try, Claude, but I won't be responsible for your health."

In the middle of their laughing Sam Baroni said suddenly, "Shush! What was that?" Silence fell upon the place while each man listened.

"What *was* that?" Edwin parroted, looking quickly about.

The rifle-crack of splintering wood shot through the tunnel. Pebbles started pelting their tin lunch buckets and the tops of their heads. For a moment the men held their breath and looked at each other, then Sam Baroni cried, "Cave-in!"

They scrambled to their feet. Overhead a timber gave way. Peter tried to stand, but the hollow in the rock he had sat in caught him by the hips and pulled him back. The rain of pebbles turned into a torrent of sliding rock and choking dust. Through the cloud, Peter saw Edwin diving headlong down the tunnel, a heartbeat before the shoring snapped overhead like a row of toothpicks. Another man stumbled in front of him and was instantly buried beneath caving rubble. Falling rock pounded Peter's legs, piling up to his knees, then his chest, shoving him solidly back against the wall, crushing the breath from him . . .

On the sidewalk outside the *Daily Miner,* Maureen said, "Well, that man was certainly the most civil of the three."

"Because he didn't laugh at your letter?" Casey asked.

"He did not, it is true. And he thought it was written just fine for the delicate ears of the politicians as well, without askin' to change one word of it. Of course, Mr. Daniels, havin' you standin' there might have reminded the fellow of his manners."

Casey laughed. "I wouldn't know about that, Mrs. Kramer, but I'm glad we got the matter of publishing your letter settled. Now, ladies, I had better get back to work." He tipped his hat to Maureen and Margaret. "Tell Peter I said howdy."

"I will."

"Good-bye, Mr. Daniels," Margaret said.

"And good-bye to you, young lady," he replied.

The far-off hoot of a steam whistle came drifting over the hills to the south. Casey's head snapped around and he strained to hear the distant signal. Along the street, men stopped to listen as well, and for an instant Cripple Creek and Fremont stood frozen.

The steam whistle was answered by another, closer to town this time, and then as if each mine was relaying the message, the whistles grew louder until The Gold King's whistle at the head of Poverty Gulch shrilled down into the streets of Fremont and Cripple Creek. People huddled together, and a buzz of questions began moving through the crowd.

"What does it mean, Mr. Daniels?" Maureen asked.

He looked back at her. "It's a warning signal. There has been an accident in one of the mines."

"Which mine?" she asked quickly, her bright blue eyes widening, her concern showing at the now tightened corners of her mouth.

Casey understood her fear. Every wife and every child lived with the "miner's dread." One morning their husband, their father would walk out his door and that would be the last time they would ever see him this side of eternity. "I don't know, Mrs. Kramer. It's one of the farther mines . . . down that way." His head inclined slightly towards the south.

"Isn't that the direction of Mr. LaFarge's mine?"

"There are lots of mines down towards Battle Mountain, ma'am."

Her view shot back at him. "But it could be."

Casey could not deny it.

"I must find out!" She grabbed Margaret's hand and started towards the road that led to Battle Mountain.

"I have a wagon, Mrs. Kramer. I'll drive you."

Turning out of town, Casey urged his horse into a gallop. Maureen held on to the iron grab bar with a white-knuckled fist. Her other hand kept the brim of her hat from flapping in the wind, and her eyes remained fixed upon the road ahead. Behind him, Margaret grabbed the sides of the bed, steadying herself. Casey swerved around a slower wagon and as he straightened out again, he saw the plume of dust from the hooves of an approaching rider. He waved an arm and hauled back on his reins, and the rider slowed.

''What happened?'' Casey said.

The rider paused long enough to shout, ''Cave-in at the Rattlesnake!''

Maureen's breath caught. ''Thanks,'' Casey said snapping the reins. The little wagon gathered speed, weaving past men on foot and slower wagons. He drifted into the big bend around Guyot Hill, then straightening out as a scattering of cabins swept past. He raced through Arequa Gulch and dipped into Eclipse Gulch, where he had to slow again for a few scattered cabins and a crowd of staring women and children standing alongside the road while their men scrambled into wagons and onto horses.

Once he was through Eclipse Gulch the head-frames of the mines on Battle Mountain came into sight. The road was filled with men making their way up to the Rattlesnake mine. Casey pulled up and set the brake. Maureen took Margaret by the hand and joined the crowd making their way up the hill. Casey went off in another direction.

''What happened?'' he asked a man coming down the hill.

''It was the Rattlesnake. There was a fall in one of the drifts.''

''Which drift?'' Casey demanded.

''The Princess' Necklace.''

Casey ran up the hill. A crowd had already gathered around the hoist shack where dust poured from its open windows.

Sam Stepton emerged from the building holding a wet cloth over his nose and mouth. Casey grabbed Stepton by the shoulders. ''How bad is it, Sam?''

Stepton was startled to discover him there, but he recovered quickly. Men were pressing in, and questions shot at him from a dozen different directions. ''I don't know yet, Casey. We are still trying to bring up the men who made it out of the main tunnel.'' At that moment the big wheel atop the head-frame began to turn. The skip stopped with a heavy clank and coughing, choking miners stumbled out of the shaft house, gulping for air.

Casey looked for Peter among them, but he wasn't there.

"How many more down there, Sam?"

"That's the last of them able to make it to the skip on their own," he said.

"Did Peter Kramer make it out?" Even as he spoke, Casey was looking around for Maureen, but the crowd was so great that he could not immediately pick her out.

"No, I don't think so."

A volunteer force of miners from the nearby works were forming to send a rescue team down for those men known to be still trapped. Phillip LaFarge appeared in the doorway of the office shack at that moment and came down to the crowd, accompanied by the slightly built Winfield Scott Stratton. Stratton owned the Independence and Washington mines, both down the hill from the Rattlesnake, and like most of the claims starting up in the District, his were barely making wages for his small crew.

When LaFarge saw Casey his stern face grew harder and he gave him a wintry glare. He glanced away and took Sam Stepton and W. S. Stratton with him a couple of dozen paces off, where they spoke among themselves a few minutes, which seemed to Casey like an eternity of not doing anything. But there was nothing anyone could do until the choking dust had settled and proper rescue plans had been made.

LaFarge turned back to the people and signaled for silence. "We've had a collapse in one of the drifts," he told the growing crowd. "As of right now, there are six men unaccounted for. Mr. Stratton has offered his crew to help dig them out. And there are more offers coming in from around the District. I haven't got anything else to tell you right now, and I won't have until we can get a crew down there. Any man here who can help is welcomed to stay. The rest of you will need to move down the hill and give us room to work."

"The names of the missing men!" someone demanded.

"I ain't got their names to give right now," LaFarge said.

He bit down hard on his cigar and ignored the rest of the questions that barraged in on him as he strode back to the office shack and shut the door.

"Mr. Daniels . . . Mr. Daniels!" Maureen pushed through the crowd, breathless, and said, "No one has seen Peter! What can we do?"

Casey's first thought was to tell her to calm down, but he knew that would be useless. "There is going to be a rescue crew going down after them in a little while," he said instead.

"Why not this instant?"

"They are waiting for the dust to settle some, that's all."

He heard his name called again, and this time it was Sam Stepton. Sam had a worried look on his face, and he waved him over to confer with Stratton. "I'll be right back," he told Maureen.

Casey had met W. S. Stratton only a few times while working on Battle Mountain. Stratton was a mild man with very light blue eyes. He was affectionately referred to as an "old-timer," although Casey knew Stratton to be only in his mid-forties. But his white mustache and fine white hair gave him the appearance of greater age, unlike James Burns, who also was snowy on top. The two men were about the same age, but no one ever thought of James Burns as being old. Stratton had said he came about his white hair honestly—through hard work and hard times. Burns had a far more fanciful explanation for his snowy top.

"Hello, Mr. Stratton," Casey said.

"Mr. Daniels," Stratton replied in his soft-spoken way, taking Casey's hand in his own small but leather-tough hand. Stratton was a shrewd man, and one of the most experienced miners in the District. But he was a loner, a melancholy man who shunned crowds. Still, he did enjoy sharing a bottle of whiskey from time to time with his cronies from "Little London." James Burns was one of those longtime friends, although Casey understood that at the moment there was some strife between the two men. Burns's young partner Jimmie Doyle had kicked Stratton off their claim over a remark about its gold possibilities. Bob Womack was another longtime friend, but Bob was too flighty for Stratton and him to ever become what might be considered close friends.

Stratton said, "Mr. Stepton tells me you know this Princess' Necklace drift that caved."

"Yes, I do," Casey said. He held back the details of the disagreement with LaFarge that had made him leave the mine, but he did say, "I've studied the geology of it carefully. It is an unstable formation. It had to be worked carefully."

"Hm. Well, I propose that you, Mr. Stepton, Mr. LaFarge, and I go down there and look over the damage. Then we can determine the best course of action to take." Stratton's ace over most of the men in the District was his cool head. He was unshakable in the face of calamity. The ex-carpenter would plot a course through disaster as calmly as he might take up pen and ruler and design a toolshed.

"That's OK with me, but I don't think Mr. LaFarge would want me down there. We've had some words, you see. Besides, Sam here knows the passages better than I do. I've not worked for the Rattlesnake for over a month."

Stratton cocked his head to one side as if giving this careful thought, all the while rolling the end of his white mustache between his thumb and forefinger. Finally he said, "I've heard good things about you, Mr. Daniels. You're a top engineer, and your opinion will be most useful right now. I'll speak to Mr. LaFarge about it."

Stratton went to the office and a few minutes later the two men returned. LaFarge viewed Casey narrowly, his chiseled features revealing not a twitch of feeling, his face as unreadable as a gambler's smile.

"Mr. Stratton thinks your knowledge of geology and engineering might be of some value to us down there. Would you join us, Mr. Daniels?" he said.

"Of course I will," Casey replied.

"Good." LaFarge glanced about at the crowd stretching down the side of Battle Mountain. "The sooner we get down there the sooner we will know how to proceed."

# TEN

CASEY PRESSED A HANDKERCHIEF TO HIS MOUTH AND NOSE to keep the fine particles out of his lungs, as did the other three men with him. The skip dropped quickly into the main shaft, falling through billowing clouds of dust, passing tunnels still lit by those lamps left behind by the men who had dashed for safety. It clattered against the timber guides on its way down, sounding like an iron shoe box filled with stones, then slowed as it neared the lowest tunnel and came to a gentle stop inches above the floor—the sure sign of a practiced operator at the clutch and brake of the steam hoist. Good operators were hard to come by, and they cost mine owners a dollar a day more than the pick-and-shovel men.

All the lamps at this level had been snuffed out by the rush of dust from the collapsing tunnel. The men stepped from the skip and held their lanterns at arm's length. The dust was thick as a London fog. Casey went ahead of them, raising his lamp to study the beams overhead.

"How do you make it, Mr. Daniels?" Stratton asked behind his handkerchief.

"The main tunnel seems sound enough, but then I expected

that. It was the Princess' Necklace drift had been the problem at this level.''

The sifting dust attached itself to their sweating foreheads and stung their eyes.

''We can safely bring men down then—at least to this point?''

''Yes, I'd say so.''

''Let's move ahead,'' LaFarge said impatiently.

Stepping carefully, they worked their way deeper into the mine. The dust was marginally less as they progressed, and by the time they reached the mouth of the Princess' Necklace drift the dust had settled enough to see clearly.

''Try not to bump anything,'' Casey said, starting into it.

''We all know that,'' LaFarge shot back.

Casey grimaced and wondered why he had agreed to go along with this in the first place. It wasn't any of his business anymore. The shoring had been built by Sam Stepton, and it was LaFarge and Sam who carried the brunt of the responsibility. To listen to LaFarge, though, one had to wonder. Then he thought about Peter Kramer, and of the woman and child up on the surface, and he knew why he had come down here.

The drift was deeper than he last remembered, and as he advanced he was aware that it was beginning to rise. That struck him as odd. If indeed the vein was rising, it would mean it apexed somewhere other than LaFarge's claim, in which case one of the other mines would be the rightful owner of all the gold. Casey crept ahead, doing some mental figuring as he went. The drift was cut more or less to the west, and if it continued in that direction it would soon be under McKinnie and Peck's Black Diamond mine.

Did LaFarge know? Casey wondered. But before he had time to explore that line of thought, he came up against a solid wall of rubble and timbers where the shoring had been snapped—as if it had been made of dry kindling. Casey shined his lamp up towards its sloping top and studied the disconformity that had worried him in the first place. The standard square shoring that LaFarge had constructed in place of his painstakingly engineered trusses had been woefully inadequate for the job.

Casey looked back at the three men. LaFarge was impatient, as if he wanted to be out of this hazy passage. Sam looked as if he was going to be ill. And Mr. Stratton was peering hard at the ceiling, almost as if he was trying to read some message hidden in the color of the rock. He was a miner through and through, that one. Stratton shifted his view to the shoring and studied it a moment, running his hand along its rough sawed surface. Casey stepped around a boulder and his foot came down on something soft. He instantly stepped back. Lowering the lamp, he discovered an arm, and a head. The rest of the body was buried beneath tons of rock.

Sam Stepton came around and hunkered down. "It's Edwin Dabble," he said, turning the battered face up.

LaFarge stared a moment at the body then. "Does he have family in town?"

"I don't think so," Stepton said.

Casey said, "Edwin's family lives in England somewhere. Cornwall, I think."

Stratton studied the body, frowning, as if Edwin had been a close friend. Then he climbed the slope of broken rock and showed his lamp over the top of it.

"The ceiling has broken away to where a man can almost crawl over the top. Might be we can get a crew up here and clear enough of this rubble to tunnel over it. If this cave-in does not extend to the rear of the drift, we can get a crew on the back side and work at it from both ends."

LaFarge scrambled up beside Stratton. Casey glanced at Stepton and in the hazy light he thought he saw a glisten in the man's eyes. Stepton quickly brushed it away.

"What are you staring at?" Stepton asked.

Casey said, "Every man who works these mines knows the danger." Stepton knew what had caused the collapse, and

Casey didn't need to point that out to him. "There could be pockets all along this drift. How many men did you have back here?"

"There was a crew of six."

Casey found a shovel and banged it against a boulder three times. He listened for a reply. Only silence, broken now and then by a pebble dropping from the ceiling.

"Maybe they ain't got anything to signal back with," Stepton said.

"Maybe."

LaFarge climbed off the rubble pile. "Either one of you two engineers see any reason why I can't immediately put a crew down here and start clearing this rubble?"

"You will have to watch that ceiling," Casey said.

"Thank you for pointing out the obvious, Mr. Daniels."

Stratton put himself between the two men and said, "It's gettin' a mite close down here, gentlemen. The way I see it, if we try to punch a hole over the top, chances are better than good that that loose breccia is gonna stay right where it is. As we start in from the ends, we can put up some temporary shoring. I've a shipment of timbers just delivered to my Independence and you're welcome to use what you need to get the job done, Mr. LaFarge."

"I've got timbers, Mr. Stratton," LaFarge said. Then he remembered the tight situation he was in and his voice mellowed some. "But thanks for the offer. All right, let's get a crew down here and dig these men out."

Maureen was waiting outside of the shaft house with Sarah Parker, Wanda Baroni, Kit Trembial, and Beth McMahon— all wives of men who had not made it out of the mine. "Where is Peter?" she asked immediately, her eyes wide and searching.

"We didn't find him. A section of tunnel has collapsed and

it is impossible to get past it. We're going to send a crew down now," Casey said.

"You could not find him?" she whispered.

"Don't give up hope, Mrs. Kramer."

"Mommy, when is Daddy coming out?" Margaret said, trying valiantly to keep a rein on the tears that threatened.

Maureen gathered her daughter to her side and said, "How did it happen?"

"Looks like the shoring gave way," Casey said.

LaFarge stepped out of the shaft house and Maureen and the other wives rushed over and barraged him with the same questions. He put them off, saying he had to get the rescue under way. He and Stratton organized a crew, and in fifteen minutes eight men with picks and shovels piled into and onto the top of the skip.

Casey knew that his services were neither welcomed nor needed here. Sam Stepton had gone down with the crew to direct the rescue and LaFarge had disappeared into the office shack. W. S. Stratton stood with a few of the other mine owners from the area—Sam Strong, Jimmie Doyle and James Burns, and J. R. McKinnie—who had come over to see what was happening.

Casey offered to drive Maureen home. "There is nothing you can do here," he said.

"No! I will stay and wait with the other women," she said.

Sam Strong said, "Casey, you know the Rattlesnake mine better than any one of us here. What happened down there?"

Sam Strong was a stocky lumber hauler from Colorado Springs who drank hard, fought hard, and played cards and the sporting ladies with a reckless abandon. Sam, who had been one of the first men to stake a claim on Battle Mountain, was an amiable fellow when sober, but sobriety had never been Sam's long suit. Casey could see by Sam's red face that he had been drinking, but he seemed in pretty good control of himself. "As far as I can tell, the shoring was not up to the job." He did not want to say any more than that. Casey was not a man to wag an accusing finger at anyone.

"That's how it looked to me," Stratton said in his quiet voice.

Sam gave Casey a sidelong glance. "Didn't you have a hand in building that when you worked for LaFarge?"

"I studied the problem, but I did not build it."

"Good to hear that. I'd not want a man working for me that didn't know how to properly build shoring."

That evening they had not yet reached the men, and every few hours a new shift went down into the diggings. Commercial wagons from Cripple Creek and Fremont brought up food and drink and did a booming business into the night.

It was almost one o'clock in the morning when word came up that the first man had been found. Sarah Parker broke down in a wild fit of hysteria when the body was identified as Claude's. The townswomen tried to comfort her, but she fell upon the crushed body when it was brought up and refused to release it until some of the men pulled her off and put her into the care of Dr. Hayes, who had stayed nearby all afternoon.

One by one the women joined Sarah—each handling her grief in her own way. Maureen was the only one left, and she clutched at a last shard of hope as the hours ticked by. Then at four-thirty that shard shattered like brittle ice. The word came up the shaft that Peter Kramer had been discovered in a niche in the wall, and as with the others, the life had been crushed out of him.

Sam Stepton stopped at the door of the mine office, swallowed hard, raised his hand to knock—then hesitated. He had no way of knowing why Phillip LaFarge had sent a man to find him, but he had a bad feeling about it. Perhaps it was only his imagination. Perhaps the lack of sleep. He'd been up all night with the rescue crews, and he was not a young man anymore. He knew that if he was honest with himself, he'd have to face up to the truth that he was getting too old for this line of work; the accident had driven that point home to him all too clearly.

He gave a weary sigh and knocked on the door.

"Yeah?" came LaFarge's impatient answer from the other side.

Stepton went inside.

LaFarge inclined his head at a chair. "Sit down. We got a matter to discuss, Sam."

LaFarge was never a cordial man, although he could be when he wanted something, but his manner was more gruff this morning than usual. Sam knew the accident had unnerved LaFarge, but he suspected it wasn't the death of six men so much that was getting at him. It was the loss of production time that bothered LaFarge, and after pondering the puzzle over a month now—ever since he had witnessed LaFarge's henchmen murder Elvin Tate, the engineer at the McKinnie mine—Sam Stepton thought he had the reason figured out.

Sam glanced at the chair, then lowered his tired body into it. "What sort of matter, Mr. LaFarge?"

LaFarge drew in on his cigar, studying Sam from beneath his dark eyebrows. "There is going to be hell to pay over what happened yesterday."

"Mining accidents happen all the time. No one looks too closely into them."

"Is that so? Have you seen the newspaper this morning?"

"No, I've been here all night, trying to get that mess below cleaned up."

LaFarge slid a copy of *Daily Miner* across his desk to him. "It's on the front page. Someone from the Rattlesnake went to them with a story about how I run this mine, and how I . . . or should I say *we* built unsafe shoring to cut down on the cost. It says I care only about pulling ore from the ground, and not a damn about the safety of my men!" LaFarge shot to his feet, knocking his chair to the floor, and began pacing. "Dammit! It's my operation and I can damn well run it any way I want! These kinds of stories will ruin my reputation."

Sam Stepton scanned the article, which was indeed a virulent attack on LaFarge. He had no disagreement with the man who wrote it, but he did not tell LaFarge that. "So, what do you intend to do?"

LaFarge picked up the chair and sat back behind the desk. Steepling his fingers, he rested his chin upon them as the cigar pumped out smoke like a locomotive, his face all sharp lines and angles. Then he said, "There is only one way clear of this, Sam, and that is for you to come clean and tell everyone you built that shoring. I'll have to let you go, of course, and you can leave the District. I'll give you a little money to get you on your feet somewhere else."

"I can't do that!"

"You can, and you will."

"But it's a lie. I tried to talk you out of changing Casey's drawings. You know that."

"I know. But no one else knows it."

Sam was shaking. "But you don't understand. At my age I ain't gonna be able to find work—in another town. The best I could hope for is sweeping out a bar somewhere."

"That's your problem, Sam."

"Sharon and me, we don't have enough money to get by on."

"That ain't my problem, Sam. You should have thought about that sooner. You can't work forever. You should have known that."

"Maybe, but I didn't, and I never thought much about stopping. I've got a good job here, Mr. LaFarge, and I do a good job for you!"

"Not anymore."

Sam stood and gripped the edge of the desk for support. His heart was racing, and sweat beaded upon his forehead. "I ain't gonna let you do this to me."

"I don't see as you have a choice, Sam. I'll tell everyone you built unsafe shoring and I fired you. It's as simple as that."

Sam's mouth went dry. He had never been a man to force his way upon people, but this was life and death! His thoughts raced, and he tried to put it all together, but when he spoke it came out all wrong.

"You do this to me and I will tell everyone how ... how you had Elvin Tate murdered after he ... he gave you a drawing about the Black Diamond mine. I will, Mr. LaFarge. Don't force my hand. I'll tell everyone what you are up to down there in the Princess' Necklace and why you are pushin' so hard to get the gold out of that vein." He hadn't intended to blurt it out like that, but there it was. His tongue was a hard lump in his mouth.

The cigar stopped pumping smoke and LaFarge's eyes narrowed. "That's a lie."

"It ain't no lie. I saw it with these own two eyes."

"You've been prying through my papers."

Sam nodded his head. "I did that—just to make sure I was right. But I never intended to tell no one, Mr. LaFarge. I'd have taken your secret to the grave if you played it square with me."

LaFarge removed the cigar and motioned to the chair. "Sit down, Sam ... sit down."

Shaking, Sam returned to the chair. Now that he had said it, he feared what LaFarge might do next. He hadn't thought this through. It had never occurred to him that he would ever have to confront LaFarge with what he had learned.

"I am truly disappointed in you, Sam. Going through a man's papers is almost like stealing from him."

"But I would not have told nobody. I'd have played it straight with you."

"You know, Sam, I believe you."

"You do?"

He thought a moment. "Perhaps I have been too hasty in asking you to leave this job. There might be another way to work this out."

"What other way?" Sam didn't like LaFarge's easy voice. It sounded too much like the tone he'd heard patent-medicine doctors use.

"Of course. Now why didn't I think of this right off?"

"What?"

"Who really did design the shoring down in that drift?"

Sam was momentarily confused. "Casey?"

LaFarge leaned forward. "Everyone knows that Casey was in charge of that work. It was no secret."

"But what you had me build down there was only a simple square shoring. Not what Casey designed."

"Who but you and me and Casey knows what was designed? All anyone needs to know is that Casey designed it, and we built it. Casey doesn't work here now. He's the perfect one to take the blame."

"I . . . I don't know, Mr. LaFarge. Casey's a good man—a good engineer. You'd be ruining him for this District."

LaFarge shrugged his shoulders. "It's either that, or I'll ruin your reputation and you'll ruin mine. That way you and I both lose. This way, only Casey loses. He's young. He'll find work someplace else. You know what *your* prospects are for finding work, Sam."

Sam didn't like it, but at least it kept his neck out of the noose. Reluctantly he nodded and said, "All right. I'll go along with that."

LaFarge stood and went to a cabinet and came back with a dog-eared roll of papers. He spread them out and Sam recognized them as Casey's original drawings. "Now, one last detail."

LaFarge took a rubber stamp from the top desk drawer, inked it, and rolled it across the bottom of the plans.

INSPECTED AND APPROVED BY_____

As the ink dried, LaFarge found an old receiving bill with Casey's signature. He spent a few minutes duplicating it upon a piece of scrap, and when he had it down pretty good, La-Farge carefully wrote Casey's name upon the blank line. Immediately, he pressed a blotter to it and shifted it slightly to give a minute smear to the signature.

"There. What do you think, Sam?" LaFarge held the two signatures side by side.

Sam didn't like this, but he had no choice but to go along. "They appear to be the same," he said. The slight smear looked perfectly natural and it cleverly hid any discrepancies between LaFarge's hand and Casey's.

"Of course they do," LaFarge said, and one of his rare smiles managed to break the surface.

That August went from one tragedy to another. Maureen didn't know she could grieve so deeply, that a loss could hurt this badly. Margaret withdrew into herself and seemed to be slipping back into her old ways, behaving as she had before they left Detroit. She refused to leave her bed for days and did not want to eat. Maureen tried to go about her daily chores as before, but she had no energy, no drive, and sometimes she'd forget herself and look at the lowering sun outside the window and wonder when Peter was going to get home from his claim. Then she'd remember and the tears would flood back.

As the days went by, more news about the disaster hit the newspapers. Casey Daniels, it was reported, had designed the ill-fated structures, and the blame for their failure was being placed squarely upon his shoulders. Casey had been Peter's friend! Peter had trusted him—trusted him with his life. Now Maureen understood that that trust had been misplaced.

She went through life mechanically, knowing it had gotten as bad as it could . . . until one morning seven days after the mine accident, when Margaret awoke from a fitful sleep complaining of a headache and sore throat. Maureen put a hand to the child's head, felt the heat, and rushed outside to the Randalls' house and asked Colleen Randall to find Doc Whiting. The doctor arrived within an hour, examined the child and, with a tightly frowning face, told Maureen the news she feared most.

Margaret had contracted diphtheria.

# ELEVEN

SAM STRONG CALLED CASEY INTO HIS OFFICE A WEEK AFTER the disaster, offered him a chair, and poured them both a whiskey. Casey knew by Sam's ruddy face that he'd been drinking, and by his tight mouth, that there was some trouble . . . and he was pretty sure he knew what it was about.

"How are things going, Casey?" Sam started off neutrally.

"That depends. If you like working alone because the men are avoiding you like a rabid dog, then I reckon things are going just fine."

Sam managed a quick grin. "That's what I like about you, Casey. You don't beat around the bush."

"It's why you called me in here, isn't it?"

Sam hesitated a moment. "It's starting to look like I might have a revolt on my hands—or worse yet, the men are talking about organizing. You know the kind of problems you have when men start thinking union. There is big rumblings about labor unions starting up in the mines of northern Idaho, and the men hear it. Oh, we've got a few loose-knit associations even here in Cripple, but nothing to worry about yet. If the men get too unhappy, though, and the grumbling starts spreading to the other mines . . . well, then we could be in for big trouble.''

"And how do you figure I fit into the problem, Sam?'' Casey said, setting the whiskey aside.

"Right now the men are grumbling.''

"Because of me?''

"They've elected themselves a spokesman. Kevin McCall.''

"I know McCall.''

"He says the men aren't gonna work no tunnels that you've had a hand in engineering. He said the men are almost of one mind on this matter. They lost friends in that cave-in at the Rattlesnake last week.''

"You believe that it was my fault?''

Sam tossed back his whiskey and immediately poured himself another. "I don't know, Casey. But I do know that the *men* think it was your fault. And LaFarge is saying he has proof.''

"That's a lie.''

"The evidence don't look too good. Maybe it's a lie, and maybe it isn't; I don't know. The important thing is, the men believe it's your fault, and right now with unrest brewing in the mines up north, and the talk of uniting spreading through the industry, I can't take any chances. We mine owners want to keep the unions out of Cripple Creek as long as we can, and if that means soothing some ruffled feathers—well, so be it. That's cheaper in the long run than what it will cost us if we allow the men to ever organize.''

"I don't know what evidence LaFarge has, but that work down in the Princess' Necklace was not my doing.''

"I want to believe you, Casey. You're a fine engineer and I can't imagine you building something that wasn't safe. Any way you look at it, it appears LaFarge is scrambling to cover his tail. But just the same, it's the men who have to be soothed over, and unfortunately, LaFarge is making a good case against you. If it was some other time . . . if the circumstances were different, I'd tell the men to can their carping or pack their bags. But this talk of unions and all—it has got a lot of mine owners nervous.''

"Then it's not only you?''

Sam winced and shook his head. "We had us a meeting last night.''

"Who was there?''

"It don't really matter who, does it? Let's just say it was some of the owners with the most to lose if the men decided to organize.''

"LaFarge?''

Sam reluctantly nodded his head. "He was there.''

"I'm not surprised. What did all of you mine owners decide at your meeting?''

Sam looked at the whiskey glass that Casey had set on the corner of his desk. "You ain't gonna let that go to waste, are you?''

"I don't usually drink whiskey.''

"Oh.'' Sam Strong got out of his chair and walked to the dingy window that overlooked the head-frame and shaft house of his mine. Beyond it some of his men were off loading a supply of timbers from a freight wagon. The morning was growing hot, and the little shack would soon be unbearable. Most of the tall trees on Battle Mountain had been leveled early on and their wood used for fuel and constructing the first buildings, the end results being a naked, rocky hillside and not a square inch of natural shade. The tailings thrown up by the mines littered the ground, reflecting the sun's burning rays mercilessly.

"The upshot of it all, I'm afraid, was that everyone figured if you left, the men would take it as a sign that the owners were on their side, and stop all this foolish talk about organizing.''

"Everyone?'' Casey wondered if Strong was including himself.

Sam turned back to the window again and did not answer that. The silence inside the shack drew out. "Sorry it has to be this way, Casey.''

"Me too." Casey started for the door.

"Wait up," Sam said, stepping back behind his desk. He opened a drawer and removed a pouch. "Your pay." He dropped the pouch of gold coins into Casey's hand.

Casey glanced at the heavy sack. "Had it all counted, did you?"

"I figured it out this morning. There's some extra in there as well. Call it severance pay."

Casey gave a short laugh. "Why not call it what it really is?"

"What's that?" Sam asked.

"Medicine for a guilty conscience."

Sam Strong grimaced. "No, it ain't that, Casey. It's blackmail money, and rightfully I should be paying it to the other mine owners, for it is them what's got the gun to my head."

Casey frowned, hefted the small pouch in his hand, then shoved it into his pocket and left.

*Twice in as many months!*

Casey walked down the rocky slope of Battle Mountain towards his cabin on Wilson Creek, brooding over his rotten luck at holding down a job. But more than that, Casey's spirit was heavy with the thought of the men who had died . . . and now he was being blamed for their deaths. He could deny it, of course. And he should he told himself—but with the mine owners stacked against him, who would believe him?

He went inside his cabin and looked at the four wooden walls. His rifle, shotgun, and fishing rod were there on nails pounded into the studs. There was a bed, a chair, a table, and a washbasin on a ledge by the back window—and that was all. Beyond the window ran Wilson Creek. The sound of its water curling around boulders mingled with the noise of the mine works up on Battle Mountain only emphasized the quietness within the cabin.

It had never struck him before, but coming home to this empty house now, with a heavy spirit pulling him down and a need to talk to someone, he suddenly realized how empty his life was—except for his job. Now he didn't even have that.

He recalled the conversation he and Peter had had that day nearly a month ago. Peter had been happy—truly happy. And in spite of the unexpected greeting he had received that afternoon, Casey had grown to know Maureen, and he understood that beneath that Irish temper lay a woman who cared deeply for her man.

Now Peter was dead and he knew that Maureen and Margaret must be suffering something terrible. What if she needed someone to talk to? Was she suffering all alone, or were the neighbors helping out? He had been inconsiderate not to have inquired after her needs earlier, he admonished himself. All at once, Casey had to know how she was coping. He had to help her if he could! He was certain it would not be long before she packed up and went home—to a sister, he seemed to recall, somewhere back east. That would be best. A woman alone in Cripple Creek had little hope of supporting herself and a daughter.

Casey hitched his horse to the little green mountain wagon and drove into Cripple Creek. He drew up in front of the tent-cabin on Silver Street. The door and windows were shut tight in spite of the heat, and the curtains were drawn. Casey wondered briefly if Maureen had not already left. The house had that closed-up appearance. Well, there was only one way to be certain. Casey set the brake, climbed off the wagon, and knocked on the door.

He heard a sudden movement behind the door, then all at once it opened and Maureen was there. She looked haggard, and her eyes were red and swollen. She stared at him a long moment and said, "So, it's you!"

The bitterness in her voice caught him off guard and he forgot momentarily what he had planned to say. "Are you all right, Mrs. Kramer?" he managed.

"I am not, and you're a fine one to ask that, Mr. Daniels.

You have torn the heart out of my life, and you ask me if I am all right!''

Like most of the folks in town, Maureen was blaming him for the accident at the Rattlesnake mine. LaFarge had been so thoroughly successful at poisoning the minds of the people that they all truly believed he had been negligent in the design of the shoring. He should have realized that Maureen Kramer would be the bitterest of them all.

"I'm sorry, Mrs. Kramer. I only stopped by to see if I could help in some way."

"Don't you think you have done enough already? It is because of you that I am a widow, and it is because of you that Margaret is sick!''

"Margaret is ill? I didn't know."

"The dear child could not eat. She grew weak and then the sickness came over her."

"Diphtheria?"

Maureen was suddenly overwhelmed and unable to keep her tears back. She buried her face in her arms, crying. Casey took her by the shoulders to try and comfort her. Instantly her head snapped up and her blue eyes burned with a fierce hatred. "Get out! Get out of here right now! You've murdered Peter and now are killin' Margaret as well! Get out!'' Maureen was screaming, and from the door of the next house a woman emerged and gave him a hard stare.

Casey backed away from the door, leaving her there, climbed back aboard his wagon and drove away. He found Doc Whiting in town.

"Yes, the little girl has diphtheria,'' the doctor said.

"Is there anything that can be done?"

Whiting shook his head sadly. He'd seen so many of the children perish under the cruel hand of this sickness that he seemed resigned to their fate. "There is not much, I am afraid. Shortly the disease will spread across the child's throat, forming a thick membrane which will have to be removed with coal oil swabs, or it might strangle her. But Margaret will have to fight it herself. The most we can do is keep her comfortable, try to keep the fever down, and see that she does not dehydrate. In the end, it will be her own strength that determines if she will live or die.''

That Margaret might die—that Maureen might lose both husband and child in a matter of days—stunned Casey. He said, ''Whatever you can do for her, Doctor—whatever—I will pay all of their expenses.''

Whiting raised an eyebrow. ''Indeed, Mr. Daniels. Are you attempting to buy a clean conscience?''

His words rang remarkably familiar—hadn't Casey himself accused Sam Strong of very much the same thing only an hour earlier? But more than ringing familiar, the words hurt. Like everyone else in town, Doc Whiting believed that Casey was responsible for the deaths of all those men. LaFarge's poisoning campaign had been complete. ''I have no reason to cleanse my conscience, Doctor. My concern is only for the child.'' He turned about angrily and strode away. His steps were directed nowhere in particular—only away from there. It was enough to be walking, and bleeding off the anger that had risen to a boil. He emerged on Myers Avenue from Fifth Street and was walking past an alleyway when a hand reached out and grabbed him by the shoulder.

Casey came about, startled, as a fist shot out of nowhere and smacked solidly into his face . . .

Oliver Sawyer stepped back finally, shaking out his bruised knuckles, and a thin smile moving across his cruel mouth. Barney Mays hunkered down and turned Casey Daniels over. Casey's face was a battered and bloodied slab of raw meat. Barney listened to the ragged gurgling that came with each unsteady breath. He grinned and looked up at Sawyer. ''Worked the pup over real good, Olly.''

''I said I'd pay him back. Never let a score go unsettled, Barney, no matter how long it takes.''

''He didn't have much of a chance,'' Lisa said. She had

followed Olly out the back door of their saloon, which was now finished except for paint, paper, and furnishings. She'd watched Olly snatch Casey off the street, haul him into the alleyway, and proceed to expertly beat the man into the ground.

"What you gonna do with him?" Barney asked.

"Let him be."

"He needs a doctor," Lisa said.

"I said let him be." Sawyer shot her a warning glance, then marched back to the saloon and into the alley doorway.

Barney grinned at her. "You heard him. Forget it. Let's go."

Lisa stood a moment, staring at Casey as he lay bleeding in the alley, and suddenly remembered where she had seen him before. He was the very man Olly had watched from the unfinished second floor of their saloon only a week or so before. The man who had been with the stunning redheaded woman and the little girl. "What was this all about, Barney? Who is this man?"

"His name is Casey Daniels. Olly and this fellow had a run-in a while back, and Olly ended up on the ground, and he swore he'd settle up."

Lisa shivered as if a cold finger had run up her spine. She looked at Casey's left hand and saw that the ring finger had no band on it. That could mean nothing, of course, or it could mean that the woman who had been with him that day last week had been only a friend. There was little she could do to help this poor fellow—not if she didn't want to end up bleeding herself. Lisa knew the price of crossing Oliver Sawyer.

Margaret grew worse, drifting in and out of consciousness. The fever burned in her scarlet forehead and her little hands shook from time to time as sweat oozed from every pore. Maureen never left her side. The damp cloth was forever present upon Margaret's brow, and Maureen sponged the child constantly. She herself was growing weaker from the lack of

sleep. There were many hours when she did not think about
Peter's death but gave herself over wholly to tending to Margaret.

Either Dr. Whiting or Dr. Hayes stopped in every day. Both
men had separate practices, but the epidemic was so widespread that every sick child instantly became part of them.

Colleen Randall had no children and she spent much of her
day with Maureen, or preparing meals. The whole town mobilized, with those women who were able to helping those who
were tending sick children.

On those few occasions when Margaret would fall into a
deep sleep, Maureen would nap in the chair at her bedside.
She missed Peter desperately. The pain of his loss was like an
iron bar crushing her spirit. And poor Margaret, fighting for
her very life . . . It was almost more than Maureen could bear.

When she would run through the events of the last couple
of months, her thoughts would always come back to that horrible day at the Rattlesnake mine. It was because of Peter's
death that Margaret had gotten sick! Maureen was sure of
that—just as firmly as she was certain that the epidemic was
caused by the nonexistent water system in this boomtown.
Then she would remember all the damning newspaper stories
after the accident, and the talk among the miners about how
the job of shoring up that dangerous section of mine had been
given over to Casey Daniels.

There was hardly a man in Cripple Creek who didn't hold
Casey responsible for the accident, but it was the wives and
children of the men who had died in it that most bitterly hated
Daniels. And of them all, Maureen harbored that most virulent
hatred, for unlike the other men who had perished, her Peter
had been a close friend of Casey's. He had trusted Casey! And
Casey had let him down!

Casey had killed Peter just as surely as he was killing Margaret!

One afternoon there was a soft knock upon her door. It was
Dr. Whiting, looking particularly weary.

"How is the little one doing, Mrs. Kramer?" he asked, lowering himself into the chair by Margaret's bedside and placing his soft fingers gently upon her forehead.

"I'm keepin' the fever down the best I can."

"You are swabbing her throat with coal oil like I showed you?"

"Yes, Doctor."

He nodded his head wearily and then removed a thermometer from his black bag and placed it between the girl's pale lips. "When was the last time you had any sleep, Mrs. Kramer?"

"I have dozed from time to time. I don't sleep regular these days."

"Hm. I can understand that, but I'd not like to have to treat you as well, Mrs. Kramer. You have someone who can watch little Margaret?"

"Mrs. Randall comes sometimes. She brings broth."

"And Margaret is taking it all right?"

"She doesn't want it, but I make sure she swallows a full cup of it three times a day, and I give her water whenever I can get her to take it—I boil it first."

He removed the thermometer and held it against the light. "One hundred and three."

"It has gone down!" Maureen said at once.

He glanced past the thermometer at her. "A single degree, Mrs. Kramer."

"But it is a good sign, is it not?" Maureen was ready to grasp at any hope, no matter how slender a thread it was supported by.

"Yes, it is hopeful." He rinsed the thermometer in a vial of carbolic acid and put it away. "The unfortunate thing about diphtheria is that unlike a broken leg, there is little anyone can do but let the disease run its course. You are apparently doing the right thing for Margaret. But it is up to her own constitution to fight it off."

"Margaret is a strong girl," Maureen said. "She will win this fight."

Whiting stood slowly and said, "I hope so. Now, Mrs. Kramer, you need to see about getting some rest or I'll have *two* ladies in this house to tend to . . . and frankly, I don't need the extra work." He put his hat on and paused at the door. "I'll stop in tomorrow."

His head throbbed like a stamp mill and every muscle in his body ached. When he tried to turn his head a red-hot poker stabbed down his spine, as if all the muscles along his neck and across his shoulders had been ripped off and tied in knots. Casey struggled to remember what had happened. Slowly, snatches of it came back to him. He recalled being pulled off the street, and that big fist driving into his face. He seemed to remember slamming against a building, then slumping to the ground. And then a face.

All at once Casey remembered where he had seen it before but he was having trouble recalling the name. As he lay there the details came back—up until the time he had passed out. How long had it been? he wondered. Was he still in that alley? It seemed to be dark. Could it be night?

His head was resting on something soft. Methodically, using his tongue, he probed his mouth, discovering two gaps in his teeth.

*Only two?*

In a morose way, Casey Daniels found some black humor in that. The way he felt, he was surprised he had any teeth left at all. Now that consciousness was full upon him, he was more keenly aware of the aches and pains that swelled in his lower back and shot down his legs. The only things that did not hurt, it seemed, were his feet—not surprising, considering the heavy work boots that he had been wearing.

Casey tried to open his eyes, and couldn't. For an instant he thought that he might be blind. A momentary surge of panic swept over him, then he realized that something had been placed over his eyes. Wincing, he raised his hand. It seemed strangely unwieldy and he quickly discovered that it was heavily bandaged. With the tips of his fingers he gingerly explored his face. His lips felt too large.

He heard a sound, and froze. A little distance away a door had opened, then closed softly. Footsteps. By the sound of them, there were at least two men coming his way. The steps grew louder, and stopped beside him.

"I see you finally decided to join the living, Mr. Daniels." Casey immediately recognized the voice.

"Doc Whiting?"

"Well, well, at least your memory is still working."

"Where am I?" To speak was an effort. It hurt his throat, and the gravelly voice that came out sounded as if it belonged to a stranger. Certainly it was not his own.

"You are in my home."

"How long?"

"You've been unconscious for three days, Mr. Daniels. For a while I was worried you might not come out of it."

Behind the bandages, he squeezed his eyelids and said, "Is there someone else with you there? I thought I heard two sets of footsteps."

Whiting gave a short laugh. "And your hearing is still working as well. I have high hopes for you, Mr. Daniels. Indeed, Mr. Stratton is here with me. He stopped in to see how you were. It was he who found you the other day in that alley. We've been wondering who did this to you, Mr. Daniels. Marshal Wilson and Sheriff Eales have been asking around, but no one admits to having witnessed it. They were hoping you could tell them when you woke up."

Casey remained silent a moment, then said, "I can't help you. I was taken by surprise."

Stratton's voice was next. "Then you have no idea who done this?"

Suddenly a name came to him: *Oliver Sawyer*. But this was his problem, and he intended to settle it his way. "Considering the reputation I've developed this last week, I'm just surprised someone didn't work me over sooner.''

"Then you think it has to do with that business at the Rattlesnake?'' Stratton pressed.

"I don't know.''

"Well, it wouldn't surprise me," Whiting put in.

Stratton reserved comment, and Casey wished he could see his face to determine what the man was thinking.

Whiting said, "Well, now that you're conscious we can start putting real food down you. You should be up and about in a few days. You were lucky nothing was broken—whoever worked you over did a thorough job of it. I'll stop in on you later.''

"Good-bye, Mr. Daniels,'' Stratton said.

Casey heard their footsteps make for the door. Then he remembered something and said, "Doc, how is that little girl doing—Margaret Kramer?''

The sound of their feet stopped. Dr. Whiting said, "She is still a very sick child, Mr. Daniels. But she's a fighter.'' He paused, then said, "Are you feeling responsible for her illness?''

Casey's anger flared, but he kept his voice steady. "Like I told you before, Doctor, I was not the cause of the accident.''

He heard a single set of footsteps return to his bedside, and Mr. Stratton's voice. "When we were down inside the Rattlesnake I saw the type of shoring that had been built. Did you design it?''

"No.''

From a little farther off, Doc Whiting said, "LaFarge has the engineering drawings which you made for that tunnel. They have your signature on them.''

"I never signed off on those drawings,'' Casey said. "And if you will go down in the Princess' Necklace drift, you will see that my designs were never built.''

Stratton said, "That might settle it. However, Mr. LaFarge has stripped out all the old shoring and has had a crew down there night and day constructing a new system.''

''You saw them, Mr. Stratton.''

Winfield Scott Stratton remained silent for a moment, then said, ''I reckon I must have overlooked the details, what with all the dust and the shock of finding a body right off.'' He hesitated again, then asked, ''You don't know why LaFarge is working that particular drift like there ain't going to be no tomorrow, do you?''

''Mr. LaFarge's business is none of my business—not anymore.''

August became September. For a while Casey kept up with the news of the town through what little Doc Whiting was able to tell him. Then the bandages came off his eyes and Casey wished they hadn't. A hand mirror showed him the extent of the damage to his face. His body was a mass of purple splotches and large scabs. It was painful to move, but Casey forced himself to limp around the small room to build strength.

Whiting had told him that the epidemic seemed to be winding down, as fewer cases of diphtheria had been discovered in the last week. Although a little boy on her street had not been so lucky, Margaret Kramer was recovering.

''Little Maggie's mother never left her side,'' Whiting told him. ''That woman has driven herself to the point of exhaustion.''

''Peter was my friend,'' Casey said. ''If there is anything I can do to help?''

''There is nothing as far as my contribution goes. I don't charge widows or orphans for my services, Mr. Daniels, and I'm not certain Maureen Kramer would take any aid if it was offered—especially if she knew it was coming from you. She is a proud woman.''

For some reason, the doctor's words hurt him more than the beating Oliver Sawyer had given him. He said, ''When is she going back east?''

Whiting looked over with an odd smile. "What makes you think Mrs. Kramer is leaving Cripple Creek?"

"I just assumed she would. What is there here for her?"

"I can't answer that. No one but she can. But I believe you might find that Mrs. Kramer is made of sterner stuff than you give her credit for."

Casey felt fully recovered by the end of September and set about looking for a new job, but he had little luck. During this time, he kept an eye on Oliver Sawyer. Sawyer had become a financial success almost overnight. The man was now running one of the busiest saloons and parlor houses in Cripple Creek. He handled the liquor and the roulette wheels, and his partner, the pretty Lisa Kellerman, was in charge of the other half of the business. Which side was most lucrative, Casey didn't know, but there was little doubt that Lisa and Olly were living high in Fremont. She was frequently seen driving a fine little phaeton, and he had taken to wearing handmade suits and smoking expensive cigars.

The epidemic that had terrorized the town that summer burned itself out in the late fall, and more and more children began to appear on the streets. They seemed particularly cheerful, bundled up in their heavy coats, once more allowed to play freely with the other children of the towns—but more than that, the epidemic had delayed the construction of the schoolhouse, and it wasn't until December, when cold winds whistled down off the mountain peaks and piled snow in high banks against the buildings and across the streets, that the first school opened its doors.

Casey saw the old year out and celebrated the arrival of 1893 with Bob Womack and a pint of whiskey at Bob's shack up Poverty Gulch. Bob was being called on more and more to serve the community, meaning that he gave his time away in exchange for a slap on the back, a "That-a-boy," and a free hand at the bar. Mining was merely an afterthought with

Bob these days, a distraction from the more important business of promoting *his* town.

Casey could see the high life was taking its toll on Bob; the man was losing weight. Also, Casey noticed an ominous trend starting. Fewer and fewer of the new arrivals were seeking Bob out for his advice on locating claims. The old cowboy's flame was not as bright a beacon as it had been only six months earlier. Soon, he was going to have to step out of the limelight, and Casey worried that when that time came, Bob would not know how to handle it.

At the moment, however, Bob was still on top of the heap—at least from his point of view. He'd recently been elected sergeant-at-arms of the exclusive Squaw Gulch Amusement Club over at Berry Village. The club boasted such eminent characters as onetime mayoral candidate George Carr and the celebrated Judge M. B. Gerry, the fellow who had tried the famous man-eater, Alferd Packer, over at Lake City in 1883. Bob's chief job at the club was to enforce its high moral standards by running off any prostitutes that came looking to turn an easy dollar, a job for which Bob was woefully unqualified, since he had an affinity for women almost equal to his affinity for a bottle of John Barleycorn.

During this time, Casey was living off his savings account, and although he was in no immediate financial trouble, he was becoming desperate to get back to work. He'd taken a job with Macklin Deats driving a freight wagon, but it was the mines that were his siren song, and after a month of driving the fourteens up Florissant Road in the dead of winter, Casey had had enough, and quit.

In February the uproar over two towns' competing side by side finally came to a head, and when it was put to a vote, the sensible folks took an eraser to the line that divided them and married Fremont to Cripple Creek. Plans began in earnest to run a water line from Beaver Creek through Gillett and into Cripple Creek, and Casey figured this would be welcome news to Maureen Kramer, who was still living in the cabin Peter had built for her up on Silver Street.

Other news was sweeping Cripple Creek as well. The people of Colorado had just elected a new governor, a Populist candidate by the name of Davis H. Waite. Waite had been rushed into office on essentially a single issue: the free coinage of silver! Silver had been Colorado's lifeblood since the fifties, and Congress was now about to monkey-wrench the works by changing from a silver standard for money to gold. So Waite had no trouble winning. But soon after he took office the fine folks of Colorado learned that along with his stance on silver, they got a lot of excess socialist baggage that they hadn't bargained on: Waite stood firmly for an income tax, an eight-hour workday, and, to the horror of the mine owners, labor unions!

One Saturday morning in February, Casey drove into town to see how Maureen and Margaret were getting along. He'd not seen Maureen since that day a week after Peter's death, although he had stopped and spoken to Margaret a time or two in town when he had come across the little girl playing with her friend, a girl named Mabs. Casey heard that Maureen had been looking for a job, but had not yet found one that paid enough to support herself and Margaret. Peter had taken out a loan to buy the lot their house was built on and now that he was dead, Maureen was having a hard time making the payments.

He sat in his wagon a moment, studying the little house that Peter had built. A cold wind rippled its canvas roof, snatching the gray smoke from the steel chimney and scattering it against the cloudless sky. Of all the homes originally built on Silver Street, all but Maureen's had been updated with permanent wood and steel roofs. Casey knew she could not afford to have the work done. He also knew that Maureen had tried to get a settlement out of LaFarge, but the mine owner had refused to meet with her—had refused to hear requests from any of the families who had lost husbands and fathers in the accident.

Casey remained on the seat of his wagon a little longer. He was only forestalling the inevitable. He had no idea what sort of greeting might await him. Maureen, like most everyone else in town, considered him the man responsible for the accident.

With hat in hand and an icy wind tugging at his hair, Casey knocked on the door. Maureen appeared after a moment. She wore a knit cap and had a heavy shawl over her shoulders. Her face was drawn, her mouth tight, her eyes dark and in shadows. He was shocked at the gauntness of her features, a look similar to what he'd seen in the faces of men who had gone through hard times. Her red hair had been pinned up into a bun beneath the cap.

Her eyes widened when she saw him and she said, "What is it you want?"

He'd half expected a hostile greeting, but he was not prepared for the defiant bitterness he heard in her voice.

"I just stopped by to see how you and Margaret were getting along. If there is something that I can do to help?"

Maureen drew herself up straight and squared her shoulders. "Margaret and I need none of your help, thank you. And isn't this a fine time to be a worryin' about widows and children! You should have done that before good men put their faith in you. The nerve of you comin' around now."

Even in her anger, her despair, and her hunger, Maureen Kramer was a beautiful woman. Casey found it unnerving that he'd be thinking that now as she glared at him, accusing him of killing her husband.

"I understand that Mr. LaFarge will not meet with you."

"He has not. He's like all the rest of the monied owners who get rich off the sweat and lives of the workin' man. Now I will thank you to leave, Mr. Daniels."

What else could he say? What could he offer her? He knew that at the moment, there was nothing. "Is Margaret all right?"

"She is—and no thanks to you."

"I am happy to hear that." He managed a small smile and put his hat back onto his head.

Maureen slammed the door, and in the chill wind Casey stood there staring at the weathering, unpainted wood of the door. He went back to his wagon, drove down into town, and spent the rest of the morning visiting with the owners of the meat markets and grocery stores. Afterwards, Casey headed for Johnny Nolon's Saloon.

Johnny's was one of the few friendly faces left to him in Cripple Creek, and as Casey trudged up Bennett Avenue, his neck bent to a cold wind, he started to think about the Witwatersrand in South Africa again. What was keeping him here? Wasn't it time that he moved on and started over again?

# TWELVE

THAT WINTER MAUREEN WATCHED THE BIG HOTEL GOING UP on the corner of Bennett and Second Street. The J. H. Wolfe Hotel opened in spring, and Maureen wasted no time making her way to Joe's doorstep looking for a job. It had been a difficult winter, but by carefully managing the few dollars that Peter had left behind, and taking in laundry, she had managed to make ends meet. Her creditors had not taken away the lot that her house stood upon, although they had made it clear that if her payments didn't soon start coming in on a regular basis they would have to foreclose.

Colleen Randall tried to persuade Maureen to sell the place and move back east with her sister again, but Maureen told her, ''Never! This is where Peter wanted us and this is where we will stay!'' Margaret was getting along well in school and had made lots of friends. It seemed that new children were arriving in the gold camp every day. The construction of the long-awaited pipeline that was to bring clean water into town was well under way, and its builders were predicting completion by the end of summer.

And now a new rumor was making its way around the District. Maureen had heard it from Kitty Barbee one day while she and Margaret were at the Barbees' house. Kitty had said that there were plans afoot to bring a railroad into Cripple Creek. It was still a couple years away, but at least there was talk. Kitty had said that most folks were predicting that a railroad would never happen, but she preferred to believe that it would, someday, and Maureen wanted to think so too.

The winter had been hard both emotionally and physically. Maureen had managed to get by because of the generous credit the grocery and dry goods stores had extended her, but she had run up large bills on her accounts, and she was determined to pay back every penny she owed. She still had Peter's claim up on Bull Hill, and although she could sell the Lucky Irish for a handsome price now that the mines around it were beginning to produce color, she resisted. Peter would have wanted her to keep it.

In the lobby of the J. H. Wolfe Hotel, a fire burned in a huge fireplace, driving off the morning chill. Beautiful chairs and sofas sat upon the carpeted floor, and the place was bustling with so much commerce that it made Joe's black eyes glisten like polished obsidian as he came across the room towards her—or was it only the reflection from that big fireplace that made them appear so? He was dressed in his customary black suit and purple vest, with its heavy gold watch chain. The wide, flat-brimmed sombrero upon his head had become Joe's trademark.

"Mrs. Kramer, is it?"

"Yes, I am Mrs. Kramer," she said. She was wearing a light gray dress beneath a black fringe-trimmed dolman that she had unpacked from the steamer trunk and carefully brushed and ironed for just this occasion. A black velvet bonnet with a yellow silk ribbon topped off the outfit, and although they were not new clothes, they were Maureen's very best.

"I'm pleased to meet you, ma'am." Joe shook her gloved hand. Taking the cigar from his mouth and holding it where the draft did not stream the smoke into her face, he said, "Now, what is it I can do for you, Mrs. Kramer?"

"I was hopin' that you might be hirin' people to work in this fine new hotel of yours."

"Oh, is that it?"

"Yes. You see, I am in need of employment." She hesitated, then said, "The winter has been very hard on us—my daughter and me—and we are in great need." The words were difficult for Maureen to speak, for she did not want Joe Wolfe to give her a job out of charity.

"And what of your husband?"

"I am a widow. My husband died last summer."

"Ah! Now I know where I have heard your name before. Yes, I recall reading about the calamity over at the Rattlesnake mine last summer. I am indeed surprised that you are still in Cripple Creek, Mrs. Kramer. If memory serves me, the other ladies have already left."

"They have, but I do not intend to leave this town, Mr. Wolfe," she said firmly.

Joe laughed. "You've got spunk, Mrs. Kramer. Tell me, have you ever done any hotel work before?"

"No, I have not. But I have clerked in a penny store back in Detroit. And I've been takin' in laundry to see us through the winter. I can clean and cook, and make up bedchambers as well as any woman. Now you tell me, Mr. Wolfe, would there be more to knowin' about the hotel business than what a woman don't already do all day long in her own house? And for no pay either, I might be addin' to that."

Joe Wolfe had an infectious laugh, and Maureen decided that the twinkle in his black eyes was from some merry fire within the man rather than from the flames in the big fireplace. "Yes, indeed, you have spunk, Mrs. Kramer." Then he frowned. "But I am afraid I have not much in the way of work to offer you."

Maureen tried not to let her disappointment show. "You have nothin' at all?"

Joe looked at her. "You *are* in a bad way, ain't you, Mrs. Kramer?"

"In truth, sir, I have run out of all the money that Peter had left us, and I haven't been able to squeeze a nickel from that tightfisted Mr. LaFarge, either. You'd think that he might feel some compassion for the widows of the men who died workin' for him."

Joe Wolfe shrugged his shoulders. "Every man got to live his life the way it seems right to him, I guess."

She nodded her head and said, "Perhaps. Well, then I won't be takin' up any more of your time, sir."

"Don't go running off now, Mrs. Kramer," he said.

Maureen turned back and saw that Wolfe was considering something.

"I reckon I can hire you on as a chambermaid. A big hotel can always use another chambermaid. It ain't much, and the pay ain't good, but it's honest work."

"I'll take the job," Maureen said at once, "and thank you very much!"

"You may not be all that happy with it after a while. I see in you a woman capable of more than making up beds and emptying chamber pots, Mrs. Kramer. You may not want to thank me just yet."

Maureen hardly heard the warning. She cared only that she had a job, and a way now to pay off the creditors. She did not know it at the time, but hers was not the only door that the bankers were hounding. In building this hotel, Joe Wolfe had run up considerable expenses. He had borrowed heavily, and his gambling debts were mounting as well. If she had known that Joe Wolfe's finances were only a little less precarious than her own, Maureen might not have been as jubilant at finding this new job of hers.

On her way home, Maureen stopped at the Bingham Brothers' grocery and mercantile store. She gave Willard Bingham her list and as he pulled items from off the shelf and set them on the counter in front of her, she said, "If you could just put this to my account, it should be the last time. I will be able to start payin' on my account in a matter of a few days. I have a job, you see, at Joe Wolfe's new hotel."

Bingham seem unconcerned about her bill. "That's fine, Mrs. Kramer. I'm in no big hurry to get paid. I reckon you're good for what you owe."

"You and all the other merchants have been most kind to me. I promise that with my first wages I will begin to pay you, and all the others, somethin' every week."

He only nodded his head, wrote up a list of her purchases, and had her sign the bill, as he had done most of the winter. He placed the bill in a box under the counter and that was that. Maureen put the food in a canvas bag, thanked him again, and turned towards the door.

As she stepped outside, a shiny black phaeton pulled smartly along Bennett Avenue by a proud, single chestnut horse drew up in front of the grocer's store. The woman who sat upon the seat was very pretty, with brilliant red hair falling to her shoulders in ringlets. She wore a stunning yellow silk dress with a matching silk Ottoman, trimmed in a brocade of orange, gold, and red. Her eyes were dark, partly hidden by her lovely lashes. Maureen knew who this woman was and immediately averted her eyes and started up the Avenue towards her home. Everyone in Cripple Creek knew Lisa Kellerman, and what she was—or at least what she had been before she and her partner had opened one of the biggest and bawdiest saloons and parlor houses on Myers Avenue.

"Mrs. Kramer."

Maureen nearly stumbled when Lisa spoke her name. She turned back and felt her cheeks burn as the lovely woman looked at her from the seat of the phaeton. At first Maureen wondered if she hadn't imagined hearing her name. "Were you speakin' to me?"

"Yes, I was." Lisa climbed off the phaeton with a certain gracefulness that did not appear to come naturally, but as if it was a skill that she had been working diligently to acquire. "I am Lisa Kellerman."

"I know who you are." Maureen's skin burned and she cursed her fair complexion, as her cheeks reddened. "How do you know my name?"

Lisa smiled sweetly, yet the smile could not hide the hardness that a life such as hers lends to one's features. "I've had my eye on you for a little while." She touched Maureen's red hair and nodded approvingly. "What a lovely color. It is all natural?"

"It is indeed," Maureen said sharply, recovering now from the surprise of this encounter and removing herself a step to the side.

"I'm sorry. I didn't mean to insult you. It is only that I must work so hard to get my hair looking like yours, and then it's only a matter of time"—she laughed—"maybe only minutes, before the men discover my little secret."

Maureen was shocked by the openly crude intent of Lisa's remark. "For what reason have you had your eye on me, Miss Kellerman?"

"Please, call me Lisa."

"Very well. Why have you been watching me?"

"Because I know your plight, dear. How you must have struggled. First with the pain of losing Peter, and then with the ugly reality of a woman alone having to make a go of it. I talk from experience on that point." Lisa laughed. "It ain't easy making your way in a man's world."

Maureen knew that to be most painfully true. What was Lisa leading up to?

"There were other women who lost their husbands in that accident as well, Mis—Lisa."

"True, and they have all left town, I believe. But it wasn't them I was interested in. It was you, Maureen."

"Why?" she asked. Lisa's friendliness, and Maureen's own curiosity, had temporarily weakened her defenses. She had the feeling that this was a woman who truly understood the trials of life, and its pains.

"Because you are the sort of woman that men find most attractive."

Maureen blinked, surprised. What was Lisa driving at.

"I've got four girls working for me now. There is room for another."

Maureen suddenly understood, and she was shocked. How could she have been so blind as to not see where this had been leading? Her mouth fell open and she did not speak at once. Finally she managed to say, "I'd never—"

Lisa laughed. "That's what most women say at first. I expected no less from you, and I'm in no hurry for your answer. Think about it, and if you get down to your last dollar and there ain't no money to put food in your little girl's mouth, remember my offer. Come to work for me, Maureen, and you'll have this town in the palm of your hand. I'm building a high-class business. We only cater to them men what can afford the best, and as this town grows, so will the purses of the mine owners, stock traders, and those men who own the banks and shipping companies. Money is no object to them— and if you come in with me, it won't be to you."

"I . . . I need to go," Maureen said quickly.

"Sure you do. Don't let me hold you up. Just keep what I have said in mind. You know where to find me, don't you?"

Maureen had no intention of ever taking Lisa up on her offer, but just the same she found herself saying that she did know where to find her. She hurried away, her cheeks burning, not looking back until she was a block up the street. Lisa's phaeton was still in front of Bingham Brothers', but she was no longer on the sidewalk. Maureen slowed her pace. Her heart was fluttering. She was incensed that that woman could even harbor such an idea. And she was angry at herself for letting Lisa Kellerman fluster her so. But the offer had come so unexpectedly, and had so thoroughly knocked her off her stride, that she only now was regaining her wit.

*The nerve of her!*

Maureen turned back towards home and strode with open indignation in her step. She hoped that if anyone had seen the two of them speaking, they would recognize her displeasure now. But what frightened Maureen most was that the indignation she thought she should be feeling was not nearly as strong as she knew it ought to have been.

Casey cut across Bennett Avenue and stepped up on the boardwalk in front of the Bingham Brothers' grocery and mercantile store. Willard Bingham was behind the counter stacking canned goods when Casey entered. There was a woman at the back of the store who appeared to be examining porcelain chamber pots. She glanced up at him, almost as if knowing that he had been watching her, and smiled. Casey grinned back, recognizing her now. Lisa Kellerman's face was known by almost everyone in town. Her saloon on Myers Avenue was the talk of the District.

"Good morning, Miss Kellerman," he said, touching the brim of his hat.

"And a very good morning to you too, sir," she said, going back to the job of inspecting the bedpans.

Casey turned and put his palms on the grocer's counter. "And 'morning to you, Willard."

"Hello, Casey. What brings you by?"

"I was in town and thought I'd stop in and see if there is a bill that needs covering."

Willard nodded his head. "In fact, she was in only a few minutes ago." Willard Bingham fished around under the counter and came up with three slips of paper. "Here you go, Casey. It adds up to . . . um, let's see." Willard put a pencil to his tongue, then summed up the numbers on each slip. "Looks to me like she has bought four dollars and fifteen cents' worth of supplies since the last time you was around."

Casey counted out the coins and paid Willard.

"You know, Casey, what you are doing is mighty commendable, but how long do you intend to keep paying that woman's bills? It is not exactly a secret that you ain't got no work yourself. And it's plain you ain't a rich man. I was in Casper Dunnagan's dry goods store the other day and he tells me you are carrying Mrs. Kramer there as well."

"There, and three or four other places. Maureen's husband, Peter, was my friend. Mrs. Kramer won't take help; she's too proud for that. And she especially won't take it from me."

"Yeah, I know. She blames you for her husband's death."

Casey frowned. "She and a lot of other folks."

"Well, just to let you know how some of us feel, Casey, I'll tell you this: It was LaFarge's mine what caved in and it is LaFarge who is responsible, even if you did build the shoring that failed."

"But I didn't—" Casey stopped himself. It was now almost eight months since the cave-in, and he wanted to let the matter die a natural death.

Willard narrowed an eye at Casey. "Go on, say it. Get it off your chest. I know if it was me who'd been accused of killing those men I'd sure be shouting my innocence to the high heavens—that is, if I was innocent."

Casey shoved his coin pouch into his pocket. "I haven't anything more to say, Willard."

"A closemouthed son of a gun you are." Willard keyed his register, opened the drawer, and deposited the coins in their proper slots.

"You just keep extending Mrs. Kramer credit, Willard, and I'll keep paying it off."

" 'Till your money gives out."

"I can get work."

"Sure you can. I'd even hire you myself. But clerking, or roustabouting, or mule-skinning ain't ever gonna satisfy you, Casey. You got to get back down into them mines. I know the look of a man who has a passion for something, and that's what I see in you right now."

"Like I said, I'll get work."

"Maybe, but it don't look too promising here in Cripple Creek."

Casey gave a short laugh. "In that case you only need to extend Mrs. Kramer credit until I run out of money."

"May not have to do it that long," Willard said.

"What do you mean?"

"I mean, the lady has found herself a job at Wolfe's new hotel. She told me so not fifteen minutes ago. And she intends to start paying back her IOUs right away."

Casey grinned. "Well, good for her. One thing you can say for Maureen Kramer, she's not a quitter."

"What do I tell her when she comes around to square up and there ain't nothing to square up on?"

"Oh, I don't care, Willard. Tell her you lost all her IOUs."

"Oh, sure, leave her to me to explain it away like that. She ain't no fool."

"Then take her money and donate it to the school fund."

"Hate to do that when she needs it so."

"I don't know what you should tell her, Willard. Only, just don't let on that I had a hand in it."

"Your secret is safe with me, Casey."

"Thanks. I better head over to Casper's place and square up with him next. So long, Willard."

Casey turned and came up short. Lisa Kellerman was standing right in front of him. She had a chamber pot in her arms and a curious grin upon her face. "Pardon me," he said, stepping around her.

"Excuse *me*, Casey," she said, the grin widening out to a perky smile.

As he left the store and stopped onto the walk outside, he heard Lisa's voice behind him, ordering a dozen chamber pots. He wondered briefly how she knew his name. Then the thought passed from his brain and he started up the street towards Casper's dry goods store.

● ● ●

Winfield Scott Stratton had been named after the famous general of the Mexican War, but now, at age forty-five, Stratton knew that *his* shot at fame was quickly running out. He owned three claims, the Independence, the Washington, and the Professor Lamb, but between them he hardly was able to scrape up enough gold to keep his small development crew working. He still had his carpenter shop in the Springs, but something kept him here, digging for the elusive prize. Stratton knew there was gold beneath his feet. The claims around him were already producing; the Black Diamond, the Strong Mine, and the Rattlesnake were just three that he could think of off the top of his head. And his claims—at least the Independence—was smack in the middle of them all!

Stratton sat down on a rock alongside the road and dropped the ore sack off his shoulder. He was getting too old for this nonsense! He stared at his boots. Once shiny and black, they were now scuffed dull, and gray as the rock that he clawed and hammered from the ground. Their soles were paper-thin, and that depressed him more than digging a worthless hole. If there was one thing Stratton did love, it was beautiful boots!

Stratton took a moment to catch his breath, then stood wearily and slung the sack of samples back to his thin shoulder and continued down the road towards N. B. Guyot's assay shop in Squaw Gulch, beneath the hill that had been named after him.

Stratton waited while Guyot crushed the samples and ran them through his furnace. When he had completed the assay, Stratton saw on Guyot's face that the results were the same as last time. Guyot sat across the little table from the waiting Stratton and showed him the results of the assay.

Stratton studied the paper, frowning. "Five dollars to a ton."

"That's what it works out to, Mr. Stratton."

Stratton's pale blue eyes scanned the paper, looking at the other trace minerals Guyot had recovered. "Pretty worthless pit, ain't it? If I was a smart man, I'd sell out to the first greenhorn who comes by and go back to the Springs. At least there's money in building kitchen cabinets and outhouses.''

Guyot pursed his lips as if waiting for Stratton to say more. When the somber man did not, Guyot said, ''You know, Mr. Stratton, if you are serious about selling, I can work you up a seller's assay that will knock the socks off any prospective buyer.'' Any assayer worth his salt could doctor up an assay to make it sparkle in the eyes of a greenhorn—and even to some old-timers.

Stratton shoved the assay paper into his pocket, and hefted the ore sack back to his shoulder. He still had samples left, and there were other assayers around to test them. Stratton never believed in sticking with only one man's opinion on a thing. ''I'll keep that in mind. Good day, Mr. Guyot.''

That afternoon Stratton shopped his samples around, and he got the same results. Later, as the shadows lengthened across Battle Mountain, he sat on the edge of his mine shaft, staring down the sixty-foot hole, dropping pebbles and drowning the bitter sting of failure with a bottle of whiskey. Behind him he heard the crunch of footsteps coming up the hill.

''That's a mighty slow way to fill up that hole, Mr. Stratton.''

''Mr. Daniels,'' Stratton said, looking over his shoulder. ''To what do I owe the honor? Come and join me in my fine parlor.'' Stratton patted a hewed log that formed the coping of his mine shaft. ''Have a sip or two of Mr. Jack Daniel's best.'' Stratton stared at the label on his whiskey bottle and grinned up at Casey. ''A relative of yours?''

Casey threw a leg over the timbers and sat down. ''That Mr. Daniel is no kin of mine—or so I've been told.'' He took a pull at Stratton's bottle, made a face, and handed it back. ''I believe I will stick with beer.''

''Every man's got his own poison.'' Stratton took another sip. ''You're looking fit. Healed up nicely, it appears—say, you ever find out who it was?''

Casey fingered a sharp yellow rock and tossed it at a rusty

shovel leaning against a tilting shack on Stratton's claim. "The past is past, Mr. Stratton. I prefer to think about the future."

"I was just pondering the future myself. What do you think has put me in this black mood. From what I hear, you ain't got much of a future in this District."

"That's why I've come up here to talk to you."

Stratton glanced over. "Looking for a job?"

"I am."

Stratton kicked a loose stone with the tip of his scuffed boots and listened to it strike the bottom of the shaft. "You know, Mr. Daniels, I don't think that cave-in at the Rattlesnake was your fault. I know the kind of man LaFarge is. I may not be much a judge of mining real estate, but I do a fair job with men. A blind man could see that he was scrambling to cover his tail. Sam Strong knows it too, and so do some others, but Sam had to fire you to keep peace with the men working his mine. Now me, all I got is a little development crew, and if I lost them all tomorrow night, I'd have me a new crew the next morning. But I won't lose 'em. And the reason why I won't lose them is because I treat my men fair. I give them a good wage and I don't work 'em too hard. Now, you take Sam Strong for instance. He was a roustabout in the Springs before he took to mining and he drives his men as if there ain't no tomorrow. LaFarge? His past I don't know much about. He's an outsider. Some say he's up from Pueblo. Others say from down south farther, maybe Santa Fe, so I don't know what motivates that man, except he's got an eye for money, and for the ladies." Stratton grinned. "Although all the ladies he dallies with make a living off of profitably losing their virtue every night—sometimes a dozen times a night."

"What are you trying to say?"

Stratton looked at the bottle in his hand. "Hell, I don't know. I reckon I forgot. A bit of whiskey and I ramble like a tumbleweed. What I think I was leading up to was that if I had a job open, I'd take you on. But the sad fact is I don't.

Can't hardly pay the few men I got working for me now. In fact, Mr. Daniels, if I don't make pay dirt soon, I'm going to have to close down this pit. I'm down sixty feet on the Independence with four crosscuts at fifty feet, and I'm hardly pulling out enough to cover shipping and refining costs. Sorry, Mr. Daniels. But I wish you luck in your search.''

Casey stood. ''Well, I'll keep looking. I hope you strike that pay dirt soon, Mr. Stratton. The District can't afford to lose men like you. Good evening.''

'' 'Evenin' to you.'' Stratton kicked another stone into his shaft and tipped back the bottle. He had to agree with Casey—it was a mighty slow way to fill up a worthless hole.

Casey halted on the edge of Stratton's claim, deciding which way to go. His view fell on a shanty up the hill, on the Portland claim. As he watched it, the door opened and James Burns stepped out. Burns and his partners, Jimmie Doyle and John Harnan, were studiously sitting upon this tiny, still unproved wedge of ground sandwiched in among the bigger claims—and apparently not doing a thing with it.

Which was odd in itself, since Burns and Doyle had so diligently searched all of Battle Mountain for an unclaimed piece of ground, and when they'd come upon this postage-stamp-sized piece of mountainside that had somehow escaped being included in the full-sized lode claims all around it, they'd immediately driven in their corner stakes, filed upon it, and named it after their hometown in the state of Maine.

They began digging a hole in January of '92; a few months later, shortly after John Harnan become the third partner, they built a shanty and all serious work suddenly seemed to end. Today, over a year later, the only ''improvement'' they'd made was the shanty and an abandoned hole on the upper corner of the claim.

These three certainly would not be looking for help, Casey reasoned, but he'd tried everyone else, and since he had already climbed halfway up the side of Battle Mountain, he figured it couldn't hurt to ask.

Casey waved an arm, caught Burns's attention, and climbed the rest of the way up the hill to the shack. "Hello, Mr. Burns."

Burns nodded his head and sleeved the sweat from his brow. As Casey drew nearer, Burns reached back and pulled the door shut. "Mr. Daniels? What brings you up here this evening?" Burns was a burly man, with a square jaw, thick mustache, and a shock of hair every bit as white as Stratton's. His clothes were soaked through with sweat and filthy with the yellow-gray dust of the dirt and rock of this hill.

Casey looked over the little claim. The hole at its corner seemed to not have been worked recently. "Any luck yet?"

A glint of suspicion came to Burns's eyes. "No, we're just scraping away at a worthless patch of ground, like most of the other fool prospectors in this District."

Casey had understood that to be the case from the stories he'd heard.

"Why are you asking?"

"I'm looking for work, Mr. Burns. I thought I'd try every mine in the District before I throw in the towel."

Burns seemed to relax some. "Well, afraid I can't help you out."

"I figured it couldn't hurt to try."

Burns pulled up a ladle of water from a barrel and took a long drink.

Sensing that Burns was in no mood to talk, Casey went down the hill. When he looked back, Burns was standing by the door of his shanty, his hand on the latch, watching him leave. Casey stepped around a building down on Sam Strong's claim, then pressed himself against the wall and peeked up the hill. Just as he suspected, Burns was only waiting for him to get out of sight before he went back inside.

*Peculiar.* What was it behind that shanty's door that Burns did not want him to see?

# THIRTEEN

THE LAST SEVERAL MONTHS, JOHNNY'S PLACE HAD BECOME A regular watering hole for Sam Stepton. Not that it helped his conscience any, but for a few hours every night he could join in with the merriment, or have himself a game of billiards— and at least it would dull the nagging truth that he had been the cause of those men's deaths, and the cause of Casey's being an outcast in Cripple Creek.

Sam had always liked Casey Daniels. Casey's abilities had impressed him when they'd worked together in Leadville, and when LaFarge had asked him to find a competent engineer to assist them at the Rattlesnake, Casey's name had been first on Sam's list. Now bitterly, Sam had to admit that Casey's downfall had been his doing all the way around; it had been he who'd gotten Casey the job with LaFarge in the first place, and it was the lie that he'd agreed on with LaFarge that had brought Casey down.

Sam Stepton had taken to the bottle to blunt the keen edge of his treachery and to blur the vision of Casey's face. He took great pains to avoid Casey these days; they had not spoken since that day eight months ago.

"Don't you think you ought to be going on home to your wife, Sam?"

Sam looked around, bleary-eyed, for the source of this voice and discovered Johnny Nolon standing there. Johnny was wearing a dark suit over a white shirt, with a cravat around his neck. His bowler hat had been recently brushed, and although he'd worked for at least fourteen hours straight, his clothes looked as fresh as if he had only put them on an hour earlier. Looking at this soft-spoken man, one would hardly have guessed that he began his career as a tough pony express rider. Johnny's fastidious dress, his gentle manner, and his huge heart made one think of a preacher rather than a saloon keeper. Sam had never seen a brawl in Johnny Nolon's Saloon; the burly miners who were known to cause trouble in other saloons and gambling halls were always on their best behavior whenever little Johnny Nolon was around.

"Hi, Johnny," Sam said.

Nolon pulled back a chair and sat across the table from him. "It's getting late, Sam. I'm about ready to close up the place for the night." A bartender in his stained white apron was drawing closed an iron accordion cage in front of the liquor bottles on the shelves behind the bar, securing it with a big padlock.

"What time is it, Johnny?"

"Nearly one-thirty. I'd think Sharon would be getting worried about you."

Sam looked back at the whiskey remaining in his glass. "She's gotten used to me coming in late."

"You've been doing quite a lot of that, Sam. Something troubling you?"

Sam glanced up, and his view sharpened momentarily before easing back to a comfortable haze. "Can't a fellow have himself a drink or two without folks thinking there is something wrong in his life?" he said impatiently.

"Sure, Sam. This here is a free country. I didn't mean to

pry. Here, let's get you up. We'll step outside for a breath of cool air, OK?''

Sam looked back at the whiskey glass on the table, took it up, then changed his mind and set it down and pushed it away. ''Yeah, all right, Johnny.'' Johnny caught him by the arm, steadying him. Out front of the saloon they stood on the sidewalk that had grown these last few months from a patchwork of boards to a continuous walk the entire length of Bennett Avenue on both sides of the street. Electric arc streetlights dropped pale pools of precisely spaced light down the center of the street. One block down, on Myers Avenue, they could hear pianos playing, and men and women laughing. The scratchy music of a gramophone was coming from an open window somewhere.

In the cool night air, Sam's head cleared a little.

Johnny said, ''You know, Sam, if there is something I can do for you, just give me a holler.''

Sam grinned. ''There ain't a thing wrong with me, Johnny.''

Nolon laughed. ''Sure, Sam. Never said there was.''

Inside Johnny Nolon's Saloon a bartender was snapping out sheets and letting them settle across the billiard tables.

''Say, you wouldn't want me to walk with you a ways? You know, just to make sure you get home all right.''

''Naw, I'll make it fine, Johnny.'' Sam squinted through the windows and watched the bartender ''making up'' the tables. ''Besides, you better get back inside and put your guests to bed.''

Everyone knew that when Johnny Nolon closed up his saloon for the night, he let the bums and homeless men of the District in to sleep on the floors and billiard tables.

''Sure, Sam. Now, you go straight home, all right?''

''Yeah, I'll go home, Johnny. G'd night.''

''Good night, Sam.''


Maureen blinked bewilderedly. ''What do you mean, Mr. Bingham? Certainly you couldn't have lost *all* of my IOUs?''

Bingham gave her a crooked smile and set the box upon the counter to show her that it was empty. "You can look for yourself, Mrs. Kramer. They ain't here, and if they ain't here, I can't expect you to pay up on them, now can I?"

"No, I suppose not," Maureen said thoughtfully. She knew exactly what Bingham had done with them. He had tossed them out, and although it was an act of kindness to be sure, Maureen had not been looking for Willard Bingham's charity, and she was not certain how to accept it now. Maureen put her coin pouch back into her handbag and looked Willard in the eye. "I intend to pay you what I owe, sir, if you can give me some idea how much it is."

"Well, since neither one of us can remember, Mrs. Kramer, why don't we wipe the slate clean and forget about it."

Maureen frowned. This was not what she had expected at all, but she did appreciate his kindness, and when she told him so, his expression soured a bit and he told her to think nothing of it, and immediately began moving pencils and paper around beneath the counter and looking anxious to get back to work.

Maureen left the Bingham Brothers' grocery store, resolving to pay back this generosity the only way she knew how—by purchasing her groceries exclusively from them. Her suspicion did not become aroused until she got essentially the same story from Casper Dunnagan at the dry goods store, then later Carl Lambert, the milliner, and Max Durante, the pharmacist.

*They are all in cahoots!* Maureen stepped out of the pharmacy on East Masonic Avenue and didn't know what to do about it. If the business owners refused to collect on her IOUs, what could she do? She walked a few paces, then halted at the corner of Second Street. The generosity of the merchants of Cripple Creek made her proud to be a member of the community. Peter had chosen well when he decided to move here! When she thought of Peter, tears always glistened in her blue eyes. Although she was alone in the world, she now had a job that paid her enough to live on, and her bills had been miraculously wiped clean. Margaret had come through the horrible epidemic and was healthy again and doing well in the new school.

Although she still had a long struggle ahead of her, Maureen knew there were good folks in Cripple Creek who were willing to help her. What the merchants had done had buoyed her spirits almost as much as Joe Wolfe's giving her a job had.

East Masonic Avenue became Myers Avenue once across Second Street. Here the character of the town took a deplorable turn. Maureen never stopped being amazed by the raucous carryings-on along this street, day and night. Even the addition of a dignified opera house had failed to bring respectability to the avenue. It had become so bad that when decent families from the good side of town would go to the opera, they made their children look away from the seedy end of Myers.

The saloons, parlor houses, and gambling dens all seemed to be competing with one another for the most noise, fights, and scantily dressed women displaying themselves from upstairs windows. Lisa and Olly's Saloon was only a few doors ahead, and as Maureen approached it, Lisa Kellerman stepped out the door and opened a peach-colored parasol to ward off the noon sun. A second woman was with her; blond, pretty, and not quite as tall. As they stepped onto the sidewalk, Lisa spied Maureen and smiled.

Maureen saw no way to avoid these women, so she steeled herself and thought only to return their greeting and then be on her way.

"Out enjoying the day, Maureen?" Lisa asked.

Maureen saw she would have to stop and speak to these women, or risk seeming snobbish. "I had business to see to, Miss Kellerman," she said.

"Don't you remember last time we chatted, Maureen? I told you to call me Lisa."

She managed a thin smile and said that she had forgotten.

"I almost forgot my manners, Maureen. This here is Kelly. She's one of my girls."

"Pleased to meet you," Maureen said, unable to put much enthusiasm in her voice.

"And me too, I'm sure," Kelly gushed. "Why, I just love your hair."

"And it's all what God gave her naturally," Lisa said. "Kelly, you remember me saying I was looking for someone to live in that last room, don't you?"

Now that they were up close, Maureen saw that Kelly was a blond by choice, not by chance—the inch and a half of hair closest to her head was a dark brown. Her face was heavily powdered, not with the light blush of Ponzi's that the women Maureen associated with wore, but something caked on, looking like it might crack and fall off in pieces if Kelly's face were to become suddenly animated. Her lips were painted a bold scarlet, and her eyes had been darkened to an unhealthy hue. Kelly had penciled in an extension of her eyebrows where nature had left her deficient, but looking her up and down, Maureen saw that she was not deficient in other areas.

Considering the penciled eyebrows and bleached hair, however, Maureen wondered if Kelly's proportions had not escaped doctoring as well.

Kelly grabbed Maureen's hand and gave it a couple of firm shakes. "We'd be please if you'd come live with us, Maureen. Why, the way you're put together, you'd fetch men like molasses fetches flies."

Maureen gave her a faltering smile and withdrew her hand from Kelly's hardy grip. "I'm not sure 'fetchin'' men is something I care to do," she said, trying to sound diplomatic about it.

Kelly's laugh sounded distinctly like a mule's bray. "Aw, you're just a little shy. You'll get over that after a day or two. Most of us started out like that. Once you see the color of them miners' money you'll forget all about how they smell. Believe me."

Maureen's mouth fell open. Lisa said quickly, "Don't you listen to what Kelly says, Maureen." She shot Kelly a warning glance and her eyebrows dipped sharply. "She's only joking around. Why, we got us two bathtubs and hot water, and we make the boys use them. All our clients are well mannered or we toss 'em out on their ears. We have two bouncers around all the time to keep the peace, and Olly, he can handle any man what comes through our door."

Maureen recovered and said, "Your offer is quite kind, I'm sure. But I already have a job, thank you."

"So I have heard. Making beds and cleaning up at the J. H. Wolfe Hotel ain't never gonna put a tin roof on that little cabin of yours, Maureen."

"How do you—?"

"Like I told you the last time—I've had my eye on you."

"But why?"

"I want you to be one of my girls, Maureen."

"Never."

Lisa shrugged and whirled the parasol casually upon her shoulders. "We shall see. In the meantime, give it some thought, Maureen. If you need money—lots of money . . . say to pay back a bill or two?—throwing in with me will be the fastest way of getting it."

"I don't have any bills that need paying."

"Oh, don't you?" There was a curious, cryptic glint in Lisa's eyes. "You were out of work an awful long time, Maureen. How did you manage to feed your little girl?"

Maureen's temper was sparking. "I made my way just fine, thank you. The merchants were most kind while I was down on my luck. Now, I really must be on my way."

"Of course. I won't keep you any longer. Only, keep my offer in mind. And if you should find out suddenly that you owe *someone* a lot of money, do stop in and see me. Good day, Maureen."

Maureen heard the thinly veiled accusation. "What are you talking about?"

She halted and looked back. "Oh, nothing at all. Only, if it was me, Maureen, I'd be real curious why all those businessmen went and lost your IOUs. That ain't exactly good business."

"They did it out of a kind heart," Maureen came back, her anger rising near the surface again. "And anyway, how do you know about it?"

"Did they?" Lisa's eyebrows arched. "I have my ways of finding things out." She took Kelly by the arm. "Come along, Kelly."

"Bye, Maureen," Kelly said, waving over her shoulder as they started away.

*What had Lisa meant? Who would she suddenly owe money to?* Maureen stood there dazed, watching the two women walking away, their fawn-and peach-colored bustles swaying in perfect synchrony. She frowned. Lisa was only trying to confuse her, Maureen decided. The woman was certainly persistent, you had to give her that.

Maureen tried to dismiss the whole conversation as she started back home to get dressed for her work shift, which started at five o'clock in the afternoon. But try as she might, Lisa's cloaked innuendo stuck in her mind, and nagged at her.

Maureen prepared an early dinner, and afterwards she put on her black dress, pinned her hair up, and slipped into the long white apron, asking Margaret to tie a neat bow at her back.

"Now, darlin', I will be back late. Don't go out of the house while I am away, but if you need anything you can run next door to Mrs. Randall's house. Remember to go to bed early. I'll not want to be findin' you waitin' up for me like you did last night. Tomorrow is your last day of school and I want you bright and cheerful."

"I will, Mommy," Margaret said. "Wake me when you get home?"

"We shall see." Maureen adjusted her hat, then bent and kissed Margaret on top of her head.

"Why are you leaving early. Your job doesn't start for another hour."

"I have a few things to tend to in town."

"What things?"

"Oh, nothin' for you to concern yourself with, darlin'. I just need to talk to some of the shopkeepers about our bills." Maureen paused on the doorstep until she heard the lock click over inside, then Margaret's face appeared in the window and she waved good-bye. In town, Maureen went immediately to the Bingham Brothers' grocery store. Lisa's remarks earlier that day had stayed with her like annoying pebbles at the bottom of her shoe, and she had to find out for herself if there was anything to them.

Willard Bingham had already locked the front door when Maureen arrived and rapped upon the windowpane. He glanced up from the cash register, where he had begun counting the day's receipts.

"I'm closed, Mrs. Kramer," he said.

"I need to speak with you, Mr. Bingham," she called back through the glass.

He frowned. Then, as if knowing she'd not take no for an answer, he came around the counter and unlocked the door. Relocking it immediately behind her, he asked, "What is it, Mrs. Kramer?"

"It's about those IOUs that you *somehow* lost."

"I thought we had settled all of that. Really, Mrs. Kramer, I'd rather you'd just forget about them."

"I would have forgotten about them . . . if you had been the only one, Mr. Bingham. But your story is very much like the story I was given from three other merchants in town. Then someone said something to me that made me wonder exactly what was goin' on."

"Someone?"

"Never mind who. But now I must know. Why were all my bills forgiven? Was this somethin' the merchants decided among themselves? If it was, is this how you handle all your accounts that belong to widows, or am I bein' treated differently? And if I am, then I want to know why."

Bingham inhaled sharply, and went back around the counter. "You won't just take things as they are, will you?"

"Not when I smell a deception brewin', Mr. Bingham. What are you keepin' from me?"

"We . . . we all felt sorry for you, that's all there was to it."

"Is it now?" Maureen placed her hands upon her hips and her gaze narrowed sternly. "When my daughter tells me a fib, she doesn't look me in the eye either. What is it you are hidin'?"

Bingham looked up. "You're a shrewd woman, Mrs. Kramer, but I wish you would forget this now."

"Mr. Bingham. I will not leave this place until you have told me the truth. Now, out with it."

"All right, Mrs. Kramer. If you must know, then I suppose I will have to tell you, but you ain't going to like it."

"Try me, Mr. Bingham."

"It was Casey Daniels. He has been paying your bills since your husband died."

"Casey Daniels?" Maureen had been prepared to accept almost any explanation . . . but *Casey Daniels*? His had been the last name she expected to hear.

"Casey Daniels!" she roared suddenly, the volcano inside her finally erupting. "Not only has he made me a widow, but he's stolen my pride as well!"

"I told you you wouldn't like it," Bingham said.

Maureen hardly heard him. Eight months of grief and pent-up anger came to the surface, and there was little she could do to stop it. She turned abruptly with a stomp of her heel against Bingham's pinewood floor that sounded like the crack of a pistol, grabbed the doorknob, and yanked. Bingham had locked it, and in her blind anger she didn't see the key still in the hole. She rattled the knob impatiently until Bingham unlocked the door. Maureen sailed down Bennett Avenue, her duties at the J. H. Wolfe Hotel forgotten. The only thought in

her head was to find Casey Daniels and spew the magma of
her wrath at him.

He had just finished a supper of diced beef marinated in a
Mexican hot sauce and wrapped in a soft flour tortilla, and a
bowl of pinto beans. There was a chokecherry cobbler baking
in his oven, filling his little cabin with a wonderful odor as he
leaned back and cleaned his teeth with a toothpick. He was
thinking about strolling down to Wilson Creek to fetch a bottle
of cold beer from his birdcage cooler when suddenly there
came a pounding at his door that sounded as if it might take
it off at the hinges.

Casey sprang out of his chair, startled. He glanced at the
rifle on the wall, then dismissed that notion and opened the
door before the person on the other side succeeded in dismantling it.

"Mrs. Kramer?"

She charged over the threshold without waiting for an invitation, like a bull in a ring, one fist clutching a hat, the other
balled tight except for a long forefinger stabbing dangerously
at him. Her blue eyes were afire, her nostrils flared, and her
red hair was scattered wildly as if she had just come through
a windstorm. Her advance backed him up against the table,
rattling the dirty dishes still upon it.

"Begorra, Daniels, you have gone too far this time! When
will your meddlin' into my life ever stop?"

"I don't know what you're talking about."

"Don't you now? Well, let me refresh your memory. How
about all my IOUs to the merchants in town bein' mysteriously
misplaced? *Now* might you be rememberin'?"

"Oh, that." Casey had been afraid the truth might leak out,
but it was a chance he'd been willing to take. Now, he knew,
he had to be willing to accept the consequences of it as well.
"Yes, I covered your bills."

"It wasn't enough for you to take my husband from me—
now you have taken my pride as well. How can I walk down

the street with my head high knowin' people are snickerin' behind my back? I have every intention of payin' back those IOUs, Mr. Daniels. Every penny of them!''

''I don't want your money, Mrs. Kramer. I did it because Peter was my friend.'' Even as he spoke it, he knew this was not entirely the truth. Since Peter's death, Maureen's tenacity, her sincerity, her devotion to her daughter . . . and yes, her beauty too, had struck a chord with Casey. His interest in this woman was growing beyond simple concern into something far more complicated. Casey feared that somehow, in spite of all her animosity, he was falling in love.

Maureen gave him a short, bitter laugh. ''Well, you will be receivin' it whether you want to or not.'' She reached into her bag and flung a handful of silver coins against his chest. ''And here is the first installment.''

She wheeled and rushed out the door before he could speak, then strode angrily away into the growing dusk.

With a heaviness of spirit, Casey slowly closed the door. He sat back down at the table, staring at the dirty dishes. The beer he'd been contemplating no longer seemed important, and the cobbler's fragrance had become bland.

Frowning, Casey bent and collected a dollar and a half off the floor. He weighed the coins in his hand, considering what to do with them, then took down an old tin box from a shelf, dropped them into it, and set it back in place.

Her wrath finally vented, Maureen's pace slowed, and as the approaching night darkened the land, she could no longer hold back the tears. She wiped her eyes, streaking the powder on her face. She only now remembered her job, and she wondered what Mr. Wolfe would say to her about arriving almost two hours late. Would he understand? Had she put her job in jeopardy by rushing out to confront Daniels?

She caught a ride into Cripple Creek on a passing wagon and immediately looked for Mr. Wolfe, to explain her tardiness. He wasn't in his office. She went searching for him, discovering the hotel strangely empty. She looked for another chambermaid to ask about Mr. Wolfe, but found none.

"Where is Mr. Wolfe?" she asked Elijah Benson, the night clerk. Benson was flipping through the pages of the hotel registry at the desk.

He glanced up from the registry book. Maureen could tell that something was wrong. "You're late, Mrs. Kramer," Benson said sharply. Then added more gently, "Well, I reckon it don't matter."

"What do you mean?" She was certain now that something was wrong.

"You ain't heard?"

"Heard what? I'm lookin' for Mr. Wolfe to explain why I am late to work."

"That won't matter now. Mr. Wolfe left town this afternoon."

"Why would he leave town?"

"From what I've been able to gather, what with his gambling debts and the mortgage on this place, it got to be too hot for him here in Cripple. He let out of here in a hurry, and George Carr went with him. I'd *heard* that they was scheming. Joe said he was heading for Oklahoma for the opening of the Cherokee Strip to make a bundle, and then he would be back."

"But what of this hotel?"

Benson shrugged his thin shoulders. "The creditors haven't said, but rumor has it they intend to close her down until a buyer can be found. They've already been through and let most of the staff go."

"Close it down? But where does that leave us?"

"Out of work, Mrs. Kramer, flat out of work."

# FOURTEEN

PHILLIP LAFARGE PARKED HIS CARRIAGE IN FRONT OF LISA and Olly's saloon. Every building along Myers Avenue was ablaze with electric light that spilled out doorways and windows, turning the street into one long carnival strip. Pianos and fiddles played bawdy drinking music, and more than one gramophone competed, adding their scratchy music to the mix. The clickety-click of roulette wheels filled the night air, and the gay voices of merrymakers sang out from the saloons and dance halls, hooting and howling, while drunks ricocheted from electric utility polls to porch posts as they made their way down the line of saloons. LaFarge stepped through the batwing doors and looked around. The place was filled with men bent over card tables, or the roulette wheel. Laughing blended with cussing, and to his left a steady stream of men seemed to be making their way up the stairs to the rooms above. He spied Oliver Sawyer and made his way through the crowd.

"Well, well, if it ain't you, LaFarge." Sawyer's eyes were impossibly large and fishlike behind the thick spectacles. "Here, lemme buy you a drink." He called to the bartender. "Whiskey for my friend here—some of that imported

Scotch.'' Sawyer took LaFarge by the arm and led him to his private table in an alcove behind a beaded curtain. ''Have a sit.'' He kicked back chairs for each of them.

''Doing well, aren't you?'' LaFarge said, lighting up a cigar.

''This was the smartest move I ever made.''

LaFarge looked at his quizzically. ''*You* ever made?''

Sawyer grinned. His weathered face had grown fat and his eyes looked unhealthy. ''Well, it was mostly Lisa's idea, but I bankrolled it.''

LaFarge shook out his match and crushed it with his shoe. ''Where did you get the money to bankroll a deal like this, Olly?''

''Oh, you know, I saved a little here, saved a little there.''

''Uh-huh.''

''It all adds up.''

''Especially when you fatten the poke with a few thousand dollars that you were supposed to pay off Elvin Tate with.''

Sawyer's smile never faltered, but his eyes hardened ever so slightly behind the thick glasses. ''What makes you say that?'' he said, an edge now in his voice.

LaFarge laughed. ''Don't worry, Olly. I won't let on how you and Barney handled Mr. Tate. Only, the next time you better be certain no one is standing around watching.''

''Who?''

''Never mind who.''

''So, why you letting on to me about it now?''

''Oh, no reason . . .''

''The hell! You never do nothing without a reason, La-Farge.''

''I didn't see Barney out there.''

''He's around someplace.''

''You two still partners?''

''We hang around. What are you driving at, LaFarge?''

He tossed back the whiskey that stood. ''Nothing . . . at least not right now.''

"Stop beating around the bush. Say what you mean."

LaFarge took the cigar from between his lips. "I don't mean nothing, Olly. I'm happy your place is such a success." He studied the smoke curling from the cigar a moment, then said, "I might need you again, and I just wanted to make certain you'd be available. I'd hate to think that all this success has gone to your head."

"Oh, blackmail, is it?"

"Nothing at all like that."

"You're a ruthless bastard. You ain't got nothing over me that I can't hold over you too."

LaFarge grinned. "Check."

"Life ain't always a game, LaFarge."

"Sure it is, Olly. And it's a game I intend to win." He parted the curtains, then looked back. "Thanks for the drink, Olly. I think I'll just stroll upstairs and see how business is there."

Sawyer stepped out of the alcove right behind him and said, "Go ahead, LaFarge. Have yourself a time with them. You can afford it."

LaFarge climbed the stairs, pushing past a man ahead of him. The stairs opened up onto a parlor. On the floor was a Persian rug, and the paper on the wall was imported from France. Walnut tables sat upon the carpet, and three women in sheer robes that revealed all their charms lounged upon the Floral sofas.

LaFarge knew each one of them, for they had all been one-crib girls before Lisa moved them up here. There was "Fire-in-the-Hole" Kelly in the pink dressing gown and Monika Maerz, also known as Sweet and Low, and finally Lynn West, a stunning blond who was really a businesswoman at heart and therefore liked her men two at a time—or so he had heard.

A half dozen men lingered about, clustered around the girls, who talked loosely and loudly and allowed the men's hands to roam about them, tempting them with whiskey and depositing gold coins in various places. Not that any tempting was required. It was all part of the game. After a while a girl would choose one of the men, take him back to her room for fifteen minutes of pleasure, and then be back to start all over again.

A door opened down the hallway and, a pretty Dutch girl named Desiree Van Vliet, stepped out, leading a grinning gent by the hand and sending him happily on his way down the stairs.

"Can I help you?" came a voice from behind him.

LaFarge turned. Lisa Kellerman was wearing a red and blue velvet dress, with a bustle and brocade bodice which she filled out nicely.

"Oh, it's you, Mr. LaFarge. Come to try out my girls?"

He smelled the heavy odor of whiskey on her breath, and she seemed unsteady on her feet. He said, "I've tried them all—all but one."

"And who might that be?"

"You."

Lisa smiled. "I'm not working anymore, Mr. LaFarge."

"Retired?"

"You might say that."

"But you could be persuaded to come out of retirement— for the right man . . . or the right price?"

"No. It's in my contract."

"You mean you and Olly? An exclusive?"

"We are business partners."

LaFarge laughed. "It's business I'm proposing to you now."

"I already told you, I don't work the line anymore," Lisa said mildly but firmly. She looked over as a door opened. "Here comes Jennifer. She's young and a real fireball, Mr. LaFarge. You can't go wrong with her."

LaFarge took a five-hundred-dollar bill from his vest pocket and slowly folded it into quarters as Lisa watched. "She's a child. I don't want her. In fact, I only want what I can't have. I want a woman with class—or one who puts on like she has it, and that is you, Lisa." As he spoke he slowly tucked the bill between her breasts, where they swelled at the plunging neckline of her dress. His fingers lingered there a few moments longer than was necessary.

Lisa hesitated, then glanced at the edge of the bill in her cleavage and quickly stepped to one side where the girls could not see her. ''You can be most convincing, Mr. LaFarge,'' she said, her voice breathless now.

He leaned towards her and kissed her hard on the lips.

''No, not here,'' she said quickly.

''My place, tonight?''

Lisa nodded. ''All right. Later, when things slow down here.''

LaFarge put the cigar between his lips. ''I'll be waiting for you.''

Oliver Sawyer met him at the bottom of the stairs. ''You're down in a hurry.''

''I decided to wait until later,'' he said, grinning. ''See you around, Olly.''


''Mommy, you are home early,'' Margaret said.

Maureen removed her hat and dropped it upon the table. ''Why aren't you asleep, darlin'?''

''It's not time yet.''

''Oh.'' Maureen's thoughts were all jumbled, and she hadn't really heard what Margaret had said.

''Is something the matter?''

Maureen fell into a chair and stared past the curtains at her reflection in the black windowpanes.

''Mommy?''

''What?'' She looked about. ''Darlin' why aren't you asleep?''

''I already told you: It isn't time.''

''What time is it?''

Margaret looked at the clock ticking softly on the mantel above the rock fireplace. ''It's just nine of the clock.''

''What's the matter?''

Maureen broke out of her trance with a sudden, sharp breath and stood, wiping the corner of her eye as she turned. ''Nothin' that need concern you, darlin'. I've just had a wee bit of a setback with my job, that's all. Now, off to bed with you. I'll tuck you in.''

After Margaret went to sleep, Maureen sat long into the night, trying to sort out her next move. If she looked at the matter in a practical light, she knew, it was obvious that her only real choice was to go back to Detroit and ask her sister to take them in again. What else was left to do? With no job and the land upon which her house sat mortgaged, and with this odious obligation to Daniels, what else was she to do?

The thought of living under Bridie's roof again made her shudder, and the tears began flowing freely. No! Never would she go back to that! There had to be another way to make it on her own, here in the home Peter had built.

After a while she went to a cupboard and carried a tin can back to the table. Inside it were the few items that Peter treasured: an old, dried-up rabbit's foot, a barlow knife, a fading tintype of his mother and father, his father's silver watch . . . and the claim paper to the Lucky Irish.

She unfolded the paper and read it over. The language of the document meant nothing to her, but she did understand that it represented ownership of a regular lode claim under the Cripple Creek Mining District law. As she looked it over, an idea occurred to her, but the hour was too late to think it through clearly. Maureen's eyes had grown heavy. She laid her head upon her folded arms, and was immediately asleep.

When Casey Daniels came into town for supplies and to collect his mail, the post office clerk handed him an envelope with his name penned in a neat hand and no return address to indicate its sender. He slit the envelope open with his pocketknife and withdrew two papers. They were from Maureen Kramer. One was the claim paper to the Lucky Irish, and the other was a brief note declaring that he was now the owner of the claim, and that that should cancel any obligations she owed him for the IOUs he had covered.

Casey stared at the papers in his hand, shocked. Then a small grin worked its way across his face. Maureen apparently knew nothing about transferring ownership of mining claims. He folded the papers back into the envelope and tucked them safely away within his inside vest pocket.

Casey bought his supplies and a newspaper, because the headline had reached out and caught his eye.

### MINERS ORGANIZE IN MONTANA!

The story told of the formation of a new labor union, the Western Federation of Miners, in Butte, Montana, its rise to life being the result of a bitter battle between miners and mine owners in the Coeur d'Alene Mining District the previous year. According to the article many of the W.F.M. organizers were in reality Molly Maguires. Casey had the feeling that this union could cause trouble for mine owners across the country, if it ever got up a head of steam. Certainly, it had competent, if not militant, leadership behind it, unlike the muddled leadership of the Knights of Labor, which had occasionally plagued Colorado mine owners in towns like Aspen and Leadville.

There would be some strong talk here in Cripple Creek about this. The only real encouraging note that Casey could see was that Montana was a mighty long way from Colorado, and that maybe the union would not bring its trouble down here for a long time.

On his way home, he drove up to Bull Hill to look over the Lucky Irish. The claim ran up the east side of the hill, almost to its summit. There was a little shack near a twenty-foot-deep pit. Over the pit, Peter had built a rough head-frame with a hand windlass nearby for hauling up the ore bucket that currently sat at the bottom of the pit.

Casey climbed down a ladder and studied the rocks in a

short tunnel that Peter had begun. There were traces of telluride—a good sign so long as it didn't turn out to be oxidized.
He had advised Peter on this, and it looked as though he had
been progressing in the right direction. Casey collected a sample of tellurium and took it to the surface. Surveying the claim,
he figured he'd do some development work on it this year to
keep the claim active. He had no real intention of working it,
but currently being out of a job, this might be something to
pursue.

He climbed to the summit of Bull Hill and looked out towards Bull Cliff. Between here and there, upon a pretty saddle
of land where a fair stand of ponderosa pine had somehow
managed to escape the woodsman's axe, was the little town
of Altman, which was in the progress of sprouting like a
mountain flower. With Pikes Peak as a backdrop nine miles
away, Altman was growing faster than any other town in the
District because of its closeness to three of the District's
richest mines; the Victor, the Pharmacist, and the Buena Vista.
Altman already had a couple of restaurants, a few grocery
stores, and, of course, a generous serving of saloons. The place
had perhaps a thousand people living in it, and the telephone
exchange was running wires and connecting it into the main
exchange at Cripple Creek.

Looking around from this lofty viewpoint, Casey could see
buildings and miners' shacks in all directions. A hundred
plumes of black smoke from the coal-and-wood-fired steam
engines smudged the sky. In the last year, men had swarmed
in and begun developing every inch of land in the District.
There were already nearly a dozen little towns springing up
all around, town with names like Elkton, Barry, Arequa,
Lawrence, and Mound City. Trees and wildlife, he mused, had
nearly become extinct in the region. The rats, of course, were
thriving, but Casey put them in a distinctly different category
from the wildlife that had roamed this area only a few short
years ago.

The place was booming, but Casey was being left out of it,

and unless he landed himself a job soon—a mining job—the boom would have passed him by.

He returned to his wagon and drove back to his cabin on Wilson Creek.

The next day when Casey took his sample to Mr. Guyot to run an assay Winfield Scott Stratton was there, wearing a long face, his pale eyes seeming more washed out than usual.

"Good morning, Mr. Stratton."

"What's good about it?"

Guyot was standing by a shelf where he kept his vials of acid and mercury amalgams, wiping his hands on a blue cloth. He glanced over. "I'll be right with you, Casey. I just have to write this up for Mr. Stratton." He sat behind a little rolltop desk and dipped a pen into the inkwell.

Stratton scratched the back of his neck and peered down at his miserably scuffed boots. "You'd think a man my age would finally know when he's been licked."

"Still no luck with your claims?"

Stratton gave a short laugh. "Luck! You know, Casey, the older I get, the more I believe that that's all this mining game is. Pure and simple, it's luck. Like the draw of a card or the spin of a roulette wheel. I think I finally learn something and try to put it to good use, and what do I get? Four-flushed by Lady Luck."

Then Stratton said to Guyot, "Tell him, why don't you. I'm too disgusted to talk about it."

Guyot looked up from his paperwork. "He's just been given some castor oil, Casey. Don't rail him none."

Stratton huffed. "Well, then *I'll* tell you. I hit a streak of telluride in my Washington mine. It showed color sure enough. I figured I had finally found my bonanza. After two years at those mines, I figured one of them was finally gonna pay off. So, I brought my sample up here and sure 'nough, it was gold. One hundred and fifty dollars to the ton, according to Mr. Guyot's assay.''

"That sounds wonderful," Casey said.

Stratton snorted disgustedly. "It sounded good to me too, until Mr. Guyot let the floor out from under me." He paused long and purposefully.

Guyot looked over his shoulder and said, "It turned out to be oxidized telluride."

Casey understood now why Stratton was so long in the face. Oxidized telluride would not separate easily. At most, Stratton could only hope for a quarter or a fifth of the assayed amount from such rock.

"That's too bad."

"Well, maybe it's the Good Lord trying to tell me something that I've been too thickheaded to listen to."

Guyot handed Stratton the assay he had worked out. "Like I told you before, if you want to sell the place I'll work you up a dandy seller's assay. Based on this sample, you should have no trouble getting out from under these claims."

Stratton folded the paper and tucked it into his pocket. "I'm seriously considering it. But first I think I'll take this over to Beaver Park and let Tomlinson run it through his stamp mill."

Stratton left, glum-faced, and trudged back up the road towards Battle Mountain.

"What can I do for you, Casey?" Guyot asked.

Casey set the rock he had taken from Peter's claim on the table. "I need an assay on this."

Guyot hefted it, looked it over, and said, "Tellurium."

"Yep. I'm in no hurry. I'll stop back in a day or two."

"I'll have it ready for you then."

By the end of May the time had come for some hard decisions. The J. H. Wolfe Hotel had been sold and the new owners had renamed it the Palace Hotel. There was no work available for Maureen there, as the new owners had hired mostly family members. Prospects for employment were thin for a woman with a reputation, at least among some merchants, for writing caustic letters to the editors of newspapers and stirring up trouble.

Maureen had run out of money and Margaret's shoes and dresses were becoming tattered. Kitty Barbee had given Margaret some of Mabs's old dresses, but that felt too much like charity to Maureen. She was determined to make her own way in this world, come what might, and it was because of that stubbornness that she now found herself vacillating on the corner of Fourth and Myers, questioning her sanity at what she was about to do.

She stood there a few minutes, steeling her nerves while watching the busy batwing doors of Lisa and Olly's Saloon. Could there be some other way that she had not yet tried? She wondered. No, she had exhausted all avenues. She had lost almost all of her cherished pride in pleading for a job that would support her and her daughter, and now it had come down to this.

Lisa had said the money was bountiful, and to hear her talk, Maureen hoped she'd only have to work a few weeks or a few months to get her financial affairs straightened out.

Maureen started forward, then drew up again for the tenth time in as many minutes.

*What can I be thinking of?*

Desperate situations demand desperate solutions, she reminded herself. What could it hurt to at least speak to Miss Kellerman about it? Lisa Kellerman had, after all, practically begged her to come and work for her.

Squaring her shoulders, Maureen tightened her grip upon her handbag and started once more for that dreaded building and its busy front door. Was anybody taking notice of her? She felt as conspicuous as if she been wearing the emperor's new clothes down the middle of Bennett Avenue. The world around her faded into a haze, and only that door—that horrible, dangerous, beckoning door—remained clear in her view.

She had rehearsed this very moment all morning—all week,

in fact, since the truth of her and Margaret's precarious situation had finally sunk into her stubborn Irish head. Even so, it seemed unreal to her, as if she were stepping through a dream from which at any moment she would awaken.

She peered over the top of the batwing doors into the building's smoky interior. A cacophony of noise assailed her ears; the rat-a-tat of a brass horn, the tinkling ivories of a piano, men's harsh voices, and the ever-present whir and chatter of roulette wheels. It almost masked the pounding of her heart. Her forehead was damp. What would she ever do if Kitty should discover her, or if Margaret found her out?

Well, that didn't matter now. She had made up her mind. She was doing what she *had* to do to survive.

# FIFTEEN

SUDDENLY SOMEONE CALLED HER NAME. IT SO STARTLED HER that she almost dropped her handbag. She whirled around breathlessly.

"Well, it *is* you!" James Burns was upon the seat of a dray, stopped in the middle of Myers Avenue. His white hair seemed to gleam in the sunlight as a grin came to his face. "Whatever are you doing in this part of town, Mrs. Kramer?"

She felt the heat rising up her neck and into her cheeks.

*Damn my fair complexion!*

"I-I," she stammered.

"This is not a place for a decent woman to be traveling alone. Now, I know you are as curious as the next person to see what goes on beyond those doors, but believe me, Mrs. Kramer, you wouldn't like it."

She inched away from the batwings and said, "No . . . no, I suppose not."

"Now, you tell me where you are going, Mrs. Kramer, and I'll be happy to drive you."

"That's most kind of you, Mr. Burns, but I wasn't goin' anywhere in particular," she said, trying to cover her shock at nearly being found out.

James Burns regarded her a moment. "I have heard you've been on hard times since your husband died."

"We have had to pull in our belts some, it is true."

"But you are making out all right?"

Maureen felt oddly conspicuous speaking to Burns with pedestrians walking past on the sidewalk, as if her problems were being exposed to the whole town to see. She stepped down off the sidewalk and into the street, close to the dray. Burns shifted over on the seat, reached down, and before Maureen knew what he was doing, she was seated next to him.

"Well, if you have no place in particular to be, Mrs. Kramer, perhaps you would not mind keeping me company as I go about my chores."

It was almost as if he had sensed her distress and, like that time in front of Hundley's stage depot, he was coming to her rescue. Why should he have showed up just at this moment to thwart her plans? she wondered. She had no answer, but a ride with him would help clear her brain some, she figured, and there was always later to do what she had to.

"Yes, of course I will ride with you, Mr. Burns."

He got the horses moving and they continued west on Myers one block, turning south on Third Street and then back east on Warren, where the business district ended and the residential district began. Here there were new homes going up everywhere, painted white and yellow and blue, like bright flowers; some with porches and every one of them with a solid tin roof or cedar shingles.

"Where are you going?"

"I've just been hauling some heavy things down to the works. I need to pick up some timbers now and take them to the mine, and then drop this wagon off back at the livery."

"How is your mine doing, Mr. Burns?"

He gave her a small smile and said, "Oh, it's backbreaking work. Maybe someday it will be worth it all."

*Backbreaking work?* Maureen had heard about James Burns and his partners, Jimmie Doyle and John Harnan. From the stories about town, the three of them did little but hang around that shanty up on their Portland claim. But she did not wish to try the man on that matter now. They were free to work their claim in any manner they saw fit. As far as she was concerned, all miners had to be a bit tetched in the head to do what they did, anyway.

"So tell me, Mrs. Kramer, how have you and Maggie—er, I mean Miss Margaret been getting along?"

Maureen had to smile, remembering the reprimand Margaret had given Mr. Burns that afternoon on the train. Thinking back on it now, it seemed like an eternity past instead of only a little more than a year ago.

"It is becomin' quite a problem," she said. "Our finances are meager, and at present, I am out of work. In fact, you might say our situation is desperate." Two months ago she would have never admitted that, but the circumstances of her life had worn her down. Lying had become too much trouble. Her pride just wasn't worth that anymore.

He looked at her oddly, and she hoped he had not seen the darker truth behind her words. Then all at once his earnest expression changed, and he laughed. "You're between jobs, then?"

"Why, yes." Maureen was surprised by his reaction, and her eyes sparked at the notion that he would take her situation so lightly.

"Well, if that isn't a stroke of luck."

"I beg you pardon, Mr. Burns?"

"I was telling my partners only the other day that we need to hire some help around the works. You would fit the bill nicely, Mrs. Kramer, if you'd be interested."

"Me? I know nothin' about minin', Mr. Burns. Whatever could I do? I certainly have not the strength to dig or haul buckets of rock."

"I never said anything about hauling rocks. I can haul rocks and swing a hammer just fine. But what I can't do is cook up a good meal. Oh, I make a passable stew, and I'm right handy at opening up a can of beans, but more than that and me and my partners are as helpless as pups. And as far as cleaning and washing is concerned, I'll tell you, Mrs. Kramer, our little cabin is in dire straits.'' He looked over at her and nodded his head as if confirming the notion. ''Yep, you'd be just about perfect for the job—that is, if you're interested.''

''I am!'' she blurted, then thought better of showing too much enthusiasm too soon and, straightening around on the wagon seat, said in a businesslike voice, ''And what would be my wage, Mr. Burns?''

''Well, as far as money is concerned, most miners are fetching three dollars a day for eight hours. Of course, there is a whole lot of danger working in the mines that you would not have to deal with. I reckon that part of a hard-rock miner's job accounts for about half of that amount, so, what would you say to a dollar-fifty—for cooking, cleaning, and going into town for the groceries?''

Maureen could hardly believe her good fortune. Mr. Wolfe had only paid her seventy-five cents a day; Burns's offer was twice that! Still, she wished to remain calm and in control of the situation. ''The wage sounds quite fair, Mr. Burns.'' Then she hesitated and said, ''But can you afford it? I mean, you haven't hit pay dirt yet, have you?''

''Well . . . er . . . no, we haven't. But we are getting close. Believe me, Mrs. Kramer, in a few months we will be into a high-grade vein . . . yep, I'm sure of that.''

Maureen frowned and looked back at the street with its bright houses and new flower gardens out front. *Miners!* They were all dreamers—the whole lot of them. Burns's optimism sounded like the malarkey that she'd heard over and over again. It was the same hopeful talk Peter used to bring home. Burns was no different. All dreamers—every one of them.

But she whispered a little prayer of thanks just the same, and accepted the job.

• • •

"You did what?" bellowed Jimmie Doyle, his back arching as he wiped the sweat from his brow. In the flickering lamp-light, James Burns saw the sudden anger flushing across his partner's face. High overhead, the mouth of their mine shaft was a lopsided rectangle in the yellow, wavering light of an-other lamp, with the shadowed shapes of a roof above. John Harnan's face appeared over the lip of the shaft, illuminated against the darker head-frame, his right hand gripping the rope that dropped down the fifty intervening feet to them.

"What's going on down there?" he said.

Doyle shouted up the shaft, "Our partner here has just gone and hired that Kramer woman to do our cooking and cleaning for us."

"He did what?"

"You heard him," Burns shouted back.

"What in the devil made you do such a thing?" Harnan called down.

Burns was about to tell him, then stopped and said, "Hell, if you want to know why, climb on down here. I don't intent to yell my lungs silly at you."

John Harnan swung a leg over the edge of the mine shaft and, instead of taking the ladder down, grabbed hold of the bucket rope and lowered himself hand over hand.

When they were all three at the bottom of the shaft, James Burns said, "It is true. I hired on Mrs. Kramer to help us out here."

"We don't need help," Doyle said.

Harnan was confused. "Hold up a minute. Who is this Kramer woman you two are talkin' about?"

Doyle said, "She's someone Jimmie met one day while coming into town. You remember Jimmie telling us about that fight over at Hundley's?"

"Oh, yeah, I recollect it now."

Burns said, "Her husband was killed in that accident at the Rattlesnake last summer. She's been down on her luck."

"Well, that ain't no reason to—"

"It's reason enough for me, John," Burns shot back. "Besides, when I ran into her today, I had the feeling she was about to do something that she might regret later."

"Still, it ain't our problem," Harnan went on. "And how are you gonna keep her from finding out about our operation here? You know what will happen if the other mine owners get wind of it."

Burns knew all too well what would happen. He had known it from the very first moment they had made their strike. Their claim, the Portland, was tiny. It had been described by some as no bigger than a hall closet. Yet fate had set them down on top of the richest vein in the District. The more they worked it, the richer it became. But because of the Law of Apex, not one ounce of the gold beneath their feet legally belonged to them.

So, they worked it in secret.

When they first realized what they had discovered, the three partners had built a shanty over the shaft. During the day they would dig the rock and at night they would don special harnesses, designed by Burns and stitched together by Burns's seamstress sisters, and haul the heavy ore down to their shack on Wilson Creek, where they secreted it away in a locked shed until they had enough to take to the mill down in Pueblo.

To date they had almost seventy thousand dollars put away from these sales, but they all knew that would not be nearly enough money to fight the lawsuits that the other mine owners would pile onto them once they found out—and find out they must, someday.

"She won't find us out. She's just gonna cook and clean, and by time we bring our rock down to the cabin, she'll be long gone, back to her own house."

"And what if she starts asking questions about what we keep in that shed, and why it's locked up all the time?"

Burns thought a moment, then said, "We can tell her it's expensive mining tools and we don't want them stolen."

"Expensive mining tools?" Doyle gave Burns a disgusted leer. "You think she will believe that?"

"Mrs. Kramer doesn't know anything about mining. Why shouldn't she believe it?"

"I don't like it," Harnan said.

Burns said, "The truth of the matter is, I believe that Mrs. Kramer was contemplating taking up with Lisa Kellerman . . . I believe her situation had become just that bad."

This gave them something to chew on, and finally Harnan came around and said, "Well, I suppose the decision has already been made, so it won't do no good sparring over it now."

Doyle was not quite so forgiving. "We are partners, dammit. You could have at least come and asked us. Once we knew the facts we would have gone along with it, Jimmie. But you shouldn't have oughta gone and done it without first asking."

"I know," Burns said. "But I had to do something right away, before she went and got herself in trouble."

"What's done is done," Harnan said. "Now let's get back to work. It's already late and there's a ton of rock here that needs to be brought down the hill."

Doyle seemed to want to continue the discussion, but he bit his tongue and followed them up the ladder. In the tiny shanty, they slipped into their harnesses. Burns fastened four heavy ore sacks onto Doyle's harness, then did the same for Harnan. Both John and Jimmie lent a hand loading up Burns, and when they were ready, they extinguished the light and, peeked around the door.

Doyle started off first, then Harnan moved onto the road. James Burns waited, hunkered down to keep the weight off his shoulders. When it was time, he stood, straining against the straps that dug into his shoulders. He had weighed the sacks once, and had calculated that with each trip down the hill to their cabin on Wilson Creek, they carried an average of two hundred pounds.

Grunting softly, he made his way along the road. At one point the way led past W. S. Stratton's little cabin on the Independence claim just below them. He always took this stretch of road a little slower, stepping as lightly as he could, trying not to make a sound. Tonight, as he passed Stratton's cabin, a lamp was burning inside, and in its unsteady glow, Burns saw the white-haired man sitting at a table alone, a bottle of whiskey to his lips, his head tilted back.

He felt sorry for the man. Stratton's claim had been one of the first on Battle Mountain, and it was because everyone thought that Stratton knew what he was doing that most of the original miners had staked claims here as well. But Stratton had not made the discovery he'd hoped for. The rumor was, Stratton was ready to shut down his mines and go back to his carpenter shop. Burns was going to miss the man when he did leave.

Lisa Kellerman pushed LaFarge off her and said, "Enough of this for tonight." She slipped out of his bed, wet with his sweat in spite of the cool mountain night air that came through the open window.

LaFarge lay there looking at her in the dark, her full breasts glistening like pink pears in the moonlight. "I suppose now you want to be paid?"

Lisa looked over and smiled. "First I want a whiskey."

"Help yourself. You know where I keep it."

She went through the dark room, knowing exactly where the cupboard was. In the last thirty days she had become intimate not only with LaFarge, but with his cabin, and with the road back to Cripple Creek late at night. Tonight there would be a full moon.

LaFarge slid out of the bed, put his arms around her waist, then bit the lobe of her ear. She put an end to it when his hand began to inch up towards her breasts. Turning out of his grasp she said, "My God, ain't you had enough for one night, Phillip?"

She looked down at him, naked in the moonlight, and laughed. "No, looks like you ain't."

"What do you think we ought to do about that?" he said.

"We? Sorry, big boy, but *I* need to get back to town. I suggest you find yourself a cold tank somewhere before you bust a vein or something."

He grabbed her roughly and pulled her to him. "That ain't what I got in mind at all. And considering what I'm paying you, you shouldn't be thinking it either."

"Your money can control a lot of things, Phillip, but it doesn't control me." She tried to break his grip but his fingers remained powerfully on her arms. Then he allowed one of his infrequent smiles and let go.

"I like a woman who isn't afraid of me."

She looked at her arms, and the marks his fingers had left on them. "Are they usually afraid of you, Phillip?" Lisa was not sure why she asked that question, or why the thought of being with a truly dangerous man thrilled her so. It was because Oliver Sawyer was such a man, and she had fallen in love with him. But over the last few months the fire of that love had grown cold. Now, it was merely a business arrangement. Sawyer was brutal and demanding—all traits that intrigued Lisa, but also traits that made any long-term relationship impossible.

LaFarge was the same sort of man, but at least the novelty of him had not worn off yet. And Lisa had to admit there was a certain thrill in leaving her business—and her business partner—and meeting LaFarge secretly at night as she had been doing since that first evening he'd asked her to come out.

LaFarge said, "What would you call it when they refer to me as 'sir' and act like wooden cigar-store Indians?"

Lisa threw back her head and laughed. "I'd call it smart, because they can see that inside here"—Lisa poked his naked chest with a finger—"where there ought to be a heart, you've got a lump of ice, and you're a lousy son of a bitch to boot."

LaFarge grinned. "Is that what you think I am?"

The whiskey bottle clinked against her glass as she hastily filled it. "That's what I know you are." She took a long drink. "But it's what I find most fascinating about you."

"Hitting that stuff kind of hard, aren't you?"

"Hell, I hit *life* hard, Phillip. Now, let me get dressed."

"Sure, go on. There will be another day."

As Lisa slipped into her chemise, she knew that LaFarge was right. There would be another day, and another after that, and another—until she tired of LaFarge and went looking again. Behind her she heard him pulling on his trousers and shoving his arms back into the sleeves of his shirt.

She was peering out the window, buttoning up her dress, when she stopped and stared hard into the night.

"What is going on down there, Phillip?"

LaFarge came over. Out of the corner of her eye Lisa saw the fire at the end of his cigar brighten. "Where?"

Lisa studied the little shanty down the side of Battle Mountain and said, "You can't see it now, but a moment ago the lights went out and I thought I saw three men step outside. It looked like they were wearing something heavy on their backs, but now they're gone."

"That's the Portland. Burns, Doyle, and Harnan's claim. I don't know what they do down there, but mining don't seem to be part of it."

Lisa brushed her hair quickly and hastily pinned it up and set her hat in place.

"There, do I look respectable?"

"You've never looked respectable a day in your life, Lisa. And that's what I love about you."

Her breath caught momentarily. 'Love'? That was the first time she had heard that word come from his lips, and she wondered if it was possible that he loved her—or for that matter, that she loved him.

At the door, he pressed a banknote into her hand. "Stop by tomorrow."

"I'm not sure I can," she said. "Maybe, if I can get away."

"Try real hard, won't you?"

She dropped the money into her handbag. "We'll see."

LaFarge suddenly drew her to him and kissed her hard and long. Then he released her and shut the door. Lisa stood there a moment, confused by this sudden shift in LaFarge. Up until tonight it had been strictly business. She thought it had been only *her* heart that was affected by it. Now it seemed that Phillip LaFarge's heart had become involved as well.

Lisa grinned suddenly at the impossibility of that thought. A lump of ice, she told herself, has no feelings.

"Where have you been?" Sawyer asked, his impossibly huge eyes blinking behind the thick spectacles. "I've been looking for you. The girls said you went out for a while."

"I went out for a drive."

"Why?"

"Because I wanted to get away. This business drives me crazy sometimes, Olly."

"Where did you go?"

"Out. What's wrong with that? It's a free country, ain't it?"

He backed off some. "Yeah, sure it is. How about we go up to your room—"

"Not tonight, Olly. I'm tired."

Lisa left him standing there and went upstairs and conferred a moment with Lynn West, who had taken over for Kelly when one of her regular customers had showed up.

"It's been a busy night," Lynn said.

Lisa said, "I'm going to retire early. Think you and the girls can handle it?"

"Aw, sure, Lisa. You look like you're beat. Don't worry about nothin'," Lynn said. "Me and Kelly will take care of business till we shut down."

The girls, and especially Lynn West, could handle any business that came in. Lisa escaped to her room and locked the door. Her brain was whirling. She was confused by LaFarge's change this evening, and the last thing she wanted now was to deal with Olly and have to answer his probing questions. She poured herself a whiskey, took a drink. Her view went around the small suite of rooms and came to the hookah on the stand by her bed. She set the glass down, peered at it then opened her dresser drawer, removed a small tin of opium, and filled the pipe.

Oliver Sawyer came up the stairs a few minutes later. Two men were sitting on the sofas. Monika Maerz lounged upon the Persian rug, eating a banana, while the gent nearby was finishing up a glass of brandy. On a table was a silver service with four bottles—two different whiskeys, one of rum, and one of brandy, and a silver bowl overflowing with grapes, bananas, and apples.

Lynn saw Sawyer standing there and came over.

"Where is she?" Sawyer asked.

"Lisa's gone to bed. She's all done in, Mr. Sawyer."

"Done in? What's she been up to, anyway?"

Lynn shrugged her bare shoulders. "Danged if I know. But it ain't unusual for her to come back dragging her tail."

"What do you mean?" Behind the lenses his bulbous eyes compressed suspiciously.

Lynn gave him a blank look. "I mean it ain't unusual for Lisa to come back late and go right to bed."

"She does this often?"

"Oh, sure. She takes her buggy out at least a couple times a week."

"Does she now?" Sawyer had noticed Lisa's interest in spending the night with him waning, but he had always put it off to the hard work of running the brothel. Now he wasn't sure. This was the first he knew of her taking late-night drives.

"You want I should go wake her up for you, Mr. Sawyer?"

"No. I'll talk to her in the morning."

"She don't usually get up before noon," Lynn said, but Sawyer had already started down the stairs.

In the saloon, he scanned the tables and spied Barney Mays

at one of them, holding a fan of cards near his chest. He caught Barney's eye. Barney set the cards on the table, facedown. "I'll be back, boys." He followed Sawyer through the beaded curtains into his private alcove. "What do you need, Olly?"

"A favor."

"Sure. Anything you want." Barney had become most appreciative since Oliver and Lisa had opened the business, and Sawyer, in return, had been generous—the whiskey and the girls were on the house. Barney had told Sawyer more than once that he felt as if he'd died and gone to heaven.

"I think Lisa is seeing someone."

"Naw. Not Lisa. The kid thinks you're the greatest thing since electricity."

"I don't know about that. She's been sort of distant these last few weeks. Now I just learned that she's been going out at night."

"Hm. That doesn't sound good, Olly. What do you want me to do?"

"Keep an eye on her the next couple days. If she goes out again, follow her and tell me who it is she's seeing."

"I can do that, Olly."

Sawyer grinned. "You're a good man, Barney. Tell Cal I said to set you up with another beer."

# SIXTEEN

MAUREEN WAS UP BEFORE SUNRISE. SHE DRESSED, ATE BREAKFAST, and laced up a pair of sturdy shoes. Margaret was awakened by the muffled sounds of her mother getting ready.

"Mommy, it's really early."

Maureen sat upon the edge of her daughter's bed. "I have work I must be off to, darlin', and it is almost two miles to Mr. Burns's cabin."

"When will you be home?"

"I don't know. I'll try not to be late. In the meanwhile, you are in charge of the house. You have your chores to do, and when you are finished, you may go and play with Mabs. I spoke to Mrs. Barbee yesterday, and she said you can spend the afternoon at their house, if you like." Maureen stood and snatched a black shawl off the back of the rocking chair.

"I wish you didn't have to go away to work."

Maureen frowned, then bent to kiss her daughter upon the forehead. "I do too, darlin', I do too. Perhaps someday I won't have to. But since your father died, we've both had a lot of growing to do."

"What do you mean?"

Maureen thought of the decision she had been prepared to

make only the day before, and a cold shudder ran up her spine. "I mean, we do what we have to—to survive. Everyone does what they have to—to survive." That answer seemed to satisfy Margaret, and Maureen was relieved that she did not have to explain further. "Now, you take care of yourself and our home, Margaret, and I'll see you later."

Maureen left her there and hesitated in the gray dawn outside the door until she heard the lock bolt slide in place. Then pulling the shawl across her shoulders against the early morning chill, she left, taking the road out of town towards Battle Mountain.

The day brightened and the walk to Battle Mountain was a pleasant one. Traffic to the mines picked up and she had offers of a ride from almost every wagon that passed by. But she was almost there and declined this first day, knowing that tomorrow she'd be able to spend an extra half hour at home and have no trouble getting a ride out to the mines.

At James Burns's little cabin, Maureen hesitated by the closed door. She listened. At first she thought no one was home and that she had arrived too late. It was after six o'clock, after all. She hoped she'd not have to go up to the claim, for she did not want to disturb the men at work. Oh, how she hated having to apologize for her tardiness on her *first* day! That would not leave a good impression at all. She knocked on the door—just to be sure one of the men had not stayed behind to wait for her.

There was dead silence beyond the door.

Unhappily, she realized that she would have to go up to the claim—and then she heard something. She knocked a second time and listened.

Yes, she was certain she had heard something this time, something like a snort or an interrupted snore in the room beyond. Then she heard a thump and a bump, a sound like pots and pans clanging together, a mild curse, and finally the door latch clicking.

"What the devil—" James Burns appeared in the open doorway. He was dressed in nothing but his red union suit, and his eyes were blurred with sleep. "Oh!" he said, and immediately placed his body behind the door so that only his face and the disheveled shock of white hair remained visible around its edge. "Why, Mrs. Kramer. What . . . what are you doing here?"

"Did you not hire me to come and clean and cook for you?"

"Well . . . well, yes, I did. But . . . but what time is it?"

Maureen placed her hands sternly upon her hips. "It's time for workin' men to be out of bed and their hands to be at the work God gave them to do."

James Burns glanced over his shoulder, then back at her. "Just give me and my partners a minute to get dressed."

The door closed and Maureen stood there amazed. The stories were all true. These three *were* only play-miners. The real mining men in the District were already up and at work while Burns and his two partners were snoring away the morning. Maureen had some serious misgivings about this new job. Neither Burns, Doyle, nor Harnan were rich men. How long could they afford to keep her employed when they slept away the morning?

A few minutes later James Burns let her into the cabin, and a more cluttered place she could not remember ever having seen. The men were scowling at her and casting pointed glances at Burns. Ignoring their looks, he introduced Maureen to each of them.

Maureen said, "Do you have any instructions you'd like to leave with me before you go to work, or do I just begin?"

"Just begin," the man named Harnan said brusquely.

"Very well. And when should I have your dinner ready?"

She thought she saw a snarl move across Doyle's face, but Burns stepped forward to block her view. "Don't worry about dinner today, Mrs. Kramer." He grinned as if embarrassed.

"Just working on cleaning up the place will keep you busy enough."

"Very well." Maureen looked around the cabin. Scattered about were their cots, the bedding draped to the floor. A table lay somewhere beneath a pile of dirty tin plates, cups, and pans. More pans filled the sink, spilling out onto the counter. The stove was buried under several nights' worth of cooking utensils. Maureen figured that every pot and pan these three men owned was dirty.

"Aye, I've got me two days' work just doin' the dishes. I can see now why you hired me, Mr. Burns."

The men crunched their hats down upon their heads and took up their canteens. As they filed out the door, John Harnan said, "Good luck with it."

Maureen figured she'd need it. She stood in the doorway watching them march up the hill and across the road until they eventually disappeared among the shacks, head-frames, and freight wagons. Then she turned back to the job at hand. Where to start? She glanced at all the dirty dishes scattered around and decided to take on the biggest battle first, feeling a little as Hercules must have when shown the Augean stables.

"Burns! That woman will have to go!" Jimmie Doyle exploded, breaking the uneasy silence that had accompanied the three men as they made their way up Battle Mountain to their claim. "Not only are you paying her a kingly sum, but she wakes us up in the middle of the night to boot!"

"It's not the middle of the night," Harnan said reasonably.

Burns frowned and kept his thoughts to himself. Maybe it had been a mistake, but it seemed the right thing to do at the time.

"And did you hear what she had to say about us?" Doyle railed. " 'Time for workin' men to be out of bed and their hands to be at the work God gave them to do.' " He did a fair impression of a nagging woman.

"She's strong-willed," Burns said in her defense. "The sort of woman a man needs behind him. One who will drive him on to better things."

Doyle snorted. "Ain't the kind of woman *I* need."

Harnan said, "Why don't you two lay off each other. To hear you, no one would guess you to be friends."

Neither Burns nor Doyle said anything, but Burns knew it to be true. They were always at each other's throats.

They reached their shanty and stood looking at each other. "I'm going back to sleep," Doyle said, and promptly leaned against the shady side of the shack and closed his eyes.

Harnan glanced at Burns. "He's right, you know. We got another long night ahead of us."

Burns agreed, and inside of five minutes all three of them were curled up on the ground, asleep.

Guyot was bent over his little furnace when Casey stepped in. "Oh, hello, Casey," he said, tapping down the flue. "Come for that assay?"

"You have it finished?" Casey asked.

"Sure do."

Casey caught the guarded inflection in Guyot's voice as the assayer took a paper from one of the cubbyholes of his battered rolltop desk and handed it to him. Casey read the report, his pulse quickening.

Guyot said casually, "Say, where did you get that sample from?"

Casey whistled softly and tucked the paper safely away in his vest pocket. "It belongs to a friend."

"I ought to know . . . for my records, you see."

Casey grinned. "I'll let you know—later."

"Playing this one kind of close to the buttons, ain't you, Casey?"

"I have my reasons."

Guyot laughed. "I know when not to stick my nose where it ain't wanted."

Casey paid Guyot for the assay work, and as the assayer was putting the money into a tin cash box that he kept in his desk drawer he said, "Have you been listening to the talk, Casey?"

"What talk is that?"

"Why, about the union coming into the District."

Casey had heard the rumors. A fellow by the name of John Calderwood who had been in on the forming of the Western Federation of Miners in Montana had moved into the District and had set up housekeeping in Altman. He was busily recruiting miners into a local union that he called the Free Coinage Union No. 19.

"I've heard that the mine owners aren't real happy."

"You blame them?"

"I think it was inevitable once the W.F.M. got rolling. But I didn't think it would come down to Cripple Creek so soon."

"Yeah," Guyot said with feeling. "It's spreading sort of like that epidemic we had last year. I understand that the man working for the W.F.M. is an old friend of our socialist governor."

Casey laughed. "That doesn't surprise me."

"Well, one thing for sure, if the miners organize, we are in for some big changes."

Casey frowned. "And some bloodshed too. The leaders of the W.F.M. are mostly ex–Molly Maguires, and as far as they are concerned the only good capitalist is a dead capitalist."

"Sounds a little like the 'Bloody Bridles' speech our wonderful governor gave a while back."

"Hopefully Governor Waite won't be around after the next election, but I'm afraid the W.F.M. will be a burr under our saddle for a long time to come."

"What a pleasant thought," Guyot said with feeling.

"Well, I need to get going."

"See you around—oh, one more thing. You and Stratton, you're friends, ain't you?"

Casey considered Stratton a friendly acquaintance, but he

had never regarded him as a friend, particularly. "We are friendly enough."

"I thought so. You hear he's leaving the District?"

This was something Casey had not heard. "No. When?"

"I just wrote up a seller's assay for him this morning on his claims. I'm spreading the word that they are for sale. I'm going to hate to see the old fellow go. Him and a few other of the original prospectors—they were the spirit of this camp. Now look what we got. A town that's beginning to look mighty grown-up, with more store owners, preachers, stock-brokers, and children than miners."

"Well, that's what we call progress. You can't stop it, can't even slow it down once men get a whiff of gold."

"No, and if you did, Casey, we'd be out of work." Almost at once Guyot regretted saying that.

Casey winced and said, "Some of us are already out of work."

"How are you making ends meet?"

"Like anyone on hard times, you do what you have to. I've hauled freight, shoveled manure, dug foundations, and helped survey a road or two."

Guyot frowned. "But it ain't the same, is it?"

"I've got mining in my blood. No other work is quite as satisfying." Casey patted the assay paper in his pocket. "But who knows, maybe I'll get back to it soon. Good day, Mr. Guyot."

"Good day to you, too."

Casey found the news of Stratton leaving the District unsettling, and instead of going to Bull Hill and doing some preliminary survey work on the Lucky Irish, he turned back to Battle Mountain and found W. S. Stratton in his shack on his Independence claim.

"I'm not one to admit defeat, Mr. Daniels," Stratton said as he shoved his few worn-out clothes into his war bag, "but there comes a time when a prudent man has to cut his losses."

"I'm sorry to see you go. If there is something I can do . . . ?"

"No, I've laid off my development crew. About the only help I need now is finding someone to buy these places off of me." Stratton picked up a battered pair of boots and looked at them sadly. "I hate to see a fine pair of boots ruined, and this country sure has a way of doing that." He shoved the boots into the bag after the clothes, dropped a few books on top of that, and then tossed in a few rocks—samples that he was going to drop off at Tomlinson's stamp mill on his way down the mountain. He drew the cords tight and slung the heavy sack over his shoulder.

Outside, Stratton tied the sack to his mule where he had already piled on his few cooking utensils, a shovel, and a couple of blankets.

"What will you do?" Casey asked Stratton as he tugged at the pack and went around adjusting its buckles, giving a stout shake at each stop.

"I still have my carpenter shop in the Springs. I'll go back to building houses, I suppose, or whatever else folks have a mind."

"You'll be back. This life is too much a part of you, Mr. Stratton. And I've become something of an expert on the subject these last months."

Stratton gave a short laugh. "Nope, I'm done with mining. You, on the other hand, you're just too bullheaded to realize when you've been licked. But a few more years under your belt will take care of that."

"Maybe so." Casey shoved his hands into his pockets and rocked back on his heels. "But I think I'll stick it out a little while longer, thank you. You take care, Mr. Stratton."

Stratton stuck out a hand. Casey clasped it. For a slightly built man, Winfield Scott Stratton had a surprisingly firm grip, and the callused skin of a man accustomed to working with pick and shovel.

"Next time you get to the Springs, Mr. Daniels, look me

up," Stratton said, gathering the reins of his mule.

"I'll do that."

"Oh, one favor, if I might?"

"Anything."

"Since your cabin is close by, think you could keep an eye on the works up here—only until the place sells. You know what happens when some folks think a place has been abandoned. They strip it clean as a whistle."

"I'll keep my eye on it."

"Thanks." Stratton looked around the hillside, littered with scrap lumber, shacks, and mounds of yellow-gray rock everywhere. Above was the Portland, with its single shack. Farther to the left stood the half dozen shacks of LaFarge's Rattlesnake mine, farther still was McKinnie and Peck's Black Diamond mine, and down slightly from that was Sam Strong's Strong mine. They had all located on Battle Mountain because of Stratton, and now Stratton was leaving. Far below was Wilson Creek and beyond that the growing town of Lawrence. The whole District was booming, with mining camps springing up into little towns everywhere. Casey saw Stratton blink and look away.

"Well, time to go," Stratton said resolutely, but there was an unspoken reluctance in his voice as well. He walked away leading his mule, his head bent slightly, and an uncharacteristic rounding of his shoulders. Watching him leave like that, Casey had the strange feeling it was a turning point in the life of this District that Stratton had helped pioneer—but where it was turning to, he had no idea.

As they tramped down the hill to their cabin, Jimmie Doyle said, "I hope she's not there. I'm in no mood to put up with her carping."

Burns only frowned.

Harnan said, "Listen to who's carping."

Doyle shot him a narrow glance. "Keep it up and you'll be patching up your face this evening."

Harnan gave a short laugh, but he let the subject drop just the same.

When they neared their cabin, they noticed a rope strung from the cabin to the shed out back, and upon it hung all their bedding. They were standing there gaping at this uncommon sight when Harnan glanced up and said, "By Gawd, I can see through the windows."

They all turned and sure enough, the glass panes nearly sparkled in the late afternoon sunlight. Burns was the first through the door. He stopped sharply just inside and stood there looking around. The countertop was empty—absolutely empty! Burns could not remember ever having seen it so. In place of the piles of pans and plat maps and dirty dishes was a green and yellow tablecloth and a beer bottle that had been pressed into service as a vase holding yellow and red mountain flowers.

The table sat upon a little rug that Burns remembered seeing once under a pile of empty dynamite crates stacked in the corner. He looked over. The corner was empty, and through the now exposed window, a stream of sunlight glanced off a floor that had been thoroughly scrubbed.

Harnan and Doyle came through the door behind him and stopped in shocked silence.

Harnan said, "I think we went to the wrong place, boys."

Doyle was sniffing the air. "Maybe so, but by the smell of that cooking, I'm voting that we should stay a while."

"But you'll be takin' your boots off first, if you please," Maureen's voice cut in.

They looked over at the stove and the pot of bubbling food there. Burns was the first to recover his tongue. "I can hardly believe this. You've worked a small miracle here, Mrs. Kramer."

She laughed. "Believe me, Mr. Burns, it were no *small* miracle."

Doyle's sniffing nose led him to the pot on the stove. "What have we here?"

"Irish stew. And considerin' the company, a most fittin' meal, wouldn't you say?"

"Yes, ma'am."

"Now, if you would set the table for me, gentlemen."

All three of them jumped to the task.

"You'll be findin' them in the cupboard, where they should be," Maureen said as she stirred the pot. "And I think you'll be amazed at how many utensils you have. I found forks and spoons in the most unlikely places. Really, gentlemen, what purpose do you suppose a spoon has under the window sash?"

James Burns said, "We use it to prop open the window when it gets hot."

"Really? And would a stick not be sufficient?"

"Er, I reckon it would."

"Then I will find you one tomorrow, and we can leave the spoons for eatin' off of."

"Yes, ma'am."

They set the table. Harnan carried the pot over and set it upon a trivet. Jimmie Doyle held Maureen's chair for her and helped it forward when she sat down. James Burns only grinned as he watched all of this.

When she left, Burns shut the door and looked at his partners. "Any complaints about my decision to hire Mrs. Kramer?"

Harnan shook his head. "No, so long as she don't find out about what we are doing up at the mine."

"She won't," Burns said, then he looked at Doyle. "And you?"

Jimmie Doyle patted his full stomach and grinned content- edly, looking around their clean cabin. "Ain't had such a good meal since I left Li'l London and your sisters' good cooking. Why, if I had a lick of sense about me, I'd marry that woman."

Burns laughed. "And what about her carping?"

"For a clean cabin, and a full stomach, a man could learn to put up with most any other baggage she might bring along."

"Well, you can get them stars out of your eyes for now, Jimmie. We got us a full night's work ahead."

They hauled in their clean bedding off the line, made up their cots, and with night full upon the mountain now, went back up to the mine.

# SEVENTEEN

THE BARBEES HAD A PLEASANT LITTLE HOUSE ON GOLDEN Avenue, with a solid shingled roof overhead. Jonce Barbee, Kitty's husband, was home from his claim and was playing a ditty on his fiddle when Maureen came in. Margaret and Mabs were sitting at the battered piano that Jonce had gotten from Mr. Burnside, the saloon owner, for the price of hauling it away. Kitty was nursing the newest member of the Barbee family, a little boy born a few months earlier whom they'd named Billie, but whom Mabs simply called "brother." It was a homey house, and Maureen had always been a little envious of the Barbees, even though she could tell that Kitty was never quite contented. Kitty had followed Jonce from the mining camps in Utah out here to Colorado, and like Maureen, she was a stubborn woman, determined to make the best of what life threw her way.

"Have you eaten anything?" Kitty asked.

"Oh, yes, thank you. I cooked a fine dinner for the men and we ate it together."

Jonce stopped his fiddling and said, "What are those three doing up there anyway? A more mysterious gaggle of men I ain't never seen."

Maureen shrugged her shoulders. "For the life of me, I don't know. Why, they were still asleep when I showed up at their door this morning! They went up to their claim, stayed all day, came down for dinner, then said they were going back to work after I left." Maureen frowned. "It is odd that they would work through the night—what are they working at? There is nothing but a little, weedy pit at the back of their claim."

Kitty said, "I'll wager it's a bottle those three are working at."

"I did not smell a trace of whiskey on their breath."

"Well, then they are just laying about up there, I suppose."

Jonce said, "I don't know that to be the case, Kitty. I know Jimmie Burns, and he's not a layabout. I've spoken to Mr. Stratton about him as well, and Stratton said that when he knew Burns in Colorado Springs, he was as industrious as a beaver, doing plumbing work for the city while acting as foreman of Hook and Ladder Company No. 1."

Maureen said, "They are gentlemen, all three of them, although the young one, Jimmie Doyle, seems a bit of a harum-scarum type."

Jonce frowned thoughtfully, resting the bow and fiddle upon his knee. "I wonder if I ought to go over there and offer to dowse their claim."

Kitty looked at him sternly. "You and that divining rod haven't brought us any luck. Don't go trying it out on other folks."

"It works just fine, Kitty," he said.

Maureen could tell by the hurt in his voice that Kitty's comment had wounded him. He set the fiddle on a small table and sat there brooding.

Margaret hopped off the piano bench and said, "Guess what Mabs and me done today, Mommy."

"What did you and Mabs do today?"

"We found a little cave, and we are going to make it into a house for our dolls to live in."

"A cave?" Maureen glanced at Kitty.

"Don't worry, Mau. The girls took me over to see it. It's just a wind-hollow under a big, flat rock. It's not dangerous, but it's deep enough to make a pretty little playhouse for the girls."

Maureen looked back at her daughter. "And where is this cave, darlin'?"

"It's just past Pisgah graveyard on the Florissant road."

"It's not far from here," Kitty interjected.

Margaret said, "We are going to bring chairs, and make a table, and eat our lunches there."

"Are you now? And where will you be gettin' all those fancy items?"

"I don't know. We'll find them around, I suppose."

"I gave the girls an old tablecloth," Kitty said.

"We have some plates we don't use, Mommy," Margaret reminded her.

Maureen said, "I suppose we can find somethin' to help outfit your new house."

The girls were excited about that, and they made plans while Kitty and Maureen visited over a cup of tea. Maureen held Billie in her arms most of the time, knowing an emptiness inside her. She would never be able to have Peter's son, and suddenly that was an overwhelming sadness which she had to fight down while showing a smiling face.

Across the room, Jonce had shrugged off his moodiness and as the women talked, he started to scratch out an old hymn on his fiddle.

Lisa Kellerman had stayed close to home the rest of that week, perhaps sensing something was afoot, but come Monday evening, she sent a boy to bring her phaeton around from the livery and, in the growing dusk of evening, rode away from town.

Barney Mays, with the help of a neat stack of five double eagles from Oliver's till, had recruited one of Lisa's girls, Jennifer Britt, to be his eyes and ears. Jennifer, true to her word and smelling more money in it, sent word to him that Lisa was going out, and so as Lisa's little buggy pulled out of Cripple Creek, Barney swung onto the back of his horse and began trailing her at a safe distance.

It didn't take an Indian scout to discover her destination. Barney halted on a rise of land near the corner of a miner's shack and watched LaFarge let Lisa into his cabin. He stayed there until darkness was full upon the land, then crept down and watched the two of them through the window. A crooked grin came to his face, and after he'd seen enough to make his blood hot, he rode back to town, found Jennifer, took out his passion upon her, and afterwards, when the fire had ceased to burn within him, dressed, paid her, and went downstairs to find Sawyer.

"Got some news you're not going to like, Olly."

"You found out who it is?" Sawyer said.

Barney nodded.

Sawyer took a bottle and two glasses and led the way to his private alcove. He filled the glasses and when Barney had taken a long pull from his, Sawyer said, "Who is it?"

"You ain't gonna like this, Olly."

"I already know that. Tell me something that I don't know."

"LaFarge."

Sawyer sat there, stunned. "You certain?"

"I seen them with my own two eyes, and they sure did seem to be enjoying themselves. I ain't no authority on it, but I think your woman has taken a fancy to LaFarge."

Oliver Sawyer sat there unmoving, a slow fire beginning to burn. Then he flung the whiskey glass to the floor and stood, knocking over his chair. "I'll kill that man!"

Barney caught Sawyer by the arm as he dove out through the beaded curtain. "Hold up, Olly."

Sawyer wheeled about with blind hatred in his eyes.

Barney didn't know if he should talk or duck as Sawyer

glared at him with huge, unblinking eyes behind his wire-rimmed spectacles. "Think about what you're about to do, Olly. Just sit down and think about it."

Sawyer remained standing, and Barney wasn't even sure he was listening.

"You have yourself a booming business here. Your life has gotten good. You've more money than you'll ever need. If you rush off now and blow LaFarge's head off, two weeks later the sheriff will give you a necktie party and you can kiss the good life good-bye."

Some of what Barney said had sunk in, and the smoke drifted from Sawyer's eyes. He snatched the bottle off the table and pumped the whiskey down his throat.

Barney went on quickly. "Your money can buy men to do what you want done. If you plan it right, your hands stay clean, and you grow richer . . . and a rich man can always find himself another woman. Think about it before you run off half-cocked and ruin everything you've built up here."

"Maybe you're right, Barney."

"You know I'm right. Give yourself a while to think of something. There ain't no hurry—neither LaFarge nor Lisa are going nowhere."

"I'll make that man pay, but it will be on my terms, not his."

That next month Margaret and Mabs spent most of their days at their new play-cave. Maureen became comfortable in her job. Jimmie Doyle's opinion of her had gone from gloom to sunshine. The house was now spotless, in spite of Doyle's careless habit of leaving smoldering cigars lying about. But it was her cooking that she suspected they appreciated most. Still, a dollar-fifty a day was heavy wages to pay someone to cook for them. Maureen didn't complain, however. Her luck seemed to have taken a turn . . . and it was about time!

Oliver Sawyer had not said another word about the affair between Lisa and LaFarge, but he'd been steadily attempting to build friendships with the mining men. There were rumblings of discontent among them, and Sawyer was always quick to lend an ear or pour some disgruntled fellow a drink on the house.

Calderwood was getting the mining men organized, promising a standard wage throughout the District of three dollars for an eight-hour day. Between his Free Coinage Union No. 19 and several smaller unions in Cripple Creek, Anaconda, and the new town of Victor, he had amassed a small army of eight hundred men. Sawyer had begun to attend some of their meetings at the Smith and Peters' Saloon in Altman, to listen to Calderwood's inflammatory speeches.

Meanwhile, life went on in the growing mining district. Cripple Creek was bursting at the seams. New city extensions were gobbling up what remained of the old Broken Box Ranch. Freeman Placer, where the Barbees lived, was one of the fastest-growing areas of town. Stock exchanges were as common as grocery stores. The Palace Hotel was quickly becoming the nightspot of the well-to-do, while Myers Avenue continued to be a stinking sore upon the city where whiskey flowed freely, women banked the miners' gold for a few minutes of pleasure, and opium dens sprang up in the back rooms of saloons and bordellos.

Casey had begun to work the Lucky Irish claim, following a narrow vein that showed lots of promise, if not a whole lot of cash yet. He took what money he needed to live on out of the works, and banked the rest in an account owned in the mine's name.

It was rumored that Stratton was ready to come back to Cripple Creek. He hadn't been gone from the District but a month and already he was getting restless in Colorado Springs, for it seemed that Li'l London at that moment was in the midst of a real estate slump. The collapse of silver prices had thrown people out of work and closed down banks, and everyone was cussing Congress for that, especially the bankers. On this point alone, most Coloradans agreed with Governor "Bloody Bridles'' Waite, and the push was on to reestablish the silver standard.

Towards the end of June a man named Pearlman arrived in Cripple Creek from San Francisco. He had learned that Stratton's mines were for sale, and that Stratton was coming back to the District, so for about a week Pearlman camped out on Stratton's abandoned doorstep, waiting.

Stratton did return at the end of June. He was relieved to be back, not only because the clear mountain air agreed with him, but because a woman in Manitou Springs had seen him clobber his stubborn mule over the head with a two-by-four, and had filed a complaint against him with the Colorado Humane Society. He had just barely escaped the animal lovers up over the stage road into the District, where men looked upon such matters in a more sensible manner. Here, at least, he felt relatively safe from being nabbed.

"Who are you?" Stratton demanded, coming upon Pearlman lounging in his old rocking chair.

Pearlman hopped out of the chair, nervously tugging his vest down over his bulging stomach. "Er . . . are you Mr. Winfield Stratton?"

Stratton glared at him from under his old, dusty gray Stetson. "Who's asking?" Stratton was cash-broke, tired, angry, and depressed . . . and what depressed him most was that his new boots, made by a Swiss-German cobbler in Colorado Springs named Bob Schwartz, had taken an awful beating on the long march up from the Springs.

"Er . . . my name is Pearlman. L. M. Pearlman."

"What are you doing on my place?"

"Well, I was told your Washington claim was for sale. I represent a number of San Francisco investors who might be interested in buying it."

Stratton's disposition softened some at this news. "It is for sale. So's the Independence, upon which you happen to be standing. You can have the Professor Lamb too if you want it.''

"I'm not interested in your other properties.''

"Why not? They're as good as the Washington.''

Pearlman hesitated, then said, "Well, the reason the people I represent want the Washington is because it's near to the Strong Mine.''

This rankled Stratton, and considering his mood, that wasn't surprising. "So that's it. You want the claim because you think that if Sam Strong found gold on his patch, you'll likely find it on mine.'' Stratton huffed, then said, "So, how much are these 'people' you represent willing to pay for the claim?''

Pearlman put on a poker face and said, "The truth of the matter is, Mr. Stratton, your claim is unproved. These last few days I've had an opportunity to examine the property and frankly, it looks unpromising.''

"Unpromising!'' Stratton's ire was growing. Maybe he hadn't found much gold, but when it came to mining, Stratton figured he'd done enough of it to know a promising claim from an empty hole in the ground.

Pearlman went on, "I'm prepared to offer you a thirty-day option on the property with five thousand down and forty-five thousand at closing.''

"Fifty thousand dollars for the Washington?''

"It is unproved,'' Pearlman reminded Stratton with a note of challenge in his voice.

Perhaps if his new boots hadn't taken such a beating, or if the animal people hadn't chased him up the mountainside, Stratton would have been more forgiving of Pearlman's assaults, but at the moment he was tasting bile. And the longer he dickered with Pearlman, the fouler the taste got. Yes, he wanted to sell the claims, but he didn't need to be talked down to by some fancy-pants fellow from San Francisco with a neat beard, fat stomach, and clean fingernails!

Pearlman added, "I think fifty thousand for an unproved claim is quite reasonable.''

Unproved claims were going for seventy-five thousand in the District, and it rankled Stratton that Pearlman thought him too stupid to realize that. Stratton wanted to sell out—he *needed* to sell out, and fifty thousand would go a long way to paying back the investors who had grubstaked him this far, but suddenly he did *not* want to sell to Pearlman. The man had rubbed him crosswise right from the start, and Stratton could be as stubborn as any man when he wanted to.

"The Washington ain't for sale."

"But you just said—"

"I changed my mind, Mr. Pearlman. I think there is gold there and I intend to find it."

"I was led to believe that you wanted to sell out rather badly," Pearlman pressed. "Fifty thousand is very generous."

"It ain't generous enough." Stratton paused, then an idea struck him. "But I'll tell you what I will do. I'll give you an option on the Independence for five thousand down and one hundred and fifty thousand in thirty days."

Stratton got a small pleasure watching Pearlman's mouth fall open. He figured that would get the man out of his hair, for one hundred and fifty-five thousand dollars was nearly twice as much as anyone had gotten to date for an unproved claim.

But it was Stratton who was rocked back on his heels the next moment when Pearlman sat down at his battered kitchen table and wrote him out a check.

Stratton was still sitting at that table an hour later, staring at the check in his fingers, when Casey rapped upon the open door and stepped inside his cabin.

"I heard you were back in the District," he said.

Stratton looked up. Mild shock was written all over his smooth, pale face, and Casey said, "What's the matter?"

Stratton handed him the check. "And that's just the down payment."

"Pearlman's been in town almost a week asking about the place."

"He wanted the Washington. I sold him the Independence instead for one hundred and fifty-five thousand."

Casey let out a long whistle. "You got some operating capital in this," Casey said, waving the check and handing it back to Stratton.

"One hundred and fifty-five thousand dollars! Can you imagine?"

"You're a rich man, Mr. Stratton."

"I suppose," Stratton said, but there was discontent in his voice, and Casey knew why. Although Stratton had enough money now to last the rest of his life, it had not come from pulling gold from the ground, but from a real estate transaction. For a mining man, there could be little satisfaction in that.

Stratton stood. "Well, Pearlman is going to have his crew here in the morning. I need to get my tools out of that shaft and move them over to the Washington."

"I'll give you a hand."

The Independence was sixty feet deep, with four crosscuts at around the fifty-foot level. He and Casey lit candles and entered the first cut, gathering up what few drill rods and hammers Stratton had left behind. They collected a shovel in the next crosscut, some gloves and an old lantern in the third. The fourth cut had been abandoned almost a year earlier and Stratton had been using it as a convenient place to store mine rubble and other clutter.

"Ain't nothing back there," Stratton said, loading the tools into the oar bucket and preparing to climb to the surface.

Old timbers, broken-up dynamite crates, and a pile of discarded tailings nearly filled it, but Casey saw that by flattening himself over the top of the rubble he could just get past it. "We might as well take a look while were down here, Mr. Stratton."

"All right, but I'm skinnier than you. I'll go." Stratton

squeezed himself through the gap. When he had disappeared, Casey gave it a try and found that by expelling the air in his lungs, he was able to just make it through. He lit a candle and crawled up beside Stratton. The crosscut was not deep and in a few moments they were at the back of it. Stratton found a drill rod. "Well, I reckon it was worth coming back here after all."

Casey sat with his back against the rock of the tunnel. A faint trace of daylight filtered down from above, through the gap at the top of the tunnel. It was cool down here, and pleasant. He was meant for this life beneath the ground, Casey reflected. Even before that summer so many years ago when he and his father and Bob Womack and a hundred other men came up here to dig that first trial tunnel, he'd found caves and dark ravines fascinating. It had always been impossible for Casey to pass by a hole in the ground and not stop to find out what was down it. After that summer in 1874, his future had been set in stone . . . literally.

Casey said, "What are your plans now?"

Stratton studied the rusty drill rod in his hand. "I don't know. This deal with Pearlman sort of puts a new slant on things."

"You can hire a crew and get to developing the Washington. You hit oxidized telluride, so you know there is gold there. Who knows—it might be right at your fingertips."

"And then there might not be another speck of it for a thousand feet." Stratton jabbed the drill rod at the side of the tunnel, absently flaking away chips of rock. "This mining business is all the luck of the draw, I'm convinced, Casey. Pearlman said he wanted the Washington because it was close to Sam Strong's mine, and this Independence ain't much farther in the other direction. Yet Sam's pulled enough gold out of his mine these last couple months that he went and bought himself a Texas ranch and took a trip to Europe. And here I sit, practically on his doorstep, and what do I find? Oxidized telluride! I tell you, Casey, it's sheer, plain, dumb luck." He jabbed the drill rod into the wall again, harder, and a flake of rock peeled away. "Well, I reckon I want to get out of here. It ain't mine any longer."

Casey hadn't really heard Stratton's last words, his view having been drawn to some newly exposed rock that Stratton had been chipping on. Casey caught his breath and levered himself forward, holding the light of his flickering candle near the chipped rock. "Look at this, Mr. Stratton."

Stratton brought his candle near as well. He stared, gulped, and glanced at Casey. "Telluride?"

"It sure looks like it."

Stratton began poking at it with his drill rod, and as he worked the outer edges, a thick vein came into view. Casey lent a hand, and inside of an hour they had determined that it was widening out. In the end, Casey and Stratton hauled out an armful of samples, replaced all the rubble at the front of the crosscut, and took the samples down to Guyot.

The samples assayed out at three hundred and eight dollars a ton, and Casey and Stratton calculated that the vein ran down at least a hundred feet—which worked out, in rough figures, to around three million dollars!

And Stratton had just sold it all to Pearlman for one hundred and fifty-five thousand dollars!

# EIGHTEEN

THE FOURTH OF JULY CELEBRATION THAT YEAR WAS THE grandest the District had ever seen. There was a big parade down the middle of Bennett Avenue, with the Anaconda Drum Corp at its head. The wealthiest members of society had taken spit and polish to their carriages and paraded them behind the Corps, men in new black hats and suits and ladies all trying to out do each other in their party fineries. Maureen felt conspicuous in her plainness, but looking around the crowd, she saw other women dressed in simple attire as well.

Revolvers fired into the air and long strings of firecrackers banged away in the street in anticipation of the fireworks to come. Street vendors selling taffy and baked pies lent a pleasant odor to the already festive air of the celebration and after the parade, Joe Moore's band entertained the people for an hour. Later in the evening they did a stirring rendition of ''The Star-Spangled Banner.'' Then, at the edge of town, the night sky exploded with a boom that shook the ground and the heavens rained red and green fire upon the people of Cripple Creek. White sprays with crackling sparkles brought cheers of delight from the crowds, but the big concussions of the red and white salutes that rocked the town were their favorite.

Maureen saw a drunken Jimmie Doyle being helped across the street into Johnny Nolon's Saloon by his partner, James Burns. Tomorrow the Three Jims would be sleeping in later that usual, she assumed. Jonce Barbee had been celebrating too, and Kitty was hauling him home by the ear, while Mabs and Margaret were having a grand time watching the boys set off firecrackers and buying candy from a roving vendor. The electric arc lights permitted the celebrations to continue long into the night. Maureen almost ran into Casey Daniels, but luckily she spied him first and turned around a corner until he'd passed her by. Even after all this time, her bitterness leaped to life whenever she saw Daniels. She always went out of her way to avoid him, and she'd bite her tongue when Margaret would come in and tell her that Mr. Daniels had spoken to her on the street or had bought her an ice-cream soda at the drugstore.

The party broke up around midnight with boastings and promises of an even grander celebration next year when, according to all reliable forecasts, the narrow-gauge railroad that was in the works from Florence through Phantom Canyon will have reached their growing city.

A few days after the big celebration, Maureen was beating a dusty carpet over a line strung between the house and the shed behind, when she remembered that James Burns had mentioned that the pantry needed restocking, and not to forget to pick up a bag of coffee beans. She went inside to make up her list for the grocer, taking an inventory of the supplies on hand and figuring out what was needed to fill the holes. That done, she took the peach can from the top shelf of the cupboard where Burns kept the grocery money and found only a nickel and four pennies at the bottom.

"Begorra, how do these men expect me to fill their larder with this?" she said aloud. She thought a minute. She was certain the grocer would extend her credit, but then she remembered the several months she'd spent living on credit, and how in the end it had cost her the Lucky Irish, the only real thing of value other than her house that Peter had left her. Credit had made her a slave to the lender, and after her experience with it, she had sworn it off, vowing never again to buy what she could not afford to pay cash for—even if, in this case, it was someone else's cash. There was only one solution, and Maureen set her feet for the men's claim.

She had never been up to the Portland claim, although she'd seen it from the road many times: a lone shack sitting up on Battle Mountain, with some clutter scattered about it—like so many other poverty-pits in the District. She knew that the three of them were up there somewhere, and she'd resolved that if James Burns wanted her to do his shopping for him, he could dig deep into his pockets and come up with the cash to see the chore through. He had warned her more than once against coming up to the claim and disturbing them, but she could see no other option at the moment.

Picking up her skirt to avoid the rocks and litter along the way, Maureen climbed the steep road to the shanty and knocked upon the door. "Mr. Burns?"

No answer.

She rapped again. "Mr. Burns? . . . Mr. Doyle? . . . Mr. Harnan?" Maureen pressed her face to a dingy windowpane. A curtain beyond it prevented her from seeing inside. Taking a turn around the little shanty, she saw that there was only one window and one door.

This is peculiar, she thought. Maureen tried the handle, and to her surprise the door opened. "Mr. Burns?" she said, stepping inside. It was dark, and there was a mustiness in the air that seemed heavily laden with dust. As her eyes adjusted she had the impression that this was the dirtiest, most cluttered shack she had ever entered. She took another step, stubbed her toe . . . and saw the truth.

Maureen gasped suddenly. What she had taken for clutter in the dusty half-light was a modified head-frame that reached to the ceiling of the shanty, and what she'd taken for dirt was just that—mounds of it filling every corner. And right in the middle of the floor was a hole . . . a big hole! She peered over the edge. It seemed to drop down forever into black nothingness. As her eyes adjusted, she caught the faint glimmer of candlelight coming from far below, out of a crosscut at the bottom of the shaft.

Maureen stood there, struck dumb by the sight, and in a few moments she heard the distant echo of their voices, as if out of a deep well.

Jimmie Doyle was scowling.

John Harnan wore a solemn face as he stared at Maureen from under narrowed eyelids.

Burns took a step or two across the tight confines of the shanty and turned briskly about on his heels. "I wish you had not come up here, Mrs. Kramer."

Maureen was sitting on a crate of dynamite, exactly where they'd discovered her upon emerging from the shaft. She'd merely looked at them curiously as one by one their faces had appeared above the edge of the shoring and their expressions had gone suddenly from flesh to stone.

"Why are you workin' this claim in secret?"

Burns glanced at his partners. Doyle looked away in disgust. Harnan gave a slight nod of his head. Burns said, "We have to, Mrs. Kramer, until we have taken enough money out of it to fight off the lawsuits."

"Why would you be havin' to fend off lawsuits, unless you were doin' somethin' that was not legal?"

Burns winced. "Well, strictly speaking, I suppose we are. Have you ever heard of the Law of Apex?"

Maureen admitted that she had not. "I'll tell you this much—the law is enough to cross the eyes of a New York lawyer," he finished.

"And to fatten his pockets," Doyle added gruffly.

"You see, Mrs. Kramer, on the side of a hill like this, mining claims are laid out like a patchwork quilt, and on paper one claim might overlap another in places. Well, what happens when you find a vein of gold? Who does that vein belong to?''

''It belongs to the man who discovered it,'' Maureen said. ''That only makes sense.''

Burns gave a short laugh. ''You're right, it makes sense, but that's not the way it works.''

Doyle broke in again, ''If it sounds easy, the lawyers step in and muddy the waters so's only they can understand what's going on.''

Burns went on, ''What happens if a vein happens to lie on a claim where another claim touches it, or even overlaps it?''

Maureen shrugged her shoulders. ''I still say it belongs to the man who found it.''

''And that's what we say too. But the Law of Apex says something else. You see, a standard lode claim in this District is fifteen hundred feet long by three hundred feet wide. The Law of Apex says that in order for a man to claim ownership of a vein, that vein must surface within the boundaries of his claim, and not only that, but if his claim is overlapped by another claim, that vein must also surface parallel to either the fifteen-hundred-foot side or the three-hundred-foot side. If instead it comes up parallel to the claim that overlaps yours, then that vein legally belongs to the other fellow, no matter how hard you've worked it. Of course, if no one knows you've discovered a vein, you can work it to death and hope you have the money to fight off the lawsuits once they begin to roll in— and a lot left over once the lawsuits are settled.''

''And that's what you three are doing here?''

Burns said, ''It's all we can do, Mr. Kramer. You see, we don't even own a standard lode claim. By the time we got to Battle Mountain, the whole blessed thing had been staked out! We searched every inch of this mountainside, measuring between other men's stakes, squinting at maps, questioning the U.S. deputy surveyors. Somewhere, we prayed, someone had made a mistake at laying out a line or measuring an angle, and sure enough, because some other fellows had shifted around their claims, they had. And here we are. It's a mere tenth of an acre! We are a little bit of a triangle on this mountainside, all squeezed in by other claims. There is the Black Diamond on one side, and the Queen of the Hills on the other. And down there a stones throw away is the Independence, and up there not but a few hundred feet is the Rattlesnake. And here we are, the Portland, a mere postage stamp of a claim, squeezed in amongst them.

"So you see, we had lost the game before we started. No matter what we found here, it was bound to be apexed by one of these surrounding claims."

"That hardly seems fair at all," Maureen said.

"It isn't," Doyle put in angrily. "And now that you know about it, everyone else will know too, and we'll be in court inside a week with not money enough yet to fight any kind of legal battle."

Maureen shot him a fighting stare and her blue eyes hardened. "Mr. Doyle, you have been opposed to me since the day I started workin' for you, yet I have done all I could to keep your house clean and put decent meals upon your table. Have I ever given you any cause to mistrust me? Do I not buy your groceries and return the proper change to the can? Have you ever come home to find somethin' of yours missin', including that fine gold watch which I fished out from between the floorboards and took into the watchmaker to have cleaned and put right for you?"

"Well," he hesitated. "Well, no."

"Begorra, man! Then why do you think I will turn against you now?"

"You mean you ain't gonna tell nobody?" Harnan asked.

She glared over at him. "It's your claim, it's your discovery, and however you choose to work it is none of my concern. I have been treated fairly by the three of you, and I will not do anything to hurt you."

Burns said, "Ah, Mrs. Kramer, you are a saint indeed."

"I wouldn't say that, Mr. Burns. But I am a fair woman."

Her voice changed, suddenly excited. "Is it a big claim?"

Burns said, "I'm not normally a bragging man, ma'am, but I'll not hesitate to venture that you are standing upon the mother lode of the District. So far we've banked almost seventy thousand dollars—and that's only what little we've been able to carry out on our backs and take down to the mill in Pueblo."

"Begorra," she said with feeling. Then the glimmer left her eyes and she recalled why she had come up here in the first place. "In that case, I don't suppose it matters that the peach can is empty, and so is your larder?" She put out her hand, and all three of them raced each other to fill it with coins.

Stratton rapped his fingers nervously upon the scarred pine tabletop in Casey's cabin as Casey worked the wire stoppers from a couple bottles of beer.

"Wish you had something stronger that this," Stratton gruffed, taking a long pull at the bottle. "What did you find out?"

For the last three weeks, Casey had been Stratton's eyes and ears at the Independence. He'd gone over there on the pretext of offering Pearlman his services as an engineer. Pearlman had already hired a certified mining engineer, but he was full of questions about the District which Casey was only too happy to answer. In exchange, Pearlman took him down into the mine and showed him the progress he had made so far. Casey had reported back to Stratton, and at each meeting Stratton had gone away less encouraged.

"They are still working the three open crosscuts," Casey told him, "but Pearlman isn't getting the results he'd hoped for. I think he's getting a little desperate. From what I gather, the investors he represents expect a big return on their money, and Pearlman is determined to give it to them. He's doubled his crew and is working them overtime."

"And the fourth crosscut?" Stratton asked.

"Pearlman intends to open it up next week."

"Next week is when his option expires!"

''He's a driven man, Mr. Stratton. I don't expect he's going to leave any stone unturned before his thirty days runs out.''

Stratton stood and strode around Casey's little cabin, his fingers flexing at his sides.

''If I'd only checked out that crosscut one more time before signing that damn option!''

''You had no way of knowing.''

''Damn luck! She's against me at every turn. She's always been against me!'' His fist slammed down upon the table, bouncing the bottle there.

Stratton had every reason to be drawn up into knots. He was sitting on a bomb whose fuse was already burned down. Pearlman was bound to find that rich vein once he sent men into that last crosscut, and when he did, he'd exercise his option and Stratton would have let the discovery of a lifetime slip through his fingers.

Stratton fell back into the chair, drumming his fingers. He finished the beer and said, ''I don't know why I let myself get so worked up. It ain't as though there is anything I can do about it.''

''Only a rock wouldn't be upset over what happened, Mr. Stratton.''

Stratton rolled the bottle between his palms a moment, then asked, ''How's that claim that you've been working?''

''It has promise. In fact, I'd apply for a patent on it if the claim were in my name.''

Stratton's thin white eyebrows lifted. ''Really? You've taken money out of that hole?''

''Enough to put food on the table. I've opened an account and have banked about eight hundred dollars.''

''Have you told her?''

''I couldn't if I wanted to. Maureen Kramer makes it a strict practice to keep out of my way.''

''She's been working for James Burns.''

"I know that, but I don't think showing up there would be the thing to do . . . yet."

Stratton studied him a moment, then a tight grin moved across his face. "You've got an eye for that woman, don't you."

Casey hadn't realized he'd been so transparent. "Well, no, er, what I mean is . . . I'm concerned about her, that's all. Life isn't easy for a widow woman, and if I can do anything to help her out . . ."

"Even if she doesn't want to be helped out by you?"

It was time to change subjects. Casey stood, took his hat from a peg at the door, and said, "I need to drive into town. You want to come along?"

"Sure, I'll ride along with you. If I stay here I'm only going to fuss and fret like an old woman."

Casey hitched up his horse and took the wagon into Cripple Creek. As they entered the town, he spied Margaret and her friend Mabs alongside the road, carrying an empty dynamite crate between them. He drew up next to them.

"Good morning, ladies," he said.

"Morning, Mr. Daniels," they answered.

"What you got there? Looks like dynamite."

"It's empty," Mabs said.

"We are going to use it for a table," Margaret added.

"A table? Well, how far are you hauling it?"

Mabs said, "To our play-cave, by Pisgah graveyard."

"Play-cave?"

"Yes," Mabs said. "It's where we take our noon tea."

Casey grinned. "That looks like it will make a fine table for your noon tea."

Margaret frowned. "It's kinda rickety, but it will do till we find a better one, Mr. Daniels."

"Well, it appears mighty heavy. Why don't you put it in back of my wagon and climb aboard. Mr. Stratton and I will carry it to your play-cave for you."

The two girls conferred, then said together, "All right."

They lifted it over the edge of the wagon and climbed up after it.

Stratton was a personal friend of the Barbees, and included Jonce in his small first-name-basis group. "How is your pa, Mabs?" he asked as the wagon started up again.

"Pa is fine, though Ma says he works too hard up at his diggin's."

"Has he made his strike yet?"

"No, but he says he's mighty close. But Ma says he ought to have listened to you and taken out a claim on Battle Mountain like you done."

Stratton gave a small wince that passed quickly. Then he was smiling again.

"Well, maybe your pa done the right thing after all."

The road climbed up towards the graveyard on the rocky side of Mount Pisgah, then swung north in a sudden tight curve. Here Mabs stopped Casey and she and Margaret hauled the box down into a ravine. Stratton and Casey climbed down as well and peeked in on the little hollow. It may have been carved out by blowing wind, but Casey thought it more likely the result of water that had flowed at one time.

The cave was about four feet deep, with a sturdy shelf-rock roof overhead. The girls had brought in empty paint cans for chairs, and a discarded box that was divided into compartments and might have once held printer's type, but now contained spoons, forks, and chipped teacups and saucers. Not a single piece matched the other, but Casey figured that didn't matter to the girls, who seemed quite proud of their play-cave.

The girls were setting up their new table and spreading a scrap-rag tablecloth over it when Casey and Stratton left them and drove back to town.

All the next week W. S. Stratton felt like he was up a tree with a wildcat above him and a grizzly bear below. His nerves were strung as tight as a Comanche's bow. He drank too much whiskey and slept badly. He'd pounce on Casey as soon as the engineer showed up at his cabin after working the Lucky Irish, and pump him for information on Pearlman's progress.

"Has he started into that last crosscut?" would be Stratton's first question.

Casey was beginning to be able to tell the time of day by it.

"Not yet." His answer was always the same, but tonight he had to add, "But he says he's about ready to try. All that's been holding him up is that he has divided his men into three crews, each working one of the crosscuts. He's more or less certain that if there is gold to be found, it will be in one of those three cuts. He's hesitated taking men out of there to start fresh on the fourth crosscut, especially since over the past twenty-eight days it's become even more cluttered with the castoffs of their work. But now he says he may be ready to."

"What am I going to do, Casey? This waiting is about to tear me apart."

"Why don't you just come out and ask the man his plans?"

Stratton looked over with a snap that should have wrenched his neck. "Are you daft? You know I can't chance showing any interest in what he's doing."

"You don't care what he's doing there. As far as you're concerned, the Independence belongs to him, and good riddance. All you care about is when you are going to get your money—or if you are going to get it."

Stratton had a reputation for ice under fire, but since this affair with the Independence, he had lost his nerve. This deal had struck too close to home . . . and his wallet. "What are you driving at?"

"When does the option expire?" Casey asked.

"Day after tomorrow."

"He's running out of time, Mr. Stratton. Pearlman thought he'd plucked a star, but now he's thinking he's holding a handful of manure. Maybe it wouldn't hurt your chances any if you make him believe that you think the mine is worthless as well. He's into you for five thousand dollars already, and he can't get that back, but if he's half the businessman he ought to be, he might be ready to cut his losses and leave. Besides, at this late date in the game, your interest in what he's doing is only understandable. After all, he still owes you one hundred and fifty thousand dollars.''

Stratton's thinking started to clear. ''Yeah, it would be like I'm only interested in getting my just dues.''

''Exactly.''

''I . . . I could invite him to dinner. Say tomorrow night. If he is truly discouraged, I might be able to convince him the mine ain't worth keeping.''

''It might be worth a try,'' Casey said.

''I'll do it. If nothing else, I'll get the straight of it from his own mouth and I'll know one way or the other what he intends.''

The invitation was sent out immediately, and Pearlman agreed to meet Winfield Stratton for dinner that next night. Stratton chose the Palace Hotel—the former J. H. Wolfe—for the meeting. When the time grew near, he dressed in his only black suit, which he kept in a trunk. He polished his boots, brushed his hat, and, steeling his nerves, walked stiffly down Bennett Avenue to the corner of Second Street. Under the wide porch that hugged two sides of the brick hotel, Stratton paused to check his reflection in a window. Satisfied that he looked relaxed, and that his tie and collar were in order, he entered the Palace Hotel.

# NINETEEN

STRATTON PROCURED A TABLE IN THE DINING ROOM AND tried to ignore the churning inside his gut. Pearlman arrived some minutes later, looking a little hazed, as if he'd just dashed off from his mining endeavors, with hardly enough time to plunge into clean clothes and tug a brush through his still dusty hair. Dinner began with both men guarding their thoughts, but as it progressed past the roasted duck, steamed vegetables, and mashed potatoes, then made its way into the chocolate mousse, they began to relax, if only slightly.

Stratton put forward a confident face and told Pearlman he was anxious to cement the deal and be out of this town, where men, he said, went broke at the rate of one hundred to one. Pearlman only frowned and dug dourly into his dessert. Stratton's stomach was in such a turmoil that he fought down the urge to vomit with each bite of his meal. He forced himself to follow each mouthful with a wide, fancy-free smile. Playacting had never agreed with him.

All and all, the meal was a disaster . . . but a perfectly well-mannered disaster, with all the rubble hidden beneath a facade of gentility, which both men had brought along by the bucketful.

Afterwards they had whiskey, and this alone did more to melt the wall than all the duck and mousse had. They took their drinks out to the lobby and settled in hard, straight-back cane chairs near a big fireplace in which pine logs crackled. The fireplace was always lighted, even on summer evenings.

"The District is certainly growing," Pearlman started off with forced optimism.

"Growing full of men going broke," Stratton answered, trying to sound indifferent about the matter, and hoping his hand didn't tremble noticeably as he sipped the whiskey.

Had Stratton blinked he would have missed Pearlman's brief frown, but seeing a glimpse of Pearlman's carefully guarded soul, he pressed on, "Yep, more men lose money in the mining business than make it. You and I both know that, don't we. It's a risky business, and I think the time is right for me to be getting out of it. Right now everyone is swimming in a pool of euphoria—snatching up anything they can get their hands on, driving prices clean out of sight. Yep, the time is right. Sell high, my pappy always used to say . . . and this real estate market has just about peaked."

Pearlman cleared his throat. "Well, if indeed mining property has peaked, you wouldn't know it by all the activity on the exchanges. And look at how this city is growing. A *city,* by Godfrey! Yes, I'll say it again. A city! Why, I've not seen anything like this in all my travels. Oh, boomtowns come and boomtowns go, but this Cripple Creek—now, *this* has the feeling of permanence."

"Perhaps, but I'd like to see what would happen if the price of gold collapses, or if there happens to be a bigger strike down the road ten miles. Then we'd see what kind of mettle this 'city' is made of."

"You really think so?"

Stratton shrugged his shoulders. "Right now we've got a whole lot of hope keeping the bubble afloat. The town's only three years old; it hasn't been tried by hard times yet. But look at the matter from another angle. Of all the hundreds of mining operations going on in the District, only a handful are producing capital. A couple on Battle Mountain, a few on Bull Hill, some scattered here and there. And not a one of them has hit the mother lode. Don't you see, it's that mother lode that keeps men digging at worthless pits, that keeps bringing miners into the District. All those other people, those shopkeepers and barbers and freight men, they are only here because of the miners. What does a cow pasture need with a grocery store, or a cobbler? No, Mr. Pearlman, I think this town's bubble is about to burst, and I'm right pleased that I'm getting out before everything falls in around my ears.''

Stratton finished his speech, shaking in his freshly polished boots. He hadn't believed a word of what he had just told Pearlman, and he hoped it didn't show.

Pearlman tried unsuccessfully to shake off a gloomy face. The course of events over the last twenty-eight days had tempered his optimism. ''I'm almost ready to agree to your theory, Mr. Stratton. I've worked my men like mules in the Independence, and the assay work I've had done shows a pitiful return on the money already invested.''

This was precisely what Stratton had hoped to hear, but he kept a tight rein on his emotions and frowned. ''It's like I said, a few men strike pay dirt—the real kind that puts men to work and builds towns. The rest of them scratch out a meager living, not knowing from day to day if they are going to make payroll, or be able to pay off the suppliers. It's a hard business, Mr. Pearlman.''

Pearlman stared at the flames leaping in the fireplace by his elbow, the dancing light flashing amber on the cut surfaces of the whiskey glass in his fingers. ''You know, Mr. Stratton, I've looked over every inch of your Independence and have come out empty-handed. Tomorrow I'm going to put my men into that abandoned crosscut, because I've only one day left on my option.'' He hesitated, and Stratton held his breath.

''Dammit all, it's been a financial disaster for me and my investors. The wires I've been getting from San Francisco have been most unpleasant. I hate to spend another day's wages throwing good money after bad."

Stratton restrained his excitement. His heart leaped; his breathing caught. But the somber frown he showed would have done a riverboat gambler proud.

Pearlman stared gloomily into the dancing flames. "See here, Mr. Stratton. I've had enough of this place. Cripple Creek has grown old and hard to wear. I'm going back to California, and I'd just as soon be out of here tomorrow morning after laying off my crew. Will you take back my option?"

Stratton started to speak, but the lump in his throat got in the way. He managed to say, "Tonight?"

"Yes, tonight. Right now."

Stratton's wildest hopes appeared to be coming true. He had played Lady Luck's game and won! Still, he could not risk telegraphing this to Pearlman. Stratton's normally soft tones were even more subdued at that instant because of a sudden lack of moisture in his mouth and the shoe-leather tongue that got in the way. "I reckon I wouldn't object to taking it back."

Pearlman pulled the option from his pocket and pushed it at him, but Stratton's hand was trembling so badly he was afraid to reach for the priceless paper. If Pearlman noticed his agitation now, he might reconsider. Stratton sucked in a breath and said, "Why . . . why don't you just drop it into the fire?"

That said, the world stopped spinning for an instant of time. The paper fluttered above the crackling logs, caught a moment on an updraft of warm air, and then was sucked down into the flames.

The Independence was his again!

Looking back on it much later, Casey figured the summer of '93 was a turning point for the city of Cripple Creek; one that had rotated upon a three-pronged pivot. The Western Federation of Miners had been formed in Montana and within weeks had extended it octopuslike tentacles down into the mining camps of the West, and into Cripple Creek in particular, establishing the first major linchpin in that town's development. A month later W. S. Stratton had sold the Independence, struck gold the same day, and gotten the mine back, all within thirty days.

Two major linchpins in as many months!

The day after Pearlman filed the option on the Independence in the fireplace at the Palace Hotel, Stratton hired Casey on, along with a crew of seven other men. The following day they were down clearing out that crosscut that Pearlman had ignored. Within weeks Stratton's crew had grown to nineteen and new buildings were being designed, contracted for, and erected on the property. Meanwhile, arrangements had been made with a smelter down in Pueblo, and the Independence was gearing up for full production.

The news of Stratton's discovery up on Battle Mountain took less than two days to make its way through the entire District, and within three days, the *Gazette Telegraph* reported this latest strike to an eager Colorado Springs audience, who were always looking for one of their own sons to do well in the gold camp.

Casey put off work at the Lucky Irish for the time being. Stratton's mine filled every waking minute those first few weeks. He sensed something important was happening; Stratton's vein of gold had already taken on such proportions that it appeared to be on the verge of eclipsing every other mine in the District. But Stratton kept the true breadth of his vein a secret from everyone except Casey. He had plans, plans that were huge, and they all hinged on hiding the true wealth of the fabulous treasure beneath his claim until he had pulled enough money out of it to put the wheels in motion.

But it wasn't until the middle of August, a mere two weeks after the soot of Pearlman's option had been shoveled out onto the ash heap of history, with production just beginning to roll at the Independence, that the third linchpin in Cripple Creek's development fell into place.

Casey and Stratton had been in Stratton's cabin around midnight, studying a set of engineering drawings that Casey had just completed, when some little distance beyond the open window they heard a noise, then a thud as something heavy fell to the ground.

Stratton glanced up from the drawings and listened. "You hear that, Casey?"

Casey went to the window, stuck his head outside, and looked around. "There's somebody out there."

Stratton grabbed the shotgun he kept by the door and they went outside. Stepping quietly, they followed the soft grunting and cussing, which grew louder towards the road. It seemed to their ears that there was a struggle going on.

Casey and Stratton split and approached the scene from converging angles. Casey came out onto the road a little below the sound, while Stratton stepped into a patch of moonlight a little above it. Between them lay something in the shadows.

They closed in on it, only to discover that that "something" was James Burns, squirming on the road beneath a collection of heavy sacks.

"Mr. Burns?" Stratton said, hardly believing his eyes. "What are you doing there?"

"Stratton," he gasped, looking up helplessly from the roadway. "I tripped, dammit. Help me up."

Casey and Stratton took an arm between them, but it wasn't easy. It felt like he weighed half a ton, and when they had hauled Burns to his knees, Casey said, "What's all that stuff you've got strapped around your chest?"

Burns fumbled with the buckles. "Rock," he said. The harness fell away with a thump, and the two men helped him the rest of the way to his feet.

"Rock?" Stratton said, staring at the pile of canvas bags at his feet. "What the hell you doing in the middle of the night hauling rock around?"

"It's a long story, Stratton," he said, disgusted.

"Are you all right?" Casey asked.

"I think so. It just knocked the wind out of me."

Stratton said, "Come on over to my cabin, Mr. Burns, and sit a while. I'm in the mood for a long story."

In the darkness, Casey saw Burns hesitate, then say, "Oh, why not? You're bound to find out anyway, now."

Back inside the cabin, Stratton dragged another chair over, took down a bottle of rye whiskey, and set three glasses around. He put an inch in each and, sitting down, he said, "Now, what are you up to?"

When Burns finished telling them about the discovery at the Portland, and of the wealth he and his partners had been secretly mining for almost a year now, Stratton was thoughtfully silent, but the wheels were turning in his brain. Stratton said finally, "You aren't going to get out of this without a big fight, Mr. Burns. Once the other mine owners get a whiff of what you've got, they'll lay on a pile of lawsuits that would choke a dinosaur. How much do you have put away?"

Burns shrugged his shoulders, and his mouth was a tight line beneath his long white mustache. Looking at the two men sitting with him, Casey was struck by the similarities. They both had hair as white as snow, with sharp, pale eyes. They were both quick-witted yet thoughtful. And although it wasn't apparent now as they sat there looking at each other, Casey knew that they shared a sincere heart that wished to do good by the District and the mining men who worked there. In that regard, they were like the bighearted Johnny Nolon—only their occupation was different.

The ways in which Burns and Stratton differed were mostly superficial. Burns's head sat upon his wide shoulders like a wedge-shaped block beneath a thatch of white hair, while Stratton's face was more elongated, and finely sculpted, with thin white hair receding deeply from his temples. Physically, Burns was a bigger man, and where Burns was known to make decisions quickly and plunge ahead, Stratton was the consummate architect, toying with an idea, turning it over to examine all sides, making his plans slowly and methodically. But once they were made, Stratton pursued them with the doggedness of a Comanche hunter. Only five years separated these two men, but Stratton looked half as old at forty-five as Burns did at forty.

"We've banked something around seventy thousand dollars," Burns said.

Stratton fell back into a thoughtful silence, then said, "You'll never hold on to the Portland with only seventy thousand."

"Are you planning the first lawsuit, Stratton?"

This took Stratton by surprise, and a moment later his blue eyes shined and he laughed. "Burns, you are a friend, and I wouldn't do that to a friend. I'm going to tell you something, something I've kept secret until now. My Independence is going to make me rich."

"We know that already."

"Ah! But nobody but a handful of men know *how* rich." Stratton grabbed the engineering drawings off the table and turned them over. On the blank back side he made a sketch of the two mines and said, "Your Portland and my Independence are sitting on the two ends of the same vein, Mr. Burns, and all this mountainside in between them . . . it's all bonanza ground!" His pencil made a big circle and stabbed the middle of it, crushing the lead. "I intend to control Battle Mountain, and the whole District. There are riches beyond belief here, but I'm not interested so much in the money as I am in making that money work for the good of the District, and the mining men in it. And that means keeping the speculators and promoters from swindling the honest mine owners."

Burns gave him a blank look. "I don't follow."

Casey knew that Stratton had been making plans for something big from the day he got the Independence back from Pearlman, but he had no idea what those plans might be. He was as in the dark about them as Burns, and just as curious.

Stratton said, "There are few owners in the District that I trust. Mostly those men who came up here when Cripple Creek was nothing more than a dream and a cow camp being overrun by a bunch of tenderfoot businessmen from the Springs. There are the Bernard brothers—I trust them—and Ed De LaVergne, Bob Womack, and a few others. And yourself. On the other hand, there are some I don't trust any farther than I can spit—in particular, that Denver wheeler-dealer.''

Casey knew Stratton was talking about Dave Moffat, a banker and railroad man. Moffat was buying up every mine he could find on Bull Hill and consolidating them as the Anaconda mine. He was also planning to bring the first railroad into the District, from Florence by way of Phantom Canyon. He had designs on controlling the whole District, and Stratton had remarked more than once that money-grabbers like Moffat were a danger.

''So what are you proposing, Stratton?''

''A partnership . . . with a man I can trust. You on the one side, and me on the other, and between us we will own all of Battle Mountain and have enough influence to control the destiny of this town.''

Casey whistled softly. Burns was speechless.

''Well, what do you say?''

After a moment Burns answered, ''I say it's a mighty bold plan, Stratton. And a mighty enticing one. But I'm going to have to talk it over with my partners first. I'll let you know in the morning.''


''Where have you been?''

Lisa Kellerman paused on the staircase with one hand upon the polished walnut railing and looked back. Oliver Sawyer was standing at the foot of the stairs. The electric lights from the saloon put half his face in shadows and glinted off his thick eyeglasses.

''Oh, it's you.''

Sawyer's huge eyes blinked behind the lenses. ''Yeah, it's me. Remember me? Your partner? The fellow who bankrolled this place?''

Lisa was tired, and in no mood to have another fight with

Sawyer, especially here in the middle of a public staircase. "What's eating you, Olly?"

"You are. You and your late-night drives. I thought we had a deal? I thought it was just you and me?"

Lisa came down the stairs and dragged the end of her yellow feathered cape under Sawyer's jutting, pugnacious chin. "What makes you think anything's changed, sweet pea?" she cooed.

"A blind man can see you've turned to ice these last couple months. Tell me the truth, Lisa: Have you got yourself another beau?"

If he was hoping to see her squirm, even just a little, he was going to be disappointed. She looked him in the eye and said, "I'd never think of it, sweet pea."

"Then let's go up to your room so as you can show me just how important I am to you."

Lisa pressed the back of her hand to her forehead. "Not tonight. I've got this pounding headache—I really do. I'm going to bed—alone, Olly." She flashed a mischievous smile. "But if you are real nice to me tomorrow . . ." She let that veiled promise linger in the air as she turned back up the stairs and wearily climbed to her quarters on the second floor.

Once safely secured behind her locked door, she undressed and filled a tub with hot water. The bath made her sleepy. She always came back from LaFarge's cabin worn out and feeling gritty. How long, she wondered, was she going to be able to keep her secret from Olly? LaFarge was becoming more demanding of her time, and she was beginning to truly look forward to their clandestine rendezvous.

*Why do I find men like LaFarge and Olly attractive?* she wondered. *What is so irresistible about wicked men?*

Lisa never understood why she was so fascinated by the dangerous life when other women sought security in gentle, ordinary men. She dried and powdered herself, looking at her tall, lean figure in the full-length mirror. After all these years, her waist was still small, her stomach flat, her breasts full and absolutely devastating to men—well, to some men. LaFarge was one of those who appreciated such assets in a woman.

Lisa slipped into a dressing gown and poured herself a drink. The tension of the day slowly drained away. When she had finished the whiskey, she turned to the water pipe by her bedside, filled it with the yellowish-brown powder from the tin she kept in her dresser, and let the friendly smoke remove any further worries from her world.

At the bar, Sawyer told Cal to set out two beers. He took them over to a whirling roulette wheel where a man named Liam O'Mally was standing with his hands shoved deep into his pockets. O'Mally was a big Irishman with a reputation for having an explosive temper. At the moment, though, he appeared placid enough, watching the little ball spin round and round, clicking wildly until it plopped into one of the seats. The men around the table groaned or snickered, money changed hands, and the wheel was spun again.

"How are you doing at the wheel, Liam?" Sawyer asked.

O'Mally looked over, and with a heavy Irish accent said, "I ain't playing, Mr. Sawyer. Ain't got no money no more. Spent it all."

Sawyer grinned. "That's the only reason to work, isn't it? To spend what you make?"

"I don't know 'bout that. I seem to be digging me a hole I'll likely never climb out of."

Sawyer laughed and handed him one of the beers. "Here, this one's on the house, Liam."

The Irishman was surprised, but grateful, and after a long drink he wiped the foam mustache from his upper lip and said, "This is mighty decent of you, Mr. Sawyer."

"Well, I appreciate hardworking men like yourself. The salt of the earth, I always say."

"I'm hardworking, no question about that. As far as the rest of that, well, I've been accused of being salty, especially when I get fighting mad."

"Really? Never would have thought so, Liam."

O'Mally grinned, showing a mouth missing half its teeth. "It's the sure truth, Mr. Sawyer. I've got fists of steel and a noggin like a pile of bricks."

Sawyer said, "Don't you work over at the Rattlesnake for Phillip LaFarge?"

"Yep, that's the outfit I carry my lunch bucket to every morning."

Sawyer took him by the arm and walked a few paces from the men and the racket of the spinning wheel. "Tell me, Liam, how do you like working for LaFarge?"

"You want the straight of it? That man is a son of a bitch. He works us like slaves, pays only two dollars and seventy-five cents a day, and is talking of tacking on an extra hour with no more pay."

"Why do you stay?"

O'Mally laughed. "Ain't got much choice. Like the other mines around, LaFarge has lent us money to get us through the tight spots, and in return I put my mark on a paper that says I got to work for him till it's paid off. Except that day will never come."

"Tough deal, Liam." Sawyer paused a moment then said, "Didn't I see you up at Smith and Peters' Saloon the other night?"

"Sure you did. I seen you there too."

"John Calderwood was talking about his union, and organizing the men," Sawyer said. "Are you thinking of joining?"

"I'm thinking about it. Ain't done nothing about it yet."

Sawyer glanced at the empty beer mug in O'Mally's hand. "You've hit bottom. Want another?"

"That's real decent of you, Mr. Sawyer."

They started towards the bar. Sawyer said, "I think it would be a smart thing for you to sign up." Sawyer signaled Cal and slid O'Mally's empty mug across to him. "You know, I'm all for the miners organizing. It's high time they take back control of their lives, and put an end to men like LaFarge pulling all the strings. I'd like to find someone to be my eyes and ears in the mines—I think I can be of some help. You know, I've made some pretty good money here, and it's men like you that I have to thank for that. This would be sort of my way of paying you fellows back." Sawyer grinned. The beer mug came back, full, and O'Mally swallowed deeply, then happily sleeved another foam mustache from his lip.

Sawyer said, "Well, I reckon I ought to check on my tables. So long, Liam." He started away, then turned back and said, "You know, it just occurred to me that you might know of someone who wouldn't mind keeping me informed as to how the organizing is going. Think you'd know of someone who'd do that for me, Liam?"

O'Mally hoisted his beer. "Hell, Mr. Sawyer, I'll keep my ears and eyes open for you. And I think I'll go up to Altman and put in with Calderwood too. I'll do it tomorrow, after my shift lets off."

"That would be just fine, Liam. And I won't forget you, either. Unlike LaFarge, I treat my business associates fair. Stick with me, friend, and you'll see just how good."


The morning after Stratton had discovered James Burns face-down on the road with two hundred pounds of rock on his back, Harnan, Doyle, and Burns were at the bottom of the Independence mine, hunkered down with thick candles flickering in their fists.

Harnan said, "I ain't never seen anything like this."

In a matter-of-fact voice, as if he were merely discussing building an addition to a house instead of digging riches from the earth, Stratton said, "Once I'm in full production in another week or two, I calculate I'll be taking two thousand dollars a day out of this shaft."

Burns looked at his two partners and said, "So, what do you think?"

Doyle said, "It's every bit as rich as our discovery."

"Richer," Harnan said, amazed by what he was seeing.

Stratton said, "We've got the mother lode, boys—the real thing. But either one of us alone don't stand much a chance of hanging on to it. I'm in a better position than you three, it's true, but just the same, if we throw in together, we'll sew up this mountain tight as a whalebone corset. So what do you say? Throw in with me, and I'll be your silent partner. I'll take a third interest in the Portland, and I'll match your seventy thousand dollars. Then I will hire us the best lawyers money can buy."

Burns said, "You know, boys, what Stratton says is true. There is no way we can hold on to our claim against the vultures of Battle Mountain once the word gets out. I'm for throwing in with Stratton."

"But a full third share?" Doyle complained.

"A third is better than losing it all," Harnan said.

Doyle considered the deal a little longer, but they were in a tight spot and slowly gave a nod of his head. "Me too."

They closed the deal with a handshake, which is all that honorable men have ever needed between them. The next day Burns filed for a patent, hired on a crew, and began openly working the mine, although they still hauled the ore out at night, by wagon now, to keep their secret from getting out a little while longer.

They did manage to keep the lid from blowing off the whole month of September. Then, one night in October, the freight wagon they were using broke an axle. The next morning the owners of the surrounding mines discovered the freighter sitting there in the middle of the road, loaded down with high-grade ore, and a red-faced Jimmie Doyle on the seat, shivering in the cold, guarding the goods.

Their reprieve had come to an end, and by the middle of November the lawsuits began pouring in.

In the beginning, twenty-seven people filed claims against Burns and company. The Three Jims and Stratton arranged a tactical meeting at Burns's cabin a few days later. Stratton brought along a fresh-faced real estate wheeler-dealer by the name of Verner Reed, and in the chill November afternoon, they tramped down from the mine office to the little cabin on Wilson Creek. Stratton asked Casey along because of his knowledge of how the vein was running and his understanding of whose prior claims were the most serious and had to be dealt with first.

Stratton rapped upon the door. It opened and Maureen Kramer was standing there, wearing an apron over her long, gray wool dress. Her view settled momentarily upon Casey, and the winter temperature instantly plummeted several degrees more. She had no alleyway to turn down now, no shop to step into this time. Casey was again riveted by her beauty, although the eyes she directed towards him were ice. He was aware of a longing stirring within him that he had tried over the past year to silence. If he could only break through that arctic exterior, he thought, if she only knew the truth—but how would she ever learn that, when she refused to give him the time of day? And she'd never believe anything he told her about the accident anyway, he told himself.

From inside the cabin Burns's voice called, "Come on in, gentlemen." Maureen stepped back to let them pass, and closed the door after them. They gathered around the table and Stratton introduced Reed. "I think you might all know each other already," he said, and as Reed was a local businessman, they did.

Burns came right to the point. "Just what can you do for us, Mr. Reed?"

Verner Reed, for all his youth, had already made a name for himself in real estate, and a small fortune in the Colorado Springs market, as the sharp cut of his tailored suit and the heavy gold watch chain that draped the flat belly of his vest reflected. He was the sort of man to whom money came easily, and was spent just as quickly. Reed opened his briefcase and laid a three-inch-thick pile of papers upon the table.

"Gentlemen," he said, "Mr. Stratton was kind enough to drop these by the other day. I've read through the claims against your property, and frankly, the way you are positioned now, when these claims go to court, they are going to yank the carpet out from under you."

This momentarily stunned them into silence. Stratton, who was already prepared for a good long fight, said, "That is pretty plain, Mr. Reed. That's why we hired you. What do you propose?"

"How are you four positioned financially?"

Stratton said, "Between us we have a quarter of a million dollars . . . so far."

Casey was watching Burns, Doyle, and Harnan. They hadn't blinked when Stratton had mentioned the sum, so apparently this was shared knowledge among them. Both mines had been working at a fevered rate since August, and considering the richness of the veins, it wasn't surprising that they had doubled their capital, especially in view of the oncoming battle.

"That's a good start," Reed said.

"There's more," Stratton went on. "Irving Howbert has given me an open line of credit. No limit."

This news did catch the Three Jims off guard. Their heads snapped around and their mouths took a dive.

Irving Howbert was one of the earliest settlers in the region, having arrived in the 1860's with his father, a Methodist minister, to look for gold. Irving's checkered career had started at age fourteen, hauling lumber to the mills in the mining camps near South Park. He and his father moved to Colorado City a year later, and young Irving began hauling lumber from the Pinery north of the present site of Colorado Springs to build homes in Colorado City before Colorado Springs was even a far-off twinkle in General Palmer's eye. With a few more years under his belt, he went into farming and claimed land of his own that later would be called "The Garden of the Gods," so named because some locals thought it would be a grand location for a beer garden.

During the Indian trouble, Irving fought the Arapaho along the Front Range, and in '64 joined the temporary Third Colorado Volunteers and was part of the Sand Creek Battle. Irving was a staunch supporter of Chivington and today will tell you that Chivington's troubles came not from the battle, but from the lies his enemies in uniform told of him afterwards.

After the Indian trouble passed, Irving Howbert became the El Paso county clerk, and from there his civil service career seemed secure. He finally resigned that job when El Paso County became too big to handle from his shoe-box office. The location of the county office, along with all the functions of the county, shifted from Colorado City to the growing town of Colorado Springs on her doorstep, and Irving's brother, Frank, took over the job of county clerk while Irving went on to head the powerful First National Bank in Colorado Springs.

It was from this position of financial strength that Irving issued his longtime friend, W. S. Stratton, a blank check to fight the battle ahead.

Reed rubbed his palms and a glint lit his eye. "Gentlemen, I believe we have a fighting chance here, but it's going to take some fancy footwork to come out of this on top."

"Whatever it takes, Reed," Doyle said, and the other men nodded their heads in agreement.

"Right. The first thing we have to do is throw the dogs off our trails. Set them yapping up the wrong tree while we start chipping away at their foundations." Reed took a paper from his briefcase and spread it before them.

Doyle took one glance and said, "What is this?"

"This is an option, Mr. Burns. You three will option the Portland to Mr. Walter Crosby for two hundred and fifty thousand dollars. I've already arranged this with Mr. Crosby."

Burns looked at Stratton, and Stratton gave him a brief nod. Doyle and Harnan were not sure about this either. "Are we selling out?"

Reed grinned. "No, you are laying down a false scent trail, that is all."

It was plain that the Three Jims were confused, but also that Stratton knew full well what Reed was up to. It made Casey wonder what else Stratton was planning that he wasn't mentioning yet.

They signed the paper. That done, Reed threw open the throttle and started the engine rolling towards the most stunning business deal of the century.

# TWENTY

ON HIS WAY OUT OF THE CABIN, CASEY TURNED AND SAID TO Maureen, "Have you been getting along all right, Mrs. Kramer?"

Maureen had been gathering up the coffee cups. She stood there a moment as Burns, Doyle, Harnan, Stratton, and Reed filed out into the crisp November afternoon, and then just the two of them were left. "I am managin' to make my way, thank you."

Casey had hoped there might be a flicker of warmth in her response, but her words were as brittle as the skin of ice on his water barrel that morning. Still, he felt that if he could press on beyond the wall she had thrown in front of him, she might hear him out. He couldn't help what his heart felt, and although he knew there was little chance of patching things up between them, he had to at least try.

"It was most fortunate that Burns needed help here."

"Help? It was only charity he was offerin' to me. I know that, though Mr. Burns will never own up to it. It was charity in the beginnin', but afterwards, he and his partners saw I was worth the cost to them. A clean house and good food will change the minds of most men."

Not knowing what to say to that, Casey went on awkwardly, "H-have you replaced that canvas roof on your house yet? The sun will rot the material in a year or so."

"I have not," she replied, taking two cups to the counter by the sink.

"You know, I've been doing a little work at the Lucky Irish. The claim shows signs that with some development work, it might be turned into a paying proposition. There isn't much money yet, but there is enough to replace that roof."

Her back was towards him. He saw her stiffen, and when she turned, her eyes had reddened. She blinked away moisture and said, "That claim is yours now. I want no part of it. I do not need your charity on top of Mr. Burns's. Now please, leave me alone." She wheeled around and began throwing cups into the sink.

Casey winced at the anger in her voice. He fingered his hat a moment, put it upon his head, and turned towards the door. Then he stopped and said, "Oh, I saw Margaret a while back. She and her friend Mabs showed me their play-cave house over by Pisgah. She is growing into a real fine girl. You ought to be proud."

Casey stepped out the door before she could reply. He had tried to chip a hole in the ice, but there was little headway to be made when Maureen still believed him responsible for her husband's death. And until she had softened enough to allow him to explain that, he could do nothing but wait.

Once Reed put his scheme into gear, events began unwinding at a reckless speed. The twenty-seven wolves yapping at the Three Jims' door were suddenly cast a hunk of red meat that to their surprise landed on the doorsteps of Mr. Walter Crosby, a rich real estate broker who had played this game before. While they circled, trying to decide who they were supposed to sue now, Reed slipped in unnoticed and began buying up all the smaller claims.

With a fistful of Battle Mountain mining claims, Reed turned the tables on the surrounding mine owners and threatened to sue them on the grounds that he now held prior claims. The fighting ground turned bloody. The big pack leaders pushed their suits, with LaFarge, McKinnie, and Peck at the forefront. They had forgotten about Burns, Doyle, and Harnan. The big game was Crosby, and they chased him right up a tree, landing him in court, exactly where they wanted him.

On court day, however, Crosby slipped their snapping fangs by surrendering his option back to the Three Jims. The wolves were again left clawing at the wrong tree. They did a couple of quick circles, then set their red eyes once again on Burns, Doyle, and Harnan. But before they could leap, Reed snatched the bait from under their nose one last time. He dissolved the three men's partnership and immediately incorporated them as the Portland Gold Mining Company.

While the wolves came to a halt, stunned by this move, the Portland Company announced a ninety-thousand-dollar dividend and share prices shot to the moon. In an instant, the Portland Gold Mining Company became one of the richest companies in Colorado.

The mine owners on Battle Mountain were scattered and helpless. They knew the sound of the specter of defeat knocking upon their door. With tails drawn up, they pleaded for a meeting with Reed. When it was all over, the floor was slick with their blood. In the end, they all sold out to the Portland Gold Mining Company . . . all but Peck and McKinnie, and Phillip LaFarge, who dropped his lawsuit but managed to hang on to his Rattlesnake mine.

The Portland mine had gone into the fray a mere postage-stamp size of a claim; what emerged was a powerful corporation sitting atop 183 acres of high-grade ground. And while this stunning development had riveted the attention of all the District, Winfield Scott Stratton had quietly hired a lawyer by the name of J. Maurice Finn, who had gone unnoticed into the business of buying up all the claims surrounding Stratton's

Independence, Washington, and Professor Lamb. In all, Finn's clandestine activities added 112 acres to Stratton's growing wealth.

The axe had fallen, and it was a sad Christmas for many that year in Cripple Creek. But one of the year's unfortunate victims, however, had had nothing to do with the startling events happenings at Battle Mountain . . .

Bob Womack had been drinking heavily, which was not unusual for the old cowboy these days. He'd been crying too, which was unusual and the tears made shiny streaks down his cheeks. Among his problems, he had been sick for almost a month, holed up in his cabin in Poverty Gulch, with the *ladies* of Myers Avenue bringing up pots of chicken soup to help him through the bout. This only reconfirmed Bob's gut feeling that all women were wonderful, and Katie bar the door if any man should make an unseemly remark about one of the "soiled doves" of Myers Avenue!

He was embarrassed that Johnny Nolon should see him in such a sad state, and he quickly brushed the tears from his gaunt, sunburned cheeks, forcing a smile. "Cripple Creek ain't what she used to be," he said, sniffling and scrubbing his long nose with the sleeve of his jacket.

Johnny sat on the barstool next to Bob. "She sure is different from when you were up here, scouting out your float trail all those years by yourself. Why, it is like night and day. There are nearly ten thousand people in the District, with a dozen little towns all over just to hold them all. And that isn't bad, is it? Why, Cripple Creek is a modern city. Look at what we have. We've electricity! Most towns back east still don't have that. A central water system too. And almost every store in town has a telephone. Now, you name me one place other than your big cities like Chicago and New York that can boast of all that."

"Oh, it ain't that, Johnny. I think Cripple Creek is a grand place. I'm proud of her, as if she was my own kin."

"Then what is troubling you?"

He winced and took another drink. "She's outgrown me, Johnny. She don't need me anymore. She's gotten so big that she does everything on her own now. When a man digs up a likely-looking rock, he takes it to one of her assayers. When a greenhorn comes to town to stake a claim, first thing he does is check in with one of the real estate brokers. When I walk down the street I'm just another face; nobody knows it was me who first found gold here, and what makes matters worse, they don't care no more." Bob sniffed and brushed at his eyes.

Johnny put a friendly arm about Bob's hunched shoulders. "Cripple Creek is like a child that grows up and moves on. Maybe the newcomers don't know all about what you did for this town, Bob, but we do—we who were here in the beginning. You did a wonderful thing, and I'll tell you this, Bob— and you can write it down in a book—history will remember you. A hundred years from now, schoolchildren will read that it was Bob Womack who discovered the greatest gold camp this nation has ever seen."

Bob managed a faltering smile. "You really think so?"

"Think so? Bob, I know so!"

Bob felt a little better, then his spirits plunged again and he swallowed some more whiskey. "And what do I have to show for it all? A bad liver, gout, and empty pockets."

Johnny thought a moment. "I know you, Bob, know you better than you might think. The money is not all that important to you. It never has been. Oh, it would be swell to hit a big strike and be sitting on top of the world like Stratton and Burns are now, but that wasn't why you spent all those years looking for gold, following that elusive float trail."

"It wasn't?"

"No. Not at all. You did it because you believed in something. You believed that there was gold west of Pikes Peak, while everyone else snickered and said, 'There goes Crazy Bob again with his nose to the ground and his head in the clouds.' You knew that what you believed in your heart was right and true, and the devil take the rest of them. And you know what else?"

"What?" Bob was feeling a mite better.

"You proved them all wrong, and you were right. You made them eat crow, while you went on to become famous."

"Famous?"

"Well, isn't that what you are . . . or will be? It wasn't the money that was important to you, Bob. It was following a dream. And now that the dream has come true, I'd say that your job is finished here. It's time for you to go on to bigger and better things."

"Yeah, bigger and better things." Bob was feeling quite a bit better. He pushed himself up straight on the barstool and for the first time he managed the affable grin which had always been Bob Womack's trademark.

Johnny slapped him on the back again and told him he was going to check on his business, but that he'd be back later to see how he was doing. Bob consumed another glass of whiskey, and in a little while he had drunk himself back into a pit of despair. The more Bob drank and thought, the more depressed he became. Finally, he found his way outside again and stomped a crooked path in the snow up to his cabin, where he rummaged around a bit until he located what he was searching for. With the claim papers to his Womack Placer mine in hand, he retraced his footsteps, which had almost filled in with drifting snow. He made it as far as Mother Duffy's Buckhorn Saloon and ordered up another drink.

Mother Duffy squeezed behind the bar, looking more man than woman with her big arms, short neck, and ruddy skin, and gave him careful study. "You're already drunk, Bob. Get yourself home before you fall in a snowbank and freeze to death."

"Jes' one more," Bob pleaded.

"Not a drop from my bar, Mr. Womack! I know ' 'tis the season,' but I think you've had about all the celebrating your system can handle for one season. You come down sick again and my gals will be out cooking you soup and babying you instead of taking care of business here.''

Bob was going to protest, but then he remembered why he had come back into town. He got off the stool, bracing his elbows upon the bar as he looked out across the crowded saloon floor. He thought he saw Christmas decorations here and there, but his eyes weren't focusing very well now. He cleared his voice.

"Hey, ever . . . everybody, listen to m-m-me.'' He always knew when he was really drunk because that confounded stutter came back. Drunk or excited—both conditions brought it on. He waved an arm and got the attention of a couple men at a table nearby.

"Who the hell are you?'' someone asked.

Bob tried to focus on the face of the man who had asked that in order to tell him, but before he could someone else said, "That's Bob Womack, you jackass. He's the man who discovered gold in Cripple Creek.''

"That . . . that's right,'' Bob said. "I was first here, and now I . . . I'm gonna be the fi-first to go.''

"What are you talking about, Bob?'' another man asked.

Bob waved the claim paper in the air. "I'm selling out, boys. Gon . . . gonna have an auction today.''

"What are you auctioning?'' a voice called out.

"My mine. The Womack Placer. It's a paying con . . . concern, and I'm sellin' out. Wh-what am I offered?''

"I'll give you fifty dollars.''

"Hell, I'll give you fifty-five, Bob,'' a husky voice countered.

"I know the place,'' someone in the back of the room said. "It's worth at least two hundred and fifty.''

"You're all taking advantage of the poor fellow. Can't you see he's in a spot? I'll give you four hundred dollars for your claim, Bob,'' another man put in.

Mother Duffy came up behind him. "Do you know what you're doing? Stop this foolishness now before you wake up regretting more than that hangover you're going to have.''

Bob ignored her and said, ''Do I hear four . . . four-fifty?''

The auction was generating some excitement and men began bidding, running the price up a few dollars with each offer. It finally reached four hundred and ninety dollars. Bob pushed the bid, but it seemed stuck there, and then someone offered five hundred dollars.

Bob tried to raise the bid. ''Ain't I got no better offer?'' he pleaded. Even drunk, he knew the claim was worth more than five hundred dollars. But no one was willing to go a penny more. Finally Bob said, ''Goin' once . . . goin' twice . . . goin'—''

''I'll give you five hundred dollars and a bottle of whiskey, Bob!'' someone yelled out at the last moment.

''Sold!''

Bob high-stepped his way through the snow towards Dave Moffat's Bi-Metallic Bank, making slow but steady progress and leaving a wildly meandering trail in his wake. He clutched the unopened bottle of whiskey firmly under his left arm and five one-hundred-dollar bills in his right hand, and he drew up at the bank as it was about to close.

''Looks like you just made it, Bob,'' the clerk said, sliding behind the counter and back inside his cage. ''What can I do for you?''

Bob set his bottle on the counter and slapped the bills next to it. ''I want to change these, Lenny.''

The teller collected his money and said, ''Sure, Bob. What do you want?''

''One-dollar bills.''

Lenny blinked. ''You want five hundred one-dollar bills?''

Bob swayed, grabbed the cage, and grinned crookedly. ''That's whats I wants, Lenny.''

''Well, all right. It will be a minute for me to get the cash from the vault.''

''Takes all the time yous wants. I gots all day.''

Lenny stepped into the vault directly behind the teller cages, and a few minutes later came back with five bundles. He began to count the bills, but Bob stopped him and said it wasn't necessary. He gathered them up, filled his coat pocket, and then, plucking up the precious bottle and anchoring it under his left arm again, swung himself around and back-stepped into the teller cage. Sorting out the direction, Bob ducked his head and set a course for the door. Lenny hurried ahead and got it open just in time.

"Are you all right, Bob?"

"I'ms jes' dandy, Lenny," Bob said in passing. "Merry Christmas."

"Merry Christmas to you, Bob."

The cold air outside slapped him across the face, sobering him slightly. Bob set his feet towards home, and sometime later that afternoon he fell through the door of his cabin and managed to get it closed and latched before passing out across his bed.

Bob was still drunk Christmas morning when he awoke, and still bundled up in his heavy coat. The angle of the sunlight through his window told him it was almost noon. His tongue felt as large as his boot, and just as tough. He craved water more than life itself, hardly aware of the cold that had filled his cabin. The fire in his stove had gone out hours ago and the oak water bucket in the corner wore a skim of ice. Bob cracked through it with a tin cup and sat on the floor drinking water until he could hold no more. His mouth was still a dry desert. He stood and grabbed his head as needles drove through it, then with nature urgently pushing at his bladder, he made his way outside to the privy behind his cabin.

He consumed another half dozen cups of water, then sat at the little table wanting to die. When he spied the still unopened whiskey bottle, his stomach suddenly wrenched and he dove outside just in time, vomiting upon the pure snow. Afterwards, he felt marginally better. He boiled himself an egg and fried up some bacon. By two o'clock he was almost fit to be seen in public, and shrugging back into his coat, Bob looked at the fistful of money he'd gotten from the bank and remembered what he intended to do with it.

Christmas afternoon found Bob Womack on the corner of Bennett Avenue and Fourth Street. Men, women, and children were visiting with each other, exchanging Christmas cheer, and enjoying the warmth of a bright sun in the clear mountain sky. The storm had passed sometime during the night and already snow was melting from the roofs and cascading off the eaves. Bob smiled, shook hands, and tried as best he could to be cheerful. To the first child that came by, he handed a dollar bill.

He did the same to the next, and then the third, and shortly there was a line of children down Bennett Avenue, each receiving a dollar bill from Bob. He didn't notice it right off, but after a while, the children began getting taller. The line never seemed to end. The children became taller, and crustier, and soon Bob discovered why. They were all rejoining the end of the line and coming through for seconds . . . and thirds! And he now saw that behind those scarves and hats pulled low were men. Full-grown men had squeezed the children out of the line!

Bob's anger flared and he swung a fist at the next man to stick out a greedy hand. He went down, and two others jumped Bob. What was left of the five hundred dollars was scattered in the wind, and as the two fellows pummeled Bob, a dozen more dove into the street raking in the tumbling goods.

By the time Sheriff Pete Eales arrived, Bob was out cold and the bullies had disappeared. Johnny Nolon rushed from his saloon and across the street to help. He and Eales hoisted Bob between them and carted him back to his cabin, where Nolon and a lady from Poverty Gulch by the name of Easy Esther nursed his wounds.

"I think Bob has had it with Cripple Creek, Pete," Johnny said. They looked at Bob and Bob looked back out of an eye nearly swollen shut. Bob knew that Johnny was right. It was time to leave.

Pete said, "Do you want me to wire Miss Lida?"

Reluctantly, Bob nodded his head.

The next day Bob's sister, Eliza Womack, arrived from Sunview, the family ranch. Bob was in a pitiful state, weeping and moaning about his bad fortune. As usual, Eliza took the matter under control—as she had the affairs of Sunview for the last twenty-five years.

"Bob," she said after changing his bandages and feeding him a bowl of soup one of the ladies of Myers Avenue had left for him, "I'm selling off what is left of the ranch."

"What will you do, Lida?" he asked.

"I'm going to open a boardinghouse in Colorado Springs, Bob, and I'd like you to be a partner in it with me.

"Me? I don't know nothing about boardinghouses," he moaned. "I'm a miner."

"Not anymore, Bob," Eliza said gently but firmly. "Your mining days are over, and it's time to do something else with the rest of your life. And besides, Bob, I need you to help me. We'll do a good job at this new business. I've already bought a piece of land on Cascade Avenue. There will be new people coming into the city all the time, and don't you think they are going to want to meet the man who first found gold in Cripple Creek?"

Eliza was a stern disciplinarian, with a brain for business that put most men to shame. But she knew the human heart as well, and could always find the right thing to say to Bob when he was down. In a little while he took to the idea, and by the end of the day Bob was grinning again and telling Johnny Nolon, who had stopped by to check up on him, that he and Eliza were going to open up the finest boardinghouse in all of Little London!

Johnny only grinned, and winked at Miss Lida. The next day, Bob and Eliza climbed aboard the stage for Colorado Springs. When they drew up in town, a boy hawking newspapers was shouting.

"Come read all about it here in the *Gazette Telegraph*! Cripple Creek's first millionaire!"

Bob looked at Eliza as they stepped down from the stage-coach. "I wonder who that is."

Eliza dug a nickel out of her purse and gave it to Bob. "Go buy yourself a copy. I can see you're dying to know."

"I'll bet you it's the Count . . . or maybe—"

"Go buy the newspaper and find out."

Bob skipped down the street, exchanged the nickel for a paper, and began reading as he walked back. For a moment Bob looked up with his eyes glazed over and a longing in them as though he were hearing the siren's call. His big Adam's apple bobbed and he said, "It's Mr. Stratton, Lida! It says here 'Mr. Stratton can write a check in six figures.' "

"What are you thinking, Bob?" she asked with caution in her voice.

Bob was not certain what he was thinking at first. His emotions were all scrambled up, as if a drunken operator was working the exchange of his brain. Then he rolled up the newspaper and, grinning, handed it up to the stagecoach driver and said to Eliza, "I think I feel mighty sorry for poor old Stratton. Look at all that money he's got to worry about now, Lida. I don't envy him one bit! No, I surely don't."

Bob took Eliza's traveling bag in one hand and his own in the other, and started off for the livery stable.

# TWENTY-ONE

FOR MANY OF CRIPPLE CREEK'S CITIZENS, SEEING THE OLD
year out was good riddance, but baby 1894 crawled onto the
same scene dragging along with it some pretty grown-up problems. The miners unions were growing stronger, and their de-
mands louder. Among other things, they wanted three dollars
a day for eight hours—at a time when the mine owners were
considering extending the work shift to nine hours with no
raise in pay.

Some saw this growing tension as a tinderbox. Oliver Sawyer saw it as his way of finally tearing LaFarge from his lofty
perch—one that LaFarge, and LaFarge alone, had managed to
keep intact while all the other independent mines on Battle
Mountain had fallen beneath the hammer blows of the Stratton, Burns, Doyle, Harnan cartel.

LaFarge worked his men like oxen, by day, and paid them
like slaves, and at night he continued his secret meetings with
Lisa Kellerman at his cabin up on the Rattlesnake mine, paying her lavishly for her services with handfuls of double eagles
from the mine's heavy cash box in his safe.

Sawyer was busy as well, plying the workers with free whiskey, and using O'Mally's influence to urge them to join the union and stir up discontent. Early one evening towards the end of January, Lisa came down the stairs and heard a commotion coming from the barroom. The roulette wheels were strangely silent, and in their place Sawyer's voice was booming, his words drawing from the crowd the drunken cheers of men working themselves up for a fight.

"Now, I will ask you again," Sawyer shouted, "does any man among you figure he's got to put up with that kind of treatment?"

"No!" was the collective cry.

Lisa stepped quietly around the corner. Sawyer was standing atop a table with at least forty men circled around him. Moving through the crowd was Barney Mays, a bottle of whiskey in each hand, making certain that no glass had a chance to run dry.

"He runs a slipshod operation. No man here can forget that it was the Rattlesnake that caved in two years ago and killed all those men—some of them friends of yours. To top it off, now LaFarge expects you to work for lower wages than Burns is paying at his Portland or Stratton at his Independence!"

O'Mally said, "It's too bad that Burns and Stratton didn't yank LaFarge off of the Rattlesnake like they done to all the other mine owners on Battle Mountain."

A roar of agreement filled the saloon. Sawyer waved his arms for silence and shouted for order. When the men had settled down, Lisa saw the sly smile that came to Sawyer's face. "LaFarge was too big for Stratton to pull down, so maybe it's up to you men to do something about that!"

"What are you saying, Sawyer?" asked a man named Bert, a mucker at the Rattlesnake.

Sawyer grinned. "Ain't telling you boys what to do now, but if it was me mucking out a mine shaft for two dollars and seventy-five cents a day, I'd be seeing red. I'd likely tar and feather that man, and if he gave me the least provocation, I might throw a rope around his neck. I wouldn't hang the son of a bitch, mind you, but I'd sure scare the shit out of him.''

Lisa knew that if this drunken crowd ever got to putting a rope around LaFarge's neck, they'd not stop until the deed had been done . . . and she knew that Sawyer understood this as well. He was planting a seed and watering it deeply with free whiskey. But why was he whipping these miners into such a frenzy, and why would he turn them loose on LaFarge, unless . . . He must know about her secret meetings! That had to be it. Barney carried another couple of bottles of whiskey from the bar. It wasn't going to be long before Sawyer had these men so drunk and worked up that they'd charge out to the Rattlesnake. She didn't know for sure how far they would go, but she had a feeling that they would not stop until there was blood on their hands.

Lisa hurried out into the failing late afternoon light, pulling the wool shawl tightly around her shoulders as she ran up the street to the livery. It had been a warm day, but now the temperature was falling, and the snow in the streets was beginning to freeze into icy ridges.

''Hitch up my buggy,'' she told old William Krenshaw, who at that moment was in the middle of shoveling out the stalls.

''Yes, ma'am,'' he said, setting aside his shovel and puffing his warm breath into the cuffs of his leather gloves, then rubbing his palms together. Lisa paced the livery, waiting for Krenshaw to bring her horse forward from one of the back stalls.

''Hurry it up, Bill,'' she said, her impatient demand accompanied by a cloud of frozen breath.

''Kinda cold to be taking a drive tonight, Miss Kellerman,'' he said, backing the animal into its traces.

She hadn't planned it this way, and was about to say so, but instead she bit her tongue and clutched the shawl tighter.

''Here you go, Miss Kellerman,'' he said finally, carrying

the reins forward. Lisa climbed up onto the cold seat, turned the phaeton out the wide doors which Krenshaw had swung open for her, and rolled out into the cold evening. Once out of town she cracked the buggy whip and urged the horse into a gallop along the icy road. It was risky pushing the animal under these conditions, but she had no way of knowing how long it would be before Sawyer would have the miners worked up to where they would descend on LaFarge.

She rattled down through Squaw Gulch, passed the little town of Lawrence on her right, and at Battle Mountain turned up the road towards the Rattlesnake, drawing to a halt at the mine office.

LaFarge appeared in the doorway, surprised at first; then the sharply cut features of his face settled into a tight smile. "I wasn't expecting you today, but the surprise is a pleasant one."

"It won't be once you hear what I got to say, LaFarge." She pushed past him and stood by the stove, opening her shawl to capture its heat. The door closed and LaFarge stood behind her. A cloud of cigar smoke broke upon the back of her head and swirled around her.

"You sound ominous, my dear. To what exactly *do* I owe the pleasure of your company on an evening like this?"

She held her palms near the stovepipe and, without looking back, said, "You have made a lot of enemies in this town, Phillip."

He gave a short laugh. "Businessmen always have enemies. I manage to handle mine."

"You only just barely scraped by with Stratton and Burns."

"True, but I did. That's the point. I'm the only mine owner that *did* scrape by."

"So far. You still won't know where you will end up until all the lawsuits are done with, and that could take months. But the 'point' is, Phillip, against those two, you were dealing with men of honor. It's going to be different this time."

He grabbed her roughly by the shoulders and turned her around. His dark eyes narrowed, and she had a sudden vision of a feral wolf. His face was all angles, his mouth a hard, straight line, broken only by the cigar clenched in his teeth. "Just say what you got on your mind, Lisa."

"All right, Phillip. I don't know how . . . or when, but I think Olly has found out about us—about our secret meetings up here in your cabin."

He relaxed and laughed. "Olly has nothing over me. He knows that I'll tell the sheriff exactly what happened to that mining engineer, Elvin Tate, a few years back."

"That would likely land you in jail as well, Phillip."

"Maybe. But Olly won't chance laying a hand on me. We both have too much to lose now."

"You're so confident, Phillip, so damned arrogant and confident. I don't know why I bothered to come out here and warn you. Well, you aren't going to easily talk your way out of this one."

"What do you mean?"

"I mean that Olly isn't stupid, Phillip. He doesn't intend to get his hands dirtied by you. Right this minute he is raising a mob. He's filling them up with free whiskey and their heads with notions about tar and feathers, and a rope around your neck. I have heard that mining men have been hanged from their own head-frames before, and the way Olly was stoking the flames of hatred against you, it's only going to be a matter of time before they fit a noose to your neck and swing you out over the main shaft of your precious Rattlesnake mine."

His expression changed, and when he removed the cigar from his teeth the grin had vanished completely, replaced with a smoky gaze that couldn't quite hide the concern behind it. "How many men has he got?"

"I don't know, but the saloon was pretty full. Maybe fifty, most of them men from right here. Their leader was a big fellow by the name of O'Mally."

"O'Mally? I know him. He's been going to those meetings in Altman, listening to the words of that man Calderwood and making trouble."

"Your trouble is only just beginning, Phillip. O'Mally joined up with Olly and Barney a few weeks ago, and—" She stopped suddenly, for all at once it was clear to her. "And now I think I know why. Olly must have been planning something like this for a long time." She gave a short laugh. "It all makes sense. Olly has more subtlety than I gave him credit for."

LaFarge's thoughts were elsewhere. "Fifty men, you say?"

"It might have been a few more, or a few less. What are you thinking?"

He pulled at his chin as he glanced around the mine office. Then he went to the door and called to one of the miners passing by. "Hitch up my carriage for me and bring it around here to the office. When you finish that, go find Sam Stepton. He should be down in the mine somewhere."

"Yes, sir, Mr. LaFarge," the man said, reversing his steps and heading to the corral and barn down on the edge of the claim.

"Phillip," she said sharply, "What are you planning to do?"

"This may be a good time to retire from the mining business, my dear. My position here is precarious at best, what with Burns and Stratton now at the reins and their lawyers ferreting out all the remaining claims on Battle Mountain. Besides which, as you so aptly pointed out, a mob of drunken miners can be most unhealthy."

"You're just going to up and leave?" Lisa could hardly believe what she was hearing.

He took a carpetbag from the closet and began filling it with a few items. She followed him into the back room, where his bed was . . . where they had spent so many nights together wrapped in each other's arms in mad, wild pleasure. He shoved some clothes into the bag, grabbed a heavy wool frock coat from off a peg. Back in the front office, LaFarge placed his humidor of cigars on top of the pile and shut the bag.

"It is only a temporary setback, my dear. I'm sure in a few days this will all blow over and I'll be back. In the meantime, I'll find a nice hotel somewhere in the Springs. I need a rest anyway."

"Take me with you," Lisa said suddenly.

He stared at her, smiling faintly. "I don't think so. This is where we part company for a while."

"But Phillip, you can't leave me. Not now that Olly knows."

LaFarge went to the safe and spun the lock, working the combination. "You'll make out. You're like me—a survivor."

"But you don't know how Olly can be when he's mad!"

"Don't I? How do you think I got this mine? You don't think Cantwell just handed it over to me, do you?"

Lisa recalled the story he told of how Sandie Cantwell had been accused of murdering a man by the name of Mueller on the Santa Fe Stage. Mueller had been found with a knife in his gut, and Cantwell was the only suspect until LaFarge stepped in with an alibi. It was out of gratitude, LaFarge had told people later, that Cantwell had sold the Rattlesnake mine to him.

"Olly?"

"Olly and Barney. They were two thugs I picked up in Denver. I snatched Olly out of a paddy wagon, and Barney from a gutter on Larimer Street. They seemed a perfect match. One had brains enough to follow orders, the other was too drunk to care. When we heard Cantwell boasting at Ben Requa's general store about this mine he'd just bought, I figured it was something I had to get my hands on. Olly and Barney were only too happy to help . . . for a piece of the action. It was Olly who distracted Mueller, and Barney who plunged in the knife. Barney has always been partial to knives." LaFarge laughed when he saw the shock on her face. "You mean in all those 'business meetings' between you and Olly, he never told you that?"

"No," she said softly. "I knew about Elvin Tate, but not this."

He pulled open the safe door, lifted the heavy cash box out, carried it across the room, and muscled it onto the desk. "Yes, it could go badly for you, my dear—if I know Oliver Sawyer. If indeed he is heading up here now with a band of drunken miners to do me in, you had better make yourself scarce. He will not take kindly to finding you here and me gone. He's not stupid. What do you think he'll do if he learns that it was you who warned me?"

"So that's it? Not even a thank-you? Just hurry me out the door and tell me, 'It's been fun'?"

His dark eyebrows lifted. "It *has* been fun."

Lisa's heart was being torn from her. "Please, Phillip, take me with you. I . . . I thought you loved me."

He laughed. "Lisa, I *did* love you. I loved you just as hard and just as often as I could. Like every other man that has passed through your wretched life. What did you expect? Fidelity? Honesty?"

"But Phillip—" She grabbed his sleeve. "Please don't do this to me. I love you."

"You love money, and I have given you that. Your business gives you more money than you will ever need."

LaFarge put his hand upon the big black cash box. It was decorated with fine, golden scrolls and secured by a large padlock. "We are alike in one respect, you and me—we love the same thing."

"Please don't leave me here, Phillip. I won't cause you no trouble. Take me with you."

He heaved his arm back and threw her off.

"Get out of here now, Lisa. Get out while you are still able," he growled.

Lisa stared at him through her tears. She blinked them from her eyes, then stood up, clutched at the doorjamb, and said, "I really thought you cared. I really did."

"Good-bye, Lisa," he said flatly, holding the door.

She gathered her shawl together, and went out into the night. The tears that glistened in the moonlight grew cold upon her cheeks as she climbed aboard her phaeton, turned the horse, and drove away.

The man brought LaFarge's carriage around and parked it in front of the mine office. "Now find Sam," LaFarge told him, setting his carpetbag on the vehicle's floorboards. He went back inside the cabin, and from his side desk drawer took a Smith & Wesson revolver, checked the loads in the cylinder, he kept it loaded with five rounds. He pushed his arms into the heavy frock coat, then hefted the cash box by its two iron handles and hauled it out to the carriage, setting it on the floorboards next to his bag.

From his vantage point high up the side of Battle Mountain, LaFarge could see the soft glow of the lights of Cripple Creek in the distance, and here and there he was able to get a glimpse of the road. The sky was clear at the moment but to the north a heavy bank of gray snow clouds was rolling in. But so far a large moon still reflected off the new snow, showing LaFarge the line of wagons and horses making its way through the little settlement of Elkton, about a half mile off.

"So," he said aloud, "she was telling the truth."

He hurried back inside and from the safe took a black book in which he'd written conflicting information in the event that some nosy auditor should decide to examine the mine's account books. Then he rifled through a bin of engineering drawings and found the one that showed the vein running from his Princess' Necklace drift straight up into the Black Diamond mine. He'd made a pretty profit working that vein right under McKinnie's and Peck's noses, but now that the Portland had taken it over, there was no sense in leaving incriminating evidence lying around. LaFarge intended to return when tempers cooled; the mine was still his, and he was not of a mind to freely relinquish it. He'd deal with Sawyer later, but first he had to put some distance between himself and that horde of drunken miners.

He crumpled the drawings and shoved them into the stove along with the book, then watched the flames crawl through the paper. He drove his carriage to the edge of the claim and left it at the back road that crossed over the Portland and down the east side of Battle Mountain, and walked back to the office. Sam Stepton was waiting for him.

"Sam," he said quickly.

"Rodney said you wanted to see me? I was just on my way home."

"I'm glad I was able to catch you before you left."

"What's the matter?"

"We have some trouble coming our way."

"What's sort of trouble, Mr. LaFarge?"

"I've just had word that a drunken mob is on their way up here to the Rattlesnake. The men have been complaining for months about not making enough money, and that troublemaker O'Mally has been stirring them up. Now it seems they are coming to take the mine's payroll."

"Have you sent word for the sheriff?"

"I sent a man for Mr. Eales just a few minutes ago, but he won't get back here in time." LaFarge paused and listened as down below the rattle of wagons and the hoofbeats of horses grew louder.

"What are we going to do?"

"I've a plan, Sam, with your help. I've already put the payroll aboard my carriage, but I need time. The men respect you, Sam. You can stall them for me while I make for town and get the gold somewhere safe."

"I don't know if they'll listen to me."

"Of course they will. I just need enough time to get on the road to Cripple Creek. That's all."

"Well . . . I can try."

"Good man." He parted the curtains and could see the lights of dozens of lanterns, and a large company of men. "They're almost here. You stall them for me, Sam."

"I'll do what I can."

LaFarge rushed into the back room and lifted the window sash. He heard an impatient banging on the door as he hitched his leg over the sill, and then he was outside. A few hundred feet later, LaFarge looked back and saw a swarm of men crowded around the front of the mine office. He began to breathe easier, and the hard line of his mouth hitched up at the corners as he climbed aboard the carriage and whipped his horse into motion.

He rattled past the new buildings on the Portland mine, over the sprawling complex of the Independence, and finally out onto the road, where he turned west and cracked the buggy whip. The scattered lights of Lawrence fell away past his left shoulder as the carriage raced along the frozen roads towards the lights of Cripple Creek.

James Burns raised a glass to the people who had crowded into the new general office of the Portland Gold Mining Company. The building had been the first to go up on the new mining operation, and he and his partners had spared no expense. Electricity had been run up from Lawrence, and a telephone wire connected the mine to the exchange in Cripple Creek. There was a telegraph wire as well, running into the mining exchanges, although the ticker machine had yet to be installed.

"I know this may be a little premature, what with all the lawsuits still unsettled, but I want to propose a toast to my partners, the esteemed Jimmie Doyle and the honorable John Harnan! And of course, to the noble and good-hearted Mr.

Winfield Stratton, without whom none of this would have ever happened!'' Burns was already feeling his whiskey, as were most of the other men there.

''Here, here,'' the guests rejoined. The guests included the Three Jims and Stratton; Verner Reed—the architect of the coup; Stratton's lawyer, J. Maurice Finn; Irving Howbert, who had bankrolled much of the battle; Sam Strong, who had just sold his Strong Mine and bought the Free Coinage over on Bull Hill; Sam and George Bernard, longtime friends of Stratton from Colorado Springs and owners of a controlling share of the Elkton mine; and J. R. McKinnie and Frank Peck of the Black Diamond, with whom the Portland's lawyers were still negotiating an agreement because of an Apex suit that had not yet been resolved. Frank Peck was engaged to Burns's sister, Mary Anne, and everyone involved in the legal dealings figured that could only help cement the final business agreements.

Casey Daniels was the final guest at this celebration, and he was certain that his presence was the only thing souring the happy event . . . and that only because Maureen had been placed in charge of the affair, and Margaret had been conscripted to help out as well. Both mother and daughter were wearing crisp new store-bought dresses for the event—purchased on the Portland Gold Mining Company's account, of course.

After the speeches, and drinks, and several platterfuls of hors d'oeuvres which Maureen had spent all afternoon putting together, the business associates retired to Burns's office and got down to a strategy meeting which was the underlying reason for their having all come together tonight.

Casey spent some time chatting with Mary Anne Burns while her fiancé was away with the men in Burns's large office. Although Mary Anne was an entertaining conversationalist, Casey's thoughts, and his view, kept wandering, and inevitably they would end up on Maureen Kramer. When

Frank Peck stepped momentarily out of the office, looking vaguely bewildered at what must have been some high-powered planning going on inside, Casey took the opportunity to say good-bye to Mary Anne, and make his way over to a table where Margaret was carefully consolidating the various leftover delicacies onto one silver platter.

"That has to be the prettiest dress I've ever seen, Margaret,"

"Thank you, Mr. Daniels. Mommy and me picked it out. Mr. Burns said we could buy anything that we wanted to at all and charge it to his account."

"Mr. Burns is a fine gentleman."

"Mommy says he's the 'top cream' when it comes to men."

Casey caught Maureen glaring over at the two of them. When Maureen discovered that she had been spotted, she whirled around and took a tray of dirty whiskey glasses into the kitchen.

"I certainly would have to agree with your mother on that. You know, *she* looks pretty too."

"Someday I will look like her."

"Yes, I am sure someday you will."

Margaret grinned and went back to arranging the finger food. Casey looked toward the kitchen and grimaced. He knew what sort of reception he'd receive, but just the same, he went and stood in the kitchen doorway.

Maureen glanced over and said simply, "Yes? Is there somethin' you'd be needin' in here, Mr. Daniels?"

How he wanted to answer that question openly and honestly, but he knew for certain the response that would have gotten him. "I wanted to talk to you."

"Unless it has somethin' to do with my duties here, in the employ of Mr. Burns, there is nothin' that we need to be discussin'."

"I think there is." Casey stepped inside the kitchen. "For over two years now you've avoided me like I carried bubonic plague. And I understand the reason why. But now you need to know the truth.''

''And you think I'd believe anythin' that came from your lips, Mr. Daniels?''

''I think you would, if you'd only take the time to listen.''

''Why do you keep insistin' on intrudin' into my life? Haven't you done enough to ruin it already?''

Casey didn't know how to say it; he only knew that he needed to get it out. ''Because,'' he started, fighting down the lump catching in his throat, ''because over the years I have grown quite fond of you, Mrs. Kramer, in spite of the way you have felt about me.''

For once, Maureen had nothing to say. She stared at him disbelievingly; then a slow fire began to burn. Casey braced himself for what was to come, but before Maureen was able to explode, the outside door burst open and a man rushed inside.

''Miners rioting over at the Rattlesnake!'' he cried. ''They've got the mine's office surrounded. Sam Stepton is trying to hold them back, but the men are all liquored up and fixing to have LaFarge by the neck! I don't think Sam can hold 'em back much longer.''

''What men?'' Casey demanded as Burns and the others came out to investigate.

''Dad-burn it, didn't you hear me? Mining men! Mostly employees of the Rattlesnake, but there are some others there too.''

Casey grabbed his hat and coat and dove out the door, with Burns and the others right behind him.

A few minutes earlier, Sam Stepton had been thinking he needed a drink. His conscience had been nagging him again, and lately the only way he knew to silence it was with a couple of whiskeys over at Johnny Nolon's Saloon. But right at this moment, standing on the porch in front of the Rattlesnake's office, looking over the angry faces of the men pressing in upon him, Sam was thankful he was sober.

"You boys just settle down," he shouted above their raucous cries.

Liam O'Mally said, "Get out of the way, Sam, or we'll run right over the top of you!"

Sam held his ground. "The sheriff has been sent for, boys. Think about what you're doing. Busting in here and taking the mine's cash box is only going to land the whole lot of you in jail."

"We don't care about no money, Sam. It's LaFarge's hide we want, and we will not leave until he gets his comeuppance. Now out of the way, Sam!" O'Mally growled.

Sam was momentarily confused, but it was plain there could be no reasoning with this mob. "LaFarge isn't here. He's gone to Cripple Creek with the cash box."

Someone said, "I believe you're siding with LaFarge, and in my book that makes you just as bad as that son of a bitch, Sam!"

"My book too!"

"Break in the door!"

The men surged forward. A rock sailed out and hit Sam in the head. Someone swung a fist, then a cudgel came from out of the dark. Sam went to his knees and fell forward as the surging tide of men washed over him and the door gave way before their weight.

Lying there on the porch in the icy cold, floating on the edge of consciousness, Sam was aware of pounding feet inside. The mob came back out, grumbling that LaFarge had slipped through their fingers. Someone had found his trail from the window over to where his carriage had been parked, and said they might catch him if they hurried. A man spotted LaFarge's fleeing carriage on the road to town. "There the son of bitch goes!" In a moment the men had piled back into their wagons and were snapping their reins and cracking their whips, rumbling down off Battle Mountain.

Sam tried to rise to his knees, but fell back. His vision blurred, and the roar inside his head grew deafening as an icy wind cooled the warm, sticky mass gathering in a pool beneath his head.

# TWENTY-TWO

THE DISTANT CLOUDS ROLLED IN, HALF OBSCURING THE moon, and a heavy snow was beginning to fall as LaFarge drove his horse on into the night, keeping one eye always over his shoulder. He had begun to breathe a little easier, and had almost decided to rein his animal in and continue at a more sane speed, when in the patchy moonlight he caught a glimpse of a wagon topping the pass at Squaw Gulch, then three more.

He urged his horse on to greater speed, his carriage skittering sideways at the sharp curves in the twisting road. The lights of Cripple Creek appeared in front of him. He slowed coming into the sprawling residential area, crossed Warren Avenue, then Myers, and swung west at Bennett. As he reached the edge of town, he put the whip to his horse. The animal strove up the long incline towards Pisgah Cemetery. Charging past it, LaFarge used his whip again. At the point where the road swung sharply north, the carriage began to slide sideways. LaFarge felt it slipping towards the rising ground on his left. His foot shot out, stabbing the brake hard. The carriage wrenched violently, its wheels bounced over a frozen rut, and with a cry of rending wood it flipped over, catapulting LaFarge clear as it made a half somersault and came down on its top, throwing the horse to the ground.

LaFarge cracked his shoulder against a rock buried beneath a bank of snow, and lay there stunned with the snow falling around him. He dragged himself clear of the rock and slowly stood. He was not seriously hurt, but his right arm was useless. He must have dislocated it—perhaps even broken it.

The wreckage of his carriage lay a dozen feet off, close enough for him to realize that only Providence had kept him from being crushed beneath it. He remembered the cash box, and in a panic searched the wreckage. When it was not to be found, he quickly scanned the ground and found it half buried in the same snowbank that had caught him as well. He dragged the box free and tried to lift it. It was almost too heavy to carry, even with two good arms. Now all he could do was drag it, and not very far.

Quickly he looked around and spied a little ravine near the road. Grabbing hold of one of the iron handles, he dragged the cash box down, hoping the falling snow would hide it and its traces before the morning's light could reveal its presence. Near the bottom of the ravine, his foot broke through a crust of snow and he sank to his waist. To his surprise, he discovered there was a shallow cave underneath. This was better than he had hoped for. Here the box would be secure all winter— perhaps longer. Not wanting to hesitate a moment longer, he shoved the cash box inside the cave.

Something impeded it. He shoved harder. There was a crash like breaking glass. Icicles, he thought, pulling himself from the declivity. When he looked back he could see no traces of the box, or the cave, other than the crushed snow around it, and judging by the snow that had begun to fall, he reasoned, by morning even that would be covered over.

LaFarge scrambled up to the road, grabbing his carpetbag from the splintered wreckage. He shoved the hand of his injured arm inside his coat and started cross-country on foot.

He was well up the side of Mount Pisgah when the wagonloads of men drew to a stop at the wreck of his carriage. LaFarge paused only a second to watch them climb down and swarm around the shattered vehicle. Some men went to the thrashing horse and began to unhitch it from its traces. No one ventured near the declivity, to his relief.

Turning away, LaFarge slipped around the side of Pisgah and made his way safely out of the District.


Casey and Burns carried Sam Stepton into the mine office and laid him upon the bed while Doyle shut the window and Harnan tossed some sticks into the stove. Maureen took one look at the bloody wound in Sam's head and said, ''This man will need a doctor right away.''

Irving Howbert said, ''I'll go into town for Doc Whiting.''

''That will take too long. Use the telephone that's just been installed in my office,'' Burns called after him.

''Someone bring me a towel and water,'' Maureen said, taking charge of the matter. Casey fetched them for her. When she saw who it was who had gone after them, she hesitated for half a second, then took the items from him and began gently cleaning the deep gash.

Sam groaned and came slowly to consciousness.

''Now don't you be strugglin', Sam,'' she said firmly, keeping pressure on the flowing wound.

''What happened here?'' Burns insisted.

''Not now! Don't you see he can't talk?'' Maureen scolded.

Sam opened his eyes and blinked. ''Where am I?''

''In good hands,'' she said.

His eyes seemed to struggle to focus, then moved to her face. ''Oh . . . it's you, Mrs. Kramer.'' Sam looked around at the faces bent over him. His view lingered longest on Casey.

Burns asked his question again. Sam said, ''It was a drunken lot. They'd come to steal the mine's cash box, but Mr. LaFarge, he got wind of it and took it into town where it would be safe.''

''That's a lie.'' Lisa Kellerman was standing in the doorway, her cheeks bright crimson from the cold, her nose running, and her usually perfectly arranged red hair lying in a tangled, windblown mass upon her shoulders.

She came into the room and looked at Sam Stepton. "He lied to you, Sam, just like he lied to me. That man has never spoken one word of truth." She paused and looked at Maureen. A ghost of a smile touched her unhappy face, then faded. To Maureen's relief Lisa pretended not to know her.

"What . . . what are you talking about?" Sam croaked.

"Those men weren't after money—they were after La-Farge. They had a rope, and they were going to use it. I know, because I came here to warn him. Olly oiled them up with free booze all afternoon, then planted the idea in their whiskey-sodden brains. He set you up, Sam. He put you there to stall them while he got away, and he took the cash box with him. He's probably halfway to Florissant by now."

"He could have gotten me killed," Sam said weakly.

"He might yet succeed, Sam," Maureen warned, trying to keep his head still, "if you don't stop movin' around."

Burns said, "For what reason did Mr. Sawyer do this deed, Miss Kellerman?"

Her head came around. "Revenge, Mr. Burns. He did it because like a fool, I was coming out here to see LaFarge." She hesitated, then went on, "I don't know what's wrong with me. You'd think I'd learn about men like LaFarge and Olly. I guess some people never learn . . . until it's too late."

There was a quiet note of despair in her voice as she stood gazing vacantly across the room. Then Lisa Kellerman turned abruptly away and, pushing past the miners who had begun to fill up LaFarge's office, went back outside, where new snow was piling up around the wheels of her phaeton. In a moment she rolled away past the window and was gone. When Casey looked back, Sam Stepton was staring at him, his eyelids obviously having difficulty staying open. His hand lifted feebly off the bed, and managed to grip Maureen's arm.

"There's something I got to say. Something that's been eating away at me for too long now."

"Don't try to talk, Sam," Maureen said.

"I got to, while I'm still able." Sam's view struggled back to Casey. "I'm sorry, Casey, sorry that I didn't come forward and tell the truth when that accident happened. LaFarge . . . he said I'd be out of a job if I spoke up, and I figured I was too old to start over again. So I went along with him when he said that Casey had designed that shoring. But the truth is, LaFarge threw Casey's drawings away. He built it cheap and fast because he was working a vein that apexed on the Black Diamond claim, and he wanted to get the gold out before anyone discovered that."

"That son of a bitch!" McKinnie growled, and then looked at his partner, Frank Peck. "He was stealing gold out of our vein and we never knew it."

"I knew it," Sam said, "but I wasn't man enough to stand up to LaFarge."

"Sam, you don't need to say no more," Maureen cautioned.

Stepton drifted towards unconsciousness, caught himself, and struggled to keep awake. "I got one more thing to say. Everyone knows you blame Casey for Peter's death. Well, it just ain't so. If anyone is to blame, it's me. I reworked Casey's designs, and then I went along with LaFarge to cover up our mistake. I wish I had told it straight when it happened." He managed to find Casey among the crowd around the bed. "I admire your gumption, boy. Any other man would have packed out of here once the District turned on him, but you stuck to it. I wish . . ." His voice faded. "I only wish I had half your strength, Casey, and I ask your forgiveness . . ."

"No need to, Sam," Casey said.

Sam's grip opened and his hand fell back to his side.

Lisa Kellerman passed Dr. Whiting's black buggy on the road, but she hardly noticed it. Her brain was clouded with a heavy shroud of hopelessness. She no longer even asked why she was like she was, for suddenly she no longer cared. Life had become one endless stream of whiskey and men, and neither one was enough to soften the pain of living. She drove her phaeton into town and dropped it off at the livery, letting it sit in the middle of the big barn unattended.

The cold drove icy needles through her shawl as she walked back to the saloon, no longer aware of the glaring music coming from the saloons and dance halls and bordellos that lined Myers Avenue, blinded even to the bright lights glaring behind the windows of the Old Homestead, Pearl De Vere's upscale brothel that had for months been Lisa's only real competition for the high-dollar clients.

Closing the door behind her, Lisa glanced at the stairs that climbed to her suite of rooms, then turned away and went across the crowded saloon and found Olly in his private alcove. She stepped through the beaded curtains as he was about to pour himself a glass of whiskey.

"What do you want?"

Lisa didn't know why she had come to him; all she knew was that somehow she needed his nearness. She sat in one of the chairs and said, "You celebrating something, Olly?"

"Maybe."

She frowned. "LaFarge got away."

Sawyer's eyes narrowed behind the thick lenses of his spectacles. "What do you know about that?"

"I warned him of what your were up to."

The whiskey bottle hung momentarily suspended above the glass, then slowly he set it back down upon the table. "You did what?"

"I told Phillip he had to leave or end up swinging. He left. I asked him to take me with him, but he just laughed and told me I was a fool."

Sawyer's face quivered and his short neck grew red, matching the glowing crimson of Lisa's wind-chapped cheeks. All at once he struck out, knocking Lisa from the chair. "You *are* a fool," he said, standing over her.

Lisa stared up at him stunned; then, grabbing the edge of the table, she pulled herself back to her feet. "I think I have finally figured it out, Olly. I think I like to be hurt—maybe because deep down inside, I know I deserve it. There is a certain exhilaration in it . . . but you know what?"

"What the hell are you talking about?"

Lisa gently placed a hand against the swelling red welt upon her cheek. "I think I've lost whatever feeling I once had. I'm all dead inside."

Sawyer grinned. "Oh, you think you've lost feeling? Well, I can promise you you ain't." Sawyer's fist struck out again, buckling Lisa over. Another blow staggered her back against the wall . . . and the noise of the busy saloon beyond the beaded curtains masked the next five minutes . . .

Lisa opened a swollen eye. Kelly, Monika, and Lynn West were hovering over her, looking worried. When they saw she had regained consciousness, they picked her up off the floor and sat her in one of the chairs.

"Oh, you poor dear," Kelly said, combing the tangled red tresses from Lisa's bloodied face.

Lynn was furious. "Something ought to be done about that man. I'm going to get the sheriff this very minute!"

Lisa managed to catch Lynn by the wrist. "No, don't bother," she said, her mouth hardly able to move, her lips purple and crusted with drying blood. "Just help me to my room."

"We can't take you out of here looking like this. My God, Lisa, what did Sawyer have in mind when he laid into you?"

Lisa managed a small smile. "He thought he could hurt me. But I told him it was no good. I'm all dead inside . . . he just didn't believe me."

"How can a man do this to a woman?" Monika asked.

"A man like Olly . . . it's the only way he knows how to treat a woman. Help me to my room."

The three women helped Lisa to her feet. She couldn't

straighten up completely. Olly had broken a couple of ribs, but she didn't say anything about it as the girls walked her past the miners in the saloon. The place was suddenly silent. Lisa kept her head up and her view straight ahead. Upstairs, they set her carefully upon the bed. The other girls came in, appalled at what they discovered. Lynn said she was going after a doctor.

"No," Lisa said sharply. "I don't want a doctor. Just leave me alone. I'll be all right."

"At least let me help you clean up," Kelly said.

Lisa shook her head. "No. I want to be alone. All of you, go back to work."

They hesitated, then one by one backed out of the room until only Kelly was left. "I'll check in on you later, Lisa."

Lisa only stared at the white ceiling. When the door latch clicked she took a hand mirror from the bedside table and was shocked . . . not by the distortion of her face, but because the face looking back at her belonged to her mother. She blinked and saw that it was herself, but the resemblance was striking. It stirred something buried deep within her memories. Lisa frowned, set the mirror back, and felt alongside her bed for a bottle she kept there. The whiskey coursed down her battered chin and burned in the open wounds, but Lisa hardly felt it.

"I *am* dead inside," she said softly to herself. She finished the bottle, and as her brain whirled, she fumbled for the hookah, filled it with opium, and lay there, inhaling deeply.

Her body relaxed, and the beating Olly had given her became just a vague memory of something that had happened long, long ago. An image of Olly's face swam across her brain and slowly transformed itself into an image of her father. Suddenly she understood. Now she knew why the beating seemed to have happened so long ago. And she understood her deadly attraction to men like Olly and Phillip. She understood everything. A contented smile moved across her battered face.

The images evaporated, and a yellow-green fog swirled in, stealing away her thoughts and her will.

Lisa's breathing slowed, all worry left her, and a few minutes later her broken heart stopped beating.

That week there were two funerals in Cripple Creek. A few hearty souls came to Pisgah graveyard to see Sam Stepton laid to rest. Casey was there, as was Maureen, Margaret, the Three Jims, Stratton, and a few other men who held Sam in high regard. The preacher said fine things, and afterwards everyone hugged Sharon Stepton and drove back into town and went their own way.

Lisa Kellerman's funeral, three days later, brought the whole District out. The procession down Bennett Avenue in Lampman's new glass-walled hearse was the finest Cripple Creek had seen since the Fourth of July parade. The hearse carrying her yellow chiffon–draped casket was followed by Lisa's driverless phaeton, overflowing with flowers sent from hundreds of admiring miners in the District. The gaiety of color turned a cold, drizzly day into an almost buoyant event. The streets were lined with men and women, and children who should have been in school. At the head of the funeral was the Elks Band, playing a funeral dirge.

Behind the hearse and the flowers walked Lisa's girls, each dressed in black, their faces hidden behind black veils, their black-gloved hands holding bouquets of pink carnations, shipped in for the occasion from greenhouses in Colorado Springs.

Olly and Barney followed in a rented carriage behind the girls, and behind them a hundred men and women, all braving the gloomy weather to say a final good-bye to Lisa.

The riot at the Rattlesnake mine was a dark harbinger. The unions were growing stronger and more demanding, and knowing that Governor ''Bloody Bridles'' Waite was standing in the wings to back them up, they laid out their strategy at the Smith and Peters' Saloon in Altman under their general, John Calderwood. The mine owners, meanwhile, encamped in

the plush surroundings of the El Paso Club in Colorado
Springs, were drawing up their battle plans as well, and in
February of 1894 they put the resolve of the unions to a test.
In unison, the mine owners—all except a few, Stratton and
Burns among them—increased the working shift from eight
hours to nine, and without a penny more in pay.

Calderwood parried by withdrawing more than five hundred
men in his Free Coinage Union No. 19 from the mines on Bull
Hill. Knowing that keeping the men fed and their families
supplied with the necessities of life was the key to winning
any strike, Calderwood set a plan in motion that included free
kitchens and a small income made up of the dues he had been
collecting since organizing the men several months earlier, do-
nations from local businessmen and contributions from
W.F.M. unions outside the District.

While getting this machinery oiled up and in place, Calderwood shrewdly kept the lines of communication open between himself and Burns and Stratton, two of the largest mine
owners in the District, who, to the shock of the other mine
owners, actually encouraged the unions. It had even been reported in the *Cripple Creek Crusher* that Burns had declared
that every man had the right to collective bargaining! Not surprisingly, while the other mines began to shut down as workers
stayed away, the Portland and Independence kept chugging
right along at full production.

The strike stretched on into March, the middle of the coldest
season of the year in Cripple Creek—a season that would usually linger through April, when the heaviest and wettest snow
always fell.

Maureen Kramer had taken her grocery basket into town
one Saturday morning and was strolling up Bennett Avenue
on her way home. She was bundled up in a long, gray wool
overcoat, with a plaid wool scarf over her head and ears, and
only her bright blue eyes showing above the blush of her
cheeks. Suddenly she spied Casey Daniels stepping out of the
door of a confectioner's shop three buildings up the street. He

was carrying a brown bag, and like herself, was so bundled up against the cold and wind that at first she had not recognized him. When she did, her natural instinct was to quickly dart into the door to her left. But she stopped herself.

Old habits die hard, she thought.

It *was* hard to face this man whom she had blamed all these years for the death of Peter. Casey had been kind and patient, while she had gone out of her way to be surly and bad-tempered. She had already confronted her own feelings on the matter of Casey Daniels, and had put the bitterness to rest . . . but that didn't mean she could within a month completely reroute the thoughts of two years.

Still, she could at least make a start of it!

Maureen arranged a pleasant face, which surprisingly was not as difficult as she had worried it might be, and as Casey started up the street, not having noticed her, she called out, "Oh, Mr. Daniels."

Why had she done that? she wondered. If she had only kept quiet he would have simply gone on his way, never knowing that she had been behind him. It would have given her more time to choose her words, to explore her thoughts . . . and her feelings. Feelings? That there might be any feelings involved startled her. How much more had her hatred blinded her to these last two years? Well, the words had been spoken, and Casey had stopped and looked back.

"Mrs. Kramer?" he said, surprised.

Was there a note of concern there as well? she wondered. She could not blame him if there was, she reflected, considering how roughly she had treated him since the accident. He waited as she closed the short distance between them. He was taller than she remembered . . . or was it only that she had never taken the time to notice? He smiled openly, but with a wariness behind it—and who could blame him?

Maureen tried her best to submerge any bitterness that might be lingering, unwanted. "What brings you into town, Mr. Daniels?" she started off awkwardly, not knowing what she really wanted to say, only that the time had come to . . . "bury the hatchet," as the people in this adopted country of hers were wont to say.

His smile widened and she knew she had been successful, at least, at coming across in a friendly manner. He held his bag open to her and said, "Care for a horehound?"

"Thank you." She took one of the hard brown candies.

Casey said, "Just running an errand for Mr. Stratton."

Maureen shivered. " 'Tis a blustery day to be runnin' errands, it is, Mr. Daniels."

He glanced at her full grocery basket. "I'm not the only one running errands."

They had started up the street again. "A workin' woman has to fit her shoppin' and cleanin' in when she can."

"I'll bet that Margaret is a big help to you."

"She helps where she can. She's a good child. She keeps the house picked up, and always has a pot of tea waitin' for me when I get home."

"Your job with the Portland Company going well?"

Maureen couldn't help but smile. The work was a dream come true. James Burns paid her handsomely, and now she was in charge of the big office building on Battle Mountain, and Burns had even put a buggy and horse at her disposal at all times. "Mr. Burns is a gentleman and a fine employer," she said. "A true Irishman, and I wouldn't be surprised if there ain't some of Hugh O'Neill's blood in him."

"Hugh O'Neill?"

She laughed. "A bit of Irish history, Mr. Daniels. O'Neill was the third Baron of Dungannon who soundly trounced the British in the early 1600s."

"Oh, I see."

"Burns and Mr. Stratton must both have a bit of Hugh's blood in them by the way they are treatin' the workin' men of this town. Why, I heard that Mr. Stratton has confounded the mine owners by giving all his men a raise in their wages."

"He has done that. He and Burns are paying the highest

wages in the District—three dollars and twenty-five cents a day, for nine hours. And the night shift only has to work eight hours to earn the same money. Here, let me carry that basket for you, Mrs. Kramer. It looks heavy.''

He took the basket before she could protest . . . not, she decided, that she would have. Maureen discovered that now that she'd let her anger go, this man was easy and pleasant to talk to. Then a prick of shame gave her pause. She knew she really ought to apologize to him—but how? Her pride had stepped in the way, and it would not be a light thing to remove. Admitting she was wrong had never been easy for her to do. She was just as likely to arch her back and march into hell as to admit that she had made a mistake. It was her pride, her damned pride! That, and the fearsome temper with which she struggled from time to time. It really did not present a pretty picture; one she fought to hide from the eyes of the world.

The road climbed away from the heart of town, and then they were walking along Silver Street, and her house was ahead. Smoke curled from the chimney high above the tattered and flapping canvas, which she had had mended several times, but which needed replacing. Not that there would be any trouble finding the money for it. All she'd have to do was ask James Burns, and next week there would be a new, shiny tin roof over their heads. But there was that pride again . . .

Casey's view had lingered an embarrassingly long while on the flapping, sun-faded sail atop the log-and-frame structure.

''You still haven't replaced it?''

''I am goin' to shortly,'' she said, which was not quite the truth.

He seemed about to say something, then stopped himself and smiled down at her. ''Well, it was very nice walking with you, Mrs. Kramer. And I enjoyed our talk.''

''Would you like to come in—for some tea?'' she asked impulsively, and instantly wished she had not. There was still too much in the way of wounded feelings to patch them over so swiftly. Maureen was confused at the easy way she had shed her years of hatred for this man, and at the moment she was uncertain that she could trust anything she was feeling. But the invitation had been spoken . . .

"Thank you, however I really ought to be on my way. Perhaps another time?"

A wave of relief washed over her—and yet there was a tinge of disappointment as well. *What on earth is going on inside your jumbled brain?* she asked herself.

Maureen gave him a pleasant smile. "Another time would be fine, Mr. Daniels. Good-bye." She opened the little gate that stood in front of her path like an orphan, for it was indeed only a token gate, since Peter had never gotten around to building the fence that would have completed it.

"Good-bye," he said, waiting until she had safely closed her front door behind her before walking back into town.

Unblinking behind the thick lenses of his eyeglasses, Oliver Sawyer listened to the report that Barney Mays had just brought back from Colorado Springs. He didn't feel the biting cold where he stood in the alleyway behind Lisa and Olly's Saloon, as the high noon sun was just reaching the stair steps there, warming the two men.

Sawyer had given Barney five hundred dollars to ferret out LaFarge, and although he had not been successful in finding and eliminating him, he did bring back some interesting news.

"The trail finally led to the Antlers Hotel—" Barney was saying when Sawyer cut him off with a short laugh.

"Where else would you expect a man with his tastes to be staying? Considering all that gold he got away with, I'm surprised he didn't end up in Chicago, or New York City."

"You got that all wrong, Olly. He weren't no guest at the hotel—he was working there. Washing dishes."

The smoldering cigar nearly fell from Sawyer's lips. "Washing dishes?" he said, unbelievingly, and then he threw back his head and roared out a laugh. "That's some come-down for a man like LaFarge, huh? So, what happened then?''

"Well, I finally played out enough money to track him down, and then it seemed a cinch. I was going to wait until he left work and catch him alone at the service entrance behind the hotel. Then . . .'' The stiletto came out of Barney's pocket and he jabbed the air, twisting the knife and thrusting it upward. He grinned, not needing to finish his sentence.

"So, what went wrong?''

Barney shrugged his shoulders and put the blade back inside his coat pocket. "One of those palms I greased with a shiny double eagle happened to be the cook at the Antlers. He told LaFarge that I'd been asking questions. I reckon he must have given my description,'cause I never used my real name. Anyway, LaFarge threw his apron aside, according to what I was told, and hightailed it out of there before I knew what was going on.''

"Damn!'' Sawyer slammed a fist into his palm. "One of these days I'll get my hands on that bastard.''

"Why not just let it go, Olly? You ran him out of town, and out of your hair, and if his holdings get sold at the tax auction like the newspaper says, there ain't no reason for him coming back to Cripple Creek.''

Sawyer's expression hardened, his bulging eyes narrowing. "He made me look the fool, a cuckold, to the eyes of this town, and I don't let no man do that and live—no matter how long it takes.''

"That might be never. I managed to get a lead on him after he fled the Antlers and found out that he'd bought a train ticket to Omaha. Hell, once in Omaha, a man can go a hundred different directions, change his name, start a new life. He knows you're after him, Olly. He ain't going to be coming back here anytime soon.''

Sawyer grinned. "I think not, Barney. I suspect Phillip LaFarge will be coming back, and not years from now.''

"I don't get you.''

"You said it yourself. He was working as a dishwasher.

Then he scrambled out of town one step ahead of your knife. And remember when he left Cripple? The remains of his carriage were smashed across the road. What does that tell you?"

Barney looked at him blankly.

"It's plain. He never got away with all that gold! He couldn't have. After he wrecked his carriage, the best he could have done was dragged that heavy chest up into the hills someplace and buried it." Sawyer took a long, satisfied pull at his cigar. "No, Barney, that chest of gold is still here in the District somewhere, and LaFarge will be back to get it someday—someday soon. All we have to do is keep our eyes open. I'll tell O'Mally to spread the word around to the men, and make it stick with some gold. A hundred dollars to the man who first spies LaFarge back in the District! He'll come back, and when he does, I'll be waiting for him."

# TWENTY-THREE

THEY CELEBRATED THE FOURTH OF JULY THREE DAYS EARLY that year, for on July 1, 1894, the District's first train, the Florence and Cripple Creek Railroad, arrived in a flurry of parades, band music, and fireworks. The whole town turned out for the event, and the party made Lisa Kellerman's funeral, and the previous year's Fourth of July celebration, pale in comparison. Fate was in an impish mood that day, however, and the train promptly wrecked on its way out of town. But that didn't quench the festive spirits any.

"Hello, Mr. Daniels," Margaret said one afternoon shortly after the big day of the arrival of Cripple's first train. Her words caught him daydreaming on the corner of Second Street and Bennett, enjoying the warm sun upon his face as he gazed past the line of buildings down Second Street and out at the hills surrounding the city, green from the spring rains in the few places where the miner's pick hadn't scarred them. He'd come into town to pick up a pair of boots the cobbler had repaired, and discovering the job not quite finished, had time on his hands to languish in the sun and dream about the future—which now, since the strike had been settled and all parties involved were working *with* each other instead of against, appeared bright and prosperous for all.

Casey looked over. Margaret and Mabs were standing there, wearing their summer play dresses. Mabs had a brown cloth sack in her hands and Margaret clutched a checked tablecloth and a little black theme book, which Casey knew was the diary she had started to keep when the strike had gripped the city in fear and the future looked bleak.

"Good morning, ladies," he said, touching the brim of his hat. "What are you two up to?"

"We are going to our play-cave," Mabs said, shifting the heavy bag from her left to her right hand.

Margaret said, "We haven't been there all winter and now we are going to clean it up and get it ready for the summer. Mrs. Barbee gave us some new dishes that she ain't using anymore."

"That she *isn't* using," Casey corrected.

Margaret frowned. "You sound like Mrs. Linker." Wilma Linker was one of the new schoolteachers—Casey knew that too.

"Sorry. I'll bite my tongue from now on."

"I haven't seen you around the house," Margaret said, holding back a smile.

"I've been busy up at the mine. Have you missed me coming by?"

Margaret glanced at his shoes, grinning and quickly shook her head.

"You know, I haven't got anything to do for a while. How about I walk along with you two ladies and give you a hand with that play-cave of yours."

"All right," Mabs said.

They started down the street together. When they passed a candy shop, Casey stepped inside and came back a minute later with a nickel bag of bull's-eyes, lollipops, and licorice sticks. The girls pondered over the selection, and after all hands had cleared the bag, they continued on their way to the declivity below Pisgah graveyard. The overhang of rock forming the roof of their play-cave was half hidden beneath a collection of junk that had blown in over the winter.

Margaret led the way. She set the tablecloth and book on the stiff grass and began clearing the debris. Casey gave a hand hauling aside a heavy pine bough that had snapped off a nearby ponderosa during one of the big snows. Margaret ducked her head and crawled inside the cave.

"Oh, my!" she cried.

"What's the matter?" Mabs said, crawling under the ledge.

Casey bent and stuck his head inside as well. Margaret was sitting against the wall of the cave staring at the pile of broken dishes and cups scattered around, and right in the middle of the mess was a big, black iron box decorated with gold-painted scrolls and secured by a big padlock.

Casey recognized it at once. "Here, let me help you with that," he said, hefting the heavy box out.

"How did *that* get there?" Mabs asked.

Casey instantly put it all together: LaFarge's mad flight from the lynch mob, the wreck on this stretch of the road, and the disappearance of all the gold that had financed the mine and the payroll.

"You know, girls, this would make a dandy table for your play-cave. I'll just take it home with me and clean it up for you."

"All right," Margaret said innocently.

Casey would find a replacement box for the girls, and a safe place to stash this one. He knew now that LaFarge would be back looking for it, and when he did, Casey figured he'd nab him—before Sawyer got his hands on him, he hoped, for everyone knew of the reward Sawyer was offering. But if word ever got out that the cash box had been found, there'd be no reason for LaFarge to come back.

"We'll just keep this our secret," Casey said.

They looked at him blankly, but nodded their heads, then immediately forgot the box and went to work straightening up their play-cave.

• • •

Throughout the rest of 1894, Casey and Maureen were frequently seen in each other's company, and slowly, the years of bitter feelings receded into the past. Maureen kept working for the Portland Gold Mining Company, now as James Burns's personal secretary, and as such, she was one of the first to notice the widening rift between Burns and Doyle—a friendship that had always stood on shaky ground.

Casey, working the Lucky Irish in his spare time, had hit a vein of gold that, although not rich by the District's standards, was producing enough of the yellow metal to warrant a full-time production crew, and a man to oversee them. Consequently, in December of '94, Casey quit his job with Stratton at the Independence and went to work full-time at the Lucky Irish.

That Christmas, Maureen took Margaret back east for a few weeks to visit Bridie and Ralph. Ralph had been injured in an accident at the steelworks and now spent his days in a shabby armchair, drinking beer and growing fat. Bridie had taken a job at a fish cannery and barely made enough money to allow them to keep their apartment. The building had fallen into disrepair since Maureen had last been there, but the scrawny Gorham Swink was still behind the desk, wearing his winter uniform—a tattered blue sweater—and forever reading his wrinkled newspaper. Nothing much appeared to have changed, except that Swink's sister had passed away a year earlier—at which time he also must have misplaced his razor, it seemed to Maureen.

She was grateful to be back in Cripple Creek, in the clean mountain air, among the familiar faces, where new buildings continued to push the limits of the city farther and farther out.

Casey picked Maureen and Margaret up at the Florence and Cripple Creek Railroad station on Xenia Street and drove them home. He drew up in front of her little house and looked over at her with a funny grin on his face.

''See anything different?''

In spite of his easy manner, Maureen sensed an underlying tautness in his voice, as if he was not quite certain what to expect next. His question had caught her unprepared, and she was about to ask what he meant when suddenly a cloud drifted out of the sun's way and a brilliant gleam stabbed at the corner of her eye. She blinked and stared.

"Look, Mommy!" Margaret said, pointing. "There is a new roof on our house."

In place of the worn and patched canvas sheet was a bright new corrugated-steel roof. "Begorra," Maureen said, stunned.

"Merry Christmas," Casey said. "I had the men start work on it the day you left. They did a good job. It should keep you two dry this winter. And you won't have to run outside day and night and scrape new-fallen snow off."

Maureen was speechless. When she regained her voice, she almost scolded him for it, but she caught herself. "I don't know what to say."

He set the brake and looked over. "Say you'll marry me, Maureen?"

Her blue eyes widened as she once again found herself groping for words. Had he really asked her to marry him?

He was watching her now, carefully guarding his thoughts so that no trace of them showed on his face.

For an instant her brain was confused, then the answer came to her, clear and sure. "I am flattered, Casey," she started slowly, "but I cannot accept your proposal."

"Why not?"

It had been almost a year since she had learned the truth about the mine accident, and about how Casey had been framed. She had settled the question in her mind, it was true, but after so many years of bitterness, she still needed more time. "I'm not ready yet to marry, Casey," she said, hoping he'd accept that simple explanation and not delve deeper into it.

He did.

•    •    •

Peering through a dingy window, Phillip LaFarge watched a steamboat puffing its way up the Mississippi River. The boat was indistinct and toylike at this distance, moving like a ghost through the gray drizzle and wispy fingers of drifting fog. Gayoso, Missouri, was the rear end of nowhere, as far as LaFarge was concerned. Boats still occasionally pulled into Gayoso to take on wood, and boatmen to take on a tankard of ale or two—and not even that very often anymore, since most of the steamers burned coal. At one time, forty years ago, Gayoso was a booming river port, but now the riverboats—and the future—seemed to be passing it by while the mighty lady, the Mississippi, nibbled away at her banks, swallowing down whole chunks of the town every spring. Soon, there would be nothing left of Gayoso except a name on some old river charts.

LaFarge bit down on the cigar and frowned. It *was* the ass-end of nowhere, but at least none of Sawyer's paid headhunters had found him down here.

*Damn him!* LaFarge cursed the day he'd ever laid eyes on Oliver Sawyer, but he had to marvel at Sawyer's tenacity. *It was only a woman. A two-bit whore who made good... A woman who happened to take a fancy to the bug-eyed street thug. Didn't the man ever let up?*

LaFarge turned from the window at the sound of the door opening. Stacey Anderson was standing there, shaking out her umbrella. Clamped under her left arm was a rolled-up newspaper. She was wearing a green cotton dress this drizzly morning, several shades greener than her eyes, and her cheeks were bright red—partly from the exertion of the steep climb up from the river, but mostly from the rouge which Stacey always wore in abundance.

Stacey was a pretty girl of twenty-three, and LaFarge had taken a liking to her right off. In the last six months they'd seen each other at least four times a week. Stacey worked for Madam Lovejoy down near Spark's Landing, which was only half a mile upriver from Gayoso where the riverboats still landed frequently. Stacey and LaFarge had a common bond: they were both being hunted. The hounds on her trail were somewhere down around New Orleans, where she'd cleaved the head of a gentleman caller one afternoon with a dull butcher's hatchet.

Stacey glanced around the room, which at the moment was empty of customers. The little saloon that LaFarge ran used to do a booming business back before the War of the Rebellion, but nowadays it was usually customerless. He ran the place for a fellow named Humphreys who had inherited it from his father. Humphreys was a sailing man, currently working a merchant ship somewhere in the islands of the Caribbean. LaFarge took the job because it involved little work with nobody looking over his shoulder. But more important it provided a bedroom out back with a good roof and decent screens on the windows. As no one ever came to Gayoso, LaFarge had found himself a safe haven.

Stacey set the umbrella aside, and giving LaFarge a little smile, reached back and threw the latch on the door. Then she came across the room and dove into his arms.

"I've only an hour," she said breathlessly, and as she spoke she pulled him back towards the bedroom.

He took the newspaper that was still clenched under her arm.

Stacey said, "It came for you on the mail boat. I told the postmaster I'd bring it up. Come on, Phillip," she insisted, tugging him towards the back room. "I ain't got much time."

"Hold on there," he said.

"Phillip!" she moaned.

He spread the paper open upon the scarred bar. It was a copy of the *Cripple Creek Crusher,* dated eight days earlier, and the name on the mailing address was Phil Smith. Stacey fixed a pout to her pretty face, but when she saw that LaFarge was not paying attention to her, she looked over his shoulder and said, "Why do you keep getting all those newspapers, Phillip?" Her voice had a soft Southern drawl, warm and inviting, like mint juleps on a summer night. "And why by that name? *Smith,* for mercy sakes? How terribly original."

He ignored her, scanning the columns of newsprint. There was much about the recent bullfight. According to the reports, after it was all over, the organizers had landed in jail, and then got out almost immediately. Joe Wolfe had fled town—again—because like the last time, he had racked up more bills than he was able to pay. LaFarge wasn't surprised. Joe had feet of wet clay, always slipping away one step ahead of the bill collectors.

In a few minutes he'd covered all the pages. Not a single mention of a found cash box. He let his breath go. In all the time he had been away from Cripple Creek he had read nothing of the box being found, and that at least gave him hope that it still remained where he had hidden it that cold night over a year ago.

"I get them, my dear," he said, suddenly pulling her roughly into his arms, "because I like to keep up with what is happening in Cripple Creek. It's as simple as that." He kissed her hard and expertly began unfastening the row of buttons down the front of her dress, nearly ripping it off her as they both fell onto the hard bed in the room behind the saloon.

Afterwards, with Stacey lying comfortably in his arms, La-Farge stared at the ceiling and his thoughts returned to the problem he'd been pondering before she came into the saloon.

*Sawyer*!

Always back to that. If it wasn't for Oliver Sawyer, LaFarge would have had the gold safely out of its hiding place a year ago. He'd be living the high life now instead of overseeing a broken-down bar in a backwater place like Gayoso.

*Damn Oliver Sawyer!*

LaFarge reached for his cigar and put a match to the charred end. Stacey shifted comfortably where she nuzzled her cheek against his chest.

But there was no way to deal with the man short of returning to Cripple Creek, and that was decidedly unwise considering all the paid eyes Sawyer had looking for him.

*Lisa had only been a whore! What was driving Sawyer so hard that he'd didn't just forget about it? Certainly with his prosperity he could afford any woman he wanted.*

Then LaFarge's thoughts came suddenly to a halt. Lisa *had* been just a whore . . . and if Sawyer had fallen for one whore, why not another?

He looked at the pretty woman next to him. Stacey smiled up at him, and her green eyes blinked. "What are you thinking?" she asked, seeing the expression that had come to his face.

"I was just wondering if you'd be interested in making lots of money, my dear."

Her eyes widened, emerald green and curious. "I'm always interested in making lots of money. The more the better."

It was a brisk September morning when Stacey Anderson stepped down from the passenger coach. Stacey didn't like the cold. She'd been born and raised in the South, and found anything much less than sixty degrees most uncomfortable. "How do I get to Lisa and Olly's Saloon?" she asked a porter.

"It's on Myers Avenue, ma'am. Just about two blocks that way, then turn right and it's another two or three blocks. You can't miss it."

Stacey thanked him, left her trunk in the station's baggage room, and in less than fifteen minutes was standing inside the batwing doors of the saloon, looking the place over. She recognized Oliver Sawyer right off from the description LaFarge had given her: a short, bulky man with a bent nose and eyeglasses thick enough to stop a bullet.

"Mr. Sawyer?" she asked after coming boldly across the noisy gaming room to where he stood by the bar, speaking to a couple of men dressed in rough work clothes. He looked over at her. She was immediately struck by the huge, unblinking eyes behind the thick spectacles. LaFarge had not exaggerated, and if he'd been correct on Sawyer's appearance, she had to trust he'd been accurate as to his deadly nature as well. She enjoyed the thrill of being around dangerous people.

"I'm Oliver Sawyer. Who are you?"

"Stacey Anderson."

"What can I do for you, Miss Anderson?"

"I'm looking for a job."

"A job? What kind of job?"

Stacey gave him a wide smile and said in a seductively smooth Southern drawl, "One where I make lots of money, and the customers come to me."

It was Sawyer's turn to grin. "Oh, I see." He looked her up and down and after a moment said, "You appear to be well qualified."

"I'm very good, Mr. Sawyer."

"Hm. I don't doubt that. Go upstairs and talk to Kelly. If she has a place for you, tell her I said to take you on—at least until I can determine your worth."

Her green eyes widened invitingly as she placed a hand lightly upon his arm. "I'd be delighted to go over all my qualifications with you in private, Mr. Sawyer . . . I promise you, you won't be disappointed."

That December, Casey escorted Maureen to the citywide Christmas Eve celebration at the Elks Club. Throughout the afternoon and evening people came and went, and the punch bowls on the long table were heavily attended as mine owners gathered around and boasted of the grand year that 1895 had been. Stratton and Burns were nodding at one another near one of the bowls when Casey left Maureen in the company of some of the town's most distinguished women and came over to replenish his cup and see how these two old friends were doing.

"It has been splendid," Stratton was saying. "The estimates are that this will be better than a six-million-dollar year."

"And the lion's share of that from your Independence and my Portland," Burns added.

"Ah, Casey! Good to see you again," Stratton said. Casey detected the slight odor upon Stratton's breath and knew that he'd been cutting his punch with rye whiskey.

"Mr. Burns . . . Mr. Stratton." Casey saluted them with his glass and said, "To a prosperous year just past and an even better one to come."

"Here! Here!" the men rejoined.

Burns said, "I thought I saw you come in with Mrs. Kramer."

"I did, but she found a conversation that was more to her liking than the ones I generally involve her in."

Stratton laughed softly, his blue eyes vaguely glazed over. Casey wondered briefly how many drinks the fellow had had. Burns said, "Mrs. Kramer is one of the finest women I know, Casey." He was into his cups as well. "If you don't ask her to marry you soon, I'm liable to ask her myself."

"I have asked her," Casey said.

"Well, then you're not being persistent enough," Stratton put in.

Casey frowned. "You can only press so hard, but I'm a patient man"—he grinned at Stratton—"and persistent. I'll wear her down yet." He turned back to Burns. "And don't you get any ideas."

They laughed. Stratton pointed at a man and woman across the room. "It looks like Oliver Sawyer has found himself a new toy."

Burns added, "Quite a good-looking toy, I'd say. I hear she's got a peaches-and-cream complexion and a Louisiana drawl to match."

Stratton frowned. "I would not know of that, Mr. Burns. But I certainly wouldn't mind hearing some of those Southern tones whispered into my ear."

"Not a chance," Burns said. "Her name is Stacey Anderson, and she's strictly private stock."

Casey and Stratton looked at Burns. Casey lifted a questioning eyebrow, and Burns grinned and shrugged his shoulders. "I already tried, boys. Kelly just shook her head at my request and turned me towards one of her other girls."

The couple made their way across the crowded floor. Up close, Casey saw that she was indeed beautiful, with startling green eyes and skin as smooth as silk. Although he tried not to live in the past, Casey hadn't forgotten the beating Sawyer had given him in that back alley years before.

Stratton refilled his glass, spiked it with some whiskey from a silver pocket flask, and offered each of his companions a nip. Casey declined. Burns thought it was time he returned to the mine. Each of the three men went his own way, as the Christmas party continued on late into the night.

April 1. The day was draped in a heavy gray fog rolling off the river when the telegram from Cripple Creek came to him. This river depressed him, and Gayoso's solitude drove him crazy at times. He tore the seal and read the short message.

> MR. SMITH.
> THE END HAS COME. OH, SO SAD.
> THE WIDOW WORE BLACK. COME SOON.
> S. A.

LaFarge could hardly believe the good news! He poured himself a drink from Humphreys's limited stock of watered-down whiskey and tossed it back. At last he was free of the bastard! With Sawyer out of the way, no one would care if he showed up again. No Sawyer, no reward—and no problem with the miners. He briefly considered Barney Mays, but the man's loyalty to Sawyer hinged upon the free flow of whiskey and women. Now, with Sawyer gone, Mays would be no bother.

He went down to Spark's Landing later that afternoon and sent a telegram to Stacey saying that he was making preparations, and to expect him in Cripple Creek in a few weeks, around the end of April.

Coming back after all this time, made LaFarge nervous. LaFarge bought a new wardrobe, and in the three weeks between receiving Stacey's telegram and his stepping off the train at the Santa Fe depot in Colorado Springs, LaFarge had cultivated a fairly decent black beard.

He stopped to study the busy platform. No one seemed to be paying attention to him. It was a bright, brisk day. The sky was clear and the sun warm upon his black coat. He set his heavy valise upon the platform and ran a finger around the uncomfortable collar. He hefted the bag again with a soft grunt, and as he started for the steps a voice behind him asked, "Can I carry that bag for you, Reverend? It appears to be awful heavy."

LaFarge looked at a black porter standing there, his arm outstretched. "No," he said gruffly, then reconsidered and let the man carry it.

"What you got here, Reverend?" the man asked, straining as he carried it down the steps to where the cabs were lining up.

"Bibles," LaFarge said. "The Colorado Midland depot," he told the driver. In a few minutes they were beyond the city limits. The horse stepped along smartly, and fifteen minutes later LaFarge was buying a ticket for Hayden Divide, and a transfer to the Midland Terminal Railroad from Divide to Cripple Creek. The Midland Terminal's tracks had reached Cripple Creek in December, making it the second railroad to service the town. The trip slashed hours from the old route, which went to Florissant and then continued by stagecoach.

He'd been away from Cripple Creek for two years, and hardly recognized the place as he viewed it from the new, redbrick, two-story Midland Terminal depot at the head of Bennett Avenue. The huge brick-and-frame skeleton of the new National Hotel filled the skyline just down the street, and every direction showed some new, larger, and finer building. LaFarge grabbed up his heavy bag and started down Bennett Avenue, careful to keep his face averted from the passing pedestrians.

He made for the Palace Hotel, recalling how the little mining camp appeared when he'd first arrived in '92, the streets nothing more than mud tracks laid out in hopeful anticipation of the buildings that would one day grow up along them. And now that day had arrived. Cripple Creek had exploded far beyond Myers and Bennett's hopes or dreams.

LaFarge registered as Reverend Smith, noting that there were only three names above his for that day, April 24, 1895. No one at the desk raised as much as an eyebrow, and there was not a single face that he recognized. The clerk was friendly and told him that his timing was perfect—the last snow had been two weeks ago. LaFarge asked that one of the bellboys carry his bag. Upstairs, he tipped the boy, and with the door closed and locked, he set the heavy valise on the bed, opened it, and removed six bricks. It would not do to raise suspicions. If he had been seen arriving with a heavy bag, he should also be seen leaving with one. The boy who had carried it up for him could vouch that it was the same if a question ever arose, as could the porter in the Springs.

He lifted the window, peered down into an alleyway behind the hotel, then he placed the bricks on the floor by the window. If all went as he hoped, he could conveniently drop the bricks outside and replace their weight with gold.

LaFarge considered contacting Stacey right away, but decided to hold off on that. He wanted to retrieve the cash box first, and be ready to leave town at a moment's notice, before risking revealing his identity here. So far nobody had recognized him, but if a man of the cloth was seen hanging around Lisa and Olly's Saloon, calling on a whore and saloon keeper, it might raise some eyebrows, and some of those might belong to men who had been on Sawyer's payroll.

He went down to the dining room that afternoon and had a

small dinner. The cost of sending first Stacey, and then himself here to Cripple Creek had used up most of his cash. But no matter—his payoff was nearly at hand. He checked his watch against the dining room clock and discovered he'd gained more than an hour traveling west, and took a moment to adjust his timepiece.

Upstairs, he waited until dark, then he pushed his Smith & Wesson revolver into his waistband, covered it with his jacket, and went down to the corner of Bennett and Second, lingering a while watching Friday night traffic in the glare of the street-lights.

It was time. His heart raced at the mixture of worry and anticipation he was feeling as he walked slowly out of town towards Pisgah graveyard. The box had to be where he'd stashed it! If it wasn't there . . . but he refused to entertain such thoughts as the lights of the town receded behind him.

His hand wrapped around the brass matchsafe in his coat pocket, and in the dark he tried to recall exactly where it was that his carriage had wrecked. If nothing else, he knew he always could find the spot by climbing up towards the grave-yard and looking down. The scene that night two years ago had been indelibly etched in his memory.

He found the dangerous curve immediately, and after walk-ing the area in widening circles, came upon the declivity. It had been snow-covered then, but he was certain this was the right place. Moving carefully in the dark, LaFarge scrambled down its steep side, where fallen branches and wind-deposited clutter slowed his descent. The place appeared as wild as he had hoped it would. What purpose, after all, would anyone have poking around here? In the winter, snow filled it nearly to the road. In the spring, like now, it was sodden from the snowmelt, with banks of dirty snow remaining where it stayed shaded. The last snowfall, he recalled the hotel clerk saying, had been two weeks earlier.

He tore at the clutter, flinging it out of his way. There was a rock ledge somewhere beneath it, he remembered in his haste

casting aside caution just as he was casting aside the wet
pieces of cardboard and heavy sheets of newsprint that half
dissolved in his fingers. His hand touched something cold . . .
the rock overhang! Falling to his knees, LaFarge thrust his
hand inside the small cave and felt around. Nothing. He
pushed farther back. Still nothing.

It wasn't there! It was gone! His hand brushed something
sharp and he yanked it back, tasting the blood as he thrust it
into his mouth.

"Damn!"

He removed the matchsafe from his pocket and struck a
lucifer along its side. In the flare, he examined the gash across
his fingertip. Ignoring the sting of it, LaFarge pushed himself
into the cave, and as the match flickered out, his worst fear
came true. He scraped a second match to life and stared at the
clutter in the cave: a pile of plates half buried beneath wet
leaves, a broken wooden crate, two shattered teacups, some
scraps of red and white checked cloth—obviously until quite
recently the abode of a family of rats. There were two old
paint cans, a crumpled brown paper bag, and some rusting
spoons and forks sticking up out of the leaves . . . and that was
all. No cash box anywhere!

The match flickered out and LaFarge ignited a third, hoping
against hope that he had only overlooked it. But no, he hadn't.
The box was gone.

Just as the match guttered something caught his eye. The
corner of a child's theme book showed under one of the paint
cans. LaFarge pulled it free and brushed the leaves from it.
He shoved it inside his coat, and then turning a handkerchief
around his bleeding finger, headed back to his hotel room.

# TWENTY-FOUR

LAFARGE DRIED THE DAMP THEME BOOK WITH A TOWEL AND
opened it, careful not to tear the soggy pages. It turned out to
be a child's diary, and it smelled mildewed; it had probably
been lying there a long time, he decided.

"*Margaret Kramer*" was written, in the uncertain cursive
of a child who had only recently acquired that skill. The name
triggered a memory buried deep in his brain. This had to be
the daughter of . . . ? Try as he might, he could not recall the
first name of the man who had died in the mine cave-in. All
that had happened so long ago.

He patted each page with the towel, carefully reading the
imperfect scrawl and working his way through the misspell-
ings. The record seemed to mainly concern itself with the labor
strike of two years previous. LaFarge had followed that affair
with keen interest through his newspaper subscription. This
account was the expression of a child's fears, which must have
been a reflection the town's fears, he figured, knowing that
children often repeat what they are told.

Her history was very detailed, and complete. After the strike
ended, the entries became fewer, with more days missing between them. Margaret had kept the little diary going for sev-

eral months after the strike—well into the summer. Suddenly
an entry caught his eye.

*July 10, 1894*

*Mabs and me went down to the cave this afternoon. It
was the first time we went ther since last fall. Mrs. Barbee
gave us some old dishes that she aint using no more, and
Mommy gave us a tablecloth. The cave was all covered
over with stuf when we got ther. Mr. D. come along with
us to and helped us clean it up. Insid we got a real shock.
All the dishes was broke and ther was a big black box
what wernt ther when we left the cave last fall. Dont know
how it got to be ther, but it sur made reck of the place.
Mr. D. took the box and said the box would make a right
fine table for us and said hed go clean it up for us.*

LaFarge reread the short account in the hope that there might
be something hidden in it that he had missed the first time,
then read to the end of the diary, which concluded on September 14, 1895, with Margaret complaining that Mrs. Linker was
bearing down on her spelling and grammar, and "how it didnt
mater none noway!"

He knew who found the cash box. But who was this man
who took it away? Margaret had only referred to him as "Mr.
D." That narrowed it down to about two or three hundred
men in the District. The logical next step was to find the little
girl, Margaret Kramer, and get the information he needed from
her.

The time had come to risk contacting Stacey. He'd need her
help in what he had to do next. Brushing at the drying mud
upon the knees of his trousers, LaFarge slipped his coat on
and tucked the revolver back into his waistband. He made his
way up Myers Avenue along the crowded sidewalk with music
and laughter spilling from every doorway. At Lisa and Olly's
Saloon, he halted and peered over the batwing doors. He told

himself that with Sawyer out of the way, and with Stacey in charge of the place, he was in no real danger here, and pushed through the doors.

It only took a moment for Stacey to see through the disguise, and instantly perceiving what LaFarge was up to, she played along as if reading the lines of a script. It would not do to show open affection to a priest, and indeed, unless she thought of something immediately, his presence here would be carefully scrutinized.

"Well, if it isn't my uncle!" she exclaimed to the people nearby.

They all shook hands with "Father Smith."

"I would have written first, Stacy," LaFarge said, "but the diocese sent me on this errand without warning. I am staying with Father Volpe at the rectory at St. Peter's tonight, but of course I wanted to visit with you."

"You want to turn me from my wicked ways, don't you?" Stacey drawled easily, and laughed. "Come, we have much catching up to do, Phil." Stacey took his arm and led him through a back door to where Sawyer had had his rooms. Stacy locked the door and began tearing the clothes off LaFarge. She flung him to her bed with animal lust, heedless of the rending of cloth and popping of buttons as her dress was torn from her.

Afterwards, their passions quieted, their breathing slowed, they lay in each other's arms as LaFarge told her about the missing cash box and of his plans to find it.

By midnight they had worked out all the details of his scheme. She let him quietly out the back door into the dark alleyway behind the saloon. When he'd gone, and the door was once again bolted, Stacey kicked the wreckage of her dress into a pile in the corner of the room and took down a new outfit. Checking her appearance in the mirror, she frowned at her ruined hair. Pinning the loose strands back in place, Stacey went out into the saloon and straight to the telephone on the wall behind the bar. She rang up the exchange, gave the operator a number, and waited while the earpiece clicked and chirped as her call worked its way through the different exchanges to Colorado Springs.

Saturday was Maureen's day off from work at the Portland Gold Mining Company, and her market day as well. At ten o'clock she left Margaret to finish up the house chores while she took up her basket and, wrapping a shawl about her shoulders, went into town. It was a mild spring day with a strong wind blowing up from the south, and as Maureen turned her steps down the hill towards Cripple's shopping district, she was thinking about the groceries she'd need to buy at Bald's Market and the material for a summer dress for Margaret that she'd seen at N. O. Johnson's Department Store.

LaFarge watched Maureen stroll down towards town then his dark eyes shifted and fixed upon the door of the little cabin. As he watched, a window curtain was pulled back and he saw the child moving around inside. LaFarge waited until he calculated that enough time had gone by; then, crushing the butt of his cigar beneath his sole and running a finger around the uncomfortable Roman collar, he stepped out onto the road and angled towards the cabin.

When he reached it, he knocked on the door quickly.

The little girl opened it, looking up at him.

"Are you Margaret?"

"Yes."

"I'm Father Smith. I'm from the church, Margaret," he said gently, putting forth a most sympathetic tone. "There has been a horrible accident. A runaway freight wagon just a few moments ago . . ." His voice cracked, then he continued with resolve. "Your mother . . . she's asking for you."

Margaret's eyes went wide and filled. "Mommy? Is she hurt?"

He nodded his head gravely and put out a hand. "Come, let me take you to her before it's too late."

Something moved inside the cabin. Another little girl now stepped into sight, standing back in the shadows, wearing an expression of fear. He had not planned for this.

"Come along with me, Margaret," he said roughly. "I'll take you to her." He glanced at Margaret's wide-eyed friend and ordered, "You stay here!" LaFarge took Margaret by the hand and pulled her after him.

"Where is my mommy?" Margaret insisted as they hurried into town.

"I'm taking you to her," he barked, dropping all pretenses now. His grip tightened as she began to hold back.

"I want Mrs. Barbee to come."

"No time. Listen, kid, if you want to see you mother before she dies, you'll come with me and quit fussing." LaFarge turned onto Fourth Street. At the alley halfway between Bennett and Myers, he suddenly stopped. They were momentarily alone, and in one swift move, LaFarge threw a hand over Margaret's mouth and, sweeping her up into his arms, carried her down the alley and through the open door into the back rooms of Lisa and Olly's Saloon.

Casey was driving his little green mountain wagon into town when ahead of him was a sight he never imagined he'd ever see again. It was a man striding purposefully towards Cripple Creek, his round, bowler hat pulled down in front, his once shiny shoes all dusty, and the jacket of his tailored three-piece suit hooked on a finger and slung over his shoulder. It wasn't all that peculiar to see men traveling like this. It was, however, a shock to see *this* man using his two hoofers instead of the fleet of carriages he had at his disposal.

Casey drew up alongside the man and grinned.

James Burns stopped and looked up at him. "Morning, Mr. Daniels. What the hell are you smirking about?"

"I'm shocked to see you reduced to walking into town. What happened?"

Burns frowned. "Ain't it just like fate to throw you a leaner.

Here I am now, rich enough to buy every rig in the District, and not one is available for me to take into town. It seems that I've let them all go off on errands, and here I am, horseless.''

"Well, climb aboard. I'm just on my way to Harper's Mine Supply for a few things.''

Burns settled himself upon the narrow seat. "I appreciate the ride. My old walking legs ain't what they used to be.''

"It's all that easy living," Casey said, getting his horse moving again. "It'll be the death of you someday.''

Burns grinned. "Yep, it certainly will . . . someday. About forty years from now will be just fine, thank you.''

"Where can I drop you off?''

"Oh, Harper's will be close enough. I'm heading over to Welty's livery to look through his catalog of the new Studebakers, and then to Harris Brothers for a couple of suits.''

"How many new suits does a man need?''

Burns shrugged his shoulders and offered Casey a cigar. "I don't know the answer to that yet, but I'm trying my darnedest to find out.''

In town, Burns went off towards Alonzo Welty's stables while Casey stepped into the supply store and gave Harper an order for the supplies he needed out at the Lucky Irish mine. It was going to take a while to get the items together, Phileas Harper told him, so Casey went outside to wait in a chair on the boardwalk, and to finish smoking the cigar James Burns had given him.

Mabs just stood there, paralyzed with fear, at first. Then suddenly the fear turned into resolve and she dashed out of the house leaving the door flung wide, and ran down Silver Street. Turning the corner, she could see Margaret in the strong grip of that priest—that odd priest with the frightening, dark eyes.

*"You stay here!"* he had told her, but all anybody had to do was ask Kitty Barbee about how obedient her daughter was when she got it in her head to be otherwise.

Mabs flew down the street after them. If Margaret's mother was hurt, Margaret would need a friend nearby, and Mabs was her best friend in all of Cripple Creek. She was only a block away now. Up ahead she saw Margaret and the preacher-man turn a corner and cross the street. Mabs skidded to a halt as a freight wagon rumbled past. When the way was clear, she thought she had lost them, then caught a glimpse of the preacher scooping Margaret up into his arms and ducking into an alleyway.

By the time Mabs reached the mouth of that alley, both Margaret and the man with the scary eyes had disappeared. Mabs was beside herself. She looked around, thinking that perhaps they had gone off in another direction . . . but no; she'd still be able to see them if they had. Mabs took a couple of tentative steps into the alley, but when the tall, dark buildings crowded around her, she backed out into the sunlight and started for home to tell her mother what had just happened.

Mabs had just reached Bennett Avenue when a gunshot rang out. She stopped at once, her attention riveted. Immediately the shot was followed by a second, and then a third, until she had counted six shots in a row. It was Fire Chief Allen's signal calling the volunteer firemen to the station.

Mabs looked quickly around, scanning the roofs of the buildings for smoke. As she wheeled back towards Myers Avenue she spied a black plume beginning to billow from the upstairs windows of the Central Dance Hall. Mabs dashed towards home, but before she'd gone a dozen steps she saw Maureen Kramer staring at the rooftops, her grocery basket clutched in tight fingers.

"Mrs. Kramer!" she cried, darting across the street heedless of the traffic, which, like the rest of Cripple Creek, was momentarily frozen with all eyes suddenly welded upon that ominous black plume.

"Mabs. What is wrong?" Maureen glanced around, then said urgently, "Where is Margaret?"

"A man took her from the house. A tall man. He told her

you had been hurt in an accident, but I saw him pick Margaret up and carry her down the alley!'' Mabs was near tears.

''Where? Show me!''

Already the crackling of dry tinder could be heard on the wind that blew in from the south. A great gray and black cloud, alive with bright, deadly embers, was moving over the town. Down Bennett Avenue the doors of the fire department's shed were thrown open and two big Percherons galloped out pulling the city's fire engine, its big bell clanging madly. People began moving in a herd down towards Myers Avenue. Mabs took Maureen's hand and dragged her across the street. At the alley, she stopped and pointed. ''He went down here, but when I got here they were gone.''

''Are you sure, Mabs?''

Mabs was staring at the yellow and red flames clawing towards sky now completely obscured by the angry, billowing smoke already streaking over the city.

''Mabs! You saw the man take Margaret down this alley?''

''Yes,'' she managed through her tears, her wide eyes reflecting the flames across the street.

Maureen took the girl by her shoulders. ''Listen to me, Mabs. Go home. Go home to Kitty, now!''

Mabs hesitated, then dashed off. Maureen dropped the grocery basket at the alley's entrance and started down it, knowing that the growing fire across the street could at any moment leap to this side and cause these dry, wooden buildings to flare up like a torch. Embers drifted overhead as she moved deeper into the gloom of the alley. The roar of the flames became louder and acrid smoke began to thicken and sting her lungs.

''Margaret!'' she called. ''Margaret, where are you!'' Maureen was desperate. Who could have taken her daughter, and why . . . and where was she now?

''Margaret!'' she cried again, uncontrollable panic gripping her.

• • • •

When LaFarge had stepped through the open back door of Lisa and Olly's Saloon, Stacey Anderson had instantly shut it behind him, thrown the heavy bolt, and for good measure put the padlock in place and snapped it shut. The little room was, in fact, a storeroom off of the sleeping quarters that Stacey had been using since Sawyer's disappearance. It was filled with whiskey barrels, dusty bed frames, extra chairs, boxes of empty whiskey bottles waiting to be refilled, old advertising placards, and some coils of rope they used to hoist the Stars and Stripes once a year during the Fourth of July.

"I thought you'd never get here," Stacey said quickly.

"Take it easy," LaFarge said, seeing the strained twitch in her face as her view darted around the room. He was still holding a hand over Margaret's mouth. "What are you so nervous about? I'm the one that snatched the kid."

He set the struggling child in a chair and said, "If you let out a peep I'll break your little neck, kid."

Margaret's face froze in terror. LaFarge cautiously removed his hand.

"Where is my mommy?" Margaret said softly, her eyes wide with fear.

Stacey said, "This is the girl?"

"It better be." LaFarge showed Margaret the tattered theme book. "This is yours, is it not?"

Margaret could only stare.

"Well?"

Stacey folded her arms and tapped her foot impatiently.

LaFarge opened the theme book to the first page. "This is your name."

Slowly, Margaret's eyes looked down at the smeared page. "I think it is. I lost it a long time ago," she managed to say. "I want my mommy."

"Just answer the questions."

Margaret gulped and began crying. Her tears spilled onto the book and darkened the already weathered paper.

Stacey stepped between them. "You're handling this all

wrong, Phillip.'' Then she said to Margaret, ''You can go home just as soon as you answer our questions.''

''He told me my mommy was hurt.''

Stacey gave LaFarge a withering stare and then said to Margaret, ''Your mother is not hurt. Now, all you have to do is answer a few questions. All right?''

Margaret nodded.

''Good. Now, according to what you wrote in this book, you found a box. Do you remember?''

Margaret shook her head.

Stacey said patiently, ''But you wrote in your book that you did.'' She showed the page to Margaret and let her read it. It was during the short minute that she was reading the entry that they heard the six closely spaced shots.

''What was that?'' Stacey asked LaFarge.

''I don't know,'' LaFarge said.

Margaret said, ''I think it's the fire call.''

''Never mind,'' LaFarge barked.

Stacey turned back to Margaret. ''*Now* do you remember about the box?''

''Yes. It was in our play-cave. But I don't know who put it there.''

LaFarge took over. ''That's not important. What I what to know is what happened to it?''

Stacey moved to the door that led to the saloon and opened it a crack, peering out. Then she turned back. ''Something's going on out there, Phillip.''

''What happened to the box?'' he demanded again.

''I don't know,'' she whimpered, cowering back in the chair as his angry face hovered near.

''Who is this person, Mr. D.?''

''He took the box and said he'd clean it up for us. But we stopped playing in the cave after that. Mabs said it was too dirty. I forgot all about it.''

''Dammit!'' LaFarge exploded, his fist forming suddenly in front of her face. ''Who is this man you call Mr. D.?''

"Mr. . . . Mr. Daniels."

"Daniels?" LaFarge had to think. "Daniels?" His thoughts went back a few years to retrieve this name that was somehow so familiar. Then he remembered. "Do you mean Casey Daniels?"

Margaret nodded her head.

"Phillip," Stacey said suddenly. "Hurry this up—there's something going on outside."

The clanging of the fire bell could be heard now, and the odor of smoke was working its way into the back room.

All at once, from outside the back door they heard a woman's voice shouting.

*"Margaret! Margaret, where are you!"*

"Mommy!" Margaret cried.

LaFarge swiftly clamped a hand across her mouth.

Stacey said urgently, "It's the Central, across the street. It's a ball of fire."

"Never mind that now. I know who has the box." He looked nervously over his shoulder at the door, and at the heavy cross bolt that held it secure.

"Who?"

"Casey Daniels. He's a mining engineer who used to work for me. He has a cabin somewhere on Wilson Creek. Let's get out of here now." LaFarge shoved Margaret away from him and started for the door to the saloon, but Stacey put herself in front of it. "Not yet, Phillip. There is some unfinished business." Her voice had suddenly hardened.

Behind him, Margaret was shouting, "Mommy! Mommy!" LaFarge ignored her, and the pounding coming from the alley door as well.

"What are you talking about?" he said, sensing that something had changed in her—something that was suddenly very dangerous. The door to the adjoining bedroom was open, and now he saw a shadow move back there. His hand eased back towards the revolver tucked in his waistband and hidden by his jacket, but he stopped before pulling it out.

Oliver Sawyer was suddenly standing in the opening, with Barney Mays at his heels.

"LaFarge," Sawyer said, grinning, his huge eyes unblinking behind the thick lenses. "I knew that someday I'd get my chance at you. I never expected it to be this easy, though."

LaFarge's view leaped from Sawyer back to Stacey, and then suddenly he understood. "You set me up! You lousy bitch."

In the background, the crackling of burning wood mingled with the shouts of firemen. Smoke was now filtering through the saloon, but all of this was only distantly registering with LaFarge as Stacey stepped closer to him.

Her big, green eyes turned wistful. "I wish it would have worked out differently, Phillip. I really do. I did come here to kill Olly, like you asked. But you see, Olly and me, well, we hit it off right away. I had to make a decision, and I decided that I'd rather stay here with Olly than to go back to Missouri. Besides, Olly has all of this." She indicated the saloon with a wave of her arm. "And all you had was a box of gold that you *hoped* had not been found. Sorry."

Behind him, Margaret had stopped shouting, and the pounding fists upon the alley door had ceased as well. Now all he could hear was the clamor out front of frantic men fighting flames, and his own heart pounding within his chest.

Sawyer stepped close with his knuckles bunched and a look of long-awaited anticipation on his owlish face. LaFarge retreated a step. From the corner of his eye he saw Barney's hand come out of his pocket holding a slender blade of steel.

"I swore no man would make a fool of me and live, LaFarge. You could have had yourself any woman you wanted. But no, you had to take what was mine. Why? To prove that you could? Well, you did that, and now you're gonna pay." Sawyer took a black leather blackjack from his pocket, slapped it menacingly against his palm, and came closer. At that same instant LaFarge reached back and drew the revolver from his waistband.

# TWENTY-FIVE

CASEY SAT STRAIGHT UP IN HIS CHAIR AT THE SOUND OF THE six revolver shoots, and like everyone else in Cripple Creek, his eyes instantly searched the roofs. He saw the menacing plume rising and streaking long gray-black fingers of smoke across the rooftops. The smoke passed across the sun, its leading tendrils turning from violet to dark purple before the mass of smoke completely obscured the sun's light and dragged a shadow over the town.

*Fire!* One thing citizens of most every western community feared nearly as much as the dread of an epidemic. Casey leaped to his feet and moved with the other folks towards the flames. He watched the fire engine turn the corner several blocks ahead. All at once James Burns was at his side.

"This could be the big one," Burns said, puffing as he sprinted along.

"I hope not," Casey replied. The pressing crowd slowed them, and when they turned the corner all of Myers Avenue looked to be ablaze. Great fountains of sparks shot skyward, caught by the wind and carried over the town, where they rained down upon rooftops. Ahead, Casey saw a woman emerge from the alleyway.

"That's Maureen!" he said to Burns.

She did not see him as she hurried towards the conflagration on Myers Avenue. Casey put on a burst of speed and in a half dozen long strides he was beside her halting her in her mad flight. "What's the matter, Maureen?"

She wheeled about and seemed not to recognize him at first. Then her vision cleared. "Casey! Oh, Casey! It's Margaret. She's in that buildin'!" Maureen stabbed a finger at Lisa and Olly's Saloon.

At first what she said made no sense to him, but the panic in her face was real. "Are you certain?"

"Yes. I heard her cryin' out but the back door was locked!"

Casey's view leaped to the building. Already the embers from the Central Dance Hall and neighboring buildings had spread to this side of the street. Women and men were fleeing the Old Homestead, some fully dressed and others wearing only a robe, clutching their few belongings. A blaze had erupted in the Topic Dance Hall, next door to Lisa and Olly's, and its flames had already spread to the saloon's front porch.

"You stay here!"

"No, I'm goin' with you."

"Burns," Casey said, putting Maureen into the man's grasp. "Keep her here." Casey didn't wait for the argument he knew would follow but instead dove down the street, under the flaming porch, and through the batwing doors. The saloon was empty except for two or three girls scrambling down the stairs with their arms full of feather capes and chiffon gowns, and several animals with either flapping wings or clawing paws.

Casey drew up among the silent roulette wheels and looked around the smoky room. He was about to call out when muffled pistol shots rang out in one of the back rooms—three quick shots, followed by a moment of silence, and then two more quick shots. He plunged down the hallway to the back of the saloon.

"Margaret! Margaret, where are you?" The crackling of burning wood came from all around him. It was only a matter of minutes before this building would be engulfed.

"I'm back here," Margaret's voice came from the other side of a doorway. The door handle rattled and she cried out, "I can't get it open."

Casey gave the knob a turn. It wasn't locked, but just the same the door wouldn't open. Something on the other side was stopping it. "Stand back," he shouted, and lowering a shoulder he drove into the door. It opened a crack. He drove into it again and slipped through.

At once he saw what had blocked the door. Two bodies lay in front of it. One was Oliver Sawyer, and the other, he noted grimly, was the woman he remembered from the Christmas party, the one with the startling green eyes. Nearby lay two other men, one atop the other. Barney Mays was on top. Casey rolled Mays off to see who the third man was. Mays's hand fell away and the handle of his stiletto remained stuck to the man's chest. It was a priest, from the look of his dress—but no. Casey looked closer and through the tangle of a black beard he saw that it was Phillip LaFarge.

Margaret flung her arms around Casey's waist. "He told me Mommy had been hurt." She was crying, and beginning to cough as the choking fumes filled the air.

"It's all right now," he said, taking her up into his arms. "Let's get out of here."

"You . . . you're not going anywhere." LaFarge had managed to hitch himself up on one elbow, and his revolver wavering ever so slightly as Casey turned back. "The box, Daniels. My cash box," he said weakly. "Where is it?"

"Kind of late for you to be worrying about that now, isn't it, LaFarge? Barney's knife has already killed you." Casey set Margaret back on the floor and gently pushed her aside.

"Not yet it hasn't," he managed. "I got to know, Daniels. What did you do with it?"

"We haven't got time for this. The building is afire and we need to get out of here—now."

"Then you'll take me out of here with you. And afterwards, you'll show me where you hid the gold." LaFarge was dying, but still clung to enough life to pull a trigger.

The crackling of dry tinder grew louder beyond the door, and the air thickening. "I don't have it anymore, LaFarge. I gave it to James Burns over a year ago. He bought your property after you abandoned it. The gold belonged to the Rattle-snake, and now it belongs to Burns. He's the rightful owner of it."

"You don't have it?" LaFarge's eyes grew distant. "Then all this was for nothing?"

"It seems so," Casey said flatly.

"No, not for nothing!" LaFarge stated, strength returning to his voice. "You'll take me out of here, Daniels. Then later, when I'm better, I'll get it from Burns."

"I don't think so, LaFarge."

"Then you'll die here with me," he growled, his anger and hatred fueling his dying body. "We will all die together!" He gripped the shaking revolver in his fist and pulled the trigger.

Casey flinched, but there was only the metallic click of the hammer striking steel. LaFarge thumbed back the hammer and tried again. Nothing. He stared at the revolver, then up at Casey, suddenly realizing what had happened. "They always say load only five," he gasped, ending with a cough that brought up blood. "They say it's . . . it's safer that way." He stared back at the revolver, then flung it away. A wan smile moved across his lips. "You can't just leave me here," he said, slowly sinking back.

"You're a dead man already, LaFarge; carrying you out won't change that. But while you're lying here waiting for the end to come, feeling the smoke crushing your lungs, you might think about how those men who died in your mine cave-in felt having the breath crushed out of them."

LaFarge slumped to the floor.

Casey took Margaret into his arms. The back door was barred and padlocked. The only way out was through the front door. But flames were already eating away at the saloon out front. Grimacing at the prospect of trying to push through that, Casey carried her out into the hall. As he reached the saloon's gaming floor, the long porch in front of the building fell in, crashing through the big plate-glass windows and flinging fire inside the building.

Margaret buried her head against his shoulder. Every avenue of escape was blocked with flames—except the stairs, which were still clear of the fire. Casey put Margaret down, told her to wait, and went back into the storeroom. LaFarge's dark eyes watched him as he grabbed a coil of rope.

Smoke enveloped the gaming room. Casey took Margaret's hand and together they raced up the stairs, where the rising smoke was even thicker. Margaret was coughing and choking. With water from a vase of cut flowers he soaked the linen cloths that sat upon a table under a basket of fruit and a silver service of liquors, and pressed them to their faces as they hurried down the narrow corridor. Casey tossed a flowerpot through the window, but the flames from the Topic Dance Hall had spread across the back of the building and were licking their way up the dry wooden wall.

He backed away and stepped into one of the small rooms, shutting the door. It showed the signs of a hasty departure; clothes had been torn from hangers in the wardrobe against one wall and bedding was scattered around. Smoke rising past the window told Casey there would be no escape that way either. He glanced quickly around and spied the rectangular shape of a trapdoor overhead. Yanking the bed across the room, he climbed on it and pushed the panel up and out of the way.

"Quickly, Margaret," he said, taking her by the waist and shoving her into the attic, and hoisting himself up after her. It was dark except for the faint lines of light through the eaves, but at least for the moment there was no smoke. Casey didn't immediately see a way out of there, and he knew he couldn't waste time searching. Lying on his back where the roof sloped down to the wall, he drove his boot up into the boards. Again and again he kicked at the boards until the end of one lifted with a tearing of shingles and a squalling of rusty nails being yanked free. Light spilled in. Casey's heart was pounding as he immediately set to work on the next board, and in another minute he'd opened a gap wide enough to crawl through.

"I can't go out there," Margaret said, pulling her head back from the hole. "I'll fall."

"I'll hold you. I'll go first, then you follow."

"No, I can't. It's too high."

The flames had worked their way up to the second floor and were beginning to eat through the ceiling, with spits of fire already licking up into the attic near the front of the building.

"Look at that," Casey said. "We don't have any choice but to climb up onto the roof. I'll hold you, Margaret. Don't be afraid." Casey wormed his way onto the steeply pitched roof and, bracing himself, reached inside and hauled the stiff and terrified little girl out. She clutched the edge of the hole, making it hard for Casey to dislodge her. When he finally did, she grabbed his arm and squeezed her eyes shut.

The angle was dizzying. The roof was fully thirty feet above the ground, but from his perspective it appeared to be double that. Casey had never been easy with heights, preferring to explore a dark recess of a cave than to climb to the sunny pinnacle of some mountain peak. He tried to put the ground far below out of mind and to concentrate instead on what he had to do next. Back in the burning gaming room, when he'd seen that his only escape was up the stairs, he had thought it might come to this, and now he was grateful that he'd grabbed the coil of rope.

"Come on, sweetheart, we need to get away from the edge." He began to work his way up to the peak of the roof, angling towards the rear of the building. The front was already sending flames high above the flimsy false front, and the tongues of fire licking up the back wall were nearly to the second floor.

Suddenly the air was rocked with an explosion. Casey clung to the ridge of the roof. On the east side of Third Street between Bennett and Myers, men were beginning to dynamite the shacks in a last-ditch effort the stop the flames from spreading beyond that point. One after another the buildings flew apart, the concussions rocking the town as no Fourth of July celebration ever had. Flying sticks rained down upon them. From this high vantage point, Casey saw that the fire had spread into the center of town and that much of Bennett Avenue was in flames. Johnny Nolon's Saloon was a raging ball of fire.

He made a fast survey of the buildings around them. Every building was burning with a fury that only a combination of a brisk wind and four-year-old dry timber could fan—every building but one, which only fickle chance had preserved thus far: Lampman's Funeral Parlor, behind the Old Homestead. Casey inched towards the corner of the saloon's roof, feeling the shingles beneath him beginning to grow warm. The fire had already climbed into the attic, and Casey prayed that the roof would hold a minute longer.

"I have to set you down, Margaret."

"I'll fall," she cried, her eyes still clamped tight as a drum.

"No you won't. Just don't move." He pried her arms from around him and set her firmly upon the coarse wooden shingles, where she remained, rigid as a corpse. He unfurled the rope and quickly tied a loop in one end. Shaking the loop out, he tried to recall what his father had taught him about throwing a lasso. He'd never been very good at it; ranching had not interested him much since that summer he and his father had spent digging a gold mine. But now his brain desperately scrambled to recall the skill. He whirled the rope overhead, the loop opened up and flattened, and when sheer instinct told him the time was right, Casey let it fly out across the alley. To his amazement, it settled squarely over the iron chimney sticking up from Lampman's roof.

I'll be damned, he said to himself. He tied the end off on one of the saloon's chimneys and pulled it taut.

"Come on, Margaret, we're getting out of here." They scooted to the edge of the roof, holding the rope as they went. "Now, onto my back. That's right," he urged gently, guiding her into place. "Arms around my neck. That's right. Hold tight. Now put your legs around my waist. Got it? Good. Just keep your eyes shut and hold tight."

He tested the rope, hoping that the two chimney stacks had been firmly installed when the buildings were erected; then, easing himself off the roof, he put his weight full upon the rope and swung out over the alley. The rope sagged, but held! It bit into his hands as he inched his way across. Margaret's weight was more than he had expected. Lampman's was only fifteen feet away. Now ten. Casey's grip was tiring. Below him the alley was an inferno.

"Hold tight," Casey said to Margaret, but he was really encouraging himself.

"I am," she said, her head pressed into his shoulder and her arms nearly choking him.

A few feet more, and he had made it.

And suddenly he realized he had not made it at all!

Lampman's roof was right there where the rope crossed over it, but hanging by his hands, Casey knew he'd never get the finger purchase he needed, or have the strength to haul both of them over and onto it. He grappled at the eaves, but there was nothing to grab on to. His grip was weakening. Panic set in, dimming the roar of the flames around him.

Casey groped again, his fingers slipping as the shingles tore his flesh. His grip on the rope began to give out. Crazy thoughts ran through his head. Could he somehow fall and still cushion Margaret? There was no way to guarantee that. The hot smoke stung his eyes, seared his lungs, burned his legs. One last time he clawed at Lampman's roof, but it was hopeless. His fingers slowly opened, and although he tried to will them to remain closed he was slipping. Thirty feet below, the alley was a swirling hell of crates, wagons, and loading docks all hidden in the midst of ravenous flames.

*I'm sorry, Margaret . . . Maureen*, he thought as the last of his strength ebbed away and his grip upon the rope and the rooftop gave out . . .

# TWENTY-SIX

JUST AS HIS OWN GRIP FAILED, A HAND REACHED DOWN FROM above and grabbed onto his right wrist. He thought at first that he must be imagining it; that it was some game the brain plays an instant before death. But no, the hand was real, the grip strong, and someone was pulling him and Margaret up.

Another hand snatched his left wrist as well, dragging him onto Lampman's roof. James Burns helped him to his feet on the slanting roof while Oscar Lampman took the petrified girl into his arms.

"That was a crazy stunt, Daniels!"

"Burns! I should have guessed you'd show up. You always show up when Maureen and Margaret need help. Have you been appointed their personal guardian angel?"

He grinned, his white hair nearly gleaming against the black, smoky clouds that engulfed the city. "Some have entertained angels unawares."

Casey frowned. "Don't let it go to your head."

Burns laughed. Oscar Lampman said anxiously, "This can wait, gentlemen. The damn place is burning down around our ears! Let's get off this roof."

The fire in the alley had begun to eat its way up the back

of Lampman's Funeral Parlor. They scurried towards the front
of the building, and Casey had a clear view of the conflagration on Bennett Avenue. The firebreak on Third Street seemed
to have stopped the flames there, but the wind had whipped
them around and was driving them back towards the big, frame
skeleton of the new National Hotel and the new redbrick Midland Terminal depot at the top of Bennett. In scattered parts
of town, the dynamiters were busy, and everywhere they
passed, the flimsy frame homes were suddenly being leveled
beneath a plume of flying lumber, furniture, clothing, carpet-
ing, and other bits and pieces of people's lives.

A trapdoor in Lampman's roof stood open. Oscar Lampman
passed Margaret down it, then Casey, Burns, and Lampman
dove after her. Casey took Margaret up into his arms as they
hurried down another ladder to a flight of stairs, past open
coffins with wreaths of flowers over them, and out into the
street . . . and none too soon. The windows on the upper floor
of the funeral parlor were alive with flames, the roof crawling
with them.

Maureen rushed up and clutched Margaret, and Casey. Her
face was grimy with blowing ash, and tears of joy and fear
made bright, pink streaks down her cheeks.

"I thought I'd lost you," she said, pushing Margaret's
stringy hair out of the child's eyes. Then she looked at Casey.
"I thought I had lost you both."

"I still don't understand," Maureen said later that evening
after dinner in her little house, one of the many on the eastern
side of town that had escaped destruction. She looked at
Casey, then at James Burns, seated around the table. "Why
did LaFarge come back here? And why did he take Margaret?"

Casey explained about the cash box, and that if word leaked
out that it had been found, LaFarge would likely have never
showed his face in Cripple Creek, what with Oliver Sawyer's
death threat hanging over his head. There was a lot that

LaFarge needed to answer for: the lives lost in the mine cave-in, Casey's life nearly ruined, Sam Stepton's death, and perhaps even Lisa Kellerman's suicide. Casey didn't want him getting away so easily, so he kept the discovery of the cash box secret. Then, when Burns bought the Rattlesnake mine for back taxes, Casey turned the gold over to him.

"Somehow, he discovered that it was Margaret who had found the cash box, and he took her to learn what she had done with it."

"He found my old diary," Margaret piped in. "I must have left it in the play-cave when Mabs and me quit playing there."

"Mabs and *I*," Maureen corrected.

Margaret frowned and returned her attention to the apple cobbler.

Maureen looked at Burns. "So, whatever happened to all the gold?"

"Oh, I still have it, Mrs. Kramer. I haven't quite decided what to do with it. It's not like I need the money, you understand, and the shareholders got a fair price for the mine when we took it over. I figured I'd use it to start a fund maybe, or give some to the Sisters of Mercy Hospital. They could use it now after all this destruction."

"A fund?"

"Yes, for widows and orphans, you see."

"I think that is most honorable, Mr. Burns."

"Why, thank you, Mrs. Kramer." Burns pulled two long cigars from the inside of his jacket pocket. "I think I'll just step outside and have me a smoke. Care to join me, Casey?"

Maureen said, "You two go and have your cigars. Margaret and me will just clean up these dishes."

"Margaret and *I*," Margaret said, looking up from her cobbler.

They all laughed as the men pushed back their chairs and went outside. The sun was just setting behind the hills ranging to the west, and the town below was deep in shadows, with few lights coming from the burned-out sections and the ash-laden sky above it blood red—an eerie sight that reminded Casey how tenuous these western towns were, even those with fancy waterworks and a reservoir of water to fight the blazes.

Burns said, "In six months we won't recognize this place."

"How so?"

"You mark my word, Casey. Every one of those buildings we lost today will be standing again, and they will be of brick this time—fine, solid things, the proper sort of buildings to welcome in the new century a few years from now. This town was built on a dream, and a dream ain't got much substance to it. Now it's going to be rebuilt not on a dream, but on gold! And gold lasts forever."

Casey stared at the dark city below. "What we had here today was a cleansing. We burned up the rubble of the past to make room for solid growth in the future."

"I suppose you can look at it that way," Burns said, studying the ember at the tip of his cigar. He paused, then said, "Speaking of the future, Casey, what are your intentions towards that woman and her daughter? She cares for you, you know. I saw it today when you went after Margaret and she thought she was going to lose you too. I'm half inclined to ask her to marry me myself if you don't get off the pot."

"Every time I've asked her, Burns, she's turned me down. I don't suppose I can blame her, though. For a lot of years she thought I had caused that cave-in—but I had hoped she would have put that all behind her by now. I'd ask her to marry her tonight, except that I know what her answer would be."

"And how would you be knowin' my mind, Mr. Daniels?"

Both men turned at the sound of her voice. Maureen was standing by the door with the light from inside the house falling softly upon her features. Neither man had heard her step out of the house. She came down the path to the gate—which was still without a fence—where the men were standing and looked up into Casey's face. "Well, Mr. Daniels?"

"I don't know your mind, Maureen," he said, suddenly lost

in her beauty. "All I know is my heart."

"And what be it tellin' you now?" she pressed.

She was putting on a stern face, but Casey saw the tilt of her mouth that meant she was trying to hold back a smile. She was waiting for his answer, and his mouth had gone as dry as an old boot. Was he really ready to say how he felt? Why was he hesitating? he asked himself. He looked to Burns for support, and got only a crooked grin for the effort.

"I reckon my heart is telling me that I loves you, and if I don't ask you to marry me at least one more time, someone like Burns here is going to come along and ask you . . . and you are going to say yes."

"Hm," she said. "You know, Mr. Daniels, a man needs to listen to his heart at least as often as he listens to his head."

"Will you?"

"Will I what, Mr. Daniels?"

"Will you marry me?" There! He had said it. The world around him blurred as he waited for her response. It seemed to take forever.

"Yes, Mr. Daniels. Yes, I will marry you."

All at once his life came into focus, the fuzzy edges suddenly sharpening up. He knew that this was the right time, and that Maureen was the right woman. Casey took Maureen into his arms and she came willingly, then pressed her lips hard against his.

"Yuck!"

They looked over. Margaret was standing there with her face screwed up.

"Grown-ups!" she said.

Burns took Margaret's hand and said, "Miss Margaret, how about you and me taking a little stroll. We'll leave your mama and Mr. Daniels alone for a few minutes. I have a notion that I'm about to lose a crackerjack secretary and you're about to get a new daddy. Come along now and I'll tell about the time I was in Cuba and fell into a pit with a boa constrictor. My hair was black as coal when I fell in, and by the time I climbed out, it was like you see it now . . ."

As Burns and Margaret walked off, Casey drew Maureen closer, felt her cheek upon his chest. They looked out across the still smoking buildings of Cripple Creek. The town was poised for a new beginning, and with Maureen at his side, and the Lucky Irish mine to bankroll them, they would be a part of it.

# AUTHOR'S NOTE

BEFORE THE 1890s, THE NOTION THAT THERE MIGHT BE GOLD on the west side of Pikes Peak was scoffed at by all the professional mining men, but it was a dream in Bob Womack's head that he could not shake loose. Colonel Demary, a respected mining man who owned a vacation shack on Bull Hill, pronounced emphatically that there was no gold in the area, and he liked nothing better than to poke fun at "Crazy Bob" as the cowboy searched out his float trail. The irony of it was that Demary's shack sat on the very spot where only a few years later the Vindicator mine would take out over twenty-seven million dollars in gold!

When Bob finally did discover the yellow metal, no one believed him. The problem was that some years before, in 1884, two men had salted a piece of ground and staged a "gold rush" hoax that became known locally as "the Mount Pisgah hoax"—even though the ruse was actually pulled off at Mount McIntyre, fully thirteen miles from Pisgah. But no one checked the geography too closely and the name stuck. Bob was never what you might call a sterling witness for the defense, what with his devil-may-care attitude towards life and his affection for the bottle and pretty women, so when he cried

"Gold," all that the people of Colorado Springs heard was "Pisgah," and they shrugged it off.

A few curious men did wander up over Pikes Peak to take a look and to stake out claims—Winfield Scott Stratton was one of them—but it wasn't until a prominent German count by the name of Pourtales put his stamp of approval on the District by buying Steve Blair's Buena Vista claim on Bull Hill that respectable investors began looking seriously at Cripple Creek.

From that point in October of 1892, the town of Cripple Creek exploded like a keg of giant powder. Its first wooden shacks spread like oil on water across the little high-mountain bowl that up until then had been known only as the Broken Box Ranch. The ranch's owners, Denver real estate men Julius Myers and Horace Bennett, quickly plotted the town of Fremont and started selling lots—mining gold in the form of real estate—while greenhorn miners from Colorado Springs dug up the hillsides, extracting the yellow metal to pay for those lots. Cripple grew like weeds on a leach field; five hundred people a month bulged the town at the seams. By the end of '93 there were fraternal lodges, literary clubs, twenty-four grocery stores, seven bakeries, ten meat markets, forty-four lawyers, thirty-six real estate and stock offices, and enough saloons, brothels, and one-girl cribs to keep the mining man well entertained.

Cripple Creek led a charmed life right from the start, arriving on the tail end of the nineteenth century and benefiting from all the latest developments that science and technology could offer. Telephones and electricity were there almost from the beginning, and it wasn't long before an electric interurban system linked a dozen little towns; for fifteen cents a man or woman could buy a round-trip ticket to anyplace in the District. After Stratton and Burns's fabulous discoveries, which read more like fiction than the real history they were, the town basked in the blessings of two of the richest and bighearted men in the District.

Stratton, always a melancholy man, became even more so after he hit pay dirt in his Independence mine. Shortly after becoming Cripple Creek's first millionaire, he moved back to Colorado Springs, into a little frame house at 115 North Weber Street that he'd built for a doctor many years earlier when he had been a carpenter. Stratton shunned the high-society life of Little London, as Colorado Springs was called, and became the subject of ridicule and gossip because he did not have a big house on Wood Avenue, attend the proper parties, own racehorses, or travel the world.

Stratton had more serious problems to tend to. What was he to do with all the money he was earning? He later made the comment that all a man would ever need was $100,000 dollars to be comfortable for the rest of his life, and I get the feeling that after a few years of being the richest man in the city, Stratton wished he had taken Pearlman's $155,000 for his Independence mine after all. Stratton worked hard at giving it away. He kept his old friend Bob Womack afloat, and he helped Senator Horace Tabor, who had become immensely rich off silver from his Matchless mine in Leadville, but was now nearly destitute. Stratton once bought bicycles for all the laundrywomen in Colorado Springs to make their jobs easier. He supported the State School of Mines, the Institute for the Mute and Blind, and dozens of charities. He gave the city of Colorado Springs a fine trolley system, and beautiful parks, and upon his early death on September 13, 1902, he left instructions in his will for the establishment of the Myron Stratton Home to provide for orphans and the elderly. The home was named after Stratton's father, and is still in existence. Stratton raised churches, fed the hungry, clothed the needy, and when asked once about the way he spent his wealth, he said, "I count my money as a gift from the Father of us all, and I am responsible for its administration as a good steward."

Stratton was all of that.

Burns, likewise, had a heart for the workingman, a trait which finally drove a wedge between him and one of his part-

ners, Jimmie Doyle. The two men parted company amidst lawsuits and allegations. Burns remained the president of the
Portland and Doyle became mayor of Victor. Harnan got bored
after a few years and left the District a rich man, only to
squander his wealth completely and return many years later
looking for a job.

The great fire of '96 was actually two great fires, separated
by a mere four days. This book ends with the first fire, which,
according to various accounts, leveled fifteen to thirty acres
of town. The second fire started in the kitchen of the Portland
Hotel and did far more damage, putting thousands more people
out into the weather, which turned cold and blustery as night
came on—typical springtime in the Rockies. Stratton was living in Colorado Springs when word reached him of the disaster. He immediately organized a massive relief effort, and
since there was no time to arrange for letters of credit, Stratton
personally backed all the expenses with his fat checkbook.
Trainloads of blankets and food, tents and medical supplies
were on their way to the mining camp within hours. When it
was all over, a bond had been forged between the two cities,
and much of the ill feelings that had begun over the villainous
activities of the striking miners two years earlier had been
healed.

These fires were really the beginning of Cripple Creek's
golden era. The rubble of the early boomtown had been con-
signed to the ash heap, and in its place rose fine brick buildings, and along with them building codes that would prevent
the haphazard growth of the past. Gold production soared in
the next few years, from six million ounces in 1895 to seven
million in '96, ten million in '97, thirteen million a year later,
and nearly nineteen million by the turn of the century—Cripple Creek's highest single year of production.

The year 1900 might be considered the pinnacle of Cripple
Creek's golden era. After that, production began to decline.
Labor wars in 1903, which affected the whole state of Colo-
rado, eventually brought about a dismantling of organized la-

bor in the District. Afterwards, mines began to merge, further squeezing labor and shrinking the population. Water was another problem. The mines were so deep by this time that huge pumps had to work overtime to keep them from flooding. Finally a drainage tunnel was driven beneath the District. It helped some, but production kept falling.

World War I broke out, pulling young men from the District and shutting down dozens of mines. The town never fully recovered from that, even though the District got a shot in the arm when the price of gold was officially set at thirty-five dollars an ounce. But it was a short-lived reprieve, for almost on its heels came World War II, from which the District never rallied—at least not as far as gold mining was concerned.

When I moved to Colorado Springs in 1969, Cripple Creek was on the verge of ghost-towndom. Only the brick buildings on Bennett Avenue remained. Myers Avenue was all but gone, except for the infamous Old Homestead brothel. North of Bennett, quite a few homes and buildings were still standing, and in the summer the population of Cripple Creek might have swelled to as many as five hundred residents. All but a few of the mines were closed, but their shafts still gaped open, inviting a curious boy to crawl through them. I found and explored my share of these abandoned mines, never realizing or caring at the time about the history accounted to them, or the danger. Over the years I watched this once glorious city return slowly back to dust as old brick walls fell in on crumbling foundations and the remnants of abandoned mining roads were washed out and covered over with pine trees.

Then something astounding happened. In 1991, almost one hundred years from Cripple Creek's conception, the people of Colorado voted to allow limited gambling in three old historic towns—Black Hawk, Central City, and Cripple Creek. Like the phoenix rising from its ashes—as Cripple Creek had done once before in 1896—the town came alive again. Following the footsteps of the first gold seekers, thousands of people flocked over Pikes Peak from Colorado Springs and countless other places to cash in on this new "strike." Money poured in and new life was breathed into dying buildings—while mostly keeping their original facades—but inside beat a new heart of twentieth-century technology; the sounds of the dance halls have been replaced by the electronic beeps of a thousand slot machines, the honky-tonk pianos by the music of dancing coins. Today, when you visit Cripple Creek, you will find new hotels, old roads resurfaced, and a town that's booming again!

I suppose that right here it might be appropriate to separate the real characters in my book from the fictitious ones. The list of genuine, bona fide Cripple Creekers is indeed long, and it might be simpler just to list the few fictional folks instead—but perhaps it would be more fun to let you, the reader, try to ferret out truth from fabrication. I will, however, list a few of the more prominent folks who walked not only these pages, but the streets of Cripple Creek a century ago. First and foremost, there was Winfield Scott Stratton. The "Three Jims" were real as well. Bob Womack, of course. So were Dr. Whiting, Irving Howbert, Johnny Nolon, L. M. Pearlman, Joe Wolfe, John Calderwood, George Carr, and the whole Barbee family—Mabel (Mabs), Kitty, Jonce, and little Billie—to name just a few.

Mabs Barbee married a young mining engineer and later, under the name of Mabel Barbee Lee, wrote a fine book called *Cripple Creek Days,* which I drew heavily from. Some other sources I used were Marshall Sprague's *Money Mountain* and *Newport in the Rockies,* Frank Waters's *Midas of the Rockies,* plus a whole pile of publications by such regional writers as Leland Feitz, Brian Lavine, Joe Vanderwalker, Leo Kimmett, and William Conte. I would like to thank them all for their fine research. Without their work, my work would have been impossible.

—Douglas Hirt
1996